THE
SLAVE
TAG

THE SLAVE TAG

A NOVEL

ROBERT BUCKLEY

CONTENTS

PROLOGUE

After two months he was getting used to sleeping on the slippery wood deck. By this time he could also keep down most of the gruel they fed him, along with the nasty, hard bread moving with insects. The ripped skin on his back was healing nicely but there would be rubbery scars around his ankles from the leg irons. But against all odds, he was surviving.

He would survive!

He understood his fate now. The village elders had talked about these people, his captors; these slave traders who showed no mercy. These mirthless, cruel people who wore strange clothing and spoke in a tongue he didn't understand. He knew he would never see his village again. Never again would he feel his mother's cool hand on his face – his father's proud embrace after the hunt. Never again would he hear his younger sister and brothers' laughter or smile at their silliness.

He left all that behind. Forever.

Two months chained to strangers on a stinking boat had changed him. He quickly learned to survive. In a way he was fortunate. Many did not survive the first 24 hours. After three days they let him come up to see the sky. He was caked with vomit and excrement and could barely stand. He was shaking and weak and terrified. He was doused with seawater that left him feeling sticky and sick. His eyes hurt.

That first day he saw two men jump over the side. Were they to swim to shore? There was no shore. There was nothing but water. They soon panicked and their thrashing attracted the big fish. The slaver traders made everyone watch what happened. No one else jumped into the water again.

The days passed quickly. Most mornings they were permitted to come up and clean themselves. Just to be able to stand straight was a great relief. He did many tasks. Whatever they asked. He slowly regained his health and strength. Eventually he found others who spoke his tongue – he even found a villager he knew. He learned there were more of them elsewhere on the boat and he hoped perhaps another family member had survived. He never found one.

If the days passed quickly, the nights passed slowly. Down below, chains were passed through his ankle irons and kept him in one place and in one position – flat on his back with no room to even turn over or sit up. The air was thick with foul odors and sounds of weeping. Early on, his own weeping. His despair and deep sorrow wore heaviest at night.

The rats came at the darkest hour. He could hear them scamper quickly down the walls and along the floor, just out of reach – searching, scratching, nibbling. If he could catch one, he would kill and eat it.

He would lay awake as long as he could and think of other things: the cool, wet, jungle mornings – the shrill screeching of colorful birds – the laughter of the village children at play – the sweet juice of papaya running down his chin.
     Yes, he was surviving.

He must survive!

PART ONE

THE KILLING

1940 – 1942

CHAPTER ONE

It was a hot, sticky evening along the banks of the Mississippi. A slight but steady down river breeze kept the mosquitoes close to the muddy shore while an occasional fish surfaced to suck some hapless, fluttering insect off the oily surface of the water.

The tug crew had been told it would be several hours before the inspection was done so Glory decided to go out for a walk along the levee. It seemed like a good chance to get away by himself and enjoy the fresh evening air. The rest of the crew stayed behind, drinking beer, smoking cigarettes, playing cards and listening to a baseball game on the radio. Glory didn't smoke and except for a special, rare occasion he didn't drink. And he sure as hell wasn't about to risk his hard-earned wages playing poker with that bunch.

"Best be back soon," said Eddie Jack, one of the older crew members. "The man says 'spection take only two, maybe three hours. But don't bet on it. Finish early and dey'll leave ya, ain't back. Hear, Glory?"

"I be back soon, don't fret none 'bout me," said Glory in what he called his *south speak*. He could talk the King's English with the best of them and knew he'd have gotten a lecture from his mama if she'd heard him just then.

"And stay away from those pretty *white* gals," shouted out Andy, much to the glee of the rest of the crew. "They got no use for an ugly ol' penniless, backwoods *N-E-G-R-O* like y'all."

Glory could hear the muffled hoots and hollers.

Andy was his best friend. His real name was Andrew Percival LeClaire, the third generation product of an amorous French plantation owner and a housemaid from Cameroon. Glory was tempted to shout back some clever reply using his *real* name, but he didn't. He knew enough about names and the way they can cause a person trouble. And *Percival* was a sure bet to create all kinds of trouble for Andy.

Lord knew his name had been a trial for him. *Glory – good heavens*, he often thought. *Who would name their own child, Glory?*

He once asked his folks to change it. A big mistake. It was after the first day of school and some older kids had given him a hard time. That evening he came home and whined about it.

"They laugh at my name, Ma. All the boys. Even some of the girls."

When she didn't give him the sympathy he felt he deserved, he whined about it to his pa when he came in from the fields that night, tired and irritable. A *really* big mistake.

"Glory's your name, boy, and don't you forget it," his pa said in his loud, no nonsense voice. "Your granny give you dat name when she first sees you in the birth bed. *Glory Hallelujah*, she shouts! Your mama, she likes it. And *I* like it. We just short it up. You get uppity with us and we'll add on *Hallelujah*. Now go do your chores and don't be pestering me 'bout it no mo."

Glory had heard the naming story many times before. He assumed adding on *Hallelujah* was an idle threat but he wasn't totally sure. In any case, he learned to live with the name, *Glory*, and after awhile, kids being kids, it was forgotten in favor of other more child-worthy things. So Glory it remained throughout the six grades his ma and pa made him go to school. And Glory it'd been ever since.

Glory was a bright boy. Seemed he was blessed with a natural ability to learn. He had a lively inquisitiveness that quickly caught Angela Grace's attention. Angela came to teach at Glory's school when he was still in third grade. She was a definite blessing to the community and brought a real education to the town including an actual teaching degree from a school up north, in *Dee-troit*, something unheard of at the time. It was mainly through her personal attention that Glory flourished in school. She knew he was special. She knew it the minute she met him and heard him speak; the careful way he expressed himself, his polite manners, and his name. It was hard to ignore the name.

When Glory finished sixth grade, it was through her dedicated pestering of the good Fathers at the private Jesuit school in Lexington that she was able to get him a two-year scholarship, including room and board. Selling his parents on the idea was a bit harder. Yet over the summer, her gentle persuasion won them over; his mother first and eventually his father. Slowly they came to realize this was an opportunity for the boy to improve his lot in life, an opportunity neither of them had ever had.

As Angela expected, Glory didn't let them down. He received top grades in all his subjects and impressed the Jesuits who admitted he was "one dern smart Negro!" But after two years his scholarship ended. The priests were willing to extend it, partly because they recognized a natural intelligence they were curious about, and partly because they knew Angela would have made their lives unbearable if they hadn't.

But truth be known, Glory was needed more than ever on the farm. Besides, he missed his family, so he returned home. His father, by then sick with bad lungs, did what he could but came to rely more and more on Glory. By the time his 18th birthday rolled along he was basically running things himself. It was during a quiet birthday party at home when he was presented with the slave tag.

Glory's great grandfather had been snatched from the Gambian Coast of Northwest Africa and taken to South Carolina in 1857. He endured a miserable trip, chained like an animal for ten weeks and sold on the docks of Charleston like a mule. Although the slave trade had already been banned for several years, slave ownership was still alive and well in the southern states.

It was common practice in those days for slave owners to hire out their "property," and by law it was necessary to purchase identity tags for them. Since his new owner neither knew nor cared what his real name was, he called him *Sam*.

Sam was big and strong for his age and was hired out as a porter. If you'd been around in those days, you'd find him loading bales of cotton, dawn to dusk, on Charleston, Carolina's busy docks. The tag he wore around his neck was stamped: SAM. No. 312. CHARLESTON. 1858. PORTER.

When the Civil War ended, Sam, by then in his late 20s, became a freed man. And like many ex-slaves, he took on his owner's last name, Alexander. Recently married, he and his wife, Tanisha, followed work to Tennessee where they finally settled down. Sam may have become a freed man, but he held on to his tag and often got it out and told his children, and later his grandchildren, about it. He wanted them all to know about the evils of slavery.

By the time Sam died in 1890, his son, John, Glory's grandfather, had already been given the tag. It was then passed on to the next eldest son, Thomas, Glory's father. And finally, on his 18th birthday, it passed to Glory. It was no small thing. Glory understood its significance. Its history and importance had been hammered into him since he was a baby. Like his father, he wore it around his neck as a constant reminder and as an inspiration for him to *do better*.

Under Glory's careful supervision and hard work, along with his ability to deal intelligently with the white businessmen in the area, the farm prospered.

Glory eventually married and a baby girl quickly came along. He and his wife, Elizabeth, named her Angela after the teacher they had both come to love and admire. But with the baby came new responsibilities and added expenses.

They needed more privacy now and had been talking for some time about building a little place of their own. Glory had been trying to set aside a little extra money when he could, but soon realized it'd be a long time before he'd have enough saved to buy the supplies necessary even to get started. Eventually, the constant pestering by his longtime friend, Andy, about joining him on the river for some *real money*, became more and more attractive. Andy was a crewman on a tugboat and was confident he could get Glory hired on.

Andy's family farm was nearby and they often got together when he was in town, occasionally meeting at one of the local dances where he'd show up with his current best girl and a pint of shine in his back pocket.

At first, Glory wasn't keen on leaving his wife and daughter, let alone his aging parents but he knew his younger brother and sister were more than capable of running the farm by this time. Besides, Andy *was* earning good money and although he never seemed to hold on to it for very long, Glory believed he'd be able to do things differently.

The pay was over twice what he earned laboring part-time back in Pineview, and the work seemed easy to him. The boss man was fair and the food was tolerable. And even though Elizabeth wasn't happy having him gone, they were both pleased he was finally able to begin saving a little money.

By August, he and Andy had made six runs together out of Memphis, usually gone for a week at most. This time the tug was pushing coal up to Minneapolis and returning to Memphis with grain – a two-week trip. Glory thought when he got back they might have enough to finally get started on their own place. And Elizabeth who was now pregnant with their second child was not as nervous at him leaving as she'd been on earlier occasions.

Things had gone well until the tug struck a partially submerged tree just south of Dubuque, Iowa. The impact was solid enough that the engineer was worried some damage might have been done to one of the huge propellers. He hoped that wasn't the case, but advised the captain it'd be better to find out there rather than risk the possibilities of problems when they were somewhere up river far from any town. Captain Placer hated to take the time, but was experienced enough to agree to the inconvenience.

The crew left the barges tied up a short ways down river and chugged into Dubuque's ice harbor to take a look underneath. If they were lucky and no harm done, they'd be underway in a few hours. However, if they discovered real damage, they could lose a day or two.

So it was that Glory decided to take advantage of the break to stretch his legs. Standing out on deck he could still make out the big houses spread along the tree-lined bluff. Lights were starting to come on throughout the town. Up river he heard a train announce its arrival with a long, drawn out whistle.

He knew Dubuque was an old town, one of the oldest in the Midwest and had a reputation for rowdiness. Nothing new there. Seemed most towns along the river were rough and tumble affairs. He'd heard enough stories to caution outsiders, white or brown, to be on their best behavior.

That was fine with Glory. He wasn't looking for any excitement anyway. He just wanted a little exercise. Life on a tugboat meant living and working in close quarters and he wasn't used to it. He liked to walk, always had. Most every evening, he and Elizabeth would take baby Angela and walk from the farm over to visit a relative or a friend, or to the top of Blossom Hill and back, hardly ever less than a couple of miles. He missed that. He surely did.

With the crew's good-natured admonitions still fresh in his mind, he jumped down on the dock, climbed up the steep levy and headed toward some of the big warehouses that lined the upstream bank. They were solid looking buildings, built with long runs of hard woods from the surrounding hills. Oak, hickory and walnut, the kinds of woods he'd like to use on his place.

He tipped his head back and sucked in a deep breath of air. "Nice," he muttered to himself. "Fresh." Almost as nice as back home and a far cry from the oil, sweat and diesel fuel fumes he had to breathe most of the day. Life was good. He was happy.

CHAPTER TWO

Across town, Tom Lavarato, Sean O'Brien and Jack Grettsmer were headed home having been kicked out of Kelly's Tavern. Their evening, which earlier had consisted of drinking beer and playing pool, had escalated into a near brawl before Kelly stepped in and stopped it.

Kelly's was a serious, drinking man's bar that catered to the packinghouse crowd, mainly first-generation German and Polish immigrants who had little, if any, formal education. Although the bar was Irish in name and nature, few of the local Irish frequented it, having a great dislike for the "bloody pig sticker bunch."

Located on the northern edge of downtown, in a dingy, drab area known by the locals as the *Flats*, Kelly's was a smoky, L-shaped room sporting a 26-foot-long, black walnut back bar and handsome, acid-etched mirror. These niceties were unfortunately wasted on its hard-core clientele who hardly spoke English and would have been perfectly content and probably more comfortable sitting on overturned beer kegs on a dirt floor.

It was commonly understood Kelly had "an arrangement" with the local police and was given a bit of leeway as long as certain financial commitments were met and complaints kept to a minimum. It was the only bar in the area foolish enough to let in the three young men. Kelly normally didn't see much of them, but now that they'd all recently graduated from high school, they'd been coming in with annoying regularity.

He tolerated Sean O'Brien well enough, but knew he was a real troublemaker. Sean reminded him of himself at that age. Hothead Mick. Mad at everyone. Chip on his shoulder. Ready to brawl at the drop of a hat.

He also knew Sean's old man was a terrible drunk. Had been for years, a mean, unpredictable and sloppy, pee-your-pants drunk. The kind he hated. Bad for business, he often said, although his crowd rarely noticed. Whiskey was the common scourge of the Irish, Kelly plainly knew, yet bootlegged whiskey was making him a rich man. And Sean's father rather craved it.

9

Ironically, Sean's brother, Pat O'Brien, was a local policeman who got both Sean and the old man out of more trouble than he should have. If it hadn't been for him, the whole bunch would've been thrown out in the alley weeks ago. Good riddance.

Yet Kelly tolerated the boys because they looked older than their years and always had plenty of spending money. All three were big, strapping lads and had been close pals all through grade school and into high school. Kelly thought it altogether strange: a Wop, a Kraut and a Mick; a mismatched trio that he felt was unhealthy and unnatural.

Jack Grettsmer lived in one of the bluff homes owned by an old money, Dubuque family who made a fortune in building supplies. Kelly didn't know his parents but had heard they had a shitpot full of money. Of the three boys, Kelly disliked Jack the most. A smart aleck who believed he was better than everyone else. "Sitting up on the hill where they could piss down on the poor working stiffs who put the meat on their tables" was the common sentiment of Kelly's crowd about bluff house owners. On more than one occasion Jack had been the instigator of an argument with some poor drunk knowing that his pal, Sean, would happily finish it for him out in the alley.

Tom Lavarato was the quietest of the three. He lived somewhere on the north end. Kelly had known his old man who used to work for the Transit Company and came in with his mates from time to time. He remembered him as a hard-working old Wop who spoke more Italian than English. He also knew he'd gotten himself killed in a freak yard accident a few years earlier. Supposedly out of respect for his old man, the Transit Company hired his son. That's all Kelly knew about him other than he seemed the least likely to be friends with the likes of Jack Grettsmer and Sean O'Brien. It was just something about him that set him apart; his manners perhaps. He always said "Thank You" when he left which was odd enough to be sure. He didn't get many "Thank Yous" from his regular crowd.

But he knew Sean well enough to know he could be real trouble. Older than his years, he was part of a large family of first-generation, shanty Irish that lived in the *Flats*.

Sean was constantly in trouble, fighting and getting thrown out of every school he ever attended. Everyone knew the only reason St. Columkille High let him stay was because of his sport skills. Yet even then he was seldom able to finish a game before being yanked out by either the referee or his own frustrated coach for losing his temper and getting into a fight. He definitely had a nasty side that only got worse when he had a few drinks. And this night they'd all had plenty and were getting louder and louder and starting to irritate his regulars. They'd still be there if Kelly hadn't ordered them to leave or suffer the consequences.

It started with an argument during a pool game. Sean and Tom had been challenged by a couple of local packers. Halfway into the game, Sean, who had already had several beers, was starting to play sloppily and accidentally nudged the cue ball with the tip of his stick. He then made the mistake of reaching over and moving it back to its original position.

Normally this would not have caused any big problem except the boys were acting like big shots and generally being obnoxious. The packers were not amused and called Sean on it.

"Hey, boy, vat you doing?" a gnarly old German said. "You move ball, shot's over."

"What're ya talking about," replied Sean with a sneer. "That were an accident. Hell, I barely nicked it with my stick and just set it right, didn't I?"

"You moved ball. Shots over!" the packer said walking up to take his shot.

"Are you kidding me?" snapped Sean. "That's chicken shit, old man. It's still my shot. Move aside and let me have a go at it."

When the pushing started, Tom and Jack started to move into the action, along with a couple of the packer's friends. Just before things got ugly, Kelly came around the side of the bar like a bull. Holding up his infamous, sawed-off cue stick for all to see, he shouted, "That's it, lads! Stop it now while you still can. O'Brien, it's time for you and your pals to get the hell outta here and don't come back until you sober up. Just what I need is another fight in here with you pissants."

Sean might have been a little drunk, but he wasn't stupid. After pausing a moment to stare hatefully at Kelly, then at the grinning packers, he stormed out, shouting, "Let's get the hell out of this stinking dump before those old ladies *really* make me mad."

It was a pathetic attempt to save face and he knew it.

"This whole damn town is starting to get to me," he ranted as the three of them stomped across the street and started down the alley. "I can't wait to get the hell out of here."

At that moment, acting on a poorly thought out whim, he bent down and grabbed a broken brick lying in the alley. Without a word to his two companions, he turned and hurled it back toward the bar. Momentarily frozen in shock, they took off running just as it crashed through the glass. They were over a block away and down another alley before they heard the shouting behind them.

"You're crazy as hell," Jack squealed merrily as they tore down the dark, wet alley. "Kelly's gonna kill us if he catches us."

"He ain't gonna kill nobody, that stupid Mick," panted Sean, "We shoulda stayed and beat the crap out of him."

"Yeah, and get our heads cracked open," puffed Tom. "I've seen him use that stick before."

"Yeah? About the time he'd try, I'd wrap it around his neck," said Sean. "All I'd have to do is tell Pat about it and Mr. *Asshole* Kelly would be tending bar with two broken arms. But damn," he added as they slowed down to a stumbling shuffle, "I'd sure like to have another beer."

By this time they were five blocks away and all sounds of shouting had died away.

"Hey," said Jack in a hazy moment of inspiration. "Let's go to the warehouse. I know where one of the guys keeps some homemade brew stashed. I've seen him sneak some when he thinks no one's looking."

"You're sure no one's there?" said Tom, not very excited about the idea. "Maybe we ought to just get the hell out of here. 'Sides I gotta get home."

"C'mon, don't punk out on us now," said Jack. "That'd be a good place to hide out for a while – ya know, in case Kelly's looking for us."

"Screw Kelly," said Sean, instantly warming to the idea. "But let's go anyway. What kinda stuff you talking about?"

"Beer," said Jack. "And super strong. So dark it's almost black. C'mon, I've got a key."

Looking behind them to be sure they weren't being followed, they trotted down a couple more blocks. Then, just before exiting the alley across from the warehouse, they spied a man walking alone down the middle of the street. But just not any man – a Negro! Whistling. Not another soul in sight.

"Well I'll be damned," whispered Sean as they backed up into the shadows and watched him heading down the dimly lit street. "If that ain't a nigger, I'm Parnell's Ghost! Where in the hell did he come from?"

It was altogether a bad piece of luck for Glory Alexander.

CHAPTER THREE

Colored folk were rarely seen in Dubuque in those days. For that matter, neither were Asians, Mexicans and most other foreign nationalities. The locals had seen outsiders from time to time, but mainly passing through town on trains or buses. But rarest of all were coloreds. The only Negro they actually knew about was Henry Johnson, the janitor down at the Julien Dubuque Hotel. And even then, old white-haired Henry lived across the river in East Dubuque, Illinois. He was known to walk to work every day, rain or shine, across the tall, noisy bridge connecting the two states. Apart from being the only colored person in town, it was considered very strange behavior.

And so it was with surprise and humor that on this particular night, another colored man would be strolling, free as you please, right down the street in front of them. Whistling.

"Where'd he come from?" said Sean, "and what in the hell do you think he's up to?"

"I don't know," said Jack, "but let's find out. Damn coon's probably planning to rob the old man's warehouse."

Of course, all the warehouse had inside it to rob was rough sawed lumber, in eight, twelve and sixteen-foot lengths, that and stacks of heavy, cast-iron piping. How anyone, on foot, was able to steal that kind of material, and why, seemed to be lost on the three of them as they quietly filed out on the street and lined up behind him.

"Hey there, boy, where you think you going?" shouted Jack as they quietly closed in on him.

Glory spun around in alarm and froze. *Whoa! Where in the hell did they come from?* His first inclination was to take off running, but thought better of it. That might give the impression he was up to no good. Besides, quick on his feet as he was, there were three of them and he might not be able to outrun them.

"Going nowhere," Glory said. "Just out walking, that's all."

He'd been harassed by white people before. Usually they were just trying to show off and act like big shots in front of friends. After some name-calling and "Ain't I tough" posturing they soon lost interest. Still, this time he was alone, in a drab area of a strange city and he didn't see anyone else around.

"So what'n the hell ya doing?" demanded Sean.

Why they're just overgrown boys, thought Glory as they moved closer to him, younger than himself but all three taller and in apparent good shape. And all three reeked of stale beer and cigarettes. *Not a good sign*, he thought. *Be calm. Just answer their stupid questions and get back to the boat.*

"Told you. Just out walking," replied Glory. "I work on a tugboat, *The John Ruxton*. We ran into a sunken tree south of town. Tug's down in the harbor getting inspected right now. You can check it out if you want."

"What's your name?" asked Tom ignoring his explanation.

Glory hesitated a moment and said, "Alexander."

"Alexander what?" said Sean.

Glory hesitated another moment and finally said, "Glory. Glory Alexander."

"Glory? *Glory*?" Jack hooted as the others started laughing. "Glory's not a name. You mean like in '*Glory In Excelsis Deo*'?" he laughed.

Sean and Tom roared at his cleverness.

"Just Glory," he replied starting to get vexed at this foolishness. "And I'm not a 'boy'. I 'spect I'm older than y'all."

They froze when they heard that. The laughing stopped and they stared at Glory, not sure how to respond to this unexpected boldness.

"Well now, a *smart ass* 'boy', at that," snarled Sean walking up close to him. "Where're you from anyway? You don't live around here, I know that for a fact. You wanna know how I know that? 'Cause you're a nigger and we don't tolerate niggers around here. Around here, niggers don't sass white folks."

"Not sassing. I'm from Tennessee, and I don't like to be called names, either," said Glory as he started around the three of them. "I got to get back 'fore they come looking for me."

"Hold on there, Mr. Smart Ass Nigger from Tennessee," said Sean as he shifted sideways to stop Glory's attempt to leave. Jack

15

and Tom stepped on either side of Sean forming an effective blocking movement. "You ain't going anywhere till you apologize."

"Hell I will," grunted Glory as he started to shove through them.

They might have let him go up to that point, but he made the mistake of pushing Sean hard on the chest. Then it happened so fast it was just a blur. Sean's fist came swinging around and up deep into Glory's stomach. Glory buckled over letting out a loud *whoosh* as Sean, in seamless motion brought his knee up into his face knocking him backwards and down onto the cobblestones.

"Jesus, Sean!" cried Tom in alarm. "What'd you do that for? Let 'im be. Let's get the hell outta here."

"Had it coming," said Jack as he bent over and roughly rolled Glory over onto his back. "He sassed us. Shit, he's all right."

Glory lay on the ground twisting back and forth and holding his stomach, coughing and trying to get his breath back. He wiped the side of his mouth and saw a trace of blood from a split lip.

"Get up, coon," Sean said. "You ain't hurt. I don't like gettin' pushed, ya got that?"

Glory struggled to his feet, wobbling a little as he stared with hatred, now mixed with fear at his assailants. He started to wobble off toward the dock when Jack shouted, "Hey there, Mr. Glory. Ain't you forgetting something?"

Glory paused a moment and looked at the three of them.

So, that's it, he thought. *Now they want to humiliate me. They aren't satisfied with ganging up on me and punching me. They want to 'put me in my place.' Well, if that's what it takes I can do it. Shame on them, not me.*

"Sorry," he muttered and started to move off.

"Hold it," said Sean. "Can't hear you."

"SORRY," shouted Glory at them. "I'm SORRY. Can I go now?"

"Let him go, Sean," said Tom in a low voice while grabbing hold of Sean's arm. "He's learned his lesson. Let's go get one of those beers."

That gave Sean an idea.

"Hey, Glory," he said. "I'm afraid you're going to go away thinking we're all mean white folks up here. We don't want that, do we fellas?"

"No, hell no!" cried Jack knowing Sean was up to something.

"You like beer, Glory?" said Sean. "Wouldn't ya like to have a nice beer with your new white friends before ya go?"

"I don't drink," said Glory turning away. "I've gotta get back."

Sean grabbed his arm and motioned for Jack to grab the other. "C'mon now, we're gonna think ya don't like us. You'd insult us something terrible if ya refuse to have one lousy beer with us."

Sean had a tight grip on one arm and Jack the other. They turned and began leading him toward the warehouse door. His stomach and jaw hurt and he wasn't sure he could run even if he could yank free. *Best to just go along with them,* he thought. *Drink their damn beer and get back to the boat. The way my luck's running, the repairs may already be done and they'll leave without me.*

The Grettsmer warehouse was over fifty years old and framed with foot-square oak timbers. A full block wide and two stories tall, it extended almost another half block toward the river.

Years earlier, the lower area had been used to store blocks of river ice sold to the packing houses, grocery stores and homes to use in their iceboxes. In those days the river was much cleaner and crews would saw huge blocks of ice and use horses to pull them across the frozen surface and straight into the building. Carefully packed in sawdust, the ice would last most of the summer. It was a popular place to hang out on a hot afternoon.

The ground level floor was the only one in use these days. About half the space was used to store metal piping and the other half held ripped hardwoods that were stored and supplied to area builders. It was a good business to be in and the Grettsmer family had made a small fortune providing the raw materials for many of the area's more elegant homes.

Sean and Tom, holding on to Glory, entered the building and followed Jack down a shadowy corridor until they reached an office area half way back toward the river. It was separated from the rest of the warehouse by a large glass partition that came down from the ceiling to waist level. Several desks and chairs were positioned around the room.

"Go in there and wait," said Jack pointing to the office. "I'll go down and grab some beer. Dieter keeps it hidden in the old icehouse. And for God's sake, don't smoke. Too much wood dust in the air. You'll blow us to hell and back."

Tom and Sean led Glory into the room and found chairs to sit on. Sean switched on a desk lamp and grinned at Tom. No one said anything, they just sat and stared at one another.

"Here we go," said Jack returning shortly with a box of clinking bottles. "Dieter's Best!"

The mismatched bottles looked like old wine bottles, dark green and brown glass and capped with some type of cork and metal twist arrangement. None had any labels.

"Wow, look at the size of these bottles," exclaimed Sean. "How do you get 'em open?"

Jack grabbed a bottle and began to untwist the metal wires. "Like this," he said, "but slow and easy so they don't blow. When you get the twists off, grab the cork and slowly rock it back and forth pulling out at the same time until ..." Suddenly the cork flew off with a loud POP! "Just like that."

He laughed and took a swig. Soon he had three more bottles opened and sitting on the table. Sean grabbed two and handed one to Glory. "Here's to your health, Mr. Glory," he smirked. "*Slainte!*"

The beer was warm and foaming. It was also bitter and strong. Sean finished his in about four gulps and loudly belched.

"Damn, that's good stuff," he said. "G'me another."

Jack laughed. "Better slow down there, son. That stuff's supposed to pack a wallop!"

Tom was sipping his beer and clearly didn't like it. Glory, who rarely drank anyway, grimaced but choked down a swallow or two. When he had finished about a third of the bottle he stood up.

"I gotta go," he said. "Thanks for the beer but I gotta get back." He started to head for the door.

"Hey, hold it there, sonny," snarled Jack. "You didn't finish the beer. What's the matter, you don't like our beer?"

"Stomach hurts," muttered Glory rubbing where Sean had hit him. "Don't want to get sick." He walked through the door and started toward the entrance of the warehouse.

"Hey, grab him," said Sean jumping up. "Did you hear what he said? That damn nigger just insulted us again. He'll drink that beer or he ain't leaving."

They caught him about halfway down the corridor and pulled him back into the office, kicking and shouting all the way.

"Hold his arms back," said Sean, now giggling stupidly as he lifted the beer bottle toward Glory's mouth. "He's gonna drink this damn beer or else."

Sean got the bottle in the general direction of his mouth and started to pour, laughing like an idiot at the same time. Tom and Jack had Glory's arms pinned back but he was shaking his head back and forth causing most of the beer to spill down over his chin and run down his neck and chest. During the struggle, the front of Glory's shirt ripped open and Sean spied something shiny hanging around his neck.

"Hey, what's this?" he said as he started to reach for it.

When Glory realized what Sean was doing, he redoubled his efforts to free himself, but Tom and Jack held tightly. Just as Sean grabbed the necklace and yanked it free, Glory screamed out, "No!" and lunged forward and clamped down on Sean's fingers with his teeth.

Sean screamed out in pain.

"LET GO YOU DAMN NIGGER!" he yowled, and blindly swung his beer bottle. What happened next took place in just seconds but was replayed in all their minds later, many times over.

The bottle smacked Glory on the side of the head with a wet thud. Why it never broke surprised Sean because he knew he'd swung it hard. Glory immediately went limp. Tom and Jack let him loose and he slumped to the floor while Sean jumped around in a circle howling in pain. The skin on two fingers of his left hand was torn and bleeding where Glory's teeth had clamped down.

"He bit me," he screamed in pain. "Did you see that? That crazy nigger *bit* me."

"Damn," said Jack in an excited voice. "You thumped him a good 'un Sean, knocked him plum out – clean as a whistle."

Tom, who had jumped back in shock at this unplanned turn of events said, "Let's get him up and in a chair or something. We can't let him just lie there. Jeez, Sean, he might be hurt, hard as you hit him."

"Hell," said Sean looking at his bleeding hand, "He ain't hurt. Didn't even break the bottle. 'Sides, everybody knows coons' heads are mainly bone. He'll be fine. Leave him be, he'll come around in a minute and we'll kick his black ass outta here."

"Hey," shouted Jack, "I've got an idea. Let's take a picture of us together. How often do you get to see a nigger around here anyway? The old man's got a new camera. I'll get it."

"Are you nuts?" exclaimed Tom. "I don't wanna be in any picture. Let's just get him outta here."

"Hell yes," laughed Sean ignoring Tom and loving the idea. "Get it but hurry up before he comes to. And if candy-ass Tom don't want in the picture, he can take it."

Jack rushed over to a cupboard and took out a black box camera. "Let's hurry," he said. "Drag a couple more lamps over here so we'll have more light. Haul him up in the chair and Sean, you get on the other side and prop him up straight."

They quickly got everything arranged and into position. Jack stood on one side sporting a wide, silly grin. Sean stood on the other side, one arm propping up Glory's drooping head, the other brandishing the dripping beer bottle. Tom stood off to the side toward the back, steadied the camera on a cabinet, aimed and snapped the shutter.

"Got it," he said.

In the rush and confusion to set things up and take the picture, they hadn't heard a door quietly open behind them. Nor had they seen someone slip silently into the room staying well back into the shadows.

"Having fun, lads?" came the sound of an ice-cold voice.

CHAPTER FOUR

The three of them whipped around at the sound of the voice and froze as Policeman Pat O'Brien stepped out of the shadows.

"Paddy," shouted Sean in relief mixed with panic at the sight of his older brother, one of the few people he truly feared. "Scared the crap outta us. Where'd ya come from? Didn't hear ya, not a'tall."

The huge policeman walked slowly toward them, taking in the scene with cold, blank eyes, holding a flashlight in one hand and swinging a sinister-looking nightstick in the other. He stopped in front of the chair where Glory was slumped over, a tiny rivulet of blood now running down the side of his head and dripping on his ripped shirt.

"And who's this, lads?" he softly asked. "One of your new playmates?"

"Awww, Paddy," said Sean. "We was just ... "

"Shut up, you little shite!" he screamed while wheeling toward his younger brother and cocking his nightstick arm. "Don't say another word!"

Then, quickly spinning toward Jack he shouted, "You. What's going on here?"

Jack fell back as if slapped. After he recovered he told him how they were heading home when they found Glory sneaking by his dad's warehouse probably getting ready to break in and how there was a fight and he got knocked out and they brought him into the warehouse until he came around. Just having a little fun.

"A *little* fun, huh? And you," spinning around to face Tom, "is that the way it was? Just having a little fun?"

"Well, yeah," stammered Tom. "I mean things maybe got a little crazy, but we meant no harm. We're gonna let him go now anyway."

"Youse were, huh?" said Pat who by this time was bent down studying Glory. "Going to let him go now, was ya? Well, let me tell you three geniuses something. He ain't going nowhere. He's dead!"

When they heard that, the three boys spun as one to stare at Glory, their mouths dropped open and their eyes grew wide.

"Dead?" exclaimed Sean. "Naw, Paddy, he's just knocked out. He ain't dead!"

"Boyos, I know a dead man when I see one," said Pat moving in to feel for a pulse. "Look at his eyes. Half open. Look at his crotch. Peed his pants. And he ain't got no pulse. But he does have the side of his head caved in. Other than that, lads, he's just fine."

The three boys continued to stare in horror.

"Yeah," Pat said. "Looks like you tough guys done killed yourselves a nigger."

"Jeez, Paddy," stammered Sean. "Are you sure? It were an accident, I swear it. Barely tapped him with a bottle – didn't I, boys? Didn't even break. Look where he bit my hand ... "

Pat whirled and backhanded Sean so hard it knocked him off his feet and half way cross the room. Shocked, Jack fell backwards in a chair and sat staring at Glory. Tom turned away and started to sob.

"I don't give a crap about no damn accident," screamed the policeman. "He's dead! That's what counts! He's a nigger, but he's still *dead* and you three killed him."

A stunned silence followed while Pat unsuccessfully searched Glory's pockets for some identification. "Who is he, anyway?"

"Called himself Glory," answered Jack in a cracked voice. "Said he worked on a tug tied up at the ice harbor. But I wouldn't take the word of a nigger even if ... "

"Shut up, smart ass," snapped Pat. "There *is* a tug tied up down there. They called in earlier for permission. Checked it out myself. And speaking of calls," he continued in a tight voice. "I got another call 'bout an hour ago. Seems some smart ass, pissant punks tossed a brick through Kelly's window. Kelly's not happy. Not happy a'tall. Don't suppose you lads know anything about that either."

"C'mon, Paddy," whined Sean, wiping the blood off his dripping nose. "No one seen us toss any brick, and no one's seen us messing with this here guy. Hell, it were an accident. We didn't mean no harm, did we fellas?"

Before anyone had a chance to say or do anything else Pat screamed, "You dumb little shites still don't get it, does ya? *Kelly* knows who tossed the brick. Everyone there saw youse get kicked out. And what youse don't know is while I'm heading here some old lady flags me down and says she sees some people scuffling down the street. Maybe she sees your faces, maybe not. Wadda ya think? Wanna whack her with a bottle, too?"

At this point, the reality of what has happened really started to sink in and the boys looked panic-stricken.

"Damn, DAMN," cried Jack who was back up and walking around in a tight circle. "My old man hears about this he'll kill me."

"Your old man is the least of your troubles, you little puke," broke in Pat. "He may be the only one that'll keep your sorry ass out of jail. Just shut up and let me think for a second."

After a moment he said, "Okay. Here's what we do. YOU!" he said pointing at Tom causing him to jump a foot. "Bring me that camera and then get the hell home to your old lady as fast as you can, hear me? Good thing your old man ain't around no more to hear what a dumb shite of a son he has. And take this with you," he said, kicking the ripped off tag across the floor at him, "Get rid of it. Toss it down a sewer! I don't want to see your sorry ass around again, you understand? Get home and keep your mouth *shut* and don't come back this way again. YOU UNDERSTAND ME?"

"Yes," whispered Tom as he handed the big policeman the camera and picked up the tag and rushed out the door.

"And you, hot shot," he said looking at Jack. "Straighten this mess back up. Wipe up that slop on the floor and get home to your rich mommy and daddy before I takes ya up there myself and tells 'em how their sorry ass, pampered little shite of a son spends his hot summer nights. And by God I *will* tell 'em if I sees ya around here again, hear me?"

"But I *work* here," whined Jack.

"Not any more you don't," snapped Pat. "You're a smart kid. Tell your old man ya don't wanna work no more. Tell him you're bored. I don't give a damn *what* ya tell him, but you're done. If I was you I'd spend some of your old man's money and go away somewheres. You don't like it, I'll show your folks the picture of you standing next to your dead friend here. And don't think I won't. I can't believe you're all so stupid to take a damn picture in the first place. You try something funny and by God I'll show it to 'em."

Jack started to argue, but quickly thought twice about it and turned away to move the lamps and chairs back to where they were originally.

Pat then turned to Sean. "And you, tough guy, grab hold of your *friend* and help me carry him outta here before someone shows up."

"Where we gonna take him?" asked Sean nervously.

"Patrol car's out back. We'll stick 'im in there."

Sean grabbed on to Glory's ankles and Pat grabbed him under the arms and they started to drag him out the door and down the hall while Jack stood watching with wide eyes.

"YOU!" he shouted at Jack. "You'd better be the hell outta here by the time we get loaded up, hear me?"

Jack turned quickly away as Pat and Sean hauled Glory's body down the steps to the lower level and out the door. The patrol car sat in the shadows.

"How'd you get in?" asked Sean, puffing with the strain. "How'd ya know we was in there?"

"Got a key. I'm a *cop*, remember? I check up on these old warehouses every night just to make sure no bums, winos or stupid little freaks like you get inside. Lucky for you it *was* me."

They dumped the body in the trunk and slowly drove down the alley and around in front of the warehouse, paused and studied the building for a few moments. Seeing no lights or other activity, Pat grunted and headed off.

"Where we going?" Sean asked nervously. "What're we gonna do with him?"

The policeman said nothing. He drove down dark, deserted streets and alleys winding his way down toward the river and north of town. Sean asked him again where they were going but when he continued to ignore him he sat back and kept quiet.

Soon they came to Lock and Dam No. 11. Pat stopped the car, got out and went up and unlocked the gate. He came back, turned off the headlamps and slowly drove down a gravel road and pulled in by the station house adjacent to the dam.

"Get out!" he growled in a low voice to Sean.

They went back to the trunk and wrestled the body out and pulled it over to the edge of the cement wall on the upriver side of the dam. Pat went back to the trunk and retrieved a length of rusty old chain and wad of bailing wire.

"Go over to that pile of scrap and haul one of those pipe sections over here."

Pat wrapped one end of the chain around Glory's neck and torso. The other end he brought down and under his crotch and back up to his neck. He then wired the ends together and threaded one end of the wire through the heavy metal pipe and brought it out and fastened it to the chain.

"Grab hold of 'im," he said.

Together they manhandled the trussed body up on the edge of the wall. The river was only a few feet below. Its swirling surface covered with the scum of leaves, bits of wood, bottles and upstream trash. Violent, angry eddies were evidence of a strong current as it fought its way under the immense sluice gates at the bottom of the dam.

With a shove of his black boot, Pat pushed Glory over the edge. He watched as the body splashed into the churning water and quickly disappeared. Sean bent over and vomited. As they walked silently back to the car and drove away, Sean, still in a state of shock, pondered how many other bodies had vanished in a similar manner.

It was a slow, silent ride back to town. Sean, now completely sobered up, was beginning to realize the enormity of what had taken place. He said nothing. His brother didn't volunteer anything.

As they approached the *Flats*, Pat turned off the headlights again and cruised slowly down the dark streets and into the alley behind the wood frame, two-story O'Brien house. Sean still lived there although Pat had moved out years ago. As they pulled to a stop, Sean turned to his older brother and said, "Really sorry 'bout this, Paddy. Didn't mean for ... "

"You've got five minutes," interrupted his brother. "Grab some clothes; underwear, socks, extra pants, shirts and get back out here."

"What'd ya mean? What'd ya talking about?" stammered Sean, panicking again. "Where we going? I said I was sorry ... "

Pat quickly reached over and grabbed him by the neck, and even though Sean tried to break loose, pulled him effortlessly toward him and snarled in a beery, tobacco stale breath, "Five minutes, you little shite. Five minutes or I swear to God I'll come in there after ya. Understand? And ya better not wake ma or anyone else," he added and roughly shoved him out into the dark alley.

Sean hurried into the house through the back door. For a moment he thought about going right on out the front, but he knew that would be a big mistake. He quickly went to his room and grabbed an old gym bag and stuffed in some clothes. He moved as fast as he could, trying hard not to wake up his two younger brothers asleep on the cot next to his. He had no idea where Pat was taking him, maybe back to his place where he could hide out for a few days.

He was upset the way things were turning out but he knew it was no use arguing. He'd never before seen Pat so mad and was still unnerved by the practiced way he'd disposed of the body. As he turned and started out of the room he almost knocked over his little sister, Deidre, who'd been standing in the doorway watching him.

"Where ya going, Sean?" she whispered.

"Shhhhhh, sis," Sean said bending down to her level. She was the only one in the family he really cared about. A thin, sickly little thing no bigger than a minute, but "with the heart of a saint," his mother liked to tell people.

"Just going to stay with a friend tonight. I'll talk to ma tomorrow. You go back to bed now, okay?

"Okay. 'Nite, Sean."

They drove away and Pat turned the headlights back on.

"Here's $18, all I got with me," he said, shoving money across the seat toward Sean.

"What's that for?" I don't need any money."

"You're leaving town. And you're leaving for good. I don't wanna see ya around here again, got it?"

"What the hell ya talking about?" said Sean in a shocked voice. "Leave town? What for? Where I'm supposed to go? Hell, I said it were an accident ..."

"You still don't get it yet, do ya, ya dumb little Mick? You and your idiot friends just *killed* someone! They may or may not ever find the body, but someone's gonna come looking and sooner or later they might figure it out. And then, there're those two dumb-ass friends of yours. We shoulda dumped them in the river, too. How long before one of them gets liquored up and brags that he killed a nigger? You ever talk to them again, tell 'em I'm holding on to that camera and if they try to get smart with me, well, you figure it out, and that includes you."

Pat drove up to the Iowa-Illinois Bridge and pulled over to the curb. Sean, still in shock was staring at him, not believing this was happening.

"This is as far as I go. Walk over to the depot and wait for the Chicago freight. Should be in an hour or so. They'll let ya ride in the mail car for $5."

"Jeez, Paddy," whined Sean. "I don't wanna go to Chicago. What the hell am I supposed to do there?"

"Here's Uncle Sean's address," Pat said handing him a scrap of paper. "I'll let 'em know you're coming. They'll put ya up for a few days. Hell, the old man named ya after him, he might even get you a job in the yards."

"But I hardly know him. Only met him once, didn't I? C'mon, why don't you let me stay with you for awhile?"

"Ya don't wanna work in the yards," Pat continued as if he hadn't heard a word Sean was saying, "join the Army. Hell, we're gonna be sucked into a damn war soon enough anyway. Tell 'em what a tough guy ya are. How you're good at killing people. They'll sign ya right up. Just don't come back here, understand? Now get the hell out!"

Sean stumbled out of the patrol car. "Damn it, Paddy, you're my *brother*. Ya can't just push ..."

The door slammed shut and Pat drove away.

Sean stood shaking and watched until the taillights disappeared from view. He looked around the deserted streets trying to make sense of what just happened. Finally he turned and slowly started across the bridge. "Screw him," he mumbled. "Hell, screw 'em all. I was gonna leave anyway."

Half way across the deserted bridge he stopped to pee in the water far below. He looked back toward town and could still make out the outline of the elegant old bluff houses. He wondered if Jack was home.

Down along the waterfront the reflections of the old streetlights rippled in crazy, zigzag patterns on the black water. And way off in the distance, he could make out the heavy, droning sound of heavy motors as a tug pushed a load of coal up river.

CHAPTER FIVE

Captain Warren Placer headed down to the crew's quarters shortly after 10:00. The inspection had been completed. They were lucky. Other than some shaft fittings that were jarred loose, the damage was minimal. After a quick repair job, it was time to retrieve the barges and start moving up river again.

The moon was out in full force and a gentle, warm breeze was blowing down river. Capt. Placer paused and gazed out at the Dubuque skyline, admiring the rugged strength the city reflected. He loved the Mississippi, especially this stretch along the Iowa-Wisconsin border, with its towering bluffs and extravagant vistas. And he loved the river towns, especially those picturesque old places like Dubuque, built out of the virgin wilderness with the strength and sweat of immigrants.

He was pleased no real damage had been done, but he now wanted to get back on schedule. Three hours lost was not terrible, and he knew he could make it up if they could speed up their lock entries and exits.

Andy saw him coming and expected the worse. And when he made his announcement that it was time to move on, his stomach sank. Glory hadn't returned and he knew something was terribly wrong. He'd started worrying earlier and even walked out on deck several times and stared up and down the riverbank hoping to catch a glimpse of his friend. It just wasn't like Glory to screw up like this. What could have happened?

He followed Capt. Placer back up to pilot room and told him about Glory's disappearance.

"Sorry to hear 'bout that, Andy," he said. "b   ut you know the rules and so does he. We can't sit here all night waiting for a crew hand to come stumbling back on board with a belly full of beer. I've got a barge they're waiting for in Minneapolis and I'm already three hours behind schedule. Get back to your job!"

Captain Placer was in no mood to listen to arguments and Andy knew it'd just be a waste of time anyway. He also knew Glory hadn't gone to town to go drinking, but what could he say? The rules were plain. Everyone knew them. It wasn't as if the Captain was being unfair.

Quickly the tug left the ice harbor and chugged the short distance back down river to hook up the barges. As far as Capt. Placer was concerned it wasn't that unusual to lose a crew hand along the way. Every once in a while, one would slip into town for "one beer" and before the evening was over, some local roughneck would get him drinking and next thing you knew, he'd end up lying in an alley with a golf ball-sized knot on the back of his head and his pockets turned inside out. A foggy memory and major headache were all he got for his evening's enjoyment.

He also knew he'd usually show up on the return trip – waiting by one of the locks, hat in hand, the picture of sorrow and piety. He'd usually take him back, docking him pay not earned and demoting him to the dirtiest, beginner jobs.

But those were the best-case, *white man* scenarios. Glory was a Negro.

In Glory's case, he *was* actually surprised. He'd quietly been watching him at work during the last few trips, and was impressed with the way he handled himself. Crewing on a tugboat wasn't exactly brain surgery but strength, agility and plenty of common sense were the benchmarks of success. Added intelligence and the earned respect of one's mates meant more responsibilities and a larger paycheck. And Glory was on his list for promotion.

He suspected something unsavory might have happened after all. According to Andy, Glory would have been back on board if he could have been. He didn't think he drank or gambled, but what the men did in the privacy of their own quarters was their business as long as they did their jobs. The best he could do was hope, regardless of what happened, that he'd be waiting when they returned this way the following week. In the meantime, his job was to keep the barge moving.

His prior good humor evaporated like an early morning mist as he pushed the men to quickly hook up the barges. Eventually, in the dark of night they slowly started back up river. Lock and Dam No. 11 was just north of town when the work began again in earnest.

CHAPTER SIX

Tom Lavarato had been the first to leave the warehouse.

He stumbled out the front door, looked left and right to see if anyone had heard the commotion before charging down the three steps and heading toward home. He was still in a state of shock and felt like he was going to be sick. It wasn't because of the beer. Other than his father lying in his casket, he'd never seen a dead person before. Now here he was involved in a killing.

He ran most of the two miles, choking and sobbing as he went, trying to stay in the shadows, praying he wouldn't see someone who'd recognize him. As he approached his old two-story house, he looked up and saw the light on in his mother's room. He knew she'd be waiting up for him, sitting quietly in the same old over-stuffed chintz chair, in the same old bedroom she had shared with her husband of 43 years. She'd most likely be reading the Bible, or listening to the radio.

He also knew she wouldn't come downstairs to challenge him – demanding to know where he'd been and why he was so late. She quit doing that months ago. Now she just needed to know he got home safely, as if somehow that gave purpose to her shattered life. She'd hear him come in and go to his room. Only then would she turn off the light and go to bed.

Tom opened the back door as quietly as he could and went to his room down the hallway behind the kitchen. His bedroom used to be upstairs but after his dad died, his old maid aunt, Ophelia, who hardly spoke a word of English and seemed reluctant to learn, had unexpectedly shown up at the funeral, and had stayed and moved in to keep his mother company.

He'd never met her before and didn't even know where she came from. There'd been talk about her over the years between his mother and father, but he was never included in the conversations. She seemed to be a source of some amusement to his father who would often kid his mother about her. Aunt Ophelia moved into his old room upstairs just down the hall from his mother's. He'd occasionally hear them quietly talking together in rural Italian.

They converted a seldom used, first floor dining area into his bedroom. He loved the privacy and was allowed to furnish it just the way he wanted, as long as it didn't require spending any money.

The family had received a small death benefit after his dad was killed, but it was barely enough to bury him and pay the medical expenses. The bus yard where his father had worked took Tom on as a courtesy to the family, but his lack of skills resulted in a meager paycheck. It was better than nothing, of course, and since the house was paid for, they were getting by.

Although it was never discussed openly, Aunt Ophelia seemed to have some mysterious form of income of her own and occasionally contributed toward expenses. Where the money came from was a total mystery to him. As far as he could tell she never received any mail and seldom left the house. Yet every once and awhile she'd appear in the kitchen, and hand his mother an envelope. No words were exchanged and his mother cautioned him not to ask.

When Tom got home that fateful night he shuffled into his room, shut the door and without turning on the light took off his shoes and fell back on the bed fully clothed, covered his face with a pillow and began to cry in earnest.

"Oh my God," he moaned softly to himself. "What happened tonight? I just helped kill a person! Oh, Lord, I'm so sorry. It was an accident. We didn't mean to hurt him. What am I going to do? What should I do?"

He lay there for hours, tossing and turning until finally, in the blackest, silent hours before dawn, he fell into a restless sleep.

He woke Sunday morning in a panic. Sunday Mass. He wouldn't take communion, he couldn't. He was now living with mortal sin on his soul and it would stay there until confession. He knew his mother would notice if he didn't go to communion and wonder why not and somehow the whole terrible story would come out. So when she called him to breakfast, he said he didn't feel good and was going to stay in bed. It wasn't the first time he'd come home drunk that summer and as unhappy as it made her, she let him be.

"Losing a father is a terrible thing," Ophelia muttered to her. "Give him time."

He stayed in his room most of the day, helpless with guilt and making outrageous promises to God that if He would somehow help him out of this desperate situation, he would do anything He wished.

Hours passed as he quietly listened to the radio for any news about the "incident." He was halfway expecting the police to arrive at the front door at any moment, pounding with their fists and shouting for him to come quietly or suffer the consequences. He was rigid with fear.

As the afternoon turned into evening without a word, he began to relax a little. And later, when his mother insisted he come and get something to eat, he finally went into the kitchen and sat down to a plate of spaghetti. He hadn't eaten anything for 24 hours and although he still didn't feel hungry, he was surprised at how quickly he polished it off.

His Aunt Ophelia sat off to the side of the kitchen in her rocker, silently watching him while he ate, her beady, black eyes boring into his skull. He was sure she somehow knew everything that had happened the night before and he dared not look at her.

He quickly finished and went back to the small bathroom by his bedroom and lost his dinner.

CHAPTER SEVEN

Jack Grettsmer left the warehouse shortly after Tom. Like Tom, he'd sobered up quickly. It hadn't taken him very long to move the lamps back to their original positions, rearrange the chairs and wipe up a small puddle of beer, blood and urine that had dripped off Glory's body onto the polished wood floor.

After a quick look around he also headed home. He stuck to the alleys, where he carefully got rid of the rags and the empty bottles, tossing them into an old trash bin. He then trotted up the steep hill toward the bluffs while looking over his shoulder for the dreaded patrol car.

Unlike Tom, Jack felt strangely excited about how things had gone that night; first the fracas at *Kelly's*, then the episode with the Negro. However, he *was* concerned about Policeman O'Brien's threat to talk to his folks. He didn't think he'd actually do it and even if he did, he knew it wasn't his fault. He didn't tell Sean to whack the guy with the bottle. Damn nigger shouldn't have been sneaking down the streets anyway.

On the other hand, if they found the body and somehow figured out what happened and he got implicated, it would undoubtedly get in the paper and that would make his father furious. And *that* was what really worried Jack. He knew his old man would keep him out of jail. He had once before. Of course, it hadn't involved a killing, unless you consider burning up a sack of cats "a killing." His dad did manage to keep that out of the paper, but he'd never seen him so angry.

"Bad publicity," he'd heard him say on more than one occasion, "can ruin a business quicker than a bad product."

The Grettsmer house stood in the middle of Bluff Street and provided a marvelous view up and down the Mississippi. It was a lovely old Queen Anne built around the turn of the century. They bought it and moved in when Jack was only five years old. It was a grand looking place with two full floors, a third if you counted the unfinished attic, a lovely wraparound porch, and adjacent coach house which now served as a garage.

The basement was filled with an immense, oil-fired Timken boiler that fed hot water through miles of Grettsmer piping and kept the house comfortable during the cruelest of Iowa winters. It was a huge house with six bedrooms and five bathrooms, almost unheard of in that day and age. Other than his parents, the only people living there were Jack and his younger sister, Anna. His mother did employ a daily maid, and there was a servant's room at the back of the house. But Mr. Grettsmer wouldn't allow a servant around at night, so she came by trolley from across town every day to clean and cook.

Jack slipped in through the servant's entrance and went straight to his room. No one was up and even if they were, no one would have bothered to ask where he'd been.

When he went to bed that night his conscience was clear enough with regard to the killing, or at least his part in it, but the more he thought about it, the more he worried about what would happen if that damn cop showed up.

When he woke up Sunday morning he not only had a monster headache, he remembered the camera! *The camera! That damn camera*, he thought to himself. What in the hell had he been thinking, taking a picture like that? And now that damn cop had it.

He stayed around the house all day, avoiding the rest of the family as best he could. That night he didn't sleep as well. As expected there had been nothing in the newspaper or on the radio all day. He doubted now there would be, but he was smart enough to realize that eventually someone might come snooping. And with a potentially incriminating photo of him floating around, maybe the damn cop was right. Maybe it was time to kiss this shit hole town goodbye.

The following morning, Jack's parents were pleasantly surprised to hear that their fair-haired son was reconsidering college after all. His earlier refusal to even talk about it had caused an ugly scene at home. His father, a Brown University alumnus, had spent the earlier part of the summer arguing, then pleading, finally begging without shame, with his old alma mater to accept Jack despite his pitiful grades. It was only after an unusually generous financial offer was made that minds were changed and an official Letter of Acceptance was reluctantly sent to the Grettsmer household.

All this was done without Jack's knowledge or interest. That became painfully clear when during a surprise birthday breakfast his father proudly presented him with a crisp $100 bill and the "magical" Letter of Acceptance from Brown. Jack managed to alienate himself completely by kissing the $100 bill and wadding up the Letter of Acceptance and tossing it in the wastebasket.

After an hour of screaming and arguing, his father stomped out of the room in a cold fury. His mother, silent during the entire sordid affair, stared out the window and thought of happier times.

Jack continued to work at the warehouse that summer avoiding contact with this father at all costs. Though it was never talked about openly, the rest of the employees eventually learned what had happened and groaned with the knowledge they'd have to put up with this sour, ill-behaved young man indefinitely.

But now, with this sudden, unexpected change of heart, his father was elated. His mother, who had given up trying to understand Jack years ago, smiled with relief. Of course, the truth be known, Jack didn't give a damn about Brown University or any other of the hot shot Ivy League colleges his old man was always ranting about. It was his ticket out of town and under the circumstances, the sooner the better.

Two weeks later he left. He refused to let his father accompany him East and ended up taking the train alone, an ultimatum that almost squashed the whole deal. He departed with a pocket full of cash, a substantial Letter of Credit to see him through the first year, and vague promises to get together with the family over the holidays.

CHAPTER EIGHT

The freight train arrived in Chicago at 4:30 in the morning. It had been a nightmare journey of constant starting and stopping. Sean felt terrible from lack of sleep, a throbbing headache and empty stomach. Disoriented, wobbly, and rather apprehensive, he climbed down from the mail car and stood on the deserted freight platform clutching his gym bag, and peered into the predawn grit of the Windy City. It started to drizzle.

When he showed his uncle's address to one of the workers, he was told the location was several miles away, in the south end of the city.

"It's a 30-minute trolley ride, pal. But they don't start running until 7:00, being it's Sunday and all."

"To hell with that!" he muttered to himself. "I've got money. I'll take a cab."

There were two cabs sitting in front of the station. Both looked empty until he walked up to one and peered inside. The driver was asleep. He tapped on the window and woke the man up.

"How much to his address?" he asked holding up a piece of paper.

The cabbie squinted and looked at the address and then at Sean, looking him up and down.

"$2.00."

"$2.00! Are you crazy? I just want a ride, I don't want to buy your damn hack!"

Leaving the cabbie sitting there too shocked to be mad yet, he went to the second cab and knocked on the door.

"I'll give you a buck if you take me to this address."

"Hop in," the cabbie said, sitting up and starting the motor.

Twenty minutes later the cab dropped him off in front of an old row house. It was dark brick, two stories tall and half as narrow as a regular house. And it was smack in the middle of an entire block of identical, attached row houses. The only difference he could see was the color of the lace curtains in the front windows.

He stood on the curb for a moment, looking up and down the empty streets trying to decide whether to stay or leave. But where could he go? He walked up the six steps and stood for a minute in front of the door, unsure whether to knock or not. He didn't hear a sound inside. Peering into the window he couldn't see any lights. Then it dawned on him.

"Damn," he muttered glancing at his cheap wristwatch. "It's not even 5:00 yet and it's Sunday. Everyone must still be asleep. I'll go find a diner somewhere and come back later."

He turned to head back down the stairs when suddenly the door opened and his Aunt Deirdre, hair covered in curlers, poked out her head.

"Sean? Is it you, luv? I've been waiting on ya here in the parlor. Your brother Pat called last night. Told us you'd be coming early and all. But never mind, luv, come in now and be quiet. Himself's still abed. I'll fix us a cuppa."

CHAPTER NINE

Tom Lavarato didn't go to Mass the following Sunday either. He told his mother he might be coming down with something, maybe the flu. So for the second time since her husband died, she went to Mass alone.

Flu or not, Tom went back to work Monday and for the second week in a row came home immediately afterwards. He may have seemed unusually quiet but his mother didn't mind, she was just happy to have him around for a change. He even stayed home Friday night, a night he almost always spent with his friends. Aunt Ophelia watched him like a predator. She knew something was amiss, but her sister told her to just hush.

Saturday evening, Tom finally left the house for the first time, but instead of meeting his pals like he told his ma, he headed to St. Michael's for confession. He was terrified. He'd known all along that he had to confess his terrible sin, and his stomach was again twisted in knots.

He arrived at church hoping there would be a crowd lined up for confession. There was. He felt a little better knowing that Father O'Malley tended to speed things up when it was busy. He got into line and when his turn came he quickly slipped into the confessional and knelt down, his pulse racing. He was never comfortable at confession. He was always embarrassed telling his sins no matter how minor they may be. But this time it was different, mortally different.

He hated kneeling there in the quiet, talcum powder-scented air, waiting for the priest to finish hearing the confession of the person on the other side. He could hear the low drone of voices and knew at any minute they'd finish. His heart was pounding like a drum and he thought he might get sick again when suddenly, it was time.

The screen in front of his face slid back and he could faintly see Father O'Malley sitting on the other side, looking down toward his lap and reciting, "In the name of the Father, the Son and the Holy Ghost."

"Bless me, Father," Tom began in a low register tone, hoping to disguise his voice. "It's been three weeks since my last confession. During this time I've taken God's name in vain seven times, and during this time I've had impure thoughts, six times. And I missed Mass twice, but I was sick and stayed at home and didn't go anywhere ..." and he paused.

"Is that all, son?" Father O'Malley asked after a moment.

The time had come.

"No, Father," he stammered. "I was part of a terrible accident a few nights ago, and I have a mortal sin to confess."

"A *mortal* sin, is it? What type of accident are we talking about, son?"

"Well, Father, an accident – like when someone gets hurt, hurt really badly, maybe even killed."

"I don't understand, son, are you telling me you were involved in an automobile accident or something?"

"No, Father," whispered Tom. "Worse than that. I think I helped kill someone!" Suddenly his voice broke and he started to cry.

There was a long pause and finally Father O'Malley asked in a low voice, "Is this Thomas Lavarato I'm talking with?"

"Yes, Father," stuttered Tom after a panic-stricken moment, horrified he'd been identified.

"Thomas, you wait for me in the back of church until confessions are over. We can talk more about this then." When not hearing a reply, he added, "Do you hear me, Thomas?"

"Yes, Father."

"Right then. We'll straighten this out later. You can go now."

Tom left the confessional on shaky legs and headed to the back of church. He felt as if all eyes were turned on him, as if everyone in the church had heard the damning recital. He walked straight ahead and, ignoring Father O'Malley's instructions, continued right out the church door and rushed home. His world was coming apart, and now his pastor knew about it.

As he turned the corner, a half block from his house, he heard someone call his name. He looked across the street and saw Jack Grettsmer, standing by his bike, waving him over.

"Where're in the hell ya been?" said Jack. "I've been looking for ya for almost an hour. Your ma said you were out with some friends."

"Nah, I went to confession but didn't stay. Line was too long."

"When in the hell is your old lady going to get a phone? I could have saved a ride over here. Good God, can't believe ya don't have a damn phone. But listen, have you talked to Sean? Do you know what his brother did with that camera?"

"Camera?" Tom exclaimed in confusion. Then it suddenly dawned on him. "Holy crap! The camera! I forgot all about it. No – I haven't talked to anyone. Why?"

"Why? Wadda ya mean *why?*" You took our picture with that dead nigger, that's *why*! What if that psycho brother of his develops the film and shows that picture to someone? Hell, that's evidence against me."

"Jeez, Jack, why would he do something like that? I mean, his own brother's in the picture, too."

"I don't know, but I wouldn't put anything past him. As crooked as he is, he might show it to my folks – get some blackmail money or something."

"Gosh, I don't think he'd do that. He'd have to get it developed – and he could get himself in big trouble if anyone found out. I betcha he's got it stashed someplace – you know – to scare us. You ask Sean?"

"Thought of that. I called his house three times. His old lady told me he wasn't there but later his old man answered, drunker than a skunk. He said Sean was gone."

"Gone? Gone where?"

"How the hell do I know?" said Jack. "I bet that damn cop brother of his had something to do with it. He's a mean one. I'd sure like to know what they did with that nigger."

"C'mon Jack, don't say that. We killed a person. Don't you know that's a serious crime, not to mention a mortal sin?"

"Crime? Mortal sin? Your ass! It was an accident. Sean's the one that hit him. We might have roughed him up a little, but he had it coming."

"But what if we get caught? We'd still be in big trouble."

"Ain't nobody gonna get caught. You didn't say anything to anyone did you?"

"No – 'course not!"

"Well there hasn't been a word about it on the radio or newspaper. Hell, bet they never find him. And even if they do, I'll be long gone."

"Gone? Where're *you* going?" asked Tom, startled at this second shocking piece of information.

"Going to college, my young, uneducated friend. My old man almost crapped his pants when I told him I'd decided to go to his stupid old school after all. I'm leaving this weekend. Going to the East coast. You should come with me and leave this turd burg behind."

"Oh sure, Jack, great idea! I'll just quit my job, leave ma alone, and take the $6 I've got saved and meet you at the station."

"Up to you, pal. In the meantime you'd better hope no one gets that film developed. Anyway, better keep your trap shut about it."

Having said that, he turned and pedaled away. Tom stood and watched him fade into the darkness.

Sure, he admitted to himself. He'd like to go with him. Somewhere – anywhere far away. But he knew he was stuck. College costs money, and besides he couldn't just leave his ma alone even if her nutty sister was there. With Jack gone and Sean missing, he was left behind to face the music alone.

CHAPTER TEN

When the *John R. Ruxton* passed through Lock and Dam No. 11 on its return trip to Memphis several days later, Capt. Placer felt anxious. He'd half expected Glory to catch up with them before then.

This was the last chance. If he was going to show up at all, he knew this would be the most likely place. The crew realized the same thing, and during the frantic scurrying around, while they prepared the barge for lock entry, worried eyes scanned the shore. But Glory was nowhere in sight. Short of running off with another woman, which Capt. Placer really didn't think happened, he now thought the most likely explanation was that once Glory missed getting back to the tug in time, he panicked and went home.

When they arrived at Memphis the following week they learned Glory was still missing. Andy had immediately gone to see his wife and parents and related what had happened. They were devastated, fearing the worse. That weekend, Andy took Elizabeth to talk with Capt. Placer. Upon meeting her and realizing what this unfortunate, pregnant young woman was going through, he felt worse than ever.

"I can't tell you how sorry we are, Mrs. Alexander," he said. "As Andy surely told you, we don't know what could have happened to Glory. I know how you must feel, but all we can do is hope for the best."

"Yes, sir," she said. "I do understand and I realize it's not your fault. It's just that ..." and she began to cry softly.

"Now, now, Mrs. Alexander. Everything's gonna be fine."

"No, sir. I'm afraid it isn't. It's not like Glory to go missing like that. Something bad happened to him, I'm sure."

"Well, we can't be certain of that now, can we? And before I forget it, here," he said, handing her an envelope. "Here's Glory's full pay for the two weeks. I want you to know his friends doubled up and covered his job so you would receive the full wages, $72."

"Thank you, sir. And thank you, Andy," she said turning to her old friend. "Please let the others know how much I appreciate it."

"Mrs. Alexander," said Capt. Placer, "I've talked to the owners and they've agreed, if it's all right with you, of course, to place a notice in the Dubuque newspaper. Someone might have seen or heard something and be able to help. We've already contacted the Dubuque police department and they know nothing, and I do believe they were telling me the truth. But a notice in the paper couldn't hurt anything. We can't promise anything might come of it but ..."

"That would be very nice of you, sir," Elizabeth interrupted showing a hopeful smile on her face for the first time. "We'd surely appreciate it, yes sir, we surely would."

"All right then, you let me take care of it," he said and paused a moment before continuing. "But if I may make a suggestion, is there any possibility you'd be willing to offer a cash reward? Say, for information leading to finding Glory? I think that might help get more attention. The owners are willing to pay for the ad, but ..."

"No, no, I understand," she interrupted again looking down at the pay envelope and then back at Capt. Placer. "Would $72 be enough?"

"That would be *more* than enough, Mrs. Alexander. Let's try $25 for now and if you'd just set aside that much, let's see what we can do. But please keep in mind, we may not get any response at all. You do understand."

"Yes sir, I understand. And I do appreciate all you're doing to help me. You'll let me know, won't you?"

"Yes, I will," he said standing up and shaking her hand. "And thanks, Andy, for bringing Mrs. Alexander in to see me. You both take care now."

Capt. Placer did as he promised and that week arranged to have a notice placed in the Dubuque paper. He doubted it'd do any good, but at least he'd tried.

CHAPTER ELEVEN

Sean lived with his aunt and uncle for the next year and a half. They moved him into a small, rear room on the second floor, and for the first time in years, gave his life structure.

It wasn't easy on any of them at first. But eventually, slowly, Sean recognized they actually seemed to care for him, and he tried the best he could to improve. Mostly, it worked.

Uncle Sean and Aunt Deirdre had two children of their own with only one still living. Brennan, their youngest child and only son, had been struck and killed by a hit-and-run driver the evening of his 12th birthday. They never really recovered from the tragedy. So, in a way, Sean coming to stay with them was as good for them as it was for him.

Their daughter, Tara, had married poorly and moved to St. Louis years ago. They only saw her and the two grandchildren infrequently, and it broke their hearts when they did. Tara's husband was not a nice man.

They never pushed Sean for an explanation of why he came to Chicago. Pat had been very vague when he called, hinting at problems at home with the old man. They knew of his father's growing death grip with whiskey that had already resulted in minimal, if any, contact with the rest of the family. It was sad because they also knew Sean's mother, Mary, was a living saint on a downward spiral to despair.

At his aunt's prodding Sean wrote his mother a few letters. Getting no response he tried calling. But when his father answered in a slurred, nasty voice he quickly hung up. Eventually he quit trying altogether. His mother paid some neighbors to use their phone and called him, once on his birthday, and again at Christmas. The conversations were always strained and always ended with a crying plea for him to come home. Of course, she didn't know the circumstances of his leaving, and he'd never tell her. He missed his sister and younger brothers, of course, and was happy to hear they were doing just fine. He asked about Pat just once and wasn't surprised to learn she had no idea. She never saw him or heard from him.

Eventually, all communication between them stopped.

Later that fall Sean got involved with a couple of local troublemakers, which ended up in an ugly, neighborhood bar room brawl. But Chicago wasn't Dubuque. For one thing, Dubuquers didn't fight with knives. For another, he had no policeman brother to bail him out, and no locals to vouch for him. I suppose you could say he was lucky; one inch lower and a main artery in his arm would have been severed. As it was, he received eighteen, painful, no anesthetic stitches and ended up spending a very scary and sleepless night in the local drunk tank.

His uncle came and got him the following morning and on the walk back to the house had a long talk with him. He explained how he understood his feelings about having to leave home and all. He told him he was most welcome staying with them, and how much his aunt missed her own children and loved having him with them. At the same time he firmly admonished that this would have to be the last time for something like this. If it happened again, he'd have to leave.

When they got back to the house, he found his aunt standing by the door with a wad of tissues in her hand. She'd been crying and was overjoyed to have him back safely. She threw her arms around him and cried on his shoulder. Exhausted, embarrassed, and perhaps for the first time in his life, truly sorry for his poor behavior, he told them both he was planning to change. And this time he did.

During the following months, Sean worked hard doing basic construction work around the downtown area. His uncle, a foreman on the city streets department, got him a job on a friend's crew and still managed to keep a watchful eye on him. Chicago was bustling in those days and there was more construction work going on than they could handle.

Sean did not let them down and was soon contributing to his room and board. With his aunt's help, he even wired small amounts of money to his mother back in Dubuque, always in care of his neighbors so his father couldn't get his hands on it. With a little more pressure from both his aunt and uncle, Sean even started to attend Mass again, breaking a long hiatus since high school.

Eventually, he started seeing a few girls he met in church. Nothing serious. A movie and a hot dog, a bus ride to Lincoln Park Zoo, that was about as serious as it got. It wasn't that he didn't like girls. The problem was they all wanted to know more about him than he cared to tell.

That December, the Japanese bombed Pearl Harbor and less than a week later, Germany declared war on America. And just that fast, everything changed and the world seemed to spin out of control.

The following year – 1942 – was both exciting and difficult for young men Sean's age. War news was everywhere, monopolizing newspapers and radio. Black and white newsreels in every theater showed war action as it unfolded.

Like many of his new friends, Sean quickly got caught up in the excitement and fervor of it all. One by one, he saw the majority of his pals enlist. Soon the glory and the pressure of it all became too difficult to ignore and, despite his aunt's frantic pleading to not do anything rash, Sean also enlisted. It happened during intermission at a local movie theater during the showing of *Flying Tigers*. It wasn't planned. It just happened.

While the Marine Hymn played over the theater's sound system and as a Marine color guard marched to center stage from the theater's wings, all the men in the theatre were invited to come on up and "do their part." Before he even had a chance to think about it, he jumped up from his seat and followed a small group toward the stage.

The recruiting team's snappy dress blues, the promise of travel to exotic places, the excitement, the adventure. It was all too much for him. In fifteen minutes he'd signed up and by the time he'd filed out after the movie ended, he had his papers in hand. He was to leave in five days!

The mood in the house that night was like a mini-Irish wake. And despite the proud announcement made by his uncle the next day, and the claps on the back he received from his work crew, his aunt took to her bed for two straight days. Sean felt terrible, but any second thoughts, even if they existed, were too little, too late.

The following week he boarded the train for basic infantry training at Camp Matthew, San Diego, California. He was on his way to "kick some Jap ass!"

CHAPTER TWELVE

Father O'Malley was not one to avoid problems. Ever since he heard Tom Lavarato talk about "killing someone" and "committing a mortal sin" he knew something was seriously wrong. Tom was a good boy. He'd known him all his life. He'd even baptized him as a baby.

Of course he also knew about his father's fatal accident – a terrible, terrible thing it was. He suspected Tom was having problems coping with the tragedy. That was only natural. But this was way over the top, there must be some misunderstanding on the boy's part. Yet when he discovered Tom was not waiting for him after confession, he began to worry. That, he also knew, was not like him at all.

The Lavarato house was not far from church. He'd planned to telephone, but on learning they had no phone, he walked to the house. He also knew Tom was at work, and when Mrs. Lavarato answered the door, he had his story in place.

"Father O'Malley!" Mrs. Lavarato exclaimed, shocked to see her parish priest standing on her front stoop. "Please, come in. I'll fix us some tea."

"No, no thank you, Mrs. Lavarato," he said smiling. "I won't be taking up your time. I was just out for a bit of fresh air and decided to stop by with a wee request."

"Yes, Father, certainly, what can I do for you?" she replied, somewhat befuddled and more than a little nervous.

"I'm wondering if Thomas would be available to help me move some boxes in the church this evening. He's a good strong lad and it would be a blessing if he could lend a hand. Shouldn't take too long."

"Move some boxes?" she said in obvious relief. "Why of course he can help, Father. Be delighted. When would you like him?"

"Oh, any time. Any time a'tall, after your evening meal, of course."

"I'll have him there by 7:00. Would that be all right, Father?"

"Lovely, Mrs. Lavarato. That'd be lovely. Have him stop at the rectory. Thank you very much. And God bless you," he said as he tipped his hat, turned and left.

"Well now, wasn't that nice," she muttered as she shut the door and turned to face her frowning sister. "That was Father O'Malley. Asked if Thomas could stop by and help him at the church. Such a nice man."

Aunt Ophelia sat quietly in the corner, dressed as always in a full length, wool black dress, and silently stared back.

When Tom got home from work that evening and learned that Father O'Malley had stopped by and asked for him, he almost fainted. He knew something like this might happen, but to have your parish priest actually walk to your house was altogether unexpected. He knew he wasn't needed to help move boxes either – he wasn't fooled by that for one second.

His mother couldn't help but notice how he picked at his meal that evening.

"Get on with you, Thomas," she chided, as he reluctantly got ready to leave. "My heavens, it won't take that long. You should be honored that Father O'Malley thinks so well of you to ask."

"Yeah, ma," he replied.

He debated not going to the church at all, but realized that wouldn't work. Where would he go? Where could he escape the humiliation? Father O'Malley would just keep after him, and eventually create a real problem at home. His wacky Aunt Ophelia would have a field day with that if she hasn't already. He knew why Father O'Malley wanted to see him and he kicked himself for spurting out the "killing" business in the confessional. He should have gone down to the Cathedral, any place where they wouldn't have recognized his voice. But it was too late now. By the time he reached the rectory, his stomach was in knots.

Father O'Malley lived in a large, two-story, red brick house. The church was next door and the grade school was behind. The nuns lived in an attached building beside the school. Alongside the school was a large playground, mostly devoid of grass, where a group of boys was playing baseball.

He rang the rectory bell and attempted to look through the lace curtains when almost immediately, Mrs. Whalen, Father O'Malley's housekeeper, opened the door.

"Good evening, Thomas," she said smiling. "Father's expecting you and just finishing his dinner. Wait in the study for him, will you? I'll just tell him you're here."

"Yes, ma'am," he replied and walked past her and down the dark hallway into a small, gloomy, book-lined room with a small couch, a roll-top desk, and chair. On the walls not covered by books, religious pictures ruled. A painting of Christ sitting surrounded with small, adoring children; the Virgin Mary ascending into Heaven, her immaculate heart exposed, her hands clasped and expectant eyes tipped upwards; a portrait of Pope Pius XII; and a photo of a young Father O'Malley taken years earlier, perhaps at his ordination. He was standing in a gravel churchyard flanked by smiling people, his family, Tom guessed, and in Ireland judging by the buildings and the odd way they were dressed.

The room smelled of incense and boiled potatoes. He stood in the middle, uncertain what to do when he heard Father O'Malley's voice coming from the hallway.

"Thank you, Mrs. Whalen. That was a grand dinner indeed. You may go on home now."

"Are you sure I can't get you anything else, Father?

"Yes, I'm quite sure, thank you. Thomas and I have some work to do."

"Very well, Father. I'll see you tomorrow."

"Good evening then, Mrs. Whalen."

Father O'Malley reached the study and entered, shutting the door behind him and walked over to his desk.

"Good evening, Thomas," he said in a voice devoid of any hint of what he might be thinking. "Sit down there on the couch, won't you? I thought we might have a wee chat."

"Yes, Father," he stammered. "I'm sorry about the other evening ..."

"Tsst tsst tsst. That's all right, lad, I understand. I do. Just sit and relax and we'll just have a short visit. Can I get you a soda pop or something?"

"No, Father. Thank you."

"All Right then, Thomas. Now, the other evening you were talking about a 'serious accident.' And something about 'someone getting hurt, hurt badly.' Do you want to tell me what you were referring to?"

"Well," fidgeted Tom. "I think I might have been wrong about

49

that after all, Father. You see, at first I *thought* I might have seen something but after I thought about ..."

"Thomas!" Father O'Malley interrupted in a sharp voice. "Don't be giving me a piece of malarkey now. I want you to tell me what happened. And I don't want to hear any sinful lies. Do you understand me? Don't be making matters worse now!"

"Yes, Father," he whispered looking down at his lap.

"Well then, look at me. Up here! I want to see your face when you're talking. Tell me what happened. You don't have to worry about anything. I'm your priest, Thomas, and I want to help you. Anything you say is just between us, us and God, of course. You do know that, don't you, son?"

"Yes, Father," he replied tipping his face up to look at the priest, tears already forming in his eyes.

"All Right then, lad," he said more softly, seeing how upset the boy was, "let's hear all about it. I doubt you can tell me anything I haven't heard before, believe me. Just start at the beginning."

In a quiet voice, Tom proceeded to tell Father O'Malley what happened, with the exception, of course, of names and places, in the hope of protecting his friends.

He started with the evening spent "in a bar with some friends" and how they were asked to leave and how they later met up with "a Negro" and, after much hesitation and a little prompting, about the scuffle in the alley, and finally, the episode with the beer bottle. He left out the part about Policeman Pat O'Brien.

Father O'Malley, to his credit, kept mostly silent during the recitation. Other than a few "Go on now," and "What happened next, lad," he kept his eyes glued on Thomas.

However, as the story progressed, it was obvious this was not at all what he was expecting to hear. He was thinking perhaps an accident in a "borrowed" car, a fight behind some building, even, God forbid, some petty crime, maybe breaking into a home or something. But this was new territory, even for him. His eyes grew larger and his face stiffer as Tom got to the part about the initial scuffle in the street. By the time Tom told about hitting Glory on the head with a beer bottle, his own head had lowered in shock and sorrow.

Tom finished and sat quietly. Father O'Malley did the same for what seemed like hours, but in reality was a matter of a moment or two.

How to respond? I must collect my thoughts, Father O'Malley thought to himself. Finally he said, "Sweet Jesus, Thomas, what were you thinking, lad? Who were the others with you?"

"Please, Father," sobbed Tom. "Don't make me tell you that."

"Never mind, son. I know who they were."

Hearing this surprising statement, Tom snapped his head up and looked at the priest.

"They were Sean O'Brien and Jack Grettsmer, weren't they?"

Tom's surprised look and silence gave him away.

"Come now, Thomas. I'm not daft now, am I? Nor blind. I know you three have been close friends for years. Who else was I supposed to think they were? Those two have been trouble ever since I've known them. What you see in them is a mystery to me. You should have known better!"

"It was an accident, Father," he said softly.

"An accident, was it?" snapped the priest. "If what you told me is the truth, it was no accident. It was no accident you stopped him in the first place. It was no accident you hauled him into a building. It was no accident that one of you, I suspect it was that hothead Sean O'Brien, hit him on the head hard enough to kill him, according to what you've said!"

By this time, Tom had lowered his head and shoulders to his lap and was sobbing uncontrollably.

"I didn't know he was going to hit him," he blubbered. "He hit Sean. It all happened so fast, we didn't even know he was dead ..."

"And that's another thing," interrupted Father O'Malley in a calmer, quieter voice. "How *do* you know he was dead? I suspect he was just knocked out. What happened to him? You never said what happened afterwards?"

After a moment's silence and in a very low voice, Tom added, "*We* thought he was just knocked out, too. We were gonna let him go but someone came and caught us and *told* us he was dead."

"What?" exclaimed Father O'Malley in surprise at hearing this new piece of information. "*Who* caught you?"

"A policeman, Father. He told me to go home and never talk about this to anyone."

"Good Lord," exclaimed Father O'Malley as he turned and looked away to collect his thoughts for a moment. "It was that no-account brother of Sean's wasn't it? Patrick O'Brien, a more dishonest policeman God never made. An absolute disgrace to the Irish race! It was *him*, wasn't it?"

Tom nodded silently, his head bowed in anguish.

"What happened then, Thomas? And this time, don't be leaving out any more details."

"That's all I know, Father," he said looking up at the priest with desperate, teary eyes. "I swear. He told me to get out and not breathe a word to anyone or he'd come looking for me. I ran home, and stayed home until the other night at church when I came to confession."

"And what about Sean and Jack? And what happened to the Negro? I'm guessing he wasn't killed after all, just a big mistake and Sean's brother wanted to scare you all to teach you a lesson. I haven't heard about any body being found, let alone a Negro's. That would surely be on the radio and in the newspaper. How do you know he's dead for certain? Surely you three boys have talked together."

"I saw Jack for the first time the other night. He told me that after I left the warehouse Sean and his brother carried him out. He said he looked dead, all right. He tried to get hold of Sean to find out what happened, but was told Sean was gone and not coming back! No one's seen him anywhere."

"Well, you can bet that brother of his knows where he is. I'm going to go down to that police station first thing in the morning ..."

"NO. NO. Father, you can't!" Tom cried in a panic. "He said if we told anyone he would get us! Father, please, I only told you because you made me. Don't do anything, please ..."

"All Right, all right, son. Settle down now," Father O'Malley said as he stood up and walked around the study. "You're right, of course. This is like going to confession and we both know I can't reveal what I've heard you say. To anyone. And I won't. What else did Jack say? What's he going to do about it?"

"Jack's leaving, too. Heading to college somewhere out East. He's scared to death of Sean's brother, and worried about his folks finding out. He says it was an accident and it was Sean's fault anyway seeing as he was the one who hit him and everything. He just wants to get away."

"And you, Thomas? What about you? What are you planning to do?"

"I don't know, Father. I feel just terrible. Can't sleep. I don't know what to do."

"Well, let's not panic now. If what you told me is the truth, and I do believe you, it does sound like an accident. A terrible accident. But at this point, we really don't know if the man is dead or not – and I seriously doubt he is. We don't even know what happened to him. Still, there *is* a serious crime involved. I'll do some discreet checking around to see if I can learn anything at all about this poor Negro. But with that Pat O'Brien involved, I doubt I will. And you, Thomas, I want you to keep this just between you and me. I don't want you talking to *anyone* about it, you understand?"

Tom nodded.

"At worst, it seems you were a hesitant participant in this sordid mess. Whatever happens, I doubt you'd be in any serious trouble. Jack probably wouldn't either from what you've said. But Sean and that brother of his would be in *big* trouble, accident or not! Meanwhile you go back to work as usual. And I want to see you back in Church Sunday, understand? I'm going to give you absolution tonight, so I want to see you at communion, too. Do you hear me?"

"Yes, Father."

"Unwilling participant or not, Thomas, you've committed a sin against your fellow man and I think you need to pray long and hard for God's forgiveness."

"Yes, Father."

"And long term, son," he asked in a gentler voice, "have you given any more thought to what we talked about earlier this year when you graduated?"

"About the priesthood? About me becoming a priest, Father?"

"Yes, or at least about *considering* the religious life. You wouldn't have to decide right away. But going to the seminary would be a good way to continue your education and with no expense to your family. I'm confident I could get you accepted this fall, if you're interested."

"I don't know, Father. I can't leave my mom alone even if I wanted to. She'd go nuts if she thought I was leaving. She needs me at home and ..."

"Thomas," he interrupted, "your mother would never tell you this, but she prays for you and your vocation to the priesthood every day of her life. We've had long talks about it on numerous occasions. Believe me, it would make her very happy."

"But Father," he stammered, in a bit of shock, "She needs me home to keep working and earning money ..."

"No, Thomas, she doesn't," interrupted Father O'Malley again. "I know you don't know very much about your Aunt Ophelia, nor am I going to tell you much, other than to say I doubt your mother will have any financial worries for the rest of her life. Your aunt may seem a little odd, I grant you that, but don't let her "old world" ways fool you. From what little I've heard about her, if even half of it's true, she's an amazing woman. Anyway, I want you to think about what we talked about and we'll visit about it later. In the meantime, we'll sort this mess out somehow. Trust me, we will. You're a good lad, Thomas, I know you meant no harm to this Negro."

"But Father, what ..."

"Good night, Thomas," interrupted Father O'Malley as he walked over and took Tom's arm and guided him toward the study door. "You go home now and think about our little visit, all right? For your penance, I want you to say the Rosary. The Sorrowful Mysteries; *all ten decades*, understand?"

"Yes, Father," he said.

Tom walked home that evening feeling for the first time in several days as if a heavy weight had been lifted off his shoulders, that perhaps God had heard his desperate prayers. Maybe, he thought to himself, there was a way out of this mess after all. That night he slept.

CHAPTER THIRTEEN

The phone in the darkened hallway outside of Jack Grettsmer's dorm room rang ten times before he finally got up to answer it.

"Hello," he answered in a groggy and irritated voice. "Who's this?"

"Jack? Is this Jack Grettsmer?" yelled a muffled voice on the other end.

"Yeah. Who in the hell wants to know at ..." He paused to look at his watch. " ... SHIT! 2:00 IN THE MORNING!"

"Jack, you lazy bunghole. It's me, Sean. What the hell you doing in bed? It's only midnight here in San Diego."

"Sean? Sean O'Brien?" said Jack in an incredulous voice.

"Yeah, Einstein. How many Sean's do you know would go to the trouble of calling you – at 2:00 in the morning? Wake up, jerk, and smell the roses," he laughed.

"Holy crap, Sean," Jack replied in an excited voice, now fully awake, "Where in the hell are you?"

"California! San Diego, California, ol' buddy. Shipping overseas tomorrow. Thought I'd give you a call. See if you're still alive."

"Damn it, Sean. Where the hell have you been all this time? And what are you doing in California? Wait a minute. You're doing WHAT? WHERE? Oh no, don't tell me you went and joined the service?"

"Yeah I did," laughed Sean. "Joined the Marines."

"The Marines? Please, tell me you didn't."

"Oh yes I did, buddy boy. Gonna keep your sorry, lazy ass safe from the Japs *and* the Krauts, like you!"

"Very funny, shithead. But tell me, where you been hiding 'fore that? I bet I've called your house a dozen times in the last few months. Finally went over when I was home for Christmas last year. Your ma told me you were visiting relatives, but wouldn't say where. I didn't see your asshole brother."

"Yeah, well that figures. I went to Chicago to stay with my aunt and uncle, you know, get outta Dodge and all. Been living and working there ever since. Then after Pearl, well, I joined up. Now getting ready to ship out. Gonna kick some Jap ass!"

"Damnit, Sean, you're still crazy as hell! You're gonna get *your* ass shot up, that's what'll happen."

"Hell no, not me. *Luck of the Irish,* and all that blarney. How about you? Ready to join up? Maybe we could get stationed together, just like old times."

"Are you nuts? Not me. I'm sticking right here in school as long as I can. I plan to study *my* ass off and keep my grades up so they can't touch me. First year was a joke. I almost flunked out, but this year, with the draft and all – I've seen the light. Studying to be a lawyer. Maybe I'll keep *your* Mick ass out of jail one day."

"Very funny, jerk. Hey listen, only got a minute or so. There're about 50 guys standing in line behind me. Tell me, whatever happened to Tommy? I woulda called him but I figure they still don't have a phone, right? And what about, you know, *that night*? Ever hear anything more about it?"

"Nah. Not a damn word. 'Course I left town shortly after you. But far as I know nothing ever came out of it. Nothing in the papers *or* the radio. But get this. You ain't gonna believe this. Your old beer guzzling buddy, Tommy, is gonna be a priest! Ain't that a kick in the ass! He's somewhere in a seminary right now. Mom sent me a clipping out of the paper!"

"No shit? A priest? Well ain't that something. Father Thomas. Damn. Well, good for him, I guess. Can't say I'm *too* surprised. When you stop and think about it, he wasn't near the screw up you and I were and – hey, hold on a minute, Jack."

In a muffled voice, "Okay – okay you guys, hold your britches will ya?"

"Listen, Jack, gotta go. Do me a favor will ya? When you talk to Tommy, tell him I called and asked about him, will ya? Tell him I'll get him a Jap flag or something, okay?"

"Yeah, sure, Sean. But wait, something I've been wondering about. What did you guys ever do, you know, with that sorry nigger?"

After a long pause Sean finally replied in a softer voice, "That was a bad deal, Jack. An accident, right? I'm sorry it ever happened."

"Yeah, yeah, but what did you *do* with him?"

"Well, it was Pat's idea," he said after a pause. "All I'll say is if I was you, I wouldn't be eating any more fish out of the Mississippi, huh? Know what I mean? Hey listen – gotta go, buddy. Hang loose."

"Wait. Hold it a sec. What'd that damn brother of yours ever do with that camera ... ?"

Too late. He'd already hung up.

Jack stood quietly in the dark hall for a few moments before shaking his head and muttering to himself, "Crazy damn Mick, went and joined the Marines! Why'd he go and do something stupid like that for?"

CHAPTER FOURTEEN

Tom Lavarato had just finished receiving his last series of shots and his arms were sore as hell. He and Father Gordon would be leaving for Africa in a few days and he had a million things he needed to get done. He was amazed his first two years at the seminary had gone by as quickly as they had. It seemed like only yesterday that he was back living in Dubuque.

"Two years, Thomas," he recalled Father O'Malley saying to him back then. "Give it two years and then we'll talk about it some more. What harm can it do, lad? You'll be getting a free college education as part of bargain and you'll not be committed to *anything* for two years."

Well, the two years were up and he decided to stick with it. When he shared his decision with Father O'Malley, the aging priest appeared truly delighted and asked permission to report the same in his sermon that Sunday. "For the sake of your dear mother," he quickly added. Father O'Malley never did believe there had been an actual death involved that night, and was convinced the three boys were being taught a tough lesson from Patrolman O'Brien. As mean as that might have been, it was God's will that it happened and now a fine young man would become a priest because of it.

A big part of Tom's decision was due to Father Gordon, an old classmate of Father O'Malley's who, unbeknownst to Tom, had been keeping an eye out for him, and quietly help ease him over the rough spots. Father O'Malley had never told his old friend why he wanted Thomas to attend the seminary in Illinois when there was one a perfectly fine one right in Dubuque. He'd only related the boy's unfortunate home circumstances, and his own, long-term intuition of the lad's calling to the religious life.

It was through Father Gordon's influence that Tom was given permission to accompany him on a visit to one of the newer mission projects in Africa. Although the Order ran missions throughout the world, Tom had shown a special interest in the African countries.

In his own mind, Tom suspected his attraction to Africa was somehow related to the terrible experience he'd been part of in Dubuque. He knew it wasn't rational, made no sense at all, but there it was. Just because the young man who'd been killed was a Negro, he was from Tennessee, not Africa. Yet, more and more it seemed like something inside him was pushing him in that direction. Does God really work like that? he asked himself. Am I supposed to be doing penance for the injustice I was involved in with a Negro by going to Africa? He didn't have the answer, and he wasn't about to ask Father Gordon.

As far as Tom knew, besides Jack, Sean and Pat O'Brien, Father O'Malley was the only one who knew what happened that night. And Fr. O'Malley's lips were sealed by the confessional. What he *did* know was there wasn't a day that passed by without thinking about it. And regardless how busy or tired he might feel, there wasn't a night that passed by without him praying for them all.

CHAPTER FIFTEEN

It seemed like years since Sean's outfit had shipped out of San Diego. In reality it'd been only a few weeks. But by now, everyone was bored stiff. The excitement of action against the dreaded enemy had long since worn off. Initially worked into a fevered, *Gung Ho* pitch, the long days and nights at sea were dragging them down. They were desperate for some action.

Their troop ship had stopped at several islands along the way. Once for three days of "acclimation training" in the hot, fetid jungles of the endless Pacific; another time to practice beach landings that involved digging in and sleeping on flea-invested, fly-swarming, hot, sand beaches. Uncomfortable as they were, these stops were still welcome breaks in the boring routine of zigzagging across the vast ocean. In their youthful innocence they were able to extract pleasure even in these temporary hardships.

Soon thereafter they'd stopped at islands which had recently seen plenty of action and where, for the first time, they got a glimpse of the aftermath of battle. This seemed to sober them up a bit for the realities of war. They didn't land at those islands, but dropped off supplies and took on wounded soldiers who had missed the overcrowded Hospital Ships. The wounded were kept separated but Sean and his group heard enough "horror stories" to realize things were not as rosy as they first believed.

Eventually, word reached them that their "pleasure cruise" was coming to an end. Scuttlebutt revealed the ship would soon be returning without them, and they realized they were nearing their drop-off zone.

Finally, after almost three weeks at sea they learned where: a small South Pacific island called Guadalcanal. No one had ever heard of it. Most couldn't pronounce the name.

The next two days were spent in renewed physical fitness drills and group meetings. They learned their job was to secure an airfield currently under construction by the Japanese. A successful campaign would ensure the Japanese would not be able to land and refuel planes used to attack the Pacific Fleet and, at the same time, enable Allied Forces' planes to move that much closer to the Japanese mainland. It was a critical exercise and one the United States could not afford to lose. They were also told it would be more of a mop-up exercise than a full-fledged fight, as it was anticipated the majority of the enemy would be blown to pieces by the time the Marines landed.

They heard the shelling from a full day's distance away. Off on the horizon, a steady string of explosions went on nonstop throughout the long night, lighting the sky with red-yellow flashes like a fireworks display run amok.

At dawn, as they finally came within sight of the island itself, the thunder of the battleships' guns was replaced by the drone of scores of planes as they came swarming over, dropping bomb after bomb until the entire island was covered by a thick blanket of cordite-laced smog.

The utter amazement of the young Marines at this unfettered display of raw destruction soon gave way to disappointment as they realized that there would, in fact, be few, if any, Japs left to fight. Nothing could live through what they had just seen and heard. No way.

And then, on top of this, they further learned that their ship would make up the *second* wave with the opportunity of any early kills going to the seasoned Third Division. Out the window went any realistic chances to get hold of a Jap sword or infamous *Rising Sun* flag promised to buddies and girl friends back home. It was quite a disappointment.

Sean and his unit were in full battle gear hours before their turn to climb down the net into landing crafts. The first wave had already landed and from what they could tell, were met without much, if any, resistance.

When Sean and the second wave hit the beach, the raw recruits tumbled out of the crafts and sloshed through chest high water onto the beach, soaked and confused.

It didn't help their morale any when they came upon dug-in squads of first wavers already drinking coffee and howling at their discomfort. And not a Jap in sight. And the jungle? It had been transformed into a mass of jagged, broken trees, still smoldering from the recent shelling.

Could their officers have been right about the enemy all being killed already? Their squad leader, a veteran from Danbury, Connecticut, thought it unlikely.

While the first wave continued to secure the beach for landing barges laden with supplies, Sean's squad, along with the majority of the second wave, lined up and started toward the jungle. They moved slowly, warily, and with the safeties on their weapons switched off. Admit it to each other or not, they were all scared stiff.

The airfield was just a few miles inland.

The Japanese, of course, were no fools. They knew what the Americans were after, and they'd learned from prior experience how they'd go about getting it. The instant the deadly American battleships had shown up on the horizon, they'd withdrawn all troops and artillery from the beach areas and moved them back and to the opposite side of the island, staying as close to the airfield as they could while still remaining hidden under the lush jungle canopy. They correctly reasoned the American guns and bombs would spare that area as much as possible in order to benefit from work they'd already done.

They also realized how critical the airfield was to the Americans, as well as to the Imperial Forces of Japan. The Emperor's orders were to fight to the last man. However, they were pitifully undermanned. The majority of people on the island were Japanese and Korean civilian workers. The actual count of combat soldiers was no match for the invasion they saw coming. This information had been radioed to headquarters and they were assured reinforcements were on the way. In the meantime, they were ordered to keep control of the airstrip. And to do so at all costs!

Initially the Marines' approach inland was slow and tense. But soon, the cautious demeanor of the young men began to relax and after a couple of hours of silent movement, good-natured banter spread up and down the line.

They hardly noticed the gradual transition of destroyed trees to undamaged ones until they were suddenly enveloped in a deep and darkened jungle environment, dripping moisture and echoing unfamiliar sounds: panicky monkeys, screeching birds, and the disturbing drone of unseen insects. They were entering an area untouched by either artillery of the ships or bombs of the planes.

The men tensed up as older, more experienced voices cautioned them to be on the alert. They were within a mile of the airfield.

Japanese eyes had been watching their approach for some time. Highly-trained snipers, artfully camouflaged and equipped with deadly accurate, scoped Arisaka Model 99 rifles were hidden in the trees.

The snipers' fates were sealed for them. They had but one task now – shoot as many Americans as possible. There would be no surrender on their part. They would fight to the death to contain the approaching enemy and give their comrades ample time to redeploy and reinforcements to appear.

The sniper was motionless. His field of vision limited to only 75 yards wide, but with a long depth of view. He knew the Yankee dogs were coming and began to see their sloppy attempts at stealth: pushing branches aside, quick jerky movements that immediately caught his eye. They were still just a little too far away ...

Sean neither saw nor heard the 7.7 mm bullet that hit him. At a distance of almost 400 yards, the lush jungle vegetation mostly deadened the soft "pop." The slug, perhaps slightly deflected by a tree branch, entered his groin area, clipped his femoral artery, and passed on through the upper part of his thigh, spinning him off his feet and backwards. His buddy beside him, still moving forward at a crouch, turned as Sean spun to the ground. He stared in confusion as his mind slowly registered the information.

Suddenly frantic shouting was heard up and down the line. "DOWN! EVERYONE DOWN. SNIPERS – IN THE TREES!"

"Sean? Sean? You hit?" his buddy yelled as he dropped to the ground and elbowed his way back.

When he got to Sean and turned him over, he saw his eyes were open but unfocused. Sean's breath wheezed in and out, and suddenly, with a grimace of pain, he started to get up only to drop back immediately with a grunt. His buddy wondered if he'd tripped. Then he looked down and saw the blood.

"Lay still, Sean," he said, holding him down with one arm "You've been hit, buddy. Hang on, you'll be okay."

Then turning on his elbow he looked up at the green jungle canopy and screamed, "MEDIC! MEDIC!"

PART TWO

THE SEARCH

2000 to 2001

CHAPTER SIXTEEN

The auction barn reeked of wet farm dogs and cow manure. Not enough to make Hank's eyes burn, but enough that he'd probably want to air out his clothes before going into his apartment.

"Perfect, this is perfect," he muttered. "This will definitely keep the genteel city folks at bay."

Going to the weekly auctions had become a ritual for Hank. He'd always been fascinated with auctions, and he particularly liked this place because of the eclectic stuff he knew would be for sale. From past experience he also knew he'd be bidding mostly against local area farmers, not seasoned antique dealers who had a good grasp on what things were actually worth. He missed going during the summer but now that fall semester was about to begin he planned to come whenever he could break away from his studies.

The barn was actually a large metal shed filled with a new collection of stuff every week. Scattered around the floor were at least fifty wooden pallets. Stacked on each pallet were six to eight cardboard boxes filled with everything you could possibly imagine; things collected from area farms after the family cleaned out and moved to the city, or old attic junk hauled in from God knows where. You never knew what was likely to show up.

The auction began sharply at 5:00 p.m. and the auctioneer moved fast. And since the bidding could be on any one of the boxes on a pallet, you never knew if the other bidders were interested in the same box you wanted, or in another. That added a little extra suspense Hank liked. Once the bidding ended, the winner chose which box he or she wanted and the bidding started up again and continued until the pallet was cleared. Then the crowd moved on to the next pallet and so it went until everything was sold.

Sometimes Hank bid on something just because it caught his fancy and he couldn't pass it up. One evening he returned home with a stuffed walleye pike mounted on a piece of driftwood, *Lac Seul – 1979*, according to a small copper plate.

"What in the world did you buy that for?" asked his roommate, Peter Lang. "That's the saddest damn thing I've ever seen. Didn't you notice half its tail's missing?"

"Hey, it was only two bucks," Hank was quick to point out, "and anyway I bought it to give to Lyle at his birthday party Saturday. What do you think – pretty cool, huh?"

"In that case, I guess. It does kind of remind me of him now that you mention it."

At first, Pete gave Hank a hard time about his auction going, insisting he was wasting his time and giving him a bad reputation from association. That was before Hank lugged home a box of old, odd-shaped bottles he'd bought for $5. One was a quart-size bottle embossed *Western Moxie Nerve Food Co. – Chicago*. He put it on eBay hoping to double his money and was delighted to see it create a bidding war and eventually sell for $176.20! That quickly quieted Pete. And pleasantly amazed Hank.

So now he was back in the auction barn hoping to find another great buy. And once again, he bought something he didn't quite bargain for.

It was stuffed in the bottom of a box of old *Saturday Evening Post* magazines dating back to the '40s, along with a couple of rusty flashlights, a pair of well worn, black men's boots, size 12, and five or six old insulators. He'd seen insulators for sale before and when he later looked them up on eBay learned that people did, in fact, collect them. He should have known that. People seemed to collect everything. He was no expert but thought the chances were pretty good he could make a few bucks. No one seemed particularly interested in any of it.

Two bucks, he thought to himself. I'll go as high as two bucks. Then he waited.

He was right. No one was even the least bit interested, so when he jumped on the opening bid of $1, he won.

"Excellent," he muttered. "I bet I can get at least $10 out of the insulators alone even if *none* of them are rare. And who knows, I may find another winner."

Hank wasn't all that interested in the money. It was the challenge he loved; the opportunity to buy something and turn it into a profit. To him, it was outfoxing the competition, even though tired old housewives looking mainly for recipe books and embroidered pillowcases, and their bored-silly husbands looking for old tools and fishing equipment could hardly be considered fair competition.

The apartment was empty when Hank returned. He remembered Pete had gone out with a bunch of his jock friends and wouldn't be in until late – a final fling before classes began. He set the box on the kitchen floor, nuked some leftover pizza, opened a can of beer and sat down to watch a little TV.

By the time Pete got back around midnight, Hank was sprawled out on the sofa sound asleep. His stinky, auction-going boots sat among pizza crumbs and two empty beer cans.

Pete spied the box on the floor and sighed. "Not again. This boy's gotta get a life. He's really starting to give me a bad name."

"Hey, Mr. 'Blue Light Special,' wake up!" he said in a loud voice as he snooped in the box. "What marvelous bargains did you bring home tonight? What the hell – don't tell me you're gonna try and resell this crap?"

"Back off, young man," yawned Hank as he got up and came into the kitchen. "You're looking at some mighty fine antiques there. Some people love old magazines and stuff. And one of *these* babies," he said holding up one of the insulators, "is going to make me rich."

"You're nuts!" said Pete. "That old bottle was just pure luck and you know it. Fat chance of that happening again. What did you have to pay for this load of junk?"

"One dolla, my friend. One thin Yankee dolla," chortled Hank as he patted the box. "And believe it or not, people *do* buy 'em. Hell, there's even a web site just on insulators and some of them sell for big bucks."

"Yeah, I'm sure," replied Pete who was still snooping through the box obviously not impressed. "I think you were taken this time, ol' buddy. Oh wow! A pair of boots, great. They should have paid *you* a buck to haul this junk outta there. Hey! What have we got here? Wow, an old flannel shirt! Now we're getting somewhere. But wait, no, it's a box *wrapped* in an old flannel shirt."

"Hey, careful there," said Hank reaching for it. "What is that? It could be something fragile."

He unwrapped the shirt and exclaimed, "Wow, it's an old camera. Well I'll be darned. I didn't even see it down there. Look at this baby, an old Brownie box camera, and in perfect condition."

"Yeah?" said Pete, suddenly interested. "I like cameras. Can I have it? That'd be fun to fool around with."

"Well of course you can have it, Peter my friend," said Hank. "What do you want to pay for it?"

"What?" Pete yelped. "I'll pay nothing for it, you cheap fart. You wanted the rest of that crap. You didn't even know it was in there. C'mon, let me have it."

"Sorry," laughed Hank. "That's not the way it works. Come along with me next time and you can buy your own stuff. I bet I can sell that baby for at least $5."

He took a closer look at it and said, "Well I'll be darned. Look, it still has film in it."

"What? How do you know?" asked Pete as he leaned in to take a closer look.

"See that small, red plastic circle on the side? See the number seven? That means six or seven photos have already been taken and the film's still in there."

"Really? That's too cool!" said Pete. "What do you think the pictures are of? Some old time, nudie cuties, I bet. Why don't you get it developed?"

"Get serious," said Hank. "That camera's older than you are! Hell, it's probably older than your parents. Maybe even your *grandparents*! That film won't be any good. Whatever was on it is most likely faded away by now."

"Oh yeah?" said Pete. "What do you know about film? You don't even have a camera."

"True," shrugged Hank. "You've got a point. Weak – but a point. Really think it could still be good? I suppose I could ask Al. He messes around with cameras a lot. I bet he'd know. It *would* be cool if there were something there."

"Call him now and ask," urged Pete.

"Don't be crazy," yawned Hank, "I can't call him now. Look at the time. 'Sides, I'm going home this weekend and I'll take the camera with me. Right now I've gotta get some sleep. Unlike some undergrads I know, I have a meeting with my advisors tomorrow that will demand some semblance of intelligence."

CHAPTER SEVENTEEN

Hank took the camera home to Evanston that weekend. Saturday night his brother, Al, came over for dinner and Hank showed it to him. Al was sales manager of a weekly newspaper that covered several metro areas surrounding the Chicago loop.

"You didn't open up the back, did you?" Al asked.

"No. I'm not stupid. It was stuck in the bottom of a box, wrapped up in an old shirt. I bet it'd been there for years sitting in some attic or basement. What do you think? Any chance of the film still being any good?"

"I doubt it," he said, twisting and turning the camera in all directions. "Depends on how old the film is and where it's been stored. Boy, it *does* look brand new. Hmmm, a Brownie Six-Sixteen. Wonder how old it is."

"I looked it up," Hank said. "Made from 1933 until 1941. It shoots 616 film and cost $3.50 when new. I only paid $1 for it along with a whole box of other stuff. Bet I could sell it for $5 or $10."

"Well," said Al, "I can develop black and white film, which this undoubtedly is, but I'm not going to take a chance on ruining it. Let me take it to work and show it to the guys in the photo lab."

The following Wednesday night Hank was just returning from the library when he heard the phone ringing. He dropped his stuff on the kitchen counter and rushed to answer it.

"What the hell's wrong with you," blasted the voice of his brother. "Is this some kind of sick joke of yours? And where've you been anyway, I've been calling all evening."

"What are you yelling for?" said Hank, confused by his tone. "I've been at the library. Why?"

"You know damn well why," shot back Al, sounding madder than ever. "Is this something you and that nitwit roommate of yours dreamt up? 'Cause if it is, I'm gonna come up there and kick both your butts!"

"Wait a minute, hold on!" said Hank more confused than ever. "Are you talking about that old camera?"

"Don't play dumb with me, Hank. Don't tell me you didn't stage that photo. Thought you'd have a little fun with big brother, did you? Well, I'll tell you something, little man, it's not one damn bit funny and if mom and dad find out about it, you're gonna be in trouble!" Suddenly the line went dead.

Hank sat stunned for a minute, looking at the phone in his hand.

Pete, who entered the apartment just as Hank answered the phone, was staring at him and asked, "What was that all about? You got a problem or something?"

"That was Al," said Hank, still in shock. "He sounded about as mad as I've ever heard him, mad at me, and possibly you. Something about that old camera I took home and a joke we were tying to pull on him. What the hell was all that about?"

"Me? Why's he mad at me? I wasn't even at the auction."

"It must have been something on the film. He accused us of trying to put a *sick joke* over on him. That's got to be it, otherwise I don't know what in the hell he's talking about."

"Well, call him back," said Pete. "Find out what the problem is. Must be some kind of mix up or something. I don't want him mad at me."

"Well there's something wacky going on all right," said Hank as he dialed. "There must have been something on that film that – Al? Listen, don't hang up on me again, damn it. Tell me what your problem is. I don't have a clue what you're talking about."

There was a long pause. "Are you telling me the truth? You swear you didn't dick with that film because if I find out ... "

"Dick with the *film*? No! Hell no," exclaimed Hank. "What're you talking about? I told you, I bought the camera at an auction. I'm planning on selling it on eBay. Did you develop the film? Did you get anything? Is that it?"

"Yeah," said Al sounding slightly mollified. "One very disturbing thing as a matter of fact. I thought for sure you and Pete must have been up to something. Sorry, I should have known you wouldn't have done something like that."

"Something like WHAT? Damn it, Al, what's so bad that it made you lose your cool like that? And I *guess* that I may or may not accept what I *think* was an apology. Same goes for Pete."

70

"Okay," said Al. "I'm *sorry*, but this really freaked me out. And it got me in trouble with Gary Woodard in the photo lab. He's black, you know."

"No, I didn't know. And I don't care," replied Hank growing more and more perturbed. "So he's black. What the hell does that have to do with anything? Can you please calm down and tell me what was on the film? Is that too much to ask?"

"Well, there were several images actually," said Al in a calmer voice. "Gary figured the film was pretty old after what I told him and doubted there'd be anything on it. He had to use some special chemicals ... "

"FOR GOD'S SAKE," shouted Hank. "Can you cut to the chase here? What'd he find?"

"All Right. Relax, will you? Two images were too blurred to make out much," said Al getting excited again. "Three were pictures taken of some old homes, pretty nice old homes, actually. But the last one was the one that set him off. He actually came to my desk and shouted at me in front of the whole office. He said that if I ... "

"WHAT? What was on it?" shouted Hank. "Damn it, you're driving me *nuts*."

"All Right, settle down. I'm looking at it right now. Looks like it was taken inside an old building, shows desks and stuff. There are three guys in the picture. All were facing the camera, posing. Two are white and one black. The white guys don't look very old, could be teenagers, maybe a little older, standing on each side of this black guy, who's sitting in a chair, sort of slumped over. Gary thinks the black guy's dead!"

"WHAT? You gotta be kidding me!" broke in Hank. "Dead? No way. There must be some mistake."

"What's going on," shouted Pete who was standing by listening. "Who's dead?"

"Shhhhhh," said Hank, gesturing to Pete to sit down and be quiet. "Al, tell me you're kidding."

"I'm not kidding, bro," replied Al. "It's a real downer. One white guy is standing there with a big grin on his face. The other guy's holding up a large bottle like he's going to hit the black guy with it. Fact is the black guy looks like he's already been hit. Maybe has some blood running down the side of his head. Damn, I have a hard time looking at it. If this is for real, it makes me sick!"

71

"Oh man," said Hank. "It's gotta be for real. I can't believe you'd think I'd fake something like that!"

"I know," replied Al. "I'm sorry, really sorry. It's just that I was so shocked when Gary came shouting at me. He must think it was something *I* faked. I just didn't think it through."

"Okay, okay," said Hank. "But what do you think we should do ?"

"Well, first thing tomorrow I've gotta get back to Gary and explain that I didn't ... "

"That's not what I mean. I mean what are we going to do about the *picture*?"

"Do about the picture? Wadda you mean 'do about it'? If this is legit, it happened years ago. Hell, we don't know a damn thing about it, who they are, when it happened or where it happened."

"Yeah, I know," said Hank. "But we just can't do *nothing*, can we? I mean, what if that black guy *was* killed, and no one did anything about it?"

"I don't understand you. Are you saying you wanna know if the bad guys were caught and punished, *assuming* this is the real deal?

"Well, yeah. Something like that. Hell, I don't know. We just can't leave it."

"All Right, tell you what," said Al after a moment. "First thing I have to do is talk to Gary. I need to straighten him out right away. Right now he thinks I'm a real creep and is probably telling everyone at work what a sick bastard Al Torney is. As far as what to *do* about it, I don't have a clue. When you coming home again?"

"I don't know," Hank said. "Fall term's just started. Why?"

"Well, let me hold on to everything until you can come back, okay? I don't even want to put this stuff in the mail. We can talk about it when you get here."

"Yeah. I guess. But boy, this is really weird. I'd really like to see that photo. You didn't show it to mom and dad, did you?"

"Are you kidding?"

"Okay – all right, I'll call when I know for certain I'm coming. Maybe next weekend."

They finished their conversation and hung up.

"What the hell was all that about?" asked Pete when Hank plopped down on the couch looking dazed. "Somehow I've got the feeling there weren't any 'nudie cutie' pictures in that camera. Right?"

CHAPTER EIGHTEEN

It was a couple of weeks before Hank returned home. When his brother showed him the photo, he was appalled. It was just as described and he had no doubt it was authentic. He'd read about things like this before – racial crimes – but it was something else to see an actual photo.

"The guy who developed the pictures," said Al, "name's Gary, wants to talk to us tomorrow. Said he'd like to help when I told him about finding out more about it. I really think he just wants to meet you to make sure I'm telling the truth. He's still pretty upset."

"That's fine with me," said Hank. "Maybe he *can* help. But I've been thinking about it some more and I think you're right, I don't see what can be done now."

"Perhaps nothing," said Al, "but Gary said he had a couple of ideas."

The newspaper office took up nearly a half city block. The photo lab was on the third floor and Gary's office was stuck back in the corner. Cameras, tripods, old newspapers and stacks of photos covered every surface of his desk and file cabinet. The walls were plastered with old photos, award plaques dating back to the 1980s and an old, moth-eaten deer head, complete with antlers. Notes and assignment sheets were impaled on the horns. The acrid odor of chemicals was thick in the air.

"Gary, meet my brother, Hank."

"Hank. Glad to meet you," said one of the largest men Hank had ever seen. He could understand why Al wouldn't want Gary mad at him.

"Knock some stuff on the floor and sit down. Coffee?"

"No, thanks," they both replied.

"Al tells me you got that old camera at an auction?"

"Yeah, I did."

"Well, I'll tell you something, that picture is some bad shit. You know what I mean? I was totally surprised when I got an image on the negative and then flipped out when I printed it. 'Suppose your brother told you 'bout that."

Hank nodded, smiling.

"The film was pretty crinkly. I could tell it was old but we have special chemicals we can use on old film and we got lucky. It must have been stored under ideal conditions if it's as old as I think it is."

"How old *do* you think it is?" asked Al. "We were wondering that ourselves. Hank learned that camera was first made in the '30s and discontinued in the '40s. 'Course it could have been used any time after that, I guess."

"Don't know for *sure*," answered Gary, spreading out enlargements of three photos, "but I've got a pretty good idea. Pics of the houses are interesting, but don't help much. If there were only some people, or cars in them, that would help date them. But there aren't. The picture with the people is the key. I've showed it around a little. It shocked the crap out of everyone by the way – and consensus is it was taken around 50 years ago, maybe more."

"Wow! Really?" exclaimed Hank. "What makes you think that?"

"Well, for one thing the clothes and hairstyles are different, mainly on the white guys. And the furniture just looks old-fashioned, heavy wooden desks, old style lamps and stuff like that. Then I noticed something else."

He reached behind him and grabbed another print and turned it around and placed it on the desk so they all could see it.

"Here's an enlargement I made. Look over at this section by the wall. I'm almost certain that's an old calendar half in the shadows. It's not that clear, but if you look carefully, you can see the basic shape and rows of numbers and days."

"Yeah," said Hank staring excitedly at the photo. "I can't really make much out. I think you're right, though. It is an old calendar. Those are definitely columns of numbers."

"Yeah, I think so too. So here's what I suggest," said Gary. "I've gotta buddy in the police department photo lab. We work together sometimes. He has access to some pretty sophisticated equipment like ultra high-resolution scanners, electron microscopes, that sort of thing. Way out of our league here. I'd like to have him take a look at the negative and try to work on that image. Might end up with something."

"That'd be great," said Hank. "If we could get a date that'd be a start, anyway."

"Right," said Gary. "In the meantime, is there any way you could find out where the camera came from? I mean the auction house got it from somewhere, right? It might be a long shot but I think it's worth checking out."

"Sure, I can ask," said Hank. "I think I even kept the sales stub."

"All Right then. I'll keep Al posted about what I learn on this end and you two guys do the same with me. If the photo's as old as I think it is, there's probably nothing that can be done anyway, but I agree with you, Hank. We just can't let it go. Might be a wild goose chase, but I'm willing to try if you are."

When Hank returned to school, he showed the photo to Pete, who thought it was some type of elaborate hoax.

"I don't think so, Pete. Consensus is it's real. Both Al and his newspaper buddies think so and I agree."

"Yeah? So what's a condensus?"

"*Consensus*, nitwit," said Hank. "Not condensus."

"Yeah. Whatever."

Pete, it should be understood, was a phys ed undergrad and not especially known for deep thinking. He was, however, a great guy and a natural athlete. He'd received a full, four-year ride to pitch on the college baseball team. Standing a solid 6'4" the local paper once described his fastball smacking into the catcher's mitt as "the sound of a screen door slamming shut." He was also a very good basketball player and a twelve-handicap golfer. Although Hank often played basketball and golf with him, he rarely was able to beat him, even on his best days.

Hank was a pretty good athlete himself. His 5' 11' frame was well proportioned without being overly muscular. His favorite sports were track and bicycling, the former of which he had lettered in throughout high school and his first four years of college. He still liked to run but no longer competitively. To keep in shape, he now alternated running with bicycling, and was a common sight speeding around campus on his 24-speed Trek.

But other than a deep love of anything to do with athletics, Pete and Hank were as mismatched as Mutt and Jeff. Still, they reveled in each other's differences and were known as close friends and had chosen to room together for the past three years.

Eventually Hank made it back to the auction. Schoolwork had been taking up most of his spare time and what little that was left over he devoted to developing his thesis. He was so busy with school stuff he'd almost forgotten about the photo. Then Al called him one night.

"Hey, 'lil brother, what's happening? Thought you might want to check in with your family every once in a blue moon. Why haven't you called?"

"I'm in grad school, remember?" Hank replied. "They're keeping us hopping. I'm just taking a little breather right now. And no, I haven't forgotten about the photo, in case you're wondering."

"Well, Gary called the other day. Asked me if I'd heard from you. I told him I'd give you a call."

"Tell him I'm going back to the auction this week. Did he say anything about his visit with his police buddy?"

"Said he had some news but wouldn't tell me what. He wants to wait and go over it with both of us. Actually, he sounded excited so I suspect he's had some luck with that calendar business. So when are you coming home?"

"Soon. I can't do it this weekend, maybe next weekend."

As it turned out Hank and Pete *both* went to the auction that week. Pete was still thinking of the killing Hank had made on that "Moxie bottle" and figured he might as well cash in on the scam.

When Hank went up to get a number, he smiled when he recognized the clerk who, by this time, also recognized him and smiled in return. About his age, maybe a few years younger, dressed in jeans and a plaid flannel shirt. She was actually quite pretty, in a healthy farm girl sort of way, and looked vaguely familiar to him now that he thought about it.

"Back again, I see," she said. "Buying more treasures to sell on eBay?"

"I wish!" said Hank, surprised. "But how'd you know?"

"Well, you don't look like an antique dealer and I doubt you're buying stuff for your room at State."

"Hey, how'd you know I go to State?" he asked even more surprised.

"'Cause I do, too. Listen, there's a line growing behind you," she said sheepishly. "I've gotta get 'em numbers or dad will ring my neck!"

"Oh, sure. Sorry. Can I ask you about something later?"

"Sure, come back after the auction's started. I shouldn't be busy then."

"Okay, see you later."

The auction wasn't scheduled to start for another few minutes but a growing crowd of people were already milling around, visiting with friends and acquaintances and looking the stuff over.

Most of the crowd seemed to be the same local farmers who were there mainly for the camaraderie. He spied Pete down one of the aisles, crouched down by a pallet inspecting the contents of one of the cartons. He walked over.

"Hey man, you won't believe this," Pete said secretively. "A box of old Playboys! Must be thirty or forty here, some dating back to the '80s! You gotta buy 'em! I bet there're worth a FORTUNE."

"Not interested, Peter, lad," said Hank shaking his head. "You wanna buy 'em, you're on your own. Just remember, it's your money."

"Oh, c'mon," pleaded Pete flipping through one of the issues. "These are collector items! Look at this – whoops, no, look at this. An old baseball article. I bet you could find something useful."

"On your own," repeated Hank. "And if you buy them, you keep them in your room, understand?"

"Man, you're mean! What do you think they'll go for? I've got $4 on me. How much would you bid?"

"I wouldn't give you five cents for the whole bunch and don't ask for a loan because the answer's no. As soon as the auction starts, I'm going back and talk to the clerk."

"Maybe you'd be willing to go 50-50 with me if ... "

"Later," Hank said as the auctioneer announced it was time to start the sale. "Remember. You're on your own." Hank got back to the office just as the clerk finished checking the last person in.

"Hi again," Hank smiled.

"Hi back," she replied. "What did you want to ask me?"

"Well, a few weeks ago, I bought a box of stuff here and ..."

"Katie Joyce," she interrupted sticking out her hand. "Name's Katie Joyce. Sorry, what were you saying?"

"Hank Torney. Glad to meet you, Katie," he said, shaking her hand. "How'd you know I went to State, by the way? We haven't met, have we? And listen, I'm sorry if I've forgotten. I've been up to my eyeballs with grad school and all ... "

"No, we've never met," she laughed, "but I've seen you whiz by me on your bike a few times. Do you always go that fast? My heavens, it looks like you're running from the law or something."

"No," laughed Hank. "Just getting a little exercise. What's your major?"

"Junior in architecture. How about you?"

"Sports psychology. Working on my master's. I'm just finishing my second year now. Architecture, huh? No wonder I haven't seen you. You guys are on the opposite side of campus aren't you?"

"Yeah, plus you're a grad student, and I'm still a lowly undergrad. I'm surprised you're still talking to me."

"C'mon, you sound like my roommate, Pete. He's inside now thinking about buying a carton of moldy old *Playboys*."

"Well you know the old saying – *one man's trash, another man's treasure.* But anyway, what was it you wanted to ask? You started to tell me about buying something?"

"Yeah. A few weeks ago I bought a box of old stuff. I kept the sales slip with the lot number," he said, handing her the small stub. "I know the date I bought it, too. I'm hoping you could tell me where it came from."

"You want to know where the box you bought came from?" she asked with a quizzical stare. "What in the world for?"

"Well," Hank said, "there was something in the box that, uh, I'd like to return to the family."

"What? Something valuable, like jewelry? You know, whatever you bought is yours and ..."

"No. Not jewelry," he interrupted, and then paused a moment. "Some photographs, old family photographs that I'm sure they meant to keep. They must have gotten into the box by mistake."

"Oh. Well that's sweet of you, Hank, but I'll tell you something. We see that a lot – young couples bringing in their old family albums to sell. I don't get it. It's so sad, but it happens all the time."

"But these seemed kinda – special," Hank said. "I'd really like to return them if I could."

"Well, let me think for a sec. You said a few weeks ago? We keep records here for a year but I need to ask my dad, first. He's sorta funny about giving out client information. Protecting someone's privacy and all. And even if he says it's okay, it'll take me some time to dig out the information. Do you need it right now?"

"No, no, of course not," Hank quickly replied. "But maybe when you have a little time, and if it's all right with your dad, of course."

"Well, I'll see what I can do. Give me your number and I'll call you soon as I can."

"That'd be great. I really appreciate it." He scribbled out his name and number and gave it to her. "I live off campus but we have an answering machine, so if we're not home just leave your name and number and I'll call you right back. Maybe you'll let me buy you a beer and pizza for your trouble."

"Sure. I'll call you one way or the other."

"Okay. Thanks, see you around."

"You might if you slow down a little. On your bike, that is?" she said with a grin.

Hank went back inside just in time to see Pete walk away from the now empty pallet with a look of disgust on his face.

"Hey, Pete. What's the problem, big guy?"

"Two damn dollars. That's the problem. Some pervert outbid me by two lousy dollars. I can't believe it."

"Yeah, that's the breaks all right," Hank said as he grabbed his friend by the arm and led him toward the exit. "C'mon, let's go. I'll buy you a beer at *Grumpy's*. Maybe it'll take your mind off all those outstanding 'sports stories' you'll never get to read."

CHAPTER NINETEEN

Hank was in the apartment studying the following Monday afternoon when the phone rang.

"This is Hank," he answered in a distracted voice.

"Sausage and mushroom. And a Pepsi," a female voice said. "I don't drink beer!"

"What? Excuse me? Who's this?"

"Katie Joyce! You promised me pizza and a beer. Remember? But I don't drink beer."

"Oh, yeah. Sure, I remember," he said, now fully alert and sitting up straight. "Pizza and beer – sorry I didn't recognize your voice."

"That's okay. But you don't have to if you don't want to."

"No, no, that's fine. I *want* to. When do you want to go?"

"Tonight. Is that too soon? I mean it *is* short notice and all. And I'll be honest. I don't think I found much to help you. We can make it another time if you ... "

"No, no," Hank said. "Tonight's fine. Yeah, tonight's great."

"Meet you at *Zoey*'s at 6:30? How's that sound?"

"Great. Want me to pick you up? I've got a car."

"No, but thanks. I'll walk. It's not far."

"All Right then, see you at 6:30."

"Who was that?" said Pete suddenly appearing in the room. What's this about pizza and beer? I'm in, by the way. I assume you're buying. Where're we going?"

"Sorry ol' buddy," replied Hank. "That was a young lady friend, and you're not invited."

"Lady friend? Whoa! What's this? When did you start dating again? I thought after your fateful 'heart to heart' with Wendy that you were through ..."

"It's not a date, bozo! It's that girl whose old man runs the auction house. I asked her for some help tracing that camera. I promised I'd treat her to a pizza for her help. Strictly business."

"Yeah, I hear you. A business thing. Man, you're so full of crap, you make me look like an amateur."

Zoey's was packed when Hank arrived, always was, weekday or weekend. A favorite with the college crowd as well as the locals, it served the best pizza in town. You could smell the tantalizing aromas of yeast and spicy sausage a block away. The first wave of customers, mainly students, had come and gone, and a new batch was lining up for a place to sit.

Katie was already there and had somehow grabbed an empty booth, a gutsy thing to do with this crowd. He spied her from across the room arguing with a trio of students who were trying to bully their way in. He walked over and quickly shooed them off.

"Whew! Saved by the bell," she said, smiling. "In another minute or two, we'd have been sitting on each other's laps, having to share our pizza with a crowd of lowly underclassmen – like me."

"Not on your life," he said, slipping in across from her.
She looked different tonight, older somehow. He hadn't noticed before how white and perfectly straight her teeth were. She was wearing faded jeans and a light blue, cotton crew neck sweater. A silver chain with a small cross hung around her neck. And just a vague hint of lipstick.

She blushed under his close scrutiny so he quickly asked, "So how early did you have to get here to save us a booth?"

"Actually, not that long ago. I joined some friends who were just getting ready to leave. You just missed them."

"Ah. That explains the empty pizza trays and stack of plates. I thought maybe you went ahead and ate without me."

"I wouldn't do that, but I *am* starving. Let's hurry and order or we'll never get served."

"Right!" Hank called over the waitress and placed their pizza order plus a couple of Pepsis.

"You didn't have to order Pepsi just because I don't drink beer."

"I know," Hank said, "but I really don't drink much myself anyway and a Pepsi sounds pretty good. So tell me, what did you find out?"

"Well, like I said on the phone, I feel a little guilty, like I tricked you into this, because I really didn't find much. Most of the stuff we sell comes from area farm families; retired folks who have sold the farm and are downsizing. I was hoping this was the case with the stuff you bought. If it were, we could tell you exactly where it came from.

"But it wasn't, was it?" asked Hank in a dejected voice.

"No. 'Fraid not. That box was brought in by one of the guys we buy from in bulk. They acquire a large bunch of stuff when a small town antique shop's going out of business. Or they'll hear about a estate sale before it's even advertised. They'll go and negotiate a set price and cart off a whole truckload of stuff at a time. It's risky business. Sometimes they'll find something really valuable – but mostly not. Most of it comes to us.

"Darn," muttered Hank. "Now we'll never find them."

The pizza soon came and they sat quietly eating for a while, Katie studying Hank's face, feeling a little confused.

"But you're not telling me everything, are you, Hank? You look totally bummed out. There's more to this than just a few old family photographs, isn't there?"

Hank didn't reply right away. He just looked at Katie. He saw an earnest expression on her pretty face and he made a decision.

"Yes. There *is* more to it. Let's finish eating and I want to show you something out in the car."

They spent the next half hour eating and chatting about school, family and friends. This was the first time he'd been out with a girl in a while and his earlier feeling of nervousness quickly vanished when he discovered how easy she was to talk with. Soon they finished and left.

"I want to show you a photo," he said. "But first I've got to explain something. Remember I told you about buying a whole box of stuff?"

"Yeah," she said, "including the old photographs."

"Well, that's not *entirely* true." Hank reached into the back seat and grabbed a large envelope. "I didn't actually find any photographs, I found an old camera."

He proceeded to tell her the whole story – about noticing the camera still had film in it. Then telling his brother, and finally about getting his brother's friend to develop it, and getting some strange and disturbing images. By the time he was finished she was bouncing with curiosity and blurted out, "Hank Torney, are you going to show me something or not?"

Hank laughed, reached into the envelope, and slipped out the 8 x 10 black and white warehouse print and handed it to her. For a moment she just sat there studying it, not saying a word. Then she turned to him and asked, "That black guy looks badly hurt. Maybe even dead. Is he?"

"We think so."

"Do you think they killed him – those white guys?"

"It looks that way."

"How terrible! I can't believe it. And you got this from the camera you bought?"

"I did."

"When was it taken? It looks old."

"We don't know for sure. That's what we're trying to figure out. The guy who developed it, who's also black, by the way, thinks it was taken at least 50 years ago. Maybe more. He was amazed we got any kind of image at all. And he was really freaked out."

"I can imagine. Do you think it could be some kind of dumb prank? I've heard about racial crimes and all. But who'd actually take a picture?"

"Exactly. We discussed that. Doesn't make much sense. He'd shown it to some police friends of his, and *they* thought it was the real thing, too."

"Are they going to do anything about it? I mean, what'd they say?"

"Well, nothing really. It's been too long ago and there's nothing to go on anyway."

"And what are *you* planning to do, Hank? What are you really trying to find out?"

"I don't really know either. If there's a way, I guess I'm trying to find out who they were. And what happened, and the where, and when ... "

"I'd like to help."

"What?"

"I want to help. Can I? There's something about this that is so wrong."

"Well, sure, I guess," he said. "I'd like any help I can get, but I'm not sure what we can do without even knowing where the camera came from. That's what I was hoping you could tell me. That would have been a big help. There's a chance we might be able to get a better idea *when* it was taken, but that's about as far as we've gotten."

"That's all right. It's kinda like a historical mystery and I love mysteries. Was that the only picture in the camera?"

"Actually, no," he said, reaching back into the envelope and withdrawing the additional 8 x 10 photos of the old homes and handing them to her. "These were on the roll, too. Not much help. No people or anything."

Katie stared at the photos for a long time, finally settling on one and tapping it said, "There's something about this one that rings a bell. I think I may have seen this house before."

"What? Where would you have seen a house like this?" chuckled Hank, amused. "And why would you remember it, anyway?"

"I'm an architecture major, remember? We study architecture – duh! And there's something unique about this house. I'm almost positive I've seen it somewhere. Can I keep it for a day or two?

"Well sure, keep it as long as you want. Right now we really don't have much else to go on, anyway."

Hank pulled up in front of Katie's dorm and parked. "Now listen," he said. "I don't want to see you getting in trouble with your boyfriend or something. Wouldn't he be upset if he knew you had pizza with some other guy?

"Why Hank Torney!" she replied with a coy look on her face. "I didn't realize this was a date."

"Well, it wasn't really," he stammered, getting red. "You're right. It's more like a research project."

"Exactly. And besides, I don't have a boyfriend. But how about you, any girlfriends? *Zoey's* was packed tonight. Word'll get around in a flash! You know how that goes."

"No. No girlfriends," he said and blushed again. "I'm in grad school you know, 'fraid I spend too much time studying and ... "

"Going to auctions," she interrupted and laughed at his squirming. "Okay then, 'research' it is then. Want me to call you if I find something?"

"Sure, and Katie, thanks. And even if you don't find anything I'd like to call you again. I had fun tonight."

"Me too," she replied, quickly slipping over and giving him a surprise peck on the cheek. "Goodnight, Sherlock."

CHAPTER TWENTY

A few days later, the phone in Hank's apartment rang twice before Pete answered in his best "I don't care who this is but it better be important" voice.

"Yeah?" he said. "Speak!"

"Is this Sherlock?" said a female voice.

"Sher-who? Who is this?"

"Oops, sorry. Is Hank there? This is a friend of his."

"Oh, yeah. Just a sec. HANK! PHONE! Some weirdo asking for Shirley or something. I 'bout hung ... "

"Hello," said Hank grabbing the phone out of Pete's hand. "This is Hank."

"Hi Hank. This is Katie Joyce. Sorry, I didn't mean to confuse your roomie. I thought it was you. Did I call at a bad time?"

"No, no, just studying. Don't worry about him. How've you been?"

"Fine thanks, but listen," she said in an excited voice. "I found something. Can you meet me over at Overton Hall tomorrow?"

"The architecture building behind the language labs?"

"One and the same."

"Sure. But how about now? Does it have something to do with our 'project'?"

"Yes, it does, and no, we can't do it now. It's too late. They lock up soon. How about over the noon hour tomorrow? Shouldn't take long."

"I'll meet you in front. Twelve sharp, but can't you *tell* me what you've found?"

"Can't. Gotta show you. See you at noon tomorrow."

"It's a date. No, sorry – it's a research thing."

"All Right," she said with a laugh. "See you then."

Overton Hall was one of the oldest and best-preserved buildings on campus. It was named after Dr. Benjamin Overton, the college's first professor of Architecture and Contemporary Design. The building, however, was anything but contemporary. It was a solid, three-story brick square covered with ivy and surrounded by mature oak trees with a grouping of six Ionic columns spread across it's welcoming entrance. It was one of the most attractive buildings on campus and appeared in all the college's information pamphlets.

Hank arrived early and was waiting at the top of the stairs when Katie came around the corner and smiled up at him.

"How much time do you have?" she asked, grabbing his arm and leading him into the building. "When's your next class?"

"I'm free until 1:00. Where're we going?"

"Upstairs. Second floor. We have our own library here and I found something yesterday. Remember I told you there was something about that neat old house in the photo?"

"Yeah, did you find it? Is that it?" he asked, getting excited.

"Think so. Come on, let's hurry," she said taking the stairs two at a time. Hank chuckled at her enthusiasm and hurried to keep up.

Approximately half of the second floor was used for labs, and the other half was filled with reference books on architecture and design. She led Hank down a hall lined with tables covered with miniature-sized, student-built models of houses, bridges, auditoriums, high rises and everything else imaginable. Hank was fascinated, and stopped to look, but Katie grabbed him and pulled him along.

"C'mon, we haven't got that much time," she said pulling him toward the library. "We can look at that stuff some other time."

"Sorry," he said, amused at her perky energy.

Katie led him over to a table, sat him down, went over to one of the shelves and brought back a large, hard-covered book and laid it down on the table. It was entitled, *Notable Midwest Homes.*

"Turn to Page 35," she said with a smug look on her face.

Hank opened to page 35, paused a moment and exclaimed, "WOW! That looks like the house all right."

"I think so too," she said as she slipped the photo out of her backpack and placed it on the table along side the book. "I haven't found either of the other two but *this one* is definitely the same. The stone fountain in the front yard's a dead give-a-way," she said. "It's the *same* fountain. And my professor said there were some other features about it that made it unique. The rooflines and proportionate size and style of the windows were very 'chic' for their time suggesting a strong Prairie Architecture influence. And then, there's the same style of columns and ... "

"Blumberg House – 135 Bluff Street – Dubuque, Iowa," Hank muttered as he studied the caption along the bottom of the page, oblivious to Katie's architecture lesson. "Thomas L. Schluss, Architect."

He paused and looked at Katie who had stopped her lecture and was smiling at him.

"*Dubuque*, Katie! Our first solid clue." He laughed in delight and reached over and gave her a big hug. "Dubuque's an old river town on the Mississippi – I've been there. This is *wonderful*. Good job!"

Katie blushed with pride and looked around the room, shrugging at the other students as they turned and stared at Hank's outburst.

"Thanks," she said. "But just because the house is in Dubuque doesn't mean that's where the other pictures were taken. You know, *the* picture."

"No, you're right. But I'd give odds that it was. And anyway, it gives me, us, a location to check out, right?"

"Sure, but *where* do we start even assuming Dubuque's the right place?"

"I don't know yet, but when I go home this weekend, I'm going to meet with my brother and that photographer guy and show them what you found. He told me they've found something useful, too. So maybe with what they learned, and with this, we'll have a better idea of what to do."

"Right, sounds like a plan."

"Think I can take this book with me?" Hank asked.

"No way. I'd get shot if they caught me, or kicked out of school at the very least. Let me make a copy. Actually, I don't think we're even supposed to do that, but under the circumstances it's worth the risk. You stay here and I'll be back in a flash."

Katie quickly left the room while Hank got up and browsed the shelves. In just a couple of minutes she was back, replaced the book on the shelf, and motioned for Hank to follow her out in the hallway. She told him to turn around while she reached down into the neck of her blouse and withdrew two sheets of copy paper – the top and bottom of Page 35.

"Couldn't get it all on one sheet," she explained, "but this should be good enough. Almost got caught but the phone rang at the last second and distracted the secretary."

"You know, you're turning into a regular undercover agent or something. Where'd you learn to be so sneaky?" asked Hank.

"An older brother," she replied, smiling. "Didn't let me get away with much. You've got to learn to be a little sneaky just to survive around our house."

"I can totally identify with that," he said as they exited the building. "Well, thanks again, Katie. Want to get together next week and I'll tell you what I find out when I go home? Maybe take in a movie or something? If you want, that is."

"Yeah, I want. That'd be fun – the movie and all. Besides I'll be dying of curiosity to find out what you learned, so you'd *better* call or else."

"Okay, gotta go or I'll be late for my class. I'll call you Sunday night." Hank quickly unlocked his bike and took off like a rocket.

"How about seeing that new ... "

She was too slow. He was already out of earshot.

CHAPTER TWENTY-ONE

Hank and Al walked into Gary Woodard's office Saturday morning with the taped-up copy of the now famous Page 35 of *Notable Midwest Homes*. Gary was totally impressed with the progress Hank had made.

"Yeah, that's the house, all right," he said after studying the photo for a few moments. "Hmmm – Dubuque, Iowa. That's great work, Hank. And now I think I can tell you *when* the photos were taken."

"Really?" Hank said with excitement.

Gary reached behind him and grabbed two photos from the top of his cabinet. "Here's the original photo showing the three guys in the office. And here's a *doctored* blow up of that part we thought was a calendar. Look at it carefully."

"I'll be darned," Hank exclaimed, bending down to study it more closely. "1940. It reads 1940! That's what – *60 years* ago? I can't believe it. Look Al, can you read it?"

"Yeah," Al said, peering at the photo. "Can't quite read the month though. It looks like it might be covered up."

"I think it's either May, July or August," Gary said.

"What makes you say that?" Hank asked. "The month's covered by this guy's shoulder."

"Well, I've studied it pretty well," said Gary, "and if you look down here at the bottom of the calendar it appears it has 31 days, you can just barely make it out."

"Yeah, you're right," said Hank looking at it again.

"Now notice the way everyone's dressed in short-sleeved shirts. May, July and August all have 31 days. So do March and October but I doubt that they'd be dressed like that in March or October and probably not even in May. Too early for summer clothes, for sure too early if it's Dubuque. So if I had to pin it down, I'd say the photo was taken in either July or August of 1940. Could be May, but I doubt it."

"Sure. Makes sense to me. Good work, Gary," beamed Hank.

"Thanks," said Gary pleased with the compliment.

"All Right then," said Hank. "If we're correct, the picture was taken, or should I say, *the alleged crime was committed,* somewhere in or near Dubuque, Iowa during the summer of 1940, and most likely during July or August. Do we agree?"

"Looks that way," said Al. "What do you think, Gary?

"Yeah, I'd say so."

"Well, thanks a million for doing this, Al," said Hank. "Not sure where we go now but thanks for all the work you've done."

"Hey, no problem. But where *are* you going to go from here? Even if the place and dates are right, you don't have any names or anything else to go on."

"Well, I thought of a couple of things," answered Hank. "One thing I plan to do is check with the Dubuque police. See if they keep records of any 'racial crimes.' The other was going to the Dubuque library to see if I can find something there. And now that we have a plausible time frame, I might even go to the newspaper."

"Good ideas," Gary agreed. "And I can probably help you out with the newspaper part. It's the *Dubuque Telegraph Herald*, by the way. And if I can make a suggestion, I'd be careful about who you show the photo to – might freak some folks out. Know what I'm saying?"

They did.

Sunday afternoon Hank headed back to school. He was looking forward to calling Katie and telling her the news. Actually he was plain looking forward to seeing her again, news or no news.

The apartment was empty when he arrived. Pete, he knew from experience, wouldn't come dragging in 'til late. He seemed seriously smitten by his girlfriend, Amy, and Hank knew he'd be hanging with her until the last possible minute before returning to campus. They'd been seeing each other for almost a year now – a new record for Pete.

Hank liked Amy – a recent grad now in her first year of teaching. She seemed to bring a semblance of common sense to their relationship; something Pete desperately needed. Pete was goofy and fun loving, and had yet to take school very seriously. Hank knew he had a good heart. He'd seen him work with groups of underprivileged area kids in local basketball camps and noticed how the kids adored him. Although he'd never told him, Hank was convinced Pete's natural sports ability would take him a long way. But he needed to settle down and get serious about his education. Hank had studied the careers of enough athletes; professional and amateur, to know a good backup plan was important for survival should things go south.

This year, Amy had carefully steered Pete into a marketing program; a broad enough program that offered Pete some good choices to make when he graduated. And to Hank's surprise, Pete seemed to be doing much better, getting decent grades for a change, although for the life of him Hank couldn't figure out how he managed when he'd seldom seen him crack a book.

When Hank called Katie, she answered on the first ring.

"What'd you find out? Tell me, tell me," she blurted before Hank even had a chance to open his mouth.

"Katie! How'd you know it was *me* calling? What if it was someone else. Don't tell me you've got caller ID or something ... "

"*No one* calls me, least of all on Sunday afternoon. I knew it had to be you. *C'mon tell me!* What'd you find out?"

"Okay," he laughed. "But I want to show you, not tell you. Still up for a movie tonight?"

"Yep, sure. How about *Angela's Ashes*? Just came to the *Bijou*. Have you seen it yet, it's really supposed to be good? Starts at 7:00 and we could get a burger at *Froggies* first, and you can show me what you have. What do you think?"

"Hold on there – slow down a bit," he laughed. "That sounds great, and no, I haven't seen it. I've read the book though and liked it. You must've stayed on campus all weekend planning this out. Sure you don't want to wait until tomorrow or next week ... "

"*C'mon Hank*," she broke in with good-natured fury. "You know I'm dying to hear what you found. That's all I thought about all weekend. I told my parents and everything and they're interested, too."

"All Right. I'll pick you up at 5:30, okay?"

"It's a date – well, sort of. See you then. They want to meet you, by the way."

"What? Who? What'd you say?"

Too late, she'd already hung up.

Hank pulled up in front of Katie's dorm at 5:30 on the nose. The front door flew open and out she bounded, big smile on her face, and dashed to the car – her loose brown curls bouncing on her shoulders. She was wearing a blue skirt and a bright red cotton sweater over a white blouse.

Hank had gotten out of the car to get her door but she jumped in before he even got close. "C'mon, slowpoke," she chided. "You're slower than my brothers."

Hank shook his head, smiled, turned around and got back in.

"You're in a good mood," he said.

"I'm *always* in a good mood. Tell me what you found out." She smelled of lavender. Hank didn't know at the time what it was, but he liked it.

"I will, I will, but I have to *show* you," he said as he pulled away from the curb. "Can you wait 'til we get to *Froggie's*?"

Froggie's was another campus favorite. Urban legend was it opened the same year as the college – 1878 – and still had the original cook and waitresses. Froggy himself ran the kitchen, lording it over the two hapless students who worked there. No matter where you sat and no matter how many people were packed in, you could always hear his loud, gravely voice yelling out commands and insults to everyone he saw. The students loved him as much as they loved the food – greasy cheeseburgers, fresh cut fries and thicker than thick malts. And like *Zoey's, Froggie's* was busy almost every night. But it was still early and it was Sunday so Hank and Katie slipped right into an open booth.

They quickly placed their orders and Hank opened the large manila envelope he had with him and spread out the two photos Gary had given him.

"Okay, you've seen this picture before," he said tapping the original photo that showed the entire scene with the three young men. "What Gary did was blow up this section here," he said making a circle over the shoulder of one of the guys. "And this is what he got!"

Katie pulled the second photo over in front of her and bent over to study it closely for a moment and looked back up at Hank with an amazed look on her face.

"It's a calendar. 1940! I can't believe it," she exclaimed looking back down at the photo. "Good heavens – that means the picture was taken ... "

"60 years ago," broke in Hank.

Katie's jaw dropped. "Ohmygosh," she blurted.

"I know. I know," he said, amused at her wide eyes and stunned expression. "It's hard to believe, isn't it? Even Gary said the crime lab guy hadn't developed film that old before. Said we were lucky to get anything at all, let alone anything this clear. Kodak rules, huh?"

"Oh Hank," Katie exclaimed, all smiles, grabbing his hand. "Now we know *where* and *when*. Is this too cool, or what?"

"Yeah, but listen to this! Gary even narrowed it down to the months of May, July or August!" He explained about the 31 days and the clothing the guys were wearing. "But, at best, these are just logical assumptions, and may not be right," he cautioned.

"Oh, pooh!" she exclaimed. "They're right on. You know they are, and besides they're the best we've got. What's the next step? What do we do now?"

Just then, Harriet, one of the more surly yet beloved waitresses, slammed down their plates of burgers and fries and double chocolate malts, and mumbled something about how they couldn't take all night, to eat up and leave, a crowd's on its way, and what a lousy place this was to work, and how she doubted they'd see her there much longer, etc, etc. Harriet, Hank knew for a fact, had been a waitress at *Froggie's* for over ten years!

"Well," said Hank, "we'd better eat up if we want to keep our heads and make the movie before it starts."

They dug into their burgers while Hank told Katie of his plans to go to Dubuque and talk to the police and check the old newspaper files at the library.

"If that poor guy was really killed," Hank said, "there'll surely be a record of it somewhere, don't you think?"

"Yeah, assuming it was reported and all."

"What do you mean?" Hank asked, looking up at Katie.

"Well, what if the crime was never reported, just sort of covered up? I bet that happened a lot back then, particularly with racial crimes."

"Yeah," said Hank as he pondered that. "Hadn't thought about that. I suppose you could be right. We'll find out soon enough. I'm driving over to Dubuque Saturday. Wanna come?"

"To Dubuque? Sure. Yes."

"Well, I plan to leave early, get there before noon and hit the library first, then visit the police station. But if you went, I could drop *you* off at the library and I'd go to the police station and join you later. Make things go faster."

"You know," Katie said after the movie. "As sad as that show was, it was still uplifting to know that the McCourts ended up as good as they did, at least Frank. I guess I had no idea how bad things were in Ireland at the time – and here I am as Irish as they come."

"I didn't realize you were Irish," said Hank. "Joyce sounds like it could be English to me."

"Oh, Lordy. Don't let my folks hear you say that. *Anything* but English! Heaven forbid. What's Torney, by the way?"

"English."

"Oh no," she exclaimed. "Sorry."

"Well, actually, it's mostly Welsh I think. At least I know my great grandfather on my dad's side came from St. David's in Pembrokeshire, Wales. And if it makes you feel any better, I think the Welsh had their share of problems with the English, too."

"Well, that should help," she sighed.

"Help what?"

"Help grease the skids when I call home and tell my folks I'm going to Dubuque with you. I doubt they'd let me go if they thought you're English."

"You're kidding – aren't you?"

"*YES*, silly. At least sort of," she laughed. "Anyway, you can sort it out when you meet them."

It was almost 10:00 when Hank pulled up in front of Katie's dorm. The night was quiet and calm as he turned off the engine. By this time there was a steady stream of students coming up the walk, or standing in the shadows, or pulling up in cars. The weekend was coming to a close.

"I really had a great time tonight. And I'm glad you're going with me Saturday. Do you want me to pick you up here?"

"Well, if you don't mind, I think I'll go home Friday night. Could you pick me up at my house? It's pretty much on the way."

"That's fine. Then I could meet your folks and let them see I don't have horns or whatever. I'll call you later this week and you can give me directions."

"Sounds good," she said smiling and started to slide toward the door.

"Katie, wait," he said grabbing her arm lightly and pulling her back toward him. "Just wanted to say 'Goodnight'," he whispered as he bent down and kissed her firmly on the lips. She didn't resist. Rather she reached up and wrapped her hand behind his head and pulled him close.

When they finally broke off, breathing heavily and fully flushed, she said in a soft voice, "Please tell me this isn't just research anymore."

"No, I don't think so."

"Good. I'm glad. 'Night Hank, I'd better go or I'll get locked out."

And she was gone.

CHAPTER TWENTY-TWO

Later that night Hank looked up Katie's profile in the school directory and learned she lived near Peoria, about 30 miles away. When he called Wednesday evening she gave him directions and warned him not to eat breakfast or her mom would kill him.

"Exactly three miles north of Wal-Mart on Hwy. 29, turn right on River Road till it comes to a T-intersection in about four miles. If you insist on going straight you'll end up in the Illinois River. At the T, turn left – north again, and in exactly a half-mile our house is on the right. You can't miss the big, green mailbox with a shamrock on it. We'll be looking for you between 8:00 and 8:30. Don't be late or my *brothers* will kill us *both*. Mom will make 'em wait so we can all eat together and they *hate* waiting when it comes to eating."

The shamrock on the mailbox was hard to miss. As Hank turned down their driveway he saw the house. A large, brick two story backed up to the lip of a steep, wooded hill offering an uncluttered view of the river valley. It was clustered among a large group of mature hardwoods. Off to one side stood an outbuilding about the size of a six-stall garage, but deeper and taller. He pulled around a circle drive and pulled to a stop in front of the house just as Katie stepped outside with a big smile and waved at him.

"Just in time," she yelled. "I was afraid we were going to have a revolt on our hands. The boys are starting to panic."

"Sorry. I missed a turn and went a couple of miles out of the way before I figured it out."

"Hey, you're not late. Don't worry about it," she said giving him a little hug. "C'mon in and meet the clan."

Katie led Hank into the living room where her parents were waiting, standing together and smiling. Mrs. Joyce was dressed in a gray knitted sweater and long black skirt and was quite attractive. He could see where Katie got her good looks. Mr. Joyce was dressed in jeans and a plaid flannel shirt and looked quite fit. They both had dark brown hair and appeared to be somewhere in their mid-fifties.

Hank had noticed Mr. Joyce before at the auction barn but had never really seen him up close. His smile was warm and inviting and his grip firm.

He could see two of her brothers lurking in the background, near the dining room. The house smelled wonderful. All of a sudden he was starving.

"Mom – Dad, this is Hank Torney."

"I'm pleased to meet you Mrs. Joyce. Mr. Joyce."

"Likewise, Hank," said Mrs. Joyce. "We're so pleased you could come and join us for breakfast. Hope you're hungry. Katherine, those two younger brothers of yours have been snitching food for the past half hour, I hope there's some left for us."

Mrs. Joyce grabbed Hank's arm and led him into the dining room where the two boys were already stationed by their chairs, fidgeting. Teenagers, Hank guessed as they smiled stiffly at him.

"Boys, where're your manners," Mr. Joyce said. "Introduce yourselves to Hank."

"Hi, I'm Michael," said the older boy, sticking out his hand.

"I'm Brennan," said the other.

Formalities over, they quickly sat and prepared to eat.

"Where's Sean," asked Mrs. Joyce looking around just as a sturdy looking young man came through the door drying his hands.

"Here!" he exclaimed as he walked to the table giving his mom a peck on the cheek. "The new boyfriend's arrived I see. Hi, I'm Sean."

"*SEAN!*" bellowed Katie in anguish.

"Sean, behave yourself," said Mrs. Joyce rolling her eyes and looking at her husband who just smiled and shrugged his shoulders.

"All Right now boys, settle down," said Mr. Joyce. "Let's say a prayer." He paused for a moment until everyone was settled and said, "Bless this food to our bodies, Lord, and give us a chance today to glorify Your Holy Name. Amen."

"AMEN," the rest of the family joined in, all except Hank who sat quietly.

Mrs. Joyce noticed Hank's silence and said, "Hope we didn't startle you, Hank dear. We pray at all our meals. I guess it's the Irish Catholic in us."

Katie turned her head slowly toward her mother and gave her a narrow-eyed, pursed lip look. Sean smiled. He knew what was coming.

"Torney," she said, pouring coffee for him. "What nationality is that, Hank? Sounds like it could be English."

"Mother!" Katie said.

"No, ma'am," Hank quickly replied.

All eyes were on him now.

"Welsh. Torney is definitely Welsh."

"Oh, Welsh. Welsh Catholic, by any chance?"

"No, ma'am. Lutheran."

"I see. That's nice. Ever thought of becoming Catholic?"

"*MOTHER!*" cried out Katie again.

"Sorry dear, just trying to get to know your new friend. Let's eat, shall we?"

All the boys were greatly amused by this banter but it didn't slow them down any. The food was plentiful and excellent; scrambled eggs, sausage, bacon, hot cinnamon rolls, pitchers of orange juice and milk, and a large carafe of freshly-brewed coffee.

Hank held his own with the best of them. Brennan, he learned, was 14, and the youngest. Michael was 16. Both were typical teenagers, loved sports, and good-sized for their ages. Sean was 24, a year older than Hank, and was one tough looking dude. He'd seen him before, helping out at the auctions, but hadn't realized until now that he was part of the family. He also learned he'd graduated from Stanford with an advanced degree in electrical engineering, worked for a firm in Peoria and was engaged to be married the following spring.

"I'm glad to see you digging in Hank," smiled Mrs. Joyce. "I suspect you don't always have a chance to fix a hot breakfast at school."

"No, ma'am, I don't. This tastes terrific. I'm afraid my breakfasts are usually Pop Tarts and cold cereal. Sometimes my roommate, Pete, gets up early and burns some pancakes for us, but that's about as fancy as it gets."

"Katherine tells us you're in grad school," said Mr. Joyce. "Psychology, is that right?"

"Yes, sir," replied Hank. "Sports Psychology, actually. I'm in my second year right now and ... "

"Sports Psychology!" broke in Michael. "That's cool. What sports?"

"Well, it could be any sport, Mike, but ... "

"Michael," Mrs. Joyce interjected softly. "We prefer to use their proper Christian names."

This time all the kids rolled their eyes.

"Yes, ma'am. Michael. It could be any sport, Michael, but I guess I'd prefer either baseball or basketball. At least those are my favorite two ... "

"Yeah! Baseball." said Brennan. "What's your favorite team?"

"Are you kidding?" said Hank getting into it. "I don't live that far from Chicago. The Cubs rule!"

"GIVE ME A BREAK!" broke in Michael. "The Cubs suck! The Twins are the only ... "

"All Right, all right, that's enough boys," broke in Mr. Joyce. "Let Hank finish his breakfast, and Michael, you can watch your language."

"Yes, sir," replied a chastised Michael.

"Finish up and go do your chores. We'd like to visit with Hank and Katherine before they leave. Sean, why don't you stay?"

That was all it took, and in a moment the two teenagers picked up their plates, thanked their mom for breakfast, and headed to the kitchen.

"Katherine told us about the photos you found, Hank," said Mr. Joyce. "And you're going to Dubuque today to find out – exactly what?"

"Well, I'm not quite sure," said Hank. "Did Katie, I mean, did Katherine tell you we have a time frame now? July or August of 1940. I guess I'd be happy if we can find out if there's any record of a crime being committed and if so, what was ever done about it."

"But that was a long time ago," said Mr. Joyce. "Do you really think you're going to learn something now? And let's say you do, what could be done about it now, anyway?"

"I really don't know, sir. But I guess we've gone this far and, if nothing else, I'd like to satisfy myself that things were righted."

"And you're really convinced this black guy was killed?" asked Sean.

"Why don't you show them the photos?" Katie suggested.

"Do you folks want to see them? I've got them in the car."

"Certainly," Mrs. Joyce said. "By all means."

Hank ran out to his car and brought in the photos and spread them on the dining room table. Of course, they were all interested in the original crime scene photo and studied it in great detail, cringing and displaying varying degrees of shock.

"Well, I guess I agree with you guys," Sean finally said. "That black guy sure doesn't look too hot. If he's not dead, he's definitely badly hurt. I can't believe they'd even take a picture in the first place."

"Why, those two white boys look like teenagers," Mrs. Joyce said shaking her head. "And you think the pictures were taken when?"

"We believe 1940," Hank explained showing them the enhanced enlargement. "This print shows a calendar, and if you look closely, you can just make out the date."

"Yes, I can see it," said Mr. Joyce. "And tell me again, why do you think Dubuque?"

"Well, Katie, I mean Katherine, recognized this house that was on the same roll of film." Hank said as he slid over another photo. "In fact we copied this page out of a book that shows the same house."

"You're right," said Mrs. Joyce studying both the photo and the page copy. "How in the world did you know that, Katherine?"

"I remembered it from one of my classes. You know how I love older homes."

"Very clever, Katherine," said Mr. Joyce. "And you're planning to take these photos to the police?"

"We've talked about that," Katie said, "and decided it might be best to just ask some questions at first. Hank's going to the police station while I go to the library."

"You know, another possibility would be to look at some old high school yearbooks," said Sean. "If mom's right about their ages, and if they all lived in Dubuque – at least the white guys, they went to school somewhere. If not Dubuque, maybe at one of the towns close by."

"Hey, that's a great idea, Sean," said Hank. "We hadn't thought of that. If we have enough time today, we'll be sure to do that."

"Speaking of 'enough time'," chimed in Katie standing up from the table, "we'd better be going if we're going to get *anything* done."

Hank gathered together his materials and thanked Mrs. Joyce again for the wonderful breakfast. By then it was 9:30 and they still had at least a two-hour drive ahead of them. As they drove away, they waved to Mr. and Mrs. Joyce who were both standing on the front porch smiling.

100

"Whew!" Hank exclaimed as they drove out of sight. "How'd I do?"

"For a Lutheran Welshman, not bad," laughed Katie. "I think Mom and Dad liked you just fine. And you obviously made a big hit with Michael and Brennan. Sean never says much, but he was watching you pretty closely. Yeah, I think you did fine."

"Is that good?"

"I'd say that's very good."

CHAPTER TWENTY-THREE

It was close to noon when Hank and Katie crossed the Iowa-Illinois Bridge and entered Dubuque. It'd been an informative drive. Hank found out quite a bit about Katie's family and was surprised to learn her dad ran the auction business as more of a hobby than anything else. He hadn't meant to pry but when he commented on the flexibility of his working hours at the auction house, she howled with laughter.

"That's just his hobby, silly," she said. "Dad's a trader; he works out of an office at home."

"Trader?" Hank exclaimed. "What kind of trader."

"Commodities, mainly," she replied. "He buys and sells grain and livestock."

"Wow, I've heard about that. A high risk business, isn't it?"

"Well, there's not much room for error if that's what you mean. But he's pretty good at it, I guess."

"And he still has time to run an auction house?"

"Well, yeah. But he's got some pretty good help, you know. Sean and I for starters," she said with a smile. "And he's got a couple of guys who've been with him for years who handle most of the day-to-day stuff. But he loves interacting with the farmers – says it helps him keep his pulse on the markets."

After crossing the river, they turned down the main street and drove to the library. It wasn't hard to find, being one of the largest buildings in the downtown area, a two-story, brick building occupying a full half block.

"Now remember," Hank said as he pulled up in front. "I'll return as soon as I finish at the police station so just take your time, okay?"

"Yes, don't worry, I can handle this just fine," Katie replied as she slipped out of the car. "See you later."

The police station was several blocks on the other side of the downtown district. Hank parked his car in the visitor's lot and walked up the steps, passing several policemen coming and going. As he entered a policewoman standing behind a waist-high window immediately greeted him.

"Can I help you?" she asked.

"Yes, thank you. I'm working on a research project and looking for information about a crime that may have been committed here in Dubuque years ago."

"What type of crime are you interested in? And how long ago?"

"Well, a violent crime – and back in 1940," he stammered suddenly realizing how lame that sounded.

Apparently the clerk did too because she asked, "Well can you be a bit more specific? Do you have the victim's name? The name of the person committing the crime? Exact dates? That sort of thing."

"Well, I have some approximate dates, all in the same year, 1940."

"All Right," she said. "But you do realize a lot of crimes are committed every year. Yet you say you're only interested in *violent crimes*?"

"Yeah, like when someone killed someone – maybe in a fight or something."

"Like a homicide," she prompted?

"Yes, a homicide."

"Do you live here in town?

"No ma'am. I'm a student at Western Illinois State. Blighton, Illinois. I'm just in town for the day."

"I see. And what were the dates you were interested in?" she asked reaching for a pad of paper and a pencil.

"July and August of 1940. And, let's say May, too."

"Okay, I'll see what I can do. Your name?"

"Hank Torney."

"Mr. Torney, you have a seat over there," she said nodding with her head toward a row of seats against the far wall. "I'll be back in a moment."

"Thanks," Hank said smiling. "I really appreciate it."

Hank looked around as he walked over and sat down. To his right, a long hallway led to a number of offices from which a steady stream of plain clothes and uniformed police were entering and leaving. It seemed pretty tame to Hank who was anticipating something more dramatic, like a scene out of *NYPD Blues* or something. At the very least, he expected to see a pair of cops leading someone in handcuffed and struggling. But this was more like a regular office building. It could have been a stationery supply store for all the excitement he was seeing.

After a minute the clerk called him back over to the window.

"Well, I'm afraid we can't be of much help at this point, Mr. Torney. I talked to our records department and was told that files that old are not computer indexed by *type* of crime. Just by name. Now if you had an *specific* date or victim's name, or the name of the criminal, or even the arresting officer's name, we might be able to help you."

The look of disappointment on Hank's face was apparent.

"Perhaps you could check out the newspapers for the period you're interested in and when you find something, come back with more information and we might be able to help you then. All Right?"

Hank didn't bothered to explain that someone was already doing that. So he thanked her for her trouble and said he'd come back if he found something. He left feeling very disappointed.

He found Katie on the library's second floor. She was sitting at a large microfilm machine slowly turning the crank and straining to scan the images as fast as she could.

"Ready for a break?" Hank asked sliding a chair over to her.

"Whew! Yeah, I am. My eyes are starting to blur. And to answer your inevitable question, I haven't found anything yet and I'm almost half way done. How about you?"

"Me neither. C'mon, let's go grab something to eat and I'll tell you about it. There's a little cafe just around the corner."

The first wave of diners had already cleared out of *Kathy's Kitchen Korner* when Hank and Katie claimed a small booth. They ordered the *Soup 'N Sandwich* special while Hank filled her in on what happened at the police station.

"So they really aren't able to help us," he said, "unless we can come up with a specific name or a date. I think the information's there, but would involve a tedious record search that they weren't interested in doing. Can't say I blame them."

"No, I guess not," Katie agreed. "I didn't have any better luck. I looked through every single issue in July and had just racked up August and started on it when you showed up. It took longer than I thought, especially when you don't know exactly what you're looking for."

"Well, let's not get discouraged yet," said Hank. "When we go back you can finish checking August while I look at May. If we still have time we can check October, too. We still have plenty of time. We don't need to leave until 4:30 or 5:00."

Back at the library, Katie started where she had left off as Hank signed up for another machine, ordered the May and October reels and started looking. They found nothing.

"What now, Sherlock? Any ideas?"

"Well, assuming we didn't miss anything, either there were no murders, homicides, or other violent crimes during our time frame, or we have the wrong months, or wrong town ..."

"Or," piped in Kathy, "The crime was never discovered, or never reported."

"Yeah, that, too. Damn, I was hoping we'd find *something* and then could go to the police station and put this thing to rest."

"C'mon now. Like you said, don't be discouraged. There could be a lot of options we haven't even thought of. We'll find something. And as long as we're here, why don't we follow up on Sean's suggestion to check out the high schools?"

"Hey, good idea!" said Hank. "I'd almost forgotten about that. Let's find out what high schools were here in 1940, and at least get the addresses and phone numbers."

It didn't take long to come up with a list. The reference librarian told them that in 1940 there were only two high schools in Dubuque; St. Columkille Catholic High School and a public school, Dubuque High.

"Do you have copies of their yearbooks on file?" asked Hank.

"We do of Dubuque High," she said. "You'll have to check with St. Columkille yourself. C'mon, what we have is over here along this back wall."

"Okay, cross your fingers," said Hank. "You take 1939 and I'll do 1940."

Hank and Katie checked all the annuals four years on either side of 1940 with no success. It really didn't take that long as each class had fewer than 120 students, and the majority of those seemed to be women. They even switched books and checked each other's work. They were hoping, of course, to spot one of the two white guys. There were no black students in any of the classes.

"Well, that takes care of Dubuque High," said Hank sounding slightly depressed. "Unfortunately, we're running out of time. If I'm going take you home and get back to school by a decent hour, we'll have to leave soon."

"I know," said Katie. "But before we do I want to check out the old house in the photo. The lady who helped me said that the house is still there!"

"Really? Know how to get there?"

"According to her it's on the bluff right above us. Should only take a few minutes." They quickly gave their thanks and left.

Bluff Street wasn't hard to find, it was right where it should be – on the bluff. They headed up the steep side street bordering the library, and after a couple of minutes turned into a lovely, old neighborhood overlooking the downtown and the Mississippi beyond. Mature oak and maple trees filled the yards of large, well-maintained homes.

After a couple of blocks, Katie spied it.

"Ohmygosh!" she exclaimed. "There it is, there it is. Pull over. Quick, pull over ... "

"Okay, okay. You scared me half to death," Hank laughed. "I see it, too."

Hank pulled over to the curb and they both stared at the house. Katie spread out the photo and the page from the book. Amazingly, the house had hardly changed at all. The fountain was still there. A circular drive had been put in, and a new room had been added to the north side. And, of course, the saplings in the original photo were now huge.

"Look at the size of the trees," said Katie in awe. "They've gotten monstrous! But the house – its lines are exactly the same, the same windows and doors, same roofline. I can't believe it. I wonder who lives there."

"Let's go find out," said Hank getting out of the car.

"Really?" said Katie, excited and jumping out to join him. "Ohmygosh, I've gotta take a picture. My professor will die when I tell him about this."

They walked onto a covered porch and rang the bell. White wicker furniture looked out over a plush green lawn. They could hear chimes going off somewhere in the rear of the home. After a moment, they heard someone coming, when Hank whispered to Katie, "You do the talking."

"What, what should I say? I don't know ... " Just then the door opened.

"Yes, can I help you?" asked this perfect, little old lady. Neatly dressed in a black dress with tiny white dots, buttoned up the front clear to the neck. A string of pearls. Soft white hair, perfectly arranged. Black, low heel shoes. Standing no more than five feet tall, she reminded Hank of grandma on the *Waltons*.

"Hello," said Katie. "We're sorry to bother you but we're wondering if you'd mind if we took a picture of your lovely house? Do you own it?"

"Why, yes I do," she said smiling and opening the door a little wider. "And of course, you go ahead and take all the pictures you want, dear. But what in heaven's name for?"

"Well, we're both students at Western State College in Blighton, Illinois, and just happen to be in Dubuque for the day. I'm majoring in architecture and design and I saw a picture of your home taken many years ago and I just wanted to see how much it's changed over the years so we drove over to take a look."

"My name's Hank Torney," said Hank offering his hand. And this is Katherine Joyce. We hope we're not disturbing you."

"Indeed you're not. My name's Anna Kiefer and I'm delighted you stopped by. You obviously like older homes?"

"Yes, we do," said Katie. "Particularly famous old homes like this one. Would you like to see an early photo of this house? We have a copy with us."

"Yes, indeed I would, but why don't you step inside and we can sit in the parlor. Would you like some tea?"

"No thank you, Ms. Kiefer," said Hank as he and Katie entered the foyer. "We really need to head back pretty quickly and can only stay for a minute."

They followed her down a short hallway and into a classic sitting room bathed in soft light from the late afternoon sun. She motioned for them to sit in a divan and took a seat in an antique high back chair beside them. A small marble top table separated the two and Katie opened the envelope and slid out the photocopy of the house. The photo of the house taken from Hank's camera slid out as well before Katie could catch it.

"Oh," Ms. Kiefer exclaimed. "I've seen this photo many times," motioning to the photocopy, "but this one is interesting." She picked up the blown up photo to look at it more closely. "This appears to have been taken *about* the same time, doesn't it? I've never seen it before. Where did you get it?"

"Uh – that was also in our files at school," said Katie quickly. "Can you tell us a little about the history of the home, Ms. Kiefer?"

"Certainly, and it's *Mrs*. Kiefer, dear, but please, call me Anna. Well, you already know it's called the *Blumberg House*. And yes, Thomas Schluss was the architect as it shows here. The house was completed in 1924 and was reportedly one of the nicest homes in Dubuque at the time boasting some of the newest improvements available. Mr. Schluss went on to design several other homes in the area, but this one is still considered one of his finest efforts.

"The Blumbergs were in banking and very wealthy. But when the Great Depression came, well, like a lot of folks, they lost everything, including this house. It was later purchased by the Grettsmer family who moved in the early 30's. The house had been vacant several months by that time and required a lot of work to restore it. But Mr. Grettsmer wanted to restore it as close to its original condition as possible, and it was only years later that Mrs. Grettsmer added this room, the solarium. Mr. Grettsmer was in the building construction trade and supplied most of the hardwoods as well as the metal pipe for the home during its initial construction. So I guess you'd say it's ironic that even though it's known as the *Blumberg House*, the Blumbergs lived in it less then four years."

"My goodness," said Katie, impressed. "You surely know a lot about it, don't you?"

Mrs. Kiefer threw back her head and laughed.

"Oh you'll think me terribly wicked," she said with a twinkle in her eye. "I suppose I should have told you from the beginning. Kiefer is my married name. Mr. Kiefer's been dead over ten years now. My *maiden* name is Grettsmer and I was born in this house."

CHAPTER TWENTY-FOUR

"Well, I still don't get it," said Hank on the drive back to Katie's. "Why *that* house on the roll of film? Don't you find that a little spooky?"

"It *wasn't* just that house," said Katie. "There were pictures of a couple of other houses on it too, remember? I just happened to recognize *that* one. Maybe the others were just as well known, at least back then. But that Mrs. Kiefer, she was one cool old lady, wasn't she?"

"Yeah, she was."

"Do you think we should have shown her the other picture – you know? Maybe she might have recognized one of the guys. She was obviously around at the time."

"No, we might have freaked her out, maybe caused a heart attack or something."

"I doubt that," laughed Katie. "She looks the type to take things in stride. I doubt too much could faze her."

They pulled into Katie's driveway around 8:30. The lights were on in the downstairs family room and the boys' bedroom.

"You want to come in for a few minutes?"

"No, I'd better not. I've gotta get back and finish a paper."

"Well, but ... "

Hank didn't let her finish. He pulled her over and kissed her. "I'll call you Monday," he said, "Okay?"

"Yeah. I had fun today."

"Me too."

"My folks didn't scare you off?"

"Nah. I like 'em."

"Good, 'cause Mom's been watching us through the living room window."

"What?" exclaimed Hank jumping back as if he'd just touched a live wire.

"Just kidding," laughed Katie moving over quickly and giving Hank another quick kiss before sliding out of the car.

"Drive carefully!" she yelled as she headed on up the porch.

"You just wait," Hank shouted as he shook his fist. "I'll get you for that."

Pete was sprawled out over the living room couch watching *David Letterman* when Hank walked in. Several empty beer cans and a pizza box covered the rickety coffee table and all but covered up the current issue of *Sports Illustrated*.

"Hey roomie!" greeted Pete. "Where're you been, man? I saved some pizza for you but I was afraid it might go bad, so I ate it."

"Thanks, pal, thoughtful of you. Katie and I went to Dubuque today. I told you I'd be late. Anyone call?"

"Wow, man. You've been seeing a lot of that young lady lately. You guys getting engaged or something? This is beginning to look serious ... "

"Any messages?" interrupted Hank, who knew once Pete got on a roll, it'd be hard stopping him.

"Yeah, your brother called earlier. Told you to call him when you got back."

"Are you sure? Gee, I don't know. It's pretty late."

"Said he didn't care. Better call him. He sounded serious."

"Yeah, all right."

The phone rang several times and Hank was about to hang up when Al's groggy voice answered.

"H'low?"

"Al? It's me, Hank. Were you in bed?"

"Hank? What the hell! 'Course I'm in bed! Why'd you call so late, jerk. You probably woke up the kids."

"Jeez, I'm sorry. Pete said you wanted me to call when I got home and didn't care how late it was."

"That air head! I said to call if it wasn't *too* late."

"Yeah, well Pete's idea of 'too late' is like three or four in the morning," Hank said turning and giving Pete the nastiest look he could come up with.

Pete, in return was holding up his open hands, palm forward and mouthing *It's not my fault,* and shaking his head in complete innocence.

"Well, now that I'm up, what'd did you find out?"

"Not much," said Hank. "A complete blank at the police station and library. But Katie's brother came up with a good idea. He suggested we ... "

"Katie? Who's Katie?" broke in Al.

"Katie. Katherine Joyce. I told you about her, didn't I? It's her dad's auction house where I bought the camera."

"She went with you to Dubuque? Does she know about the photos and stuff?"

"Yeah, I thought I told you that. Anyway she knows the whole story and her brother had a great suggestion."

"Her brother? Why don't you take out an ad in the paper?"

"C'mon. No big deal. It's not like we're trying to hide anything. Anyway, he suggested trying to identify the white guys in the photo by checking in old school yearbooks. Her mom thought ... "

"Geeesh!"

"... her mom thought those two white guys looked around high school age. I think they're on to something with the yearbook idea."

"So did you look 'em up?"

"We checked out the public high school while we were at the library – no dice. But there's also a Catholic high school we didn't have time to check out. Katie's gonna order copies of their old yearbooks through our library here at school."

"Why didn't you check them out when you were there?"

"Ran out of time. I had to get Katie home and I had to get back here and do some work tonight. Got a paper due next week."

"Yeah, and what's with this 'Katie' person? Does Mom know about her? Sounds like you're already in thick with *her* family. Are you planning on telling the folks about her or are you two just going to run off and elope?"

"Very funny, Al, very funny. You sound like Pete. Don't worry, you'll meet her soon enough. Oh, almost forgot. Remember that house in the photo? Well it's still there and we went and saw it. It really hasn't changed much. And we met the lady who lives there – a widow who, and you've gonna love this, was *born* there! Is that wild?"

"Did you show her the one photo – you know ... ?"

"No. Might've freaked her out! Listen, I've gotta go. Sorry I woke you. Call you soon."

"Jeez, Pete," said Hank turning to his roommate. "Why in hell'd you tell me to call so late? I woke up their whole family."

"Shhhhhh," said Pete mesmerized by something he was watching on TV. "Check this out. Those two guys invented a 'Pumpkin Cannon.' There're gonna show a film clip of 'em shooting a pumpkin across the Delaware River and look, they've taped a dollar bill on the side. Get it?" he whooped, bouncing up and down on the sofa. "Washington crossing the Delaware on a pumpkin. Is that too cool or what?"

"Night, Pete," said Hank, shaking his head and heading to his room. "See you in the morning, and keep the sound down, will you? Unlike other people I know, I go to school here and I've need to get some work done."

CHAPTER TWENTY-FIVE

The next couple of weeks seemed to fly by. Hank was scrambling to get his thesis in shape and Katie was buried in her own class work.

When possible, they still managed to get together for lunch or coffee in the Commons. Finally, they received their first major breakthrough.

Hank was home studying when Pete yelled at him, "Hank – phone! Your heartthrob sounds panicky. Better hurry, Romeo."

Pete was right about one thing, Katie did sound panicky. When he picked up the phone, she blurted out, "Hank. I found something. You won't believe this. Can you come right over to the library? I'm at the microfilm machines."

"Now?" he said, looking at his watch. "Did you find something? Can you tell me over the phone?"

"Puleeese! I need to show you. The library's only open for another 45 minutes, but this won't take long. You need to see this."

"Okay, okay. I'll be right there. Don't panic."

"Hurry."

Hank grabbed his helmet, ran down stairs, jumped on his bike, flipped on his lights and took off like a madman. Hank and Pete lived three blocks off campus and Hank covered the distance in two minutes and then another five across campus to the main library. He skidded to a stop, locked his bike and jogged up the stairs and to the research room. Katie looked up when he entered and waved him over. She was flushed with excitement, and apparently had already earned some displeasure from surrounding students who were still frowning at her.

"C'mere," she whispered a little too loudly resulting in a new round of "shhhhhh's."

"What'd you find?" whispered Hank as he slid a chair over, amused at her obvious excitement.

"Remember when we were at the library and how we skipped the month of September because we were only concerned with months with just 31 days?"

"Yeah."

"Well, when I ordered the Columkille High yearbooks I also ordered the newspaper films again – just to double check. The newspaper film came Monday and the past few days I rechecked May, July and August. Tonight I was going to skip to October when I thought I might as well check September while I was at it. Look what I found."

She moved aside and motioned Hank in closer. The microfilm was cued to the top of page three of the main news section for Sunday, September 19, 1940. Slowly she turned the knob and the page started to scroll down. Hank leaned his head in, scanned back and forth and squinted to read the moving words. Suddenly she stopped and turned to look at Hank.

"I don't get it," he said. "What am I supposed to be looking for? I don't see anything. What did you ... " Then he froze.
"Oh my gosh!"

Toward the bottom was a quarter page ad.

$25 CASH REWARD
For information leading to the whereabouts of
Glory Alexander, Negro male, 25 years of age,
5' 8" tall. Last seen the evening of
August 25th near the Dubuque Ice Harbor.
Contact the Delta Shipping Company,
25 Levee Street, Memphis, Tennessee.

"Do you think that's him?" he said in a low voice while staring at the screen.

"Yeah, I do," she said. "Has to be. The age seems right, don't know about the height. And he is a 'Negro male.' How many 'Negro males' do you think came up missing in Dubuque in August 1940?"

"Okay – you're right. *Glory* Alexander. What a strange name. The Delta Shipping Company. Memphis, Tennessee. Think the place is still in business?"

"Don't know. Shouldn't be hard to find out."

Just then the library sound system announced that it was closing in 15 minutes and advising patrons to please gather together their things and get ready to leave.

"Let's print this," said Hank.

In a couple of minutes they had their copy, rewound the film and turned off the machine.

As they exited the library, Hank gushed over Katie, telling her what a wonderful job she had done noticing the ad. She beamed from ear to ear. They sat on the library steps and discussed possible next steps.

"All Right," said Hank. "Assuming our guy *is* Glory Alexander, what does this all mean? I suppose we can now assume that there was definitely some bad stuff involved. Otherwise, why put an ad like that in the paper?'

"Exactly," chimed in Katie. "And if that's true – that is, if he turned up missing on August 25, *why* didn't we find anything about it in the paper? While I was waiting for you I've rechecked around that date *twice* and there's *nothing*."

"I don't know," replied Hank, "unless, like you said earlier, for some reason it was never reported. I hate to say this, but he *was* black, you know. And they were *white* teenagers. They were either very clever, or somebody helped cover up for them. Anyway, now that we have a name and a date, we can go back and check again."

They decided to split up the assignments. Hank said he'd try and run down the Delta Shipping Company. Katie said she'd go back and recheck all the dates through September and then do October. They left promising to touch base with each other later in the week.

Later that night, Hank called Al and filled him in on what Katie had found. Al was almost as excited as he was and said he'd be sure to tell Gary Woodard about it in the morning. After they hung up Hank went online and tried to find information on the Delta Shipping Company. No hits. He then tried to find it on the Memphis Chamber of Commerce site. No luck there, either. Frustrated, he got up from his computer just as Pete came through the door and asked him what's happening.

He showed him the copy of the ad and Pete read it and asked, "You think this is the same black dude in the photo?"

"Yeah, I do. Everything seems to check out. But I can't find Delta Shipping on the Internet, nor can I find them listed in the Memphis Chamber list."

"How 'bout the Memphis Library. They'll look it up for you. They love stuff like that and they have access to all the old city phone books. Betcha they'll find 'em in a minute."

"Hey, that's a good idea, Pete," said Hank impressed, turning to look at him. "How'd you think of that?"

"Heck, I use libraries all the time. They'll look up anything. I never go in a library if I don't have to. I just send 'em an email, even our own library here at school."

"You're kidding, of course," he said, looking at Pete who just shrugged innocently.

"No, you're not, are you," said Hank, smiling and shaking his head. He quickly got back online and fired off a query to the Memphis main library asking what they could tell him about the Delta Shipping Company; a Memphis company in business in 1939.

Now, according to Pete, just sit back and relax.

Hank and Katie had a date that Friday night. A fellow grad school buddy and his wife were having some friends over for spaghetti and meatballs and Hank was going to bring a bottle of Chianti. When he got home from the store there was an email message waiting for him from the Memphis library.

"Wow," he thought to himself. "That *was* fast. Ol' Pete's definitely on to something."

He opened the message and read:

Dear Mr. Torney, regarding your inquiry about the Delta Shipping Company, it was founded here in Memphis in 1925 and operated continuously as barge shippers until 1945, at which time The Coastal Transport Company, New Orleans, Louisiana, acquired it. The main office is now located in New Orleans in the Hanford Building, Suite 756, 276 Logan Street, New Orleans 70122. They can be reached by phone at 504-486-2839. However, they still maintain a terminal here in Memphis at 25 Levee Street, Memphis, Tennessee 38101 and the number here is 901-544-9021. If your question is of historic nature, you may also consider contacting the Memphis History Center, 235 Trevor Street,

Memphis 38102, telephone 901-564-7349. If there is anything else we can help you with, please let us know.
   Kathy Parent, Reference Librarian

Hank printed off a copy of the message and took it with him when he went to pick up Katie. She came bouncing out of the dorm and jumped into the car and exclaimed in a rush, "Am *I* hungry, and I *love* spaghetti and meatballs." She threw her arms around him and gave him a quick, hard kiss on the lips. "Oh, I'm in such a good mood tonight."

"You're always in a good mood, kiddo," Hank laughed. "When are you ever in a 'bad mood'?"

"Oh, just cross me, Buster, and you'll find out," she threatened holding up her fist. "Hey, what's this?" she said picking up the email message that was sitting on the seat.

"Just got that that tonight," said Hank. "Read it and see what you think."

Katie read the message.

"Oh, Hank, a new lead! What are you gonna do with it?"

"Well, I guess I'll call them and see if I can find out anything about our friend, Glory."

"Gosh, do you really think they'll still have records that go back that far?"

"All I can do is ask."

CHAPTER TWENTY-SIX

Monday morning Hank called The Coastal Transport Company. He might as well have been calling *Lower Slobonia*. A woman answered the phone with a Southern drawl as thick as lava. She had absolutely no idea what he was talking about, had never heard of Delta Shipping Co., and insisted he had the wrong number. In desperation, he asked to speak to someone in management and was mercifully transferred.

This time a man answered, introduced himself as John Andrews, Sales Manager, and listened patiently as Hank asked his questions.

"Well, Mr. Torney," he said. "I can tell you that, yes, I am familiar with the Delta Shipping Company – although just barely. But if I understand you correctly, you're looking for someone who was a *possible* employee over 50, maybe 60 years ago? I can tell you right now that we have no records that go back that far. Is this person a relative?"

"No sir, I need to find out some information about him for a research project I'm working on."

"Well, as I've said, we have no records *here* that will help. Have you contacted our Memphis office?"

"No sir, not yet. I thought I'd try you first."

"Well, I suggest you give *them* a call. Do you want their number?"

"No, sir, I already have it."

"You might ask for the manager, Bill Watkins. Tell him you and I have talked. And good luck. I hope you find what you're looking for."

"Thank you, Mr. Andrews."

Hank dialed the number of the Memphis office.

"Coastal Transport" chirped a shrill voice. "Can I help you?"

"Yes, I'd like to speak with Bill Watkins, please."

"And whom should I say is calling?" responded the operator whose voice made Hank think of Lily Tomlin on those famous

Laugh In episodes. After a few moments, a gruff voice came on the line.

"Hello. Bill Watkins here."

"Mr. Watkins, my name's Hank Torney. I just spoke with John Andrews in your New Orleans office who thought you might be able to help me."

"Yeah? What can I do for you?"

"Well, I know this may sound a little strange, but I'm looking for any information I can find about a former employee of yours, a Mr. Glory Alexander, who worked for you back in 1940."

There was a long pause.

"Mr. Watkins, are you there?"

"Yeah, I'm here. Did you say 1940?"

"Yes sir, August of 1940, to be exact. Do you have records that go back that far?"

"1940. That was back when the Delta Shipping Line was in business, right?"

"Yes sir, I believe it was."

"Did you say *Glory* Alexander?"

"I did. I know it's an unusual name, but that might make it easier to find, wouldn't it?"

"Are you a relative of this person or something?"

"No sir. I'm, uh, working on a research project and ... "

"Yeah, whatever," interrupted Mr. Williams. "And you said John Andrews told you to call me?"

"Yes sir, he did. I just talked to him."

"Well, lemme speak to our dock foreman. He's been around a long time. Might remember something. We *used* to have a bunch of old records boxed up somewhere. Get back to us this afternoon. Ask for Tony. I'll tell him you're gonna call. Okay?"

"Yes sir, and thank you. I'll call back around 1:00 or 1:30."

After lunch Hank called back and asked to speak with Tony.

"Just a moment, Mr. Torney, and I'll connect Mr. Rabino."

After a long pause, the thick voice of a dedicated smoker came on the line.

"Tony."

"Mr. Rabino, this is Hank Torney. Mr. Williams asked me to call you."

"Sure, and it's Tony. Something about some old records right? You need to find someone – a Glory Alexander? What kinda name's that? Back in 1940? What'd this guy do, anyway?"

"Well, I don't know if he did anything – you mean like break the law or something?"

"No, no. I mean what was his *job*? Did he work here in the warehouse? On the docks? One of our barges?"

"I don't know for sure, but he came to Dubuque, Iowa, when he was working for you so I suspect he worked on a barge."

"Dubuque, huh. Well that helps. You know we still barge up through Dubuque – clear to Minneapolis and back. 1940? Well we still have records that go back that far – why we keep 'em, I don't know. Tell you what, I'm busy right now. When I have a little time, I'll take a look. Give me your name and address and if I find something I'll copy it and send it up to you."

Hank gave him his name and address.

"All Right then, I'll do what I can."

"That's great. Thanks a million, Tony."

That evening Hank called Katie and told her about his calls. "Let's assume Glory *was* an employee of the company," he said. "I mean why else would they spend the money to place a 'Missing Person' ad in the Dubuque paper."

"Yeah, I agree," said Katie.

"And if he *was* an employee, they may know his address and other personal information. That way we might be able to run down any family members and tell them what we found."

"But Hank, it's been so long," said Katie. "I mean it's been 60 *years*! We don't even know if there's anyone alive who'd even remember him. We may never know."

"But we need to at least try, Katie! What if he was married, and had children? Chances are they'd still be alive. Heck, his wife could even still be alive. Don't you think they'd want to know what happened to their father – her husband, gone missing without a word? Not knowing if he were dead or alive? Not knowing why he never came home. Wondering if he ran off, or was hurt and injured, or whatever. What are we doing all this for anyway?"

There was a prolonged silence on the other end of the line. Finally, Hank realized that he'd almost been shouting and said, "Katie?"

She replied in a soft voice, "I'm here."

"Katie, I'm sorry. I didn't mean to shout like that. I got carried away. Guess I'm starting to take this all so personal. I shouldn't have jumped on you like that. I'm sorry."

"No, Hank," she replied in a subdued voice. "You're right. I guess I've been thinking of this too much as just a game, a challenge, a puzzle to solve. You're right. It's definitely more than that now. Those were real people. And we need to do what we can, as you say, to bring closure."

"Thanks, babe. Gosh, I'm glad I met you. I wish you were here right now so I could give you a great big, long, make-up kiss."

"That wasn't even a fight," she laughed, back to her normal, cheerful self. "But I like the 'kiss' part. Did I tell you I talked to our reference librarian and she told me the Columkille yearbooks should be here soon?"

"Perfect. That's great. Now we're making some real headway. I've got some old records coming and you've got the books ordered. Let's relax and see what happens. Hey, by the way, my folks are coming up next weekend for the Danville game and they'd like to meet you. Are you going to be here that weekend? I'm sure they'll want to take us out for dinner."

"Sure. I'd like to meet them, too. Sounds like fun."

"All Right, but I must warn you. Amy, Pete's girlfriend is coming to the game, too, and I'll have to ask them to join us. Her folks don't live that far from our house. Mom really likes her, but thinks Pete is absolutely *wonderful* – like he walks on water or something! She really thinks he's a great influence on me. Some kind of super-student. In her eyes, he can do no wrong and for some reason she thinks he's really *clever*. Maybe she's getting senile or something."

"HANK!" Katie replied in a mock shocked voice. "Don't say things like that about your mother. And anyway, I think Pete's kind of special myself and ... "

"Okay, okay, forget I said anything," said Hank, laughing. "Listen, gotta go. I've got a ton of work to do on my paper before tomorrow. I'll call you later this week. Sorry I spouted off at you."

"Night, babe!"

"Yeah, g'night."

That week, the balmy, sunny days of Indian summer slowly began sneaking away from campus. Almost overnight – quietly – the lovely green leaves that had earlier morphed into crimson and gold were starting to fall. Faster and faster. Students dug heavy sweaters out of bottom drawers. Brisk frosty mornings greeted them as they walked across campus, and fresh excitement was in the air. Fall Semester was coming to a close and Winter Semester was within sight.

Friday morning before the Danville game, Katie got a call from her librarian friend, who told her the books she had ordered had just come in. She quickly called Hank, catching him before he left for class, and they agreed to meet at the library over the noon hour.

"We could have saved this until later, you know," Katie said as Hank arrived and found her waiting for him on the front steps. "We don't have to return them for two weeks."

"Don't kid me," Hank replied, grabbing her arm and pulling her into the reference room. "You're as curious as I am. I know you are."

"Guilty as charged!" she admitted and quickly retrieved the books and headed to a study table. "How should we do this?"

"I'll take 1939," said Hank. "You take 1940. Then, we'll switch if neither of us find anything. Ready?"

"Let's go," said Katie. She grabbed a book and quickly opened it. Like all yearbooks, she figured there was a section showing head and shoulder portraits of all the graduating seniors and that's where she started. Hank, on the other hand, methodically started at page one and slowly began turning the pages from the beginning.

It took less then ten minutes. Hank had just gotten to page 25 when he heard Katie gasp and exclaim in an odd voice, "Ohmygosh!"

"What is it?" he said. "What's wrong?"

She didn't say anything. She just closed her eyes and slid the book over, her finger tapping the bottom of the page.

Hank grabbed the book and glanced down and quickly skimmed back and forth over the photos and then stopped. He withdrew the warehouse photo from the envelope he was carrying and moved it alongside. There was no question about it. There was one of them, almost the identical twisted smile.

He read the caption. "Jack Grettsmer –The graduate most likely to own the City of Dubuque in 20 years."

It took a moment for the excitement and shock of actually identifying the student to pass. Then, almost simultaneously, the second shock hit them. Jack Grettsmer. *Grettsmer*! Anna Kiefer's brother?

CHAPTER TWENTY-SEVEN

After Katie and Hank spotted and identified Jack Grettsmer, things quickly fell into place.

"No wonder the picture of that house was in the camera. He obviously lived there." Katie said. "That solves *that* mystery. Might have even been his camera."

They started searching again and in a few pages found the photo of the second young man. "Sean O'Brien – The graduate most likely to win the Heisman Trophy," he read. It was amazing how closely their photos matched the faces in the black and white crime scene photo.

"My heavens, they look so young!" said Katie. "They must have just graduated when all this took place. What were they thinking? What in the world could have happened?" And then, as something new and even more terrible occurred to her, she moaned, "And they're *Catholic!*"

Hank turned back to the 1939 annual and looked them up. They were both there, of course. Looking a little more innocent, a little smaller in stature.

"Let's keep going," he said. "There was a third person there that night. That old camera model doesn't have a self-timer. Someone else had to take the picture."

"That's right," said Katie as she started to move on through the album. "Look, here's another picture of Sean O'Brien with the football team but Grettsmer's not in it."

"Hey, how about this," said Hank in an excited voice pointing to a page of photomontages in the 1939 annual. It was a photo of three male students clowning around; hanging on to one another. Two were obviously Grettsmer and O'Brien.

They studied the photo; heads tilted, scrunched up faces, tongues sticking out, hands poking up behind each other's heads making horns.

"The Three Musketeers," he read. "All for one, one for all, even when they're acting like total morons. Has anyone ever seen Sean

O'Brien, Tom Lavarato or Jack Grettsmer do anything without the other two???

"Tom Lavarato. Now there's a new name. What'd you think? Is he in your book?"

"Yeah, here he is," said Katie. "'Thomas Lavarato – The graduate most likely to save the world'. What's that supposed to mean? Nice looking kid. And with that name, probably Italian. Think he was the one who took the picture?"

"He'd be my first choice. Sounds like the three of them were pretty close buddies."

"And just think, we were in Jack Grettsmer's house!" said Katie. "And the lovely, old lady must be his *sister*. I can't believe it. Do you think she knows anything about this?"

"I doubt it. And let's keep this to ourselves for the time being. I want to talk to Al and Gary before we do anything else. They're going to flip! Wow, I can't believe we actually found them. Can we take these books out of the library?"

"No, but we can copy the pages," Katie said.

"Okay, let's make copies of each page. Then I've got to get back and clean up the apartment before my folks show up tomorrow. Pete promised to help, but I'll be surprised if he's anywhere around. I'll probably be up late so I won't have to worry if Mom wants to come in and inspect. Pete, Amy and I will meet you in front of your dorm at 1:30. Okay?"

"It's a date, Sherlock."

"You know, kiddo," said Hank after they'd returned the books and left the library. "This was a *huge* find. I can't believe we've been so lucky. If things don't work out for us in school, I think we could both get jobs as private eyes. We're doing pretty good for a couple of amateurs!"

On cue Pete turned up around 9:00 p.m. Hank, by that time, had pretty much finished cleaning the living room and washed and put away a week's worth of dirty dishes. He'd also straightened up his bedroom and was ready to get started again on his thesis. The place actually looked pretty good. Almost livable.

"Oh my gosh," cried Pete in a phony, theatrical voice, as he entered the door. "This must be someone else's apartment. I can see the floor in this one. And look thither, I believe that's what they call an empty sink."

"Thanks for all your hard work, *buddy*," replied Hank. "I recall you promised to help."

"I did. I did, dear roomie," said Pete. "But what's the hurry? Your folks aren't coming till tomorrow. The night's still young, lad."

"Can it!" said Hank sharply.

"All Right, all right. I'm sorry," said Pete in a contrite voice. "I've been over at Lennie's beating the entire free world in pool. Guess I let the time get away from me. Tell you what I'll do, I'll pop for dinner. Pizza or Chinese?"

"Chinese! Cashew chicken, pork egg roll, steamed rice and extra sweet and sour sauce. Sticks."

"You got it, you Foreign Devil you. Be back in 20." And with that he whipped around and left.

Hank smiled. It was difficult to stay angry with Pete. While he was gone, Hank took advantage of the quiet apartment to call his brother and fill him in. First he told him about talking to the two shipping companies, saving the best for last.

"Wait until you hear this," Hank teased. "Today, Katie got the Columkille yearbooks from Dubuque and guess what?"

"Don't tell me you found them."

"Yes."

"YOU DIDN'T," yelled Al.

"Oh yes we did! No question about it at all – 1940 graduates, names of Jack Grettsmer and Sean O'Brien. And we believe the third one, the person who took the picture, was a buddy of theirs – Tom Lavarato."

"WOW! I'm totally impressed. And so will Gary be when I tell him. Gosh, I can't believe it. You actually found them. What are you going to do now?"

"Haven't a clue. But you want to hear something really weird? The house in the photo? The one Katie and I went to visit in Dubuque? That was one of their houses – the Grettsmer kid's, and the old lady we talked to – Anna Kiefer, she must be his sister. How bizarre is that?"

Hank and Pete were up early Saturday morning and took a quick three-mile jog around campus. They then headed for breakfast at *The Hungry Goat* to preserve the integrity of their clean kitchen and back to shower and straighten up their rooms before Hank's folks arrived sometime around noon.

Mary and Ralph Torney were the youngest looking 50-somethings you'd be likely to meet. They seriously kept in shape and dressed fashionably. Mrs. Torney's hair was still a shiny, sleek auburn while Mr. Torney's black hair was starting to show a distinguished flash of gray around the temples. She was one of the original stay-at-home mothers and he managed a very successful insurance agency.

They lived in the same Evanston brick ranch Hank grew up in. Although they were financially capable of living pretty much wherever they wanted, a loyalty to old friends kept them rooted to the same neighborhood for over 25 years. And besides, there were the grandkids to consider. Hank's brother, Al, and wife and two children lived in nearby Oak Park. His sister, Sarah, her husband and their three children lived in Milwaukee. None of the three, including Hank, were more than a two-hour drive from home and that's the way the parents liked it. They dearly loved their family and kept close tabs on them. Hank knew he was a lucky young man.

Shortly after lunch Pete spotted them from the second story window and yelled out, "Hank, your folks are here!" and without waiting, bounded down the stairs like some big puppy eager to have his ears scratched.

"Peter!" Mrs. Torney yelled as she saw him rushing down the sidewalk. "How are you, dear?" She wrapped her arms around him and gave him a kiss on the cheek. "How wonderful it is to see you again."

"Thanks Mrs. T. It's good to see you, too," he said breaking away and shaking Mr. Torney's hand. "Sir."

"How are you, Peter? You're looking fit. Anxious for basketball to begin?"

"Yes, sir. I sure am. We're going to be *too* tough this year!"

Just then Hank showed up and gave both his mom and dad big bear hugs.

"Oh, Hank, you look so thin? Are you eating right? Peter, dear, is he eating right? It looks like he's lost weight?"

"C'mon in," said Hank breaking off the conversation and leading them toward the apartment, ignoring the ritual discussion of how thin he looked. He could have gained 25 pounds and would still get the same reception. A *mother thing* he knew. "The joint's a little messy, but I think we can find you a place to sit and I've got a fresh pot of coffee going."

"Lovely, dear, but when are we going to meet Katherine, and where's Amy, Peter?"

"After the game, Mom," said Hank. "It's too hectic before and we really don't have that much time anyway. Kickoff's at 2:30 and we'll need to get there early 'cause there's gonna be a mob. Pete and I are picking up the girls and sitting in the student section. We'll walk with you part way and then meet you outside right after the game."

"Oh drat!" pouted Mrs. Torney. "I was hoping to meet her before that, but okay. That's fine. And we're all going out to eat together afterwards, right? You and Amy *are* coming, aren't you Peter," she said turning to him to confirm it.

"Yes, Mrs. T. Looking forward to it. Oh yeah."

It was a glorious day. It was a classic game. Western State won by three points with a 35-yard field goal with less than a minute left. The stadium erupted! Hank and Pete led the girls outside through a jubilant crowd to where they had planned to meet Hank's parents by one of the concession stands. His parents were already standing there when they finally forced their way through the living stream of screaming students.

"Now, that was a game," shouted Mr. Torney as they spun off and joined them. "State's got quite a team this season! They looked great."

"And you must be Katherine," smiled Mrs. Torney as she stuck out her hand to Katie. "I am so happy to meet you, dear."

"Hello Mrs. Torney, Mr. Torney, and I'm glad to finally meet you, too. Hank's talked about you both often."

"Amy," Mrs. Torney said, giving Pete's girlfriend a little hug. "It's so good to see you again. How's teaching going?"

"Fine, Mrs. Torney, thanks for asking. Mr. Torney, good to see you again."

"Thanks, Amy, same here. C'mon everyone, let's head back and get the cars. I'm starving. We can talk during dinner."

Christophers was an old-fashioned roadhouse on the edge of town – just the basics: steaks, chicken and fish, but prepared with pride. A favorite with parents and students alike, the place would be packed, but Mr. Torney had made reservations over two months earlier and double-checked the night before. They were golden.

Their reservation was for 6:00 and the two cars pulled into an almost full parking lot right on time. They were led to a table just off the main section, with a view of Carter's Lake in the background. When the waitress came for drink orders, Mr. and Mrs. Torney each ordered a glass of wine and told the others to order what they wanted. The girls ordered iced tea.

"Pete," said Mr. Torney. "I know you're in training, but you'll at least have one beer, won't you?"

"Well, sir, thanks, but I don't know, uh, no, I'd better not, uh, well, I suppose *one* won't hurt. *Heineken*." Hank did a deep eye roll and ordered the same.

It was a lovely, relaxed dinner. Mr. Torney quizzed Pete about the upcoming basketball season and Hank asked Amy all about her student teaching assignment. Mrs. Torney chatted with Katie about, well, about everything. It was obvious they hit it off right from the start, as Hank knew they would. Sometime during the meal, Pete bent his personal training rules a little further and agreed to one more *Heineken,* somehow managing to look very guilty about it. Hank bit his tongue.

Katie told Mrs. Torney all about her family, where they lived, her three brothers, her dad's auction business mixed with commodity trading, and her major in architecture and design. Mrs. Torney told Katie about Hank's brother and sister, Mr. Torney's business, and selected stories of Hank's embarrassing escapades from cradle to college. She was witty and quick and Katie laughed at all the right places. Hank mellowed.

Then out of nowhere, Mr. Torney turned and said to Katie, "Hank's brother tells us you two have been working on some kind of project together. Of course Hank never tells us *anything*," he said with a sideways, good-natured glance at his son.

"Well, yes," stammered Katie. "We are. It's sort of a – history, mystery thing ... "

"It's not a big deal, Dad," Hank jumped in, rescuing Katie who was starting to turn a bright crimson, a reaction not lost on Mrs. Torney. "I was planning to tell you and Mom about it later. Just what did Al tell you?"

"Well, not much," his father admitted. "Something about some old photographs, and a possible crime committed back in the –

what, '40s? And you two are trying to find out more about it? Sounds kind of fascinating to me."

"A crime?" said Mrs. Torney, slightly startled. "What kind of crime, dear?"

"We're not even sure if it was a crime, Mom, but if it was, it was racially motivated. It all started when I bought an old camera at Katie's father's auction and noticed it had some film still in it. I gave it to Al and he had a friend at the paper develop it, and it turned out there were some old photos that seemed to show a possible crime scene, along with pictures of some old houses, one of which Katie recognized from her architecture classes. In Dubuque, Iowa."

"Wow, it sounds like you two have made quite a bit of headway already," said Mr. Torney. "I hope you're not neglecting your classes over this."

"Oh no, Mr. Torney," jumped in Katie, relieved it was out in the open. "Most of the research has been done in our school library or over the phone. We kind of work on it when we have some spare time."

"Well, that's good, dear," said Mrs. Torney. "And we want to hear all about it, but let's not dwell on it now. Poor Peter and Amy are going to think we're ignoring them," she said smiling and patting Pete's hand.

"No ma'am, not at all," said Pete. "Actually, I've been helping Hank out on the project a little myself. You know, giving him a little advice here and there."

"Why that's wonderful to hear, Peter," Mrs. Torney beamed. "I'm so happy you and Hank are looking after one another."

"Yes, ma'am. But if you'll excuse the two of us, Amy and I need to take off now. She has to drive back tonight so I'm going to take her back to her car so she can get started before it's too late. Thanks for the terrific meal. We really appreciate it."

Hank's parents said goodbye and Mrs. Torney gave Pete a big hug and told them to drive carefully.

After they'd left, they ordered coffee and Mrs. Torney said, "My, isn't Amy a lovely young lady? Seems so well-rooted. Pete's so fortunate to have someone like her around. Now I don't worry about his silliness as much."

Hank froze. He couldn't believe his ears. He turned to his mother with wide eyes and exclaimed, "Mom! I can't believe what

I've just heard. His *silliness*? What happened to Sir Galahad – your Knight in Shining Armor?"

"Oh Hank," she laughed. "You know I just adore Peter. But he doesn't fool me one bit. I just choose to go along with it all. I think it's good for his self-esteem, don't you agree, dear? Now, I want to hear all about this 'mystery-history' thing of yours. Start from the beginning."

By the time they pulled up in front of Katie's dorm, Hank had told them all he and Katie knew about the photos, recognizing and visiting the old Grettsmer house in Dubuque, how they just found out who the three boys were and why they believe the black man in the photo was Glory Alexander.

"Wow," said Mr. Torney. "I've got to give you two credit. You've taken this further than I would have. I'm amazed at how much you've been able to find out. But what I said earlier still stands. Your grades should be coming first, know what I mean?"

"I know, Dad, and you're right!" said Hank. "We've been pretty careful not to let this mess up our studies or anything. But neither Katie nor I want to stop now. Hopefully, I've got some material coming from Memphis. We want to go through that and see if we can find out anything about the black guy. And we want to drive back up to Dubuque again and see what we can find out about those three guys. But we can do that some Saturday or Sunday."

"But Hank, dear," said Mrs. Torney. "What can you hope to find out that will make any difference now. I mean it's been 60 years! Even if you find out about those dreadful boys, chances are they're not even alive anymore. They'd have to be – what? At least in their late 70s? And surely, you can't mention this to the older woman whose brother was involved."

"No, of course not, Mom," said Hank. "We'll be very discreet. It's just that we've gone this far, we want to put some kind of closure to it."

"But Hank, dear, don't you think that ... "

"All Right, Mary," broke in Mr. Torney. "The kids know what they're doing. And I agree with them. I think they should see this thing through. It's actually a fascinating story, and I'm kind of curious where it might end up. But right now, you and I have to hit the road ourselves, if we're going to get back home at any decent time. Good luck to you two and keep us informed."

After a round of hugs and some last minute instructions, the Torneys drove off, leaving Hank and Katie standing in front of her dorm, waving goodbye.

"Oh, I just love your folks, Hank," Katie said turning into Hank and giving him a big bear hug. "They're so much fun! Think I did all right?"

"You'd do 'all right' anywhere, babe. Look up here. I wanna give you a heavy-duty kiss. That bottle of *Heineken* kinda made me crazy and I'm afraid I won't be able to control myself!"

"Well, you'd better try, tiger," she said wrapping her arms around him and looking up into his eyes. "All my friends are watching us from the second floor!"

CHAPTER TWENTY-EIGHT

A large, registered envelope from Coastal Shipping arrived at Hank's apartment the middle of the following week. Hank and Pete were both in class so when the postman knocked on the door, Mrs. Conrady, their landlady, signed for it.

Mrs. Conrady was a widow who ran a tight ship. Her large two-story home, in one of the more established neighborhoods adjacent to campus, was neat as a pin and well maintained, inside and out. Ever since her husband died six years earlier, she rented the upstairs to male only college students and was known to keep a close eye on *her boys*. It was both a blessing and a curse thought Pete.

She had three simple rules: 1. Music played at a moderate level (as determined by her). 2. No lady visitors after 8:00 p.m. 3. No parties, ever!

One did not deviate from these rules if one knew best. Pete learned the hard way.

Through careful observation, he discovered Mrs. Conrady had a hair appointment every Saturday morning at a small salon in the strip mall near campus. She was gone from 8:30 until 10:30 during which time he took advantage of the situation to crank up his CD player to a, let's say, more than moderate level. This routine went on for several weeks until one day, during an unfortunate lapse of concentration, Pete left to get some class notes from a friend in one of the frat houses. He left fully intending to return in 15 minutes. Alas, time slipped by and he was gone for an hour. When he returned he found Mrs. Conrady waiting for him on the front steps. He saw her and heard *U2* blasting out of the upstairs window at the same time.

The strangest thing about it, he later reported to Hank, was she never said a word. Not one word! She just stood there, arms folded in front of her, staring intently at him as he crept up the walk, whimpering apologies all the way, slinked around her and rushed up the stairs and into the apartment, where he literally dove at the CD player cord and pulled it out of the wall socket.

"That woman is evil!" he later told Hank. "Totally and maliciously evil. If you could have seen her eyes. Like burning embers. I swear her pupils weren't even round, but rectangular, like a goat's. It was horrible!"

"Yeah, well can't say you weren't warned," replied Hank. "Next time you go down to have a button sewn on your shirt, you can ask her about her eyes."

Mrs. Conrady gave Hank the envelope when he returned after his afternoon classes. He knew he should call Katie, but he just couldn't wait and carefully slit open the sealing tape and looked inside. The first thing he spied was a single sheet of paper: *Hank, This is all I found dealing with the John Ruxton. She was the only tug that went to Dubuque during the 1930s and 1940s. I thought there might be more stuff but this is it so I just copied everything and put it into folders for you. Anyway, hope it helps. Good luck, Tony.*

Hank wasn't sure if he was pleased or disappointed since there really didn't seem to be much there. On the other hand, it shouldn't take long to go through it. He started removing the folders. Most were labeled and he quickly discovered the majority dealt with maintenance records, repair expenditures, manifests, galley supplies, etc. It was toward the bottom of the pile when he came across something promising; a folder labeled PAYROLL.

He quickly opened it and found a collection of ledger sheets. At first he didn't know what he was looking at but soon figured out it was a listing of the boat's entire payroll history. He glanced at the first date – March 1928 and jumped to the bottom of the pile – September 1943. "This must be the entire time the boat was in service," he said to himself. "Or at least it covers the period when Delta Shipping owned it."

The sheets appeared to be in calendar order. Each page showed the names of employees, a two or three word job description, total hours worked by week and a final weekly and monthly total for each worker. Hank quickly flicked down to August 1940 and scanned the names.

It almost jumped off the page. "Good Heavens!" he exclaimed. "There he is!"

There were 12 names listed and next to the bottom was the name he had hoped to find, *Glory Alexander*. Beside the name were the weeks he'd worked, with a total hourly figure per week, and a dollar figure inserted at the end. According to the report, in August 1940, Glory had worked two weeks, a total of 112 hours and had earned $72.

But Hank was confused. The date of the second week was after the time Glory had been missing. How could that be? Why would they have placed an ad in the paper if he weren't missing? Then he noticed a small asterisk, barely legible, beside the monthly total. And at the bottom, another asterisk with the words: *See report attached.*

The next page was a copy of what must have been an envelope and written on the face of the envelope were the words: <u>*Glory Alexander.*</u> After that were a couple sheets of paper in excellent handwriting.

On the evening of August 25, 1940, while in the Dubuque ice harbor for repairs, deck hand Glory Alexander reportedly debarked and went for a walk. Friend and co-worker, Andy LeClaire, reported his disappearance. When he did not return by the time the repairs were completed, it was my decision, according to common and accepted practice, to proceed without him. Upon returning to Memphis, still with no word of the whereabouts of Mr. Alexander, his immediate family (wife, Elizabeth and infant daughter, Angela) were notified and subsequently awarded Mr. Alexander's full pay, pursuant to an agreement with the rest of the boat's crew. It was also agreed upon, and at no expense to his family, to place a notice in The Dubuque Telegraph Herald, a copy of which is attached. As of this date, December 12, 1940, no meaningful reply has been received.

Signed:
Captain Warren Placer
John R. Ruxton

A tear sheet of the newspaper notice and invoice, stamped PAID came next. There were also two letters. One showed a crude stick drawing of a person hanging from a tree along with the scrawled words: *I think I seen him hanging around. Send the money.*

The other letter was merely a printed message: *I wonder if that was the nigger I seen running from my garden with a watermelon under each arm. If so, he's long gone!*

The last piece of paper was a receipt: *Paid to Mrs. Elizabeth Alexander, wife of Glory Alexander, the sum of $72 cash money, for work rendered. Signed:*

Elizabeth Alexander, Hardeman County, Tennessee

Andrew P. LeClaire (witness), Hardeman County, Tennessee

Capt. Warren Placer, Memphis, Tennessee

September 14, 1940

When Pete returned to the apartment early that evening he found Hank sitting in the darkened room alone, eyes closed, papers strewn across the desk.

"Hey, man, what's up? You okay?"

Hank stirred and looked at Pete with bloodshot eyes, "Yeah, I'm okay, Pete. Long day."

"Cool – but get some sleep tonight, buddy boy, you look like crap!"

Hank called Katie later that afternoon and asked her to join him for a cup of coffee in the Union.

"Sure, Hank, I'll leave now. You sound terrible, what's the matter?"

"Tell you when I see you. I'm pretty bummed out."

"Really, well maybe I can cheer you up."

Katie was waiting when Hank walked into the Memorial Union. He'd ridden his bike and was tucking his muffler into his jacket pocket. He managed a weak smile and a quick peck on the cheek.

"Bad news, huh?" she asked when he sat down.

"Well, not bad news, exactly. I found what I was looking for. But *sad news*, yeah. Let me show you."

He spread out the ledger page for August 1940 and pointed to Glory's entry. Then he showed her Capt. Placer's special entry page and let her read that along with the two "hate responses." She frowned and shook her head. Finally he showed her the receipt signed by Glory's wife, a witness and Captain Placer.

"I see what you mean," she said in a soft voice. "It *is* sad. He *was* married and they had a baby girl. His poor wife. Just think of what she must have been going through, not to mention his parents, assuming they were alive."

"I know, I know. What in the world was wrong with those guys?"

"Think any of his family is still alive?"

"I do," said Hank. "The daughter, Angela, would only be in her early 60s. But his wife, Elizabeth, I don't know. Could be. Depending on how old she was when this happened, I guess she could be in her late 70s now. That's not that old. I suppose they could *both* be alive."

"Where's Hardeman County?" asked Katie looking at the signed paper. "Looks like that's where they lived."

"I looked it up – just east of Memphis, maybe 50 miles or so, bordering Mississippi on the north."

"Well, I'd say you did good," smiled Katie. "If we could find any of the surviving family, it would be a proper thing to let them know what happened. Like you said, it's worse never knowing, even if it's bad news. What do you think?"

"I agree. But Dad was right. I'm up to my ears in thesis stuff now and I know you're busy, too. We can't let this get in the way right now."

"I know. I know. And we should go back to Dubuque one of these days, shouldn't we?"

"Yeah. I've been thinking about that, too. Now that we have names and dates I want to make another stop at the police station. And for sure we need to stop and see Mrs. Kiefer. She'll know about Jack. We also need to check with the high school to see if they have an alumni office. They may be able to help, too."

"Okay, sounds good. Let me know when. If we do it on a Saturday, shouldn't be a problem."

"Right, same with me. Come on, I'll walk you back to the dorm."

As fall moved through the Midwest, the rhythm of life on campus quickly changed. Football season, with its pageantry of brass bands and tailgating parties, was well underway.

Hank and Katie had fallen into a comfortable pattern, meeting and sitting together at every home game. Pete was a bit miffed at first but Katie's friends understood what was going on and approved. Besides, Pete was already heavily scheduled for daily practice as the beginning of basketball was just around the corner. And since Hank had the apartment more or less to himself those days, he was able to catch up on his schoolwork.

Thanksgiving plans were already being solidified and Hank and Katie decided that would be a great time to take advantage of the long weekend to head back to Dubuque. After some very tricky parental negotiations, it was decided they would drive to Katie's home for Thanksgiving, have the main meal there, and then stay over night. Early Friday they would drive to Dubuque and spend as much time there as necessary, and afterwards drive to Evanston and spend the weekend with his folks.

Hank's mom wanted to show her off to friends and family on Saturday, and have a belated family Thanksgiving meal. They would then either return to school Saturday evening, which was Hank's plan, *or* stay over and return on Sunday, which was Hank's mother's plan. Her argument was that Hank had already been to Katie's house *twice* and on *Thanksgiving*. And this was the *first* time Katherine had visited them and she was intent on spoiling her.

Hank felt he was being grossly manipulated. Katie just smiled. She understood how it worked.

Over the next few days Hank tried, unsuccessfully, to find anything he could about Glory's family. He ended up calling the Hardeman County courthouse and had a frustrating experience with a seemingly bored clerk. He had to admit to himself, however, that he had very little to go on. Alexander apparently was a fairly common a name in Hardeman County. But the real problem was caused due to the amount of time that had passed – over 60 years.

CHAPTER TWENTY-NINE

Thanksgiving was a gorgeous, crisp, fall day. When Hank and Katie drove up the circular drive of her home they found a touch football game going in full swing. The *Wacky Warriors*: Mike Joyce and future sister-in-law, Linda, were already two touchdowns behind. The *Gruesome Gobblers*: Brennan and Sean Joyce had just high-fived after a recent score.

"Reinforcements!" the two younger brothers screamed when they spied and rushed the car. Before they even had time to say hello, Hank was quickly snapped up by the *Warriors* and Katie was recruited by the *Gobblers*.

After 15 frantic minutes, and a couple of miraculous TD passes, first from Hank to Linda and then from Mike to Hank, the *Warriors* had tied the game. The *Gobblers*, thirsty for revenge, were marching steadily down the lawn toward the birdhouse goal line when Mrs. Joyce appeared on the front porch and yelled for everyone to stop what they were doing and come in and clean up for dinner.

"Mom – not yet," yelled Brennan in anguish. "We're about ready to score."

"Now!" she yelled back. "If you want to eat."

The game ended immediately. She'd uttered the magic words.

The entire event reminded Hank of a Norman Rockwell painting. The dining room was decorated with deep rich, fall colors, pine boughs and candles. The table had been extended and absolutely sparkled. Mrs. Joyce had put out the best china and silverware and starched linen napkins, each tucked in a sterling silver ring holder. She ushered Hank in to meet Katie's 78-year-old grandmother, Elsie, and then seated him between them.

Katie had earlier primed Hank and she was right; Elsie was indeed "a stitch." She was certainly inquisitive, and had a wonderful sense of humor. She asked all about Hank's family, friends and his studies at school. Then, out of the blue, she said, "And what exactly does a sports psychologist do, Hank?"

Immediately, the rest of the conversations around the table came to a screeching halt. Obviously, this was a topic that had come up before.

"Well," Hank cautiously began, "it varies a bit depending on the team and level of professionalism required. A lot of my time will just be making myself available to the players. Helping them work through personal problems with family, school and issues with other team members. In most high schools and small colleges, the coach or assistant coach would be the person who does this, but with larger schools and larger teams, it's just not practical. And when you get to the college and professional level, a higher degree of training is needed.

"But probably the greatest share of my time will be working with both team and players, one on one, helping them focus on what they are doing right. This is particularly true in individual sports like tennis and golf. For example, they say that golf is 10% skill and 90% mental. That might be an exaggeration, but it's probably not too far off. One of the key skills of a top-notch golfer is the ability to blank out everything that's going on around him or her. Just completely focus on that putt or chip. It's harder to do than it sounds, but it's a skill that can be learned."

"Well, that sounds *so* interesting, Hank. Katherine tells me you might have to look at schools out of state. We have some wonderful ones right here in Illinois, you know."

"Yes ma'am," Hank said, shooting a glance at Katie who wisely kept her eyes on her plate. "No, I'm not ready to move anywhere. I have a lot more school to finish yet. I'll be looking at lots of different possibilities before I decide anything."

"How about the Twins?" interjected Brennan. "Minneapolis isn't very far away."

"Who'd wanna work with the Twins?" broke in Mike. "I wouldn't cross the street ... "

"All Right everyone," broke in Mr. Joyce. "Let Hank eat in peace. We can all talk about this after our meal."

And what a meal it was, perfect in every way. A honest-to-goodness old-fashioned Thanksgiving dinner with all the trimmings. The two younger boys ate with reckless abandon and Hank was sure Mrs.

Joyce bent the rules as they tore along. They were not only starving, but apparently wanted to finish in time for kickoff of the Vikings-Cowboys game.

After the meal the men moved into the den and spread out on favorite chairs, couches and the floor. Hank was motioned to a recliner and encouraged to loosen his belt and kick back. Mrs. Joyce and her mother moved into the kitchen to get the dishes started and Katie and Linda cleared the tables, chattering away about school and Linda's wedding plans.

Sometime during the first quarter, orders were taken for pie and ice cream. So it went throughout the afternoon and into the early evening. By 8:00, the two exhausted boys came back in, after tossing the football around in the yard for the past hour, and went up to their rooms to relax and get ready for bed. The grownups were settled back in the den drinking coffee and talking.

"All Right, guys," said Mrs. Joyce, turning to Hank and Katie. "The boys have gone upstairs. Tell us what's happening in your project.

Katie showed them the pictures of the young men in the high school annuals and the copy of the ad that ran in the paper. Hank told them that now that they had names and dates they were first going to double check with the police station. Hopefully they would find some clues as to whether the crime was ever recorded – and if not, why. Then they were going to return to the old Grettsmer home and visit with Mrs. Kiefer again.

"I called her the other day," said Katie, "and told her I have a photo of the house that I took, and I want to give it to her. We said we'd stop before noon. That's why we need to get out of here early in the morning – like 6:00 or so. We'd like to be in Dubuque by 8:00 – 8:30 at the latest."

Hank added, "We're hoping to verify if Jack was, indeed, her brother and what became of him."

"Well, sounds like you've got a plan," said Mr. Joyce. "Have you found out anything about the black fellow?"

"Glory Alexander? Yes, a little," replied Hank. "I talked to the company he used to work for and they sent me copies of some old records from the tugboat he worked on when he came up missing. *The John Ruxton*. Here's a ledger sheet showing his name. Let me read you the entry the captain put in the file.

Hank read them Capt. Placer's report and showed the receipt Mrs. Alexander and Andy LeClaire had signed.

140

"His wife's name was Elizabeth and I think this Andy must have been a good friend of his. At least they both lived in Hardeman County, Tennessee. I called the local courthouse but apparently didn't have enough information for them. And I really don't think their records go back that far. Even if they do, there're not on any computer database."

"Did you try looking up any census records?" piped up a voice from across the room.

Everyone turned to look at Elsie. She was sitting quietly in a leather recliner, supposedly taking a little nap. Apparently not.

"Write down what you know," she said, "and I'll take it to my Genealogy Club. We meet once a month and we're always looking for new projects. We've pretty much exhausted our own families. Would be interesting to look up some nice black folks for a change."

"Mama," exclaimed Mrs. Joyce. "That's a marvelous idea. We all thought you were asleep."

"No dear, just resting my eyes but I do believe I'll turn in now if you don't mind."

"Not at all. Fact is I'm about ready to go upstairs myself and read," said Mrs. Joyce. "C'mon I'll go and turn the lights on for you. That old hallway gets pretty dark at night.

"Katherine, you and Hank stay up long as you want but remember you've got to get up early if you want to get going by 6:00. You'd better not make it too late. Does Hank know where he's sleeping?"

"Yes, Mom, Sean's old room."

"All right then, good night everyone."

Mrs. Joyce and her mother's departures marked the official end of the evening. Shortly thereafter Sean and Linda headed back to Peoria. Mr. Joyce went into his office to check his email and Katie took Hank down the hall to show him Sean's old bedroom.

"I promised Michael and Brennan I'd stop and tell them about the time I met Coach John Wooden," said Hank.

Katie led him to their room. When they opened the door, both boys were sound asleep, spread out over their beds, half covered, sports magazines spread out everywhere. The lights were all on and the CD player was cranking out some strange, unrecognizable music.

"Well, so much for your Wooden story," she said as she covered them up, turned off the music and lights and closed the door. "It'll just have to wait till next time. Here's your room," she said, turning and crossing the hall.

"Okay, but tell 'em I tried," he said. "They're great kids. They do play hard and I'm sure they're exhausted. To tell you the truth, I'm bushed, too. See you in the morning. 5:30. Don't let me oversleep."

Katie and Grandma Elsie were talking in the kitchen when Hank walked in at 5:45. Coffee and toast were already on the table.

"Morning," said Hank. "Coffee smells great!"

"Good morning, Hank, dear," said Elsie. "Get a good night's rest?"

"Yes, ma'am, I did. I hope you didn't get up for us."

"Heavens no. I get up this early every morning. Of course, I get to take a little nap in the afternoon, too," she chuckled. "Sit down and have a cup of coffee and a glass of juice. I fixed some rye toast, but I can scramble up some eggs, too. Just takes a sec."

"No, grandma, this is just fine. Thanks."

Hank and Katie quickly ate. Heading out the door she gave her grandmother a big hug and then the grandmother hugged Hank.

"I'm awful glad to have met you, Hank. You kids drive carefully and be sure to let us know what you find out, all right? We'll do the same."

"Goodbye, ma'am," said Hank. "We sure will. And thanks for breakfast."

"Bye, grandma. Love you."

CHAPTER THIRTY

They pulled into the Dubuque Police parking lot at 8:15. The same lady was working at the reception desk.

"Good morning, ma'am. You probably don't remember me but I was here a few weeks ago asking about information on an old crime?"

"Yes," she said. "You're the student working on some kinda project?"

"That's right. Well, I have a little more information now and I'm wondering if we could try again. Name's Hank Torney and this is Katherine Joyce."

"Right. Why don't you two take a seat and I'll find someone to help you."

Hank and Katie walked over and sat down along the sidewall while the clerk picked up the phone.

"Lt. Rea? This is Gloria. Remember that student I told you about who stopped by looking for some information on an old homicide?" She listened a moment. "Yes, that's the one. Well, he's back and now there're two of 'em. Say they have some new information."

A few minutes later the door to the main corridor opened and a 50ish looking man stepped into the lobby. No jacket, white shirt and plain blue tie. A strong cigarette odor trailed him across the room.

"Hi guys," he said. "I'm Lieutenant Rea."

"Lieutenant. I'm Hank Torney and this is Katherine Joyce. Thanks for seeing us."

"Hey, no problem. C'mon back and we'll see what we can do for you."

Hank and Katie followed him down the corridor to a small, windowless office with just enough room for a desk and chair, a couple of well-used file cabinets, and two visitor chairs which he waved them into. A large industrial calendar was the only thing hanging on the walls.

"Sgt. Jones tells me you've been here once before. Something about a crime that happened back in the '30s or '40s?"

"1940, sir," said Hank. "August 25th, as a matter of fact."

"Oh, so you have the date and everything. Well, that'll make it easier to look up. Records that far back aren't on any computer database but we do have hard copies we can check, particularly if it was a 'violent crime.' You got the date out of the newspaper, I assume?"

"Yes sir, we did," Hank said, turning and looking quickly at Katie. "Actually, this is what we found." He handed Lt. Rea a copy of the 'Reward' ad.

"Hmmm," mumbled Lt. Rea as he read the ad. "Glory Alexander – a black man – from Tennessee. Strange name. Interesting, but it says nothing about a crime. Was there anything else you found? A story about a crime?"

"No, sir. But we strongly believe there was and are hoping you might have something in your files."

"So what you're saying is you *think* a crime was committed, but you really don't know for sure and you came up with that date from this notice?"

"Yes, sir."

"You guys realize this was a long time ago, don't you, and even if anything did happen back then, there'd be nothing anyone could do about it now."

"Yes sir, we do. But we've been working on this awhile and would like to find out as much as we can."

"I see," said Lt. Rea. "And you're both students where – Western State?" he said looking down at his notes. "Is this some type of project you're working on?"

"Yes, sir."

"Yeah, well, you two just sit here a minute and I'll go and talk to one of our clerks and have them check our old files. It might take a while, if you've got something to do and want to stop back later ... "

"No, we'll wait if you don't mind, as long as we're here and all."

"No problem. Be back in a second."

Lt. Rea left the room and quickly walked down the hall and walked into another office and picked up a phone.

"Gloria? Rea here. Listen, do me a favor will you and call Western State and check on those two kids – Hank Torney and

Katherine Joyce. See if they're really students, first of all, and if so, find what they're studying. Give me a call when you find something out.

"Jack," he said turning to another officer sitting nearby. "Would you go down and check the old case records for August 25, 1940. See if there was any kind of local violent crime recorded back then – or a week or so on either side. Vic was supposedly a black guy named Glory Alexander. Then come let me know, will you?"

Lt. Rea walked down to the break room and got a cup of coffee and returned to his office. Hank and Katie were talking when he entered.

"Hey, can I get you guys something? Coffee or a soda?"

"No thanks, Lieutenant, but we do have another question?" Hank said.

"Sure, what is it?"

"Do you have rosters of the police force back in 1940? Like old yearbooks, or something like that?"

"Well, we have records of who was working for the department year by year – just names and specific assignments. Would that be of interest?"

"Sure, that'd be great, and for the same period of time, August, 1940."

"Okay, let's see what we get," he replied as he turned to his computer and typed in some commands. He stared at the screen for a few moments and made a few adjustments. "Here we go – 1940, August. Looks like a pretty short list. Be glad to print it out for you."

"That'd be great," said Hank.

In a moment the printer kicked out a page and Lt. Rea grabbed it and laid it on his desk. Hank and Katie slid up and scanned it quickly. It was a list of 18 names. Along side each name was a short job description. They spotted the name, Pat O'Brien, at the same time and looked at each other nervously. Besides the name was listed, "Night Patrolman."

"This policeman here," pointed Hank. "Pat O'Brien. Is there any more information you have on him?"

"What kind of information?"

"Oh, I don't know, uh, like what happened to him."

"Why just him?" asked Lt. Rea looking at Hank as if he knew more than he was saying.

145

"His name sounds familiar, I guess. But maybe that would be too much trouble."

"No, not really," said Lt. Rea. "We keep personnel files forever. But it'll take a few minutes. Are you going to be in town for awhile?"

"We are," replied Hank. "For a few hours, at least."

"Okay, tell you what. Stop by before you leave and I'll have everything waiting for you at the front desk. How'd that be?"

"That'd be great. Thanks, Lieutenant."

"No problem," he said.

After Hank and Katie left, Lt. Rea called Personnel and asked for any information they had on a Patrolman Pat O'Brien back in the '40s. As he hung up Gloria called and told him she'd learned the two students were indeed enrolled at Western State. The girl is an architecture major and the boy is a graduate student in psychology.

At this point Lt. Rea was getting more than just curious. Why did they seem so certain about a violent crime being committed while nothing was in the paper other than that odd notice? And just *why* did the name of Patrolman O'Brien sound familiar to them?

Quickly he asked, "Have they left yet?"

"Just heading out the door."

"Any patrolmen hanging around?"

"No. Wait, just a sec – Flemming's coming in right now."

"Damn," Rea said under his breath, "Not that hot head. Anyone else?" he asked.

"Nope."

"Okay," he sighed. "Put him on."

After a quick pause, a gruff voice answered, "Flemming here."

"Listen, this is Rea. Two college kids just left the building. You can probably still see 'em."

"Uh, yeah, I see 'em. Want me to stop 'em?"

"No. I just want you to *follow* them and let me know where they go. Nothing else. *Nothing*, got it?"

"Yeah, sure. I'm on it. What'd they do?"

"They've done *nothing*, I'm just curious 'bout something. Just follow them, all right?"

He hung up before any more questions were asked.

"Why didn't you show him the photo?" asked Katie as they got back to the car. "He was having trouble connecting the notice with any violent crime, and I guess I would too if I were in his place."

"You know, I almost did," Hank admitted, "but I was afraid it might upset him in some way, like if there was a violent crime committed and not reported to the police. I was afraid he might take some personal affront to it. But I'm glad we thought about asking for the list of cops working there back then. And then learning one of the policemen was an O'Brien. Might be just a coincidence, but I really don't think so. That could be the reason why the crime was never reported. The guy could have been related to that Sean kid in some way and covered it up."

Hank and Katie pulled into Mrs. Kiefer's driveway and walked up to the house. Anna Kiefer answered the bell on the first ring and looked delighted to see them. "C'mon in kids. How nice to see you again. Hank and Katherine isn't it?"

"Yes, that's right, Mrs. Kiefer," said Hank.

"Oh, *please* call me Anna, won't you? Mrs. Kiefer sounds so, so *old*," she said smiling. "Let's go into the solarium. I've fixed some tea and we can sit and visit for a while. I really don't get that many visitors these days and I'm so glad you stopped by."

The three of them sat down and Mrs. Kiefer poured them each a cup of tea from a lovely old silver tea set and placed a plate of warm chocolate chip cookies on the table.

"Tell me how school's going. Katherine, you're in architecture, I seem to recall. And Hank, did you tell me what you were studying?"

"No ma'am ... "

"*Anna*, please!"

"No, Anna. I'm in graduate school in psychology. And it's going great. I'll be getting my master's next year."

"Excellent. And how about you, Katherine, how's architecture treating you?"

"Just fine," said Katie. "Thanks for asking. That's one of the reasons I love Dubuque – all the lovely old homes. And by the way, here's a photo I took of your home when we were here last. We thought you might like a copy."

"Well, thank you, dear," she said looking at the photo Katie handed her. "My, it's lovely, absolutely lovely. I'll have it framed and placed with some of the other pictures I have."

Ah, the magic word, "pictures" thought Hank as he snuck a peek at Katie and winked.

"Do you mind if we look at some of your pictures?" he asked, innocently. "I love old photos and I couldn't help noticing a whole wall of them in the other room."

"Heavens no. C'mon," she said, smiling, and led them into the formal living room and up to one of the walls displaying several photographs. "They're mainly old family photos, but we've framed a few interesting old city scenes you may enjoy. My father loved taking pictures and a lot of these were taken by him except for the formal family photos, of course."

"Who are these people?" asked Katie looking at a couple of old family photos.

"These are my parents – taken in New York City, and these are my husband's parents – taken in Germany. My, don't they all look so stern?"

"How about this one," asked Hank looking at a larger, more recent photo. Is this your family?"

"That's right," she said. "My parents, my brother, Jack, and that skinny little squirt is me. I believe I was all of eight years old when it was taken." She didn't notice the two of them focusing in on the image of her brother. "And this one is the four of us on vacation at the Wisconsin Dells. That was taken around 1938 or, maybe '39. It was a special trip for my 8th grade graduation. Jack was already in high school."

"Is Jack still alive?" asked Hank fighting to keep the excitement from showing.

"No, no. Jack died, oh dear, over 20 years ago. A heart attack. He became a lawyer, lived in Boston."

"That's too bad. Were you two very close?" asked Katie, giving Hank a quick frown to back off.

"Well, no. Not particularly. I don't think Jack was really very close to anyone. He was just the typical big brother. Always annoyed at his little sister hanging around."

"So you two were in high school at the same time, how'd that work out?" Katie asked with a smile. "I have an older brother, too."

"Oh, just fine, I guess. I was just a freshman when he was a senior and I'm sure I drove him crazy, but we survived."

"Well, he's a good looking young man. I bet he had a lot of girl friends," said Katie.

"Oh, I'm sure he had his share," Mrs. Kiefer said. "If so, he never told me about them. He mainly hung out with his buddies. Drove dad crazy. One was Italian and the other Irish and neither came from what our father would call 'a proper background.' She smiled and shook her head to show her disagreement with her father's attitude.

"My father was *very* old fashioned, you see – very *German*. But the Irish boy, Sean O'Brien, oh my, I think every girl in the school was in love with him. I know *I* had a terrible crush on him. A big football hero and a definite rascal. Always in trouble."

"Did you ever date him?" asked Katie mystified.

"Oh, heavens no," said Mrs. Kiefer with an exaggerated shocked expression. "My father would have disowned me. Besides, by the time I was mooning over him, *he* was a senior, and I, of course, was a lowly freshman. He'd never have given me the time of day. He was so gorgeous! But what a waste."

"Why's that?" asked Hank.

"He was killed just a few years after he graduated, in the Second World War. One of the first Dubuquers to die during that terrible time. I remember I was with some friends at a local swimming pool when we heard the news. It was announced over the loud speaker. It was terrible. I remember it was the middle of summer yet the whole school assembled in the gym the next day and said a Rosary for him. I was crushed. A lot of girls were. He was so young. I went home afterwards and cried in my room all afternoon and couldn't even tell my parents what was wrong."

"That's so sad," said Katie, tearing up.

"And the Italian boy," asked Hank. "What ever happened to him?"

"Tommy Lavarato was his name. Dark complected, very Italian, quiet and polite – unlike Jack and Sean. You know I really never spoke to either of them, only saw them around school. If I remember correctly, he went into the priesthood. Yes, I'm rather sure he did. But it was that wild Irish lad, Sean, that all the girls mooned after."

Patrolman Flemming sat slouched in the patrol car, supremely bored. He'd parked a half block down the street and had already run the Illinois plates on Hank's car. He found it was, indeed, owned by a Hank Torney. Disappointed it wasn't listed as stolen, he called in his report informing Lt. Rea what he had found and where the students were at the moment, at the old Grettsmer Home.

Lt. Rea was more puzzled than ever and muttered something to that effect over the phone. But when Flemming volunteered to go up and "interview" Mrs. Kiefer, whom was a well-known and respected "old money Dubuquer," he was told in no uncertain terms to stick with his assignment and report back where they went next.

He was not happy with this "baby-sitting job," as he thought of it, but knew he'd better do as he was told. Lt. Rea was already on his case after some "minor" injuries had resulted from his involvement with a DWI last month. "Drunks and smart ass kids," he muttered. "They're all a pain in the arse."

Just after Flemming hung up, Personnel returned Lt. Rea's call and informed him that a Patrolman Pat O'Brien had been a member of the force from August 1935 until he was relieved of duty in March 1943. Worked the night beat.

"What the hell!" said Lt. Rea. "*Relieved of Duty?* Does that mean what I think it means?"

"Yeah, probably. A bad egg."

"Damn," Lt. Rea muttered to himself. "Something strange is going on here. What in the world are those two kids on to? I've got a bad feeling 'bout this."

He picked up his phone and called Gloria again. "Hey, is Buck Larson still around?"

"Gimp? Sure. See him every once and awhile down at *The Tap*. Stops in for some beers and shoots the breeze. Jeez, that guy can talk. And for a guy his age I can't believe he can drink as much ... "

"Yeah. Yeah. See if you can get him on the phone."

CHAPTER THIRTY-ONE

When Hank and Katie finally left Mrs. Kiefer's house, Hank saw the patrol car parked down the street but didn't give it much thought. So he didn't notice when it pulled out behind him as he left. He and Katie were hyped up after their meeting with Mrs. Kiefer and had decided to go right to St. Columkille High School and see what else they might be able to find out about the three boys.

"Well, Jack Grettsmer's dead. So's Sean O'Brien. I suspect Tom Lavarato is, too," said Hank. "I'm hoping they have a good alumni office that keeps track of their grads. Hopefully we can put some closure to this part of the mystery."

"It was so sad," said Katie. "Hearing that lovely old lady talk about those guys as if it were last week. Do you think she knows anything at all about what happened?"

"I doubt it. And I guess it'll remain our secret. Can't think of any reason to stir up the past at this point, can you?"

The school was easy to find and not that far from the Grettsmer house. It also sat high on the bluff and still looked solid and well maintained. They pulled up in front and parked. **St. Columkille Catholic High School • 1924** was chiseled on a long, stone slab stretching over the front door.

"We have around an hour before the Administrative Offices close. I called them last week to be sure," said Hank.

Patrolman Flemming pulled in behind them, this time, a little closer and with less caution. His patience was being sorely tried.

"Good morning, ma'am," said Hank to an attractive, casually dressed lady in the office. "My name's Hank Torney. I called last week about stopping by and checking on some former students of yours?"

"Yes, I remember. You talked to me, as a matter of fact. My name's Sister Mary Catherine."

"Oh, I'm sorry," said Hank, embarrassed. "I didn't know you were a sister, I mean – I thought ... "

"No need to apologize," she said laughing and sticking out her hand. "Even sisters can wear jeans and sweaters these days."

"I'm Katherine Joyce," said Katie, amused at Hank's discomfort. "We're both students at Western Illinois State."

"Well, c'mon in and sit down," she said as she turned and walked back to her desk.

"Who're you looking for? We keep pretty good tabs on our alumni here – comes in handy during fund raising campaigns."

"Well, we're interested in these three boys," said Hank, handing her the copied page of the yearbook. "They all graduated in 1940."

Sr. Mary put on a pair of glasses and studied them.

"We know a little about a couple of them," Hank said, "but were hoping you might be able to ... "

"Jack Grettsmer," interrupted Sr. Mary who was already clicking away on her computer. "Grettsmer. That's an old Dubuque name, you know. I believe there're even still some family members around. But Jack, I'm almost certain he's died. The family's been very generous to the school over the years and – yes, here he is. Jack Grettsmer. Graduated 1940. Deceased, May 1979, Boston, Massachusetts. My, not all that old. Wonder what happened to him?"

"I believe he died of a heart ... " Katie started to say.

"Sean O'Brien. That seems to ring a bell, too," she continued, unfazed and again blazing away at her computer, all business now, excited. On a mission. "Oh yes, of course. Here he is. I remember now. Sean O'Brien, Graduated 1940, Deceased, August 1942. Killed during the battle of Guadalcanal. First Dubuque resident and St. Columkille graduate to fall during W.W.II. Oh dear, what a shame!

Okay, so far we're batting 1,000. Last name, Thomas Lavarato. Gosh, *that* name sounds familiar, too," she said, still typing furiously. "And my memory's not even that good. "Aha! Here *he* is. *Father* Lavarato, now. Why wait a minute! I *know* him. I've even *met* him. He's a missionary. Been here to talk at the school at least twice. And apparently very much alive it seems. At least he was as of June 30th of this year, the last time we updated all of these. So there you are. Three out of three! How'd I do?" she looked up smiling and obviously very pleased with herself.

"Terrific! You did terrific, sister," said Hank in a semi-state of shock. "I can't believe it. I don't suppose by any chance you could tell us how we could get hold of Father Lavarato?"

"Heck yes! That should be easy. I'm sure he was ordained here in the Dubuque Diocese and our offices are right here at St. Raphael's Cathedral, only about five minutes from here. If you want me to, I could give them a quick call?"

"That'd be super," said Hank turning to Katie with a look of disbelief on his face. "If you could get an address and telephone number, it would be very helpful."

"Sure, hang on." She picked up a phone off her desk, punched a speed dial number and sat back and winked at the two of them.

"Delores? Hi. Mary Catherine. How're you doing? Great, glad to hear it. Listen, I've got a couple of young people here interested in getting in touch with Father Thomas Lavarato? Yeah, Lavarato, the missionary from Africa, graduated from here in '40. Yep, one and the same. No, I don't know why, hold on."

Covering the speaker and looking up at Hank and Katie she asked, "You family?"

They shook their heads "no."

"Friends?"

"Sort of," shrugged Hank.

"Listen, Dee, they're close friends, okay? Why? Is there some secret where he is or something? No? Well that's great. Give me the info and I'll write it down."

She scribbled an address and telephone number on a small pad of paper and listened some more before thanking her friend and hanging up.

"Well, here 'tis," she said handing the paper over to Hank with a big smile. "Apparently there have been some health issues but he's fine now. He's around 80 you know. Spent most of his life in Africa and that can really beat you down but I hear he's a tough old bird. Sister Delores says he's now living in Philadelphia but plans to return to Africa sometime before the end of the year. Spends most of his time raising money for his mission in Burundi, you know."

"Wow," said Hank. "You don't know how much you've helped us. You're amazing. This really means a lot to us."

Katie was vigorously nodding her head in agreement.

"No sweat! But tell me something," she said. "You've got *my* curiosity up. Why those three students? What makes them so special? You didn't know any of them, did you?"

Hank and Katie quickly looked at each other and Katie opened her mouth to say something when Hank quickly said, "You're right, Sister, we don't know them personally. But we're working on a research project and we're just in the, uh, fact gathering stage, you might say. And we really appreciate your help."

"Well, you're certainly welcome," she said with a shrug. "I'm not sure I did *that* much, but if it helps with your project, that's fine with me. And give me a call if you need something else."

As they walked to the car, Hank couldn't help but notice the police car again and this time the policeman, sitting and staring at them, not even trying to hide his presence anymore. Hank decided to keep it to himself. No sense mentioning it to Katie who was so excited with the news, she was bouncing all over the seat.

"Wow? I can't believe it," she said. "He's still alive. Who'd have thought? What are you going to do now? Call him or something?"

"I don't know. I haven't thought that far ahead yet. But I'd like to make another stop at the library before we leave. Now that we know the date when Sean O'Brien was killed I bet there was a story or something. As long as we've got the time, let's swing by there before we return to the police station, but let's grab a sandwich or something first."

They drove to the same little cafe near the paper and pulled into the tiny parking lot and went in. This time there was no mistaking it. The patrol car pulled up and Hank and Patrolman Flemming stared at each other for a moment until he pulled into a nearby "No Parking" zone.

"Listen, I didn't want to say anything before," Hank said as they were seated, " but do you see that patrol car across the street?"

Katie looked out the window and nodded, "Yeah, what about it?"

"Well, he's been following us ever since we left Mrs. Kiefer's. I didn't think anything about it at the time, but then I saw him parked by us at the school, and now he followed us here. I'm not sure what's going on but I'm thinking about going over and asking him."

"Oh Hank, please don't," pleaded Katie, placing her hand on his arm. "You weren't speeding or anything, were you?"

"No. I made sure of that when we left the school."

"Well, just ignore him, then. We'll leave as soon as we finish at the paper and you can ask Lt. Rea about it."

"Let 'em stew for a while," said Patrolman Flemming to himself knowing full well Hank had seen him. "He makes one mistake and I'm pulling his sorry butt over, the hell with it, and Rea, too. I'm too old to be messing around with punk kids – probably dealing drugs or something. Meanwhile here I sit, while there're in there feeding their faces. I feel like a damn fool."

Hank and Katie quickly finished lunch and went to the library. They went directly up to the librarian they'd worked with last time.

"Hi you guys. How're you doing? How's your project coming?"

"Really good," said Katie. "We're in town for the day and just thought of something else you might be able to help us with."

"Sure."

"Well, we just learned about a young guy, name of Sean O'Brien, who was killed during WWII. He was a 1940 graduate of St. Columkille High and supposedly one of the first people from Dubuque that was killed. We're wondering if there were a story in the paper about it."

"Gosh, I'd think so. Let me see if his name's on our database. Sean O'Brien, right?" she asked turning to her computer and began to type. After a few moments she exclaimed, "Yep, here he is. Sean O'Brien. Recent Columkille graduate killed on Guadalcanal. August 18, 1942. Page 5. Let's go get the film and check it out. What's so special about this guy? Is he part of the project?"

"Yeah, he's part of it," said Hank.

Meanwhile, Patrolman Flemming was sitting outside steaming. He'd followed Hank and Katie from the cafe to the library. They'd walked – he'd driven the patrol car, feeling ridiculous. And he told Lt. Rea that, too, when he'd called in to report.

"Just stick with 'em!" he was told.

Damn waste of time, he thought to himself. A wild goose chase.

They found the story quickly in the main section, which was filled with war news.

DUBUQUER EARLY WAR CASUALTY

Marine Private Sean O'Brien, 21, recent past resident of Dubuque, was reported killed in action during the Battle of Guadalcanal, August 9th. O'Brien, a 1940 graduate of St. Columkille High School, was part of the early wave of Marines to fall under heavy enemy fire and fought valiantly, according to his Commanding Officer Duane Barnhardt. O'Brien is survived by his parents, Mary and John O'Brien, a younger sister, Deidre, two younger brothers, Dennis and Michael, and an older brother, Dubuque Patrolman Patrick O'Brien. A Memorial Service will be held at St. Patrick's Catholic Church on Tuesday morning, August 22nd at 10:00.

"Well, that's it," she said. "Short and sweet. What a shame, only 21 years old. Anything there helpful?"

"Very," said Hank. "Think we can get a printout of that article?"

"Sure, no problem. Take just a second."

When Hank and Katie walked back to their car, Hank smiled and waved at Patrolman Flemming who sat glaring at them. Hank was in a good mood, and so was Katie. The link of Pat O'Brien to Sean O'Brien made perfect sense to both of them. A suspicious mind might think he had something to do with the crime never being reported.

The big news of the day, however, was the fact that one of the young men in the photo, namely Father Thomas Lavarato, was still alive. It had been a great day so far. But, as it turned out, waving at Patrolman Flemming had been a bad idea.

"Wise ass punk," thought Flemming as he followed them to the nearby lot. "Dissing the law's the way I see it. Maybe it's time to teach them two a lesson." As they pulled out of the parking lot he pulled up right behind them and followed them up the street, just a few feet behind them.

"What the heck's he doing now," said Hank looking nervously in the rear view mirror. "He's right on my tail. What's he trying to do, get me in an accident?"

"Just drive," said Katie turning quickly to look. "He must be nuts or something. Wait till we tell Lt. Rea what's going on. Let's get back to the station."

Hank *was* nervous. He kept looking in his rear view mirror, afraid the patrol car was going to ram into him. At the same time he was trying to drive and not sure which was the best way back. As he reached the corner and started to turn right, Katie shouted out, "No, no, the other way!" Hank had already started to turn, but when Katie shouted at him he cut left sharply and changed direction causing the car to swerve before he quickly got it under control.

"Sorry," said Katie. "Didn't mean to shout."

"No, it's not you. It's that stupid cop. He's really bugging me."

At that moment Patrolman Flemming decided the time had come and he quickly flicked on his red lights and hit the siren for a short burst.

"Great, he wants us to pull over," said Hank.

He slowly pulled over to the side of the road. They were in a residential district, quiet and peaceful. The patrol car pulled in behind them. The siren was quiet but the red light was still turning. For a few moments, nothing happened. They just sat there.

"Are we supposed to get out or something?" asked Katie, obviously nervous and concerned.

"No, he'll come to us. For some reason he's giving us a hard time. I'll get his name and we'll let Lt. Rea deal with him. All Right, here he comes. Let me do the talking."

Hank rolled down his window as Patrolman Flemming approached his side of the car. He stood there a minute just looking in at both of them.

"Is there a problem, Officer?" asked Hank.

"You were driving a little erratically back there. You been drinking?"

"No sir, I haven't been drinking. I've been trying to avoid getting rear-ended. Why were you tailing me so closely and why have you been following us?"

"I'll ask the questions, Slick. License?"

"Name's Hank Torney," said Hank as he reached into his billfold and handed over his license. Patrolman Flemming spent some time studying it, making a big display of checking the photo. Finally he bent down and peered in at Katie giving her the once over before saying, "You too, miss. License."

Katie started to get her billfold out of her purse when Hank said, "No Katie. You don't have to show him your license. You're weren't driving."

"That's okay," she said, her voice quivering.

"No," said Hank looking right at Patrolman Flemming. "He's got no right asking for your license."

At this point it could have gone either way. Flemming could have saved face by yelling at Hank, and even writing him a ticket for reckless driving or illegal parking – anything, and that would have been the end of it. Unfortunately Flemming was already out of control. He felt he'd spent the entire morning screwing around with these kids who were without a doubt up to no good. To complicate things further he didn't like getting talked back to, and especially by punk kids. So he made a mistake.

"You don't tell me what I can do or not do," he roared and quickly reached in to grab Katie's purse out of her hand.

It all happened in the blink of an eye. Katie, in a panic, pulled the purse away and gripped it up next to her chest. Hank, without thinking, pushed the patrolman's arm extended in front of him, smashing it into the dash. Flemming howled with pain and pulled away from the car, looking down at his left hand, two fingers of which were already beginning to swell and bruise.

"Get outta the car, punk!" he screamed at Hank. "You've just assaulted a police officer."

He yanked open Hank's door and pulled him out on the street and turned him roughly toward the car and leaned on him. All the while he was unhooking his handcuffs from his belt and slapping them on Hank's wrists. Not an easy thing to do with a bum hand.

Grabbing him by the shoulder with his good hand he shoved him back to the patrol car and into the back seat and slammed the door. "I'll be back to see you in a minute, Slick," he sneered and turned and walked back to the passenger side of the car.

"All Right, sweetheart," he snarled. "Your boyfriend's not here to tell you what to do. Give me your license. Now!"

Katie was fighting back tears and furious. She turned her body away from the window and held her purse down by her side, out of his reach. "Don't you dare touch me," she said looking straight in his face.

Furious at being dissed once again he suddenly shoved his upper body inside the window and lunged toward the purse. Katie gave a yelp and quickly pulled the purse behind her back where he couldn't get at it without pulling her out of the car. Then she yelled, "You just keep away from me, you – you – FLATFOOT!"

For a second they were at what could have been just a comic stalemate. Patrolman Flemming froze when he heard what she'd called him. Then suddenly he backed away breaking into laughter. "Flatfoot? FLATFOOT? Where in the hell did you ever hear that?" he said wiping his eyes. "Girlie, you've been reading too many Dick Tracy comic books. Good Lord – Flatfoot! That's great."

Whatever it was, it seemed to defuse what was quickly turning into an ugly situation. Patrolman Flemming stood there chuckling to himself, looking at his hand, which had started to throb, and said, "Okay, forget it. Keep your damn license. And if you have any sense you'll keep your silly mouth shut, too." With that he whirled away, leaving Katie, shocked, and staring at him as he turned and headed back to the patrol car.

Hank had no idea what had just happened. Because of the angle of the patrol car and the heavy metal, mesh screen separating the back from the front seat, his vision was extremely limited. But when Patrolman Flemming got back in the car, Hank yelled at him, "What in the world's wrong with you, anyway. Let me speak to Lt. Rea."

Flemming ignored him and got on the radio and called in and reported to Lt. Rea that he'd stopped the car because of Hank's reckless driving, and how he'd been physically accosted by him and had him handcuffed in the back seat, and should he bring him in for further questioning.

Hank couldn't exactly hear what was said, but there was no mistaking the muffled screaming that leaked through to the back seat. It seemed to go for several minutes before Flemming, much subdued at this point, and once again bright red in the face, hung up and sat breathing heavily.

Finally he got out, came back and opened the door, pulled Hank out and undid the cuffs. After muttering something about some kind of a mix-up he told him that if he were smart he'd get the hell out of town as quickly as he could before he changed his mind.

"And better tell your lady friend to watch her mouth," he said, trying not to smirk. "And as far as you go, Slick," he said holding up his slightly discolored, left hand, "I won't forget this."

Hank started to say something but before he had a chance, Flemming pivoted around, got in the patrol car and drove off leaving Hank standing alone, rubbing his wrists.

"What a maniac," muttered Hank under his breath as he walked back to the car. "What in the hell was all that about? Wait till I talk to Lt. Rea."

But when he got into the car he found Katie sitting there fuming, eyes moist with tears.

"Katie, honey," he said, "what happened? Did he say something to you? Did he touch you?"

"No. No. Nothing like that. He tried to get my purse, but I wouldn't let him. I called him a name and he laughed at me. Please, let's go. I'll be fine."

"What'd you call him?"

"Never mind. Let's just leave."

"C'mon – what did you say?"

"I called him a flatfoot!"

"A flatfoot? You really called him a *flatfoot*?" Hank said with a grin on his face.

"Yes I did! And I don't care. He was such a jerk – made me so mad. C'mon let's go home."

"Well, we need to go back and see Lt. Rea first. We need to tell him about that nut, and besides, he said he'd have some information …"

"Please, Hank. I just want to go now – I'm so upset I'm not sure what I'd say if we run into him again. 'Sides – look at the time. We're gonna be late the way it is. Can we please just go and you can call Lt. Rea tomorrow?"

CHAPTER THIRTY-TWO

Once again Hank and Katie crossed the Mississippi and headed toward Chicago. Katie remained rather subdued and quiet while Hank pondered the incident with Officer Flemming.

"So what made you call him a *flatfoot?*" he finally asked. "Where on earth have you ever heard such a term anyway?"

"Oh, I don't know," she said, pouting. "I guess I heard my brothers calling each other names when they were playing *Cops and Robbers*. I got the impression it wasn't a nice thing to be. That's all I could think of. Is it really bad?"

"Well, not exactly," Hank said, smiling to himself. "Although it *is* a little dated. I remember it from my comic book days. It was used when talking about patrolmen who walked their beats. I suppose it could be considered a *little* derogatory."

"Well I don't care," she said in a huff. "You didn't have him grabbing for your purse. All you did was sit in the back of the police car – handcuffed."

When that sunk in, they *both* burst out laughing.

They pulled into his driveway at 4:30. His mother welcomed them at the door and immediately ushered them into a huge family room where Katie was introduced to the whole family. Everyone was dying to meet "the new girlfriend." There were his brother Al, his wife, Mary Ann, and their two kids, and his sister, Sarah, and her husband, Greg, and their three kids.

Katie worried there was no way she could remember all the names as the questions came fast and furious. They wanted to know all about her life beginning at conception. She was doing pretty well holding her own until, to her and Hank's relief, his dad saved the day arriving with five large pizzas from Graziano's, one of Chicago's Best. End of interview. Time to eat!

While the youngsters were herded to a table in the kitchen, the adults grabbed plates and spread out around a comfortable family room and dug in. Over a great selection of deep-dish pizza, Hank filled them all in on the great progress he and Katie had made that day. He told them what they had learned about the deaths of both Jack Grettsmer and Sean O'Brien. He then shocked them all by telling them one of the men was still alive and a Catholic Priest – a missionary, to boot, in Africa.

He finished by giving them a "blow-by-blow" account of their experience with Officer Flemming and really laid it on thick about Katie's merciless *flatfoot* attack that set them all howling. Katie turned red as a beet.

"Gotta tell ya, 'lil brother," said Al. "I'm seriously impressed. So, what's up next?"

"I'm not sure," said Hank. "At this point I think we've gone about as far as we can without doing some travel. I really don't want to *call* Father Lavarato and ask him where he was on the night of August 25, 1940. If he was the one who took the picture, and I strongly suspect he was, I'd like to be there in person. And as far as finding out more about Glory Alexander, I may need to go down to Tennessee for many of the same reasons. Katie's grandmother and her genealogy club are doing some research on his family for us and that might help."

"Now, Hank," his dad broke in. "I hope you're not forgetting what we talked about."

"I know, dad. Katie and I have talked to her folks about that very thing and I think we're being pretty careful with our time and not taking any more away from class work than we have to. Actually, up to this point, we've been able to do most everything either on weekends, or during holidays."

"That's fine," his dad continued. "I just want you two to keep focused."

"Right. And we are."

"Well that's good, but *now* you're talking about traveling all over the country. How are you planning on doing all that?"

"Oh, excuse me," his mother broke in, "but speaking of traveling, Peter called earlier today from Amy's house – I didn't know he was having Thanksgiving at her folks? Sounds serious. I ran into her mom at the store just the other day and she never said a word. Anyway, Peter wanted to make sure you and Katherine didn't forget you guys were getting together for *a light refreshment,* I believe is the way he put it, at *Guido's* around 8:00. He said he had a 'very important' message for you, Hank. Wouldn't tell me what it was, though."

Guidos, an Evanston neighborhood favorite, was bouncing when Hank and Katie arrived. The place was jam-packed with locals and the college crowd as well, and Hank waved to several old friends standing at the bar or sitting in booths along both walls.

"Hank!" shouted Pete from across the front room. "Over here."

Pete and Amy were already seated in one of the large corner booths. Guido, himself, was bending over talking to them and a half empty pitcher of beer was sitting on the table. Hank pulled Katie through the crowd and introduced them.

"Hey, college boy, why you no longer come around and see your old friends, huh?" Guido said, shaking Katie's hand and giving Hank a big bear hug. "*Guido's* not good enough for you no more? Why you waste your time with this one, huh?" he said to Katie. "I can tell already. He's no good enough for you. Hey, Johnny," he yelled at the bartender. "Another pitcher of the cheap stuff for my friends here. You guys be good now or I tell you to leave – got it?"

"Thanks, Guido. We'll be good," said Pete as Guido left to work the crowd. "C'mon you two, slide in. "I've got an urgent message for Mr. Jail Bait, here."

"What're you talking about?" said Hank as he and Katie slid around the table. "Hi Amy, good to see you again, how's school going? Kids driving you insane yet?"

"Hardly. I'm loving it," she said.

Hank turned back to Pete and asked, "So, what's with the *Mr. Jail Bait* bit?"

"You got a call this afternoon, hot shot, just as I was getting ready to leave."

"Yeah, who was it?"

"Guess."

"PETE!"

"All Right already – a Lieutenant Rea from the Dubuque Police Department! That's who. Said he wanted to talk to you as soon as possible. Gave me his work number, his cell phone number, AND his home number. Wants you to call him right away. I tried to get him to tell me what was going on, but he wouldn't say. So what's up?

What'd you two do now? Drunk and disorderly? Shoplifting? What? Need the name of a good lawyer? Sounds like you're in deep doo doo this time, partner."

"Yeah, so pour us a beer," said Hank, completely ignoring the subject. "You guys want to split an order of onion rings ... ?"

"Hey," broke in Pete. "Don't do that to me. Tell me what's going on. I'm dying here!"

Hank and the girls laughed at Pete's frustration and Hank finally settled in and told them the whole story. Meeting with Lt. Rea. Going to the Grettsmer home and finding out about Jack Grettsmer. Visiting the school and finding out about Tom Lavarato and Sean O'Brien. And then the problem with the police officer with special emphasis on the now-famous *flatfoot* attack by Katie.

"You really called him a flatfoot?" howled Pete. "Wow, that is *so* great. Right out of the comics. Man, I haven't heard that term for years – since I was in grade school. *Flatfoot*! How cool is *that*?"

"All Right. All Right. Don't get carried away," said Hank. "Everyone's been on poor Miss Katie's case. I should have kept it to myself."

"No. That's just fine," said Katie. "Enjoy it while you can. You two will have your day of reckoning soon enough, and when you do, I'll be there waiting."

CHAPTER THIRTY-THREE

Hank called Lieutenant Rea early Saturday morning. The phone was picked up on the first ring.

"Hank," Lt. Rea said, "Thanks for calling. I want to apologize for what happened between you guys and Officer Flemming yesterday. I don't want you to think badly of me or my men. Officer Flemming's really a good cop – granted a tad intense but ... "

"A tad!" Hank exclaimed. "I'd say that's putting it mildly. What got into that nut anyway? We were minding our own business until he came along."

"Well I'm afraid that was my fault. I asked him to keep an eye on you two and ... "

"What? Why'd you do that?" said Hank.

"Please, let me finish. Flemming recently transferred here from Detroit. He worked there with lots of street gangs and is having trouble adjusting to the low level of crime here in Dubuque. He really meant no harm."

"Well," said Hank, "I still want to know why you felt we had to be followed around like criminals."

"Again, I apologize. That was *my* decision. All the strange questions you were asking just waved too many red flags. Then I did some checking and learned you two weren't being exactly truthful about working on a 'school research project.' Although that's not a crime it was just another red flag."

"Wait. Hold on a second," said Hank. "I never said we were working on a *school* project. I said we were *students* working on a *research project*. It just happens to be a private project."

"Okay, I misunderstood. But as I said, either way, that's your business. I'm just sorry it turned out the way it did."

"Well, we are too. We were planning to stop by before we left but Katie was so upset, we just headed on back. She and Officer Flemming kind of got into a shouting match."

"Yeah – I heard about that," he chuckled. "The *flatfoot* bit."

"So were you able to find out anything for us?" Hank said, slightly subdued.

"We checked and no – we didn't. We looked at the records for a month on either side, too. No crimes that involved *any* type of death. Nothing. But we did have some information on that patrolman you asked about – Pat O'Brien. I suspect he fits into your *research* somehow. He was relieved of duty in the early '40s. I should tell you that's just another way to say he was fired.

"Fired?" said Hank. "Why do you 'fire' a policeman?"

"I called an old timer who actually knew him. He told me O'Brien was a 'bad egg.' Said he must have gotten involved with things he shouldn't have and apparently got caught. It was kept quiet, out of the newspapers, and according to this guy some kind of involvement with the mob was his best guess. You should realize back then Dubuque was a lot wilder than it is today. I'm not making excuses, that's just the way it was. Anyway, no one knows for sure what happened to him, but my friend seemed to think he went to Chicago. End of story. I'm telling you this because I feel bad for what happened yesterday. It sounds like you two are on to *something* and I thought this might help. Any chance you'll tell me what it's about? Maybe I really *could* help."

"I appreciate your candor, Lieutenant," said Hank. "And what you told me helps fill in a few blanks, but I'm not sure what more you can do at this point. We're pretty sure an attack was made on that black man while he was in Dubuque on that date because of an old photo we found. I know it was years ago, ancient history I guess, but we're committed to finding out what really happened. We're still piecing it together."

"And I'm guessing Officer O'Brien is part of the story," said Rea. "And Mrs. Kiefer?"

Hank paused, then recalled seeing the patrol car parked down the street by her house. "Yes, but she knows nothing about this. I'd like to keep it that way."

"I see. Well, if it's anything concerning the police department, even
though it been years ago, I'd like to avoid any embarrassing publicity. People are always looking for excuses to give us a hard time, you know what I'm saying?"

"I do. When we figure it all out, I'll tell you about it."

"Fair enough, Hank. Good luck, then. Come back again and give us another chance."

By Saturday afternoon Mrs. Torney had pressured Hank and Katie into staying over one more night so they all could have dinner with Hank's grandmother who lived in a high rise on Chicago's north side. That was fine with Hank and Katie was excited to meet her anyway.

The Lancaster Arms sat on a premium piece of property facing Lakeshore Drive and Lake Michigan. It was a large 10-story condominium bordered on two sides by a tall hedge and a straight line of mature Ginkgo trees. A gorgeous place, Katie thought as Hank's dad pulled up to a large gate and were greeted by a uniformed guard.

"Evening, Mr. Torney. How are you tonight, sir?" he asked.

"Fine, Walter. And you?"

"Just fine, sir. I'll ring Mrs. Torney and let her know you're on the way up."

"Thanks. We're eating downstairs this evening, so I'll leave the car up front if that's all right. We shouldn't be too late."

"No problem, Mr. Torney. Enjoy your evening, and give my respects to your mother."

Mrs. Torney lived in a large unit on the top southeast corner. The door was ajar as she sat waiting for them in the doorway in her wheelchair, elegantly dressed for dinner. A tall, attractive maid stood by her side, beaming at the approaching group.

"Hank," Mrs. Torney squealed. "Give your grandmother a big hug!"

Hank grinned and bent down, gave her the hug she demanded and a big kiss on her cheek. "Good to see you, Grams, Happy Thanksgiving. I want you to meet a friend of mine. This is Katherine Joyce. She goes to Western State, too."

"How are you, dear," she said reaching up with both hands to greet her. "I am *so* pleased to finally meet you. Apparently the last one in the family to do so ... " she said, giving Hank a fake scowl. "C'mon in everyone. We've got a little time to catch up on things before dinner and I want to know what Hank and Katherine have been up to."

Everyone moved into the apartment while Hank also gave a hug to the maid.

167

"Good to see you again, Betty, how have you been?"

"Just fine, Hank, just fine. Mrs. Torney's been so excited to see you. That's all she's been talking about all day."

"Well, I'm excited, too. How's she been doing, by the way?" he asked in a lower voice.

"Oh, you know. Mostly good days – some bad. She sure misses your granddaddy, though."

"Yeah, I know, I know. I do, too. C'mon let's join the rest of them. If we stay out here too long Katie's gonna get jealous."

"Oh, chile," she laughed and pushed his shoulder as they walked into a large corner living area. "You still be ornery."

As always, Hank was momentarily stunned by the million dollar view that opened up in front of him. Even though he'd seen it many times before, he never tired of it; Lake Michigan spreading off into the distance in front, Centennial Park to the left, and downtown Chicago, with its magnificent, twinkling skyline to the right. He looked at Katie and saw her staring, mesmerized, similarly affected.

Betty came in wheeling a tray holding a large pitcher, lead crystal glasses, several bottles of *Perrier*, and two bottles of *Schlitz* beer.

"Betty's been kind enough to mix up a batch of Compari Cocktails for anyone who's interested," announced Mrs. Torney. "And no one can mix that elegant drink as well as she can, so come sit down and let's talk. And don't panic, Hank. You'll notice I have some *Schlitz* beer for you although it's becoming harder to find these days."

"Way to go, Grams! But don't worry, you'll always find *Schlitz* for sale around here. Chicagoans love their *Schlitz*, you know."

"Yes, I know," said his grandmother rolling her eyes. "You've told me all about it before."

"Why's that?" asked Katie, taking a tentative sip of her Compari Cocktail. "Mmmm, that's good," she added smiling at Betty.

"When Chicago suffered through the Great Fire in 1871 most of Chicago's breweries burned to the ground," said Hank. "Joseph Schlitz, a German immigrant who ran a brewery in Milwaukee, donated and shipped down thousands of barrels of his beer. That endeared him to the city and Chicagoans don't forget, at least I don't. Besides, it's good beer."

168

"Yes, I'm sure you're right, dear," his grandmother said dismissing the subject with a wave of her hand. "But I want to know more about this mysterious, extracurricular project you and Katherine are working on. Your parents have told me some things, but I want to hear it from you."

"Really, mother, I don't think we have the time," broke in Mr. Torney, looking at his watch. "What time are we expected downstairs?"

"Now you hush, son," Hank's grandmother said, turning to Mr. Torney. "I told them not to expect us before 7:00 so we have plenty of time. Go on, Hank, tell all. Betty!" she called out. "Come back in here and listen to this, I think you'll find it interesting."

Hank spent the next twenty minutes giving them the condensed version of how the whole thing had started and what had happened since, even filling them in on the conversation he had had with the Dubuque police chief the day before.

"My goodness!" exclaimed his grandmother when Hank had finished. "That is a great story! And, Katherine, if I understand Al correctly, *your* grandmother is researching the family of this poor, unfortunate black man?"

"Yes," said Katie. "She and her genealogy club."

"And you believe one of the original boys is still alive?" said Mrs. Torney.

"Yes, Grams. He's a missionary in Africa, but apparently living in Philadelphia right now. I'm hoping to go see him if possible."

"Well, all I can say is that is the strangest story I've ever heard. Intriguing is what it is! And Hank and Katherine, I admire your tenacity. I can't believe you two have gone to all that time and trouble. Which brings me to the next subject. Betty, would you go in and bring me that envelope on my dresser? The one with Hank's name on it."

"Yes, ma'am," Betty said, turning and leaving the room.

"I've got something for you, Hank dear. I was going to give it to you for Christmas, but when I heard what you've been up to, I think it would be better to give it to you now. You can think of it as an *early* Christmas present."

Betty returned with an envelope and handed it to his grandmother.

"Here, dear, this is for you," she said. "Go ahead and open it."

Hank ripped open the envelope and slipped out a United Airlines frequent flyer mileage card with his name on it.

"What's this, Grams? I'm not a frequent flyer. I don't have any frequent flyer miles."

"You do now, sweetheart. 250,000 of them."

"What? Where did you get this? I mean, why did you do this? I mean, it's great and all, but *250,000 miles!* Grams that must have cost a fortune, I can't accept this."

"Now don't be silly. Of course, you can. And to be honest, it hardly cost a thing. I've got so many frequent flyer miles I wouldn't be able to use a fraction of them, even if I were planning on going somewhere. Which I'm not. So I transferred some to you."

"Well, I don't understand," said Hank, stammering. "Where did you get them?"

"When your grandfather was alive, he traveled abroad on business quite a bit. International patent attorneys do that, you know. In the last couple of years he worked, he must have gone back and forth to Japan dozens of times. And before you go off thinking you're my favorite, whether you are or not," she said, smiling, "you should know your brother and sister are getting their own cards as well."

"Wow, that's great, Grams," he said giving her a quick hug. "Thanks! These *are* going to come in handy. "

"My thoughts exactly. I'm sure there's at least enough to get both you and Katherine to Philadelphia and back. Now, let's go to dinner!"

Germaines, one of Chicago's top-rated French restaurants took up the entire ground floor of the building and was packed. Anxious couples were lined up trying to finagle their way inside. But when the Torneys arrived shortly after 7:00 the maître d' stopped in mid stride and came rushing over to greet them and personally led them to a large private table in the corner.

"We are honored to have you with us again, Mrs. Torney. Please let me know if there is anything, anything at all I can do to make your evening more pleasant."

"Thank you, Lawrence. I certainly will. Is Anthony working tonight?"

"Of course," he smiled. "He's waiting for you."

And as if on cue an elderly, elegant-looking waiter mysteriously appeared at her side.

"Mrs. Torney," he said with a half bow.

"Anthony," she said with a laugh. "How good to see you again. You're looking absolutely dashing, as usual. We're all famished and looking forward to your recommendations. I assumed you've saved us something edible this evening?"

And so went the evening. Lighthearted banter. Impeccable service. Frequent table visits from nearby friends and acquaintances. And, of course, a memorable meal. Anthony, indeed, knew his stuff.

The following morning, Hank and Katie said their goodbyes and headed back to school. Along the way Hank explained how his grandmother had been confined to a wheelchair after being diagnosed with a degenerative hip disorder three years ago.

"She's never said a word of discouragement to anyone, ever! And everyone knows how painful it is. I feel really bad only seeing her every few months."

"How long's your grandfather been gone?"

"Five years. They were very close and I know she really misses him. We feel very fortunate that Betty is still able to stay with her. She moved in shortly after Granddad died and she and Grams have become best of friends."

"Well, that was some gift. 250,000 frequent flyer miles. Wow! What are you going to do with them all?"

"Well, Grams had a good idea. We should *both* go to Philadelphia and see Father Lavarato. I bet if we left early enough we could fly there and back the same day. Think your parents would go for that?"

"Oh, I'm sure they would. I'd really like to meet this guy and see what he's like. Maybe I won't even mention it to them."

"No, no. We don't want to do that," Hank said quickly. "And anyway, we're getting ahead of ourselves. We don't even know if he'll see *us*."

CHAPTER THIRTY-FOUR

The gap between Thanksgiving and Christmas was on them before they knew it. Hank and Katie thought the perfect time for their trip to Philadelphia would be during Christmas break and Katie agreed that would make an easier sell to her parents. Soon after returning to school Hank called United and got flight schedules from O'Hare. He learned if they could leave on the 7:30 morning flight, they'd arrive in plenty of time to meet with Father Lavarato and catch the 6:00 evening flight back. Seats were available then – but were filling up fast. He went ahead and reserved two tickets. All they had to do now was call Father Lavarato and see if he would meet with them.

"Hello?" answered a soft, accented female voice.

"Is Father Lavarato there?" asked Hank.

"Who is calling, please?"

"This is Hank Torney. I was given Father Lavarato's number by the diocesan office in Dubuque."

"One moment, please."

"Hello," said a man's voice. "Tom Lavarato here."

"My name's Hank Torney, Father."

"Hank Torney? Do we know each other?"

"No, Father. Not personally. I know you graduated from St. Columkille's and you've talked to the school about your missionary work. Is that right?"

"Yes," he said with a soft chuckle. "But that's been a while now, hasn't it?"

"Yes, Father, I suppose it has."

"Well, what can I do for you, Hank. I'm afraid I'm not up to returning to Dubuque for any more talks if that's why you called."

"No, no, that's not it at all, Father. Actually I'm going to be in Philadelphia over the Christmas break and wonder if I could meet with you? I'm working on a research project and would be really interested in talking with you."

"Well I don't know, Hank. I'm quite busy now. I'm planning on returning to Africa in a few weeks and I've got a lot of things I need to get done."

"Father, I promise I won't take much of your time. I'd just like to ask you a few questions. I'll be in and out before you know it. And it really would be a big help.

"Well, I suppose we could meet. When are you planning to be here?"

"I've got midterm exams next week – but Christmas break begins on the 19th so how about that weekend – say Saturday the 23rd? Would that work for you?

"Yes, Saturday would work fine. What time?"

"How about 11:00?"

"11:00? All Right. I'll see you then. Goodbye now."

"Uh, excuse me, Father. Is your address still on L Street?"

"Right. 1245 L Street. It's a small house very near Holy Innocents Church. That'd be the easier way to find it. Holy Innocents Church. On L and Hunting Park Avenue, in North Philly. Do you know the area?"

"I'll find it, no problem. 1245 L Street, Holy Innocents Church, North Philly. Thank you *very* much, Father. See you at 11:00 on Saturday the 23rd."

"I can't believe it," Hank said to Katie after hanging up. "We did it! He didn't even ask why I wanted to talk to him so I didn't have to 'bend the truth.' I bet he thinks I was a student he talked to years ago in Dubuque. No going back now – we've got the tickets reserved. It looks like a go."

"That's great," she replied. "All we have to do now is convince my parents."

The hardest part of convincing Katie's parents came when she said they were planning to go so close to Christmas.

"But it's only for one day," she pointed out. "I'll be home the same night, I promise." They weren't thrilled about it but eventually gave in. They suggested that her brother, Sean, come and pick her up at the airport and take her home Saturday evening. That way, Hank wouldn't have to drive so far out of his way.

Their flight landed on time. They exited the airport and jumped into the first cab they saw. Hank gave the cab driver the address, and when he started to refer to a map Hank said it was very close to Holy Innocents Catholic Church in "North Philly." This worked and off they went.

Once they found the church, finding the house was easy. It *was* close, half way down a long block of similar houses that looked like they were all built back in the 60's. The street was lined with mature trees and looked comfortable and well maintained. A lovely, young black girl answered the door, and led them into a small living room and invited them to sit as she went to get Father Lavarato.

"She's beautiful," Katie whispered. "What's her accent?"

"Not sure. African, I bet," Hank said, looking around the room which was decorated with a variety of African-looking masks, musical instruments and wall hangings.

"You must be Hank Torney," said the man who entered the room and extended his hand. "I'm Tom Lavarato."

"Pleased to meet you, Father," said Hank jumping to his feet. "Thank you so much for seeing us. This is Katherine Joyce. We're both students at Western State in Illinois. I'm afraid I didn't mention she'd be with me. I hope it's all right."

"Of course. Hello Katherine. Welcome to Philadelphia."

"Thank you, Father," said Katie, smiling. "This is my first time here."

"Please, call me Tom. 'Father' makes me feel older than I already am, which is plenty old enough, believe me," he said in a friendly voice. "And sit. Please, sit back down."

Father Lavarato stood around 5' 11" and looked like he didn't have an ounce of fat on him. He was dressed in khakis and a red, long sleeve knit shirt and was wearing a pair of battered, old loafers with no socks. His white hair was cropped short but was thick and full. His grip was strong and firm and his hands heavily callused. He wasn't wearing glasses and his eyes appeared to be a dark, dark brown, almost black.

Other than a wicked-looking scar that ran across his left cheek, and being around 80, Hank thought he looked in great shape. However, he would never have picked him out of a lineup trying to match him with the high school graduation picture he had tucked away under his arm.

"How about a cup of tea?" he asked.

"That'd be wonderful," answered Katie. Hank nodded in approval.

"Mariama," he called out.

The young lady who had let them in the house instantly appeared in the doorway and Father said something softly to her in a foreign tongue. She quietly turned and left.

"She speaks English, you know," he said, smiling. "But she has some difficulties and is easily embarrassed, particularly around people she doesn't know very well. We speak Swahili together, or sometimes Chaga, which is really her native language."

"What a lovely name. *Mariama*," said Katie.

"It means 'Gift of God' in Swahili. And she truly is. It's not her real name but I thought it described her so well and could be easily pronounced by foreigners, especially Americans."

"What's her real name?" asked Hank.

"I don't know, actually. And she won't say."

"She won't tell you? Why's that?" said Katie, mystified.

"Well, you may have heard this story before during one of my Dubuque visits, but I'll give you the condensed version."

Hank and Katie exchanged quick guilty looks as he went on.

"As you know, I run a small missionary parish in Eastern Africa – have for years. It was a peaceful place until the '50s when the Belgians lost control of the area and the Tutsis and Hutus started in on one another. For decades things got progressively worse until September 1987. One night several family groups that lived in the area came rushing to the mission seeking protection from the rebels. Mariama came with her family. She was just a child at the time ... "

Just then Mariama returned with a serving tray holding a teapot, cups and saucers, and a small plate of cookies.

"Thank you, Mariama," Father Lavarato said in English.

"Yes, thank you," chimed in Hank and Katie.

Mariama gave a shy smile and left.

"Anyway," he continued, checking to be sure she'd gone, "she was just a small child and we all crowded into the church. Thirty four people; including myself."

He stopped to pour some tea and, Hank sensed, to collect himself.

"This time it was different," he said. "They followed the people right into the church. They'd never done that before. I tried to stop them. But I couldn't. They killed them all."

"Oh, Father," gasped Katie, "That's terrible."

No one said anything for a moment.

"They tried to kill Mariama, too, but I grabbed her and shoved her behind me and backed up to the altar. They never meant to harm me, but when I refused to release her, one furious young man came at me with his machete and ..." At this point he paused, smiled and stroked the scar on his face.

"The others pulled him away but to this day I'll never forget the look on his face. He was like a madman – so young yet filled with so much hate. I'll never understand it. I was lucky. My Guardian Angel was working overtime that day."

"Oh Father," cried Katie, close to tears. "That's so awful. What happened then?"

"Well, eventually they left and we fled as soon as we could. I had an old Jeep that for some reason they ignored, another miracle. We drove to a local hospital, about 80 kilometers away. Once we got there, they sewed me up and we left the country soon after."

Hank said, "Wow. That's quite a story. I'm sorry if I stared when we met. I wondered how you got it. The pain must have been terrible."

"You know, that's the strange part. I really don't recall much pain at all. I guess I was in shock. And if there's a bright side to the story, this little blemish has opened up a lot of pocket books for the mission. I shamelessly exploit it wherever I go fund raising," he said with an easy laugh.

"But for Mariama," he continued, "I'm afraid the event was much more serious. The experience traumatized her severely. She wouldn't speak for years, not a word. Finally, little by little, she began again. But she's never told us what her name was. We suspect she's blocked out that period of her life completely. Anyway, I renamed her when I adopted her."

Noticing the surprised look on both of their faces he quickly added, "Well, I say 'adopted' but I'm not sure how official it would be here. In Africa, it's done all the time. If not, there'd be more orphans running around than there are regular kids. Anyway she's been with me ever since. I'm afraid she's become terribly protective of me. I believe she's somewhere in her teens now. I like to shock people when I introduce her as my great granddaughter," he said, laughing. "At any rate, she can't go back. She has no one left and, to tell you the truth, it's probably not safe for her."

He paused and looked at them quizzically.

"But I'm *sure* I've told you this story before at the school. You don't remember it?"

Again Hank and Katie exchanged quick glances and Hank finally began.

"I'm sorry, Father ..."

"Please – Tom."

"I'm sorry, Tom. I think I may have misled you. We didn't go to school in Dubuque. In fact, neither of us had ever been to Dubuque before a few months ago."

"I don't understand," he said, looking puzzled. "I thought you were students doing a research paper on the mission."

"Well, not exactly. We're doing research on, uh, a different matter."

"Really?" he said, looking back and forth between the two of them. "And what matter is *that*?"

At this point Hank reached down and opened his briefcase and started flicking through papers. He was nervous as a cat and fumbled around until he finally found what he was looking for and took out copies of Father Lavarato's graduation photo along with photos of Sean O'Brien and Jack Grettsmer. He carefully placed them side-by-side on the coffee table.

"Do you recognize these people?" he asked.

Father Lavarato bent down and peered at the photos, slowly glancing from one to the other, finally reaching and picking up his photo and turning to Hank. A broad smile spread across his face.

"Where in the world did you get these?" he asked. "Good Heavens, this is my old high school graduation photo. And what's with the photos of Jack Grettsmer and Sean O'Brien? Why do you have *them*? I haven't seen these pictures in what, gosh, 60 years I guess."

"You and these two were pretty good friends, weren't you?" asked Hank.

"Yeah, we were. Best of friends," he said looking at Hank and then Katie. "But why do you have them? I don't understand."

All of a sudden he looked a little nervous and unsure of himself – as if he knew bad news was on the way. "And how did you know we were friends?" he finally asked. "And why would you even *care*? Maybe you'd better tell me why you're both here."

"Do you know what happened to them?" asked Hank.

"Yes, of course. Sean joined the Marines and was killed early in WWII. Jack died relatively early too, back east, in Boston. But that was a long time ago. Are they part of this 'research project' you say you are working on?"

Hank sighed, looked at Katie and back at Father Lavarato. The moment of truth had arrived. Earlier he was thinking of calling the whole thing off. What was he going to gain dredging up the past; particularly now? My God, he thought to himself, the man is 80 years old. What was the point? What if they were wrong and he had nothing to do with the crime? What if someone else, after all, had taken the photo in the warehouse? Yet, after a long pause, Hank reached in his folder and withdrew the large photo of the crime scene. Father Lavarato was watching him carefully, looking for some clue as to what was going on. Hank silently placed the photo on the table.

"Do you recognize this photo, Father – uh – Tom?" he asked.

Father Lavarato reached down and picked it up, looking back and forth at Hank and Katie noticing the nervousness on both their faces.

"Another old photo?" he said as he stood and took it over to the window for better light.

Hank and Katie watched him closely. For several seconds his eyes slowly moved over the figures in the photo. Gradually his puzzled expression began to fade and his hands began to tremble lightly. His eyes betrayed a kindling recognition that seemed to drift off into a distant memory and stop frozen as the scene came to life in his mind's eye.

"Sweet Jesus," he said, and started to collapse.

CHAPTER THIRTY-FIVE

Hank and Katie both rushed to grab Father Lavarato as he started to slump to the floor. Gently, they led him back to the couch.

"Father? Are you all right?" Hank asked in an alarmed voice.

He sat down heavily and shrugged off Hank's hands.

"I'm fine," he said. "Just give me a minute."

Just then Mariama came in and took in the scene with shocked eyes. Alarmed, she yelled something and rushed to Father's side. Hank couldn't understand what was said, but Father pushed her hands away and replied in her language, obviously reassuring her that he was all right.

"He's had a shock," said Katie to Mariama. "Could you get a glass of water, please?"

Mariama paused, and then left hurriedly.

"Sorry," said Father Lavarato looking from Hank to Katie. "Took my breath away for a minute. What's going on here," he said pointedly to Hank. "Where did you get that photo and why are you here?"

"You took the picture, didn't you, Father?" asked Hank.

Father Lavarato looked away and stared into space and finally, in a soft, resigned voice said, "Yes. I took it. My God, that old Brownie. I'd forgotten all about it. We never knew what happened to it. Such a long time ago."

"Over 60 years ago. August 25th, 1940, to be exact," said Hank.

Again it was Father's turn to be shocked as he turned to Hank with a look of intense puzzlement on his face. "I'm confused," he said. "What *do* you want? Are you with the police or something? How do you know all this? You'd better tell me what's going on here or I'm going to ask you to leave."

"Father – Tom, we're not from the police," Hank said. "We're just students. And, of course we'll tell you everything but I need to start at the beginning. It's a long story and it's going to take some time. Do you have the time?"

"Are you kidding?" he replied. "I'll make the time." Then he looked at Mariama who'd returned with the water and rattled off some instructions.

She looked a little concerned but turned and left the room again.

"I told her to make some calls and cancel a meeting I had. This is more important, of course. Please, tell me again who you are and where you're from."

Katie, now sitting by him on the couch, repeated their names and where they lived and studied in school.

"Earlier this year," Hank said, "I bought an old camera at a farm auction in Illinois. It was the Kodak Brownie you just mentioned. Just by accident I noticed it still had film in it. I was curious and eventually found someone who could develop it. Here is another one of the prints we got." Hank handed him the photo of the Grettsmer house.

"Jack's house," Father Lavarato said with a nostalgic smile. "I was in it only once. When Jack's folks were away. It was a lovely old place, I remember that."

"Still is," Hank said. "But anyway, it was the other photo that got our interest. People who saw it first thought it was just a bad joke – some kind of nasty prank. But when we studied it closer, we decided it wasn't. And that's how it started."

"It was an accident," Father Lavarato said in an anguished voice. "A terrible accident. We never meant to hurt that young man, you've got to believe me. We'd been drinking, the three of us, and we'd gotten into trouble at a local bar and ran off. If we'd just gone home, none of this would have happened. But we didn't."

"It was in Dubuque, Iowa, wasn't it" said Katie.

"Yes, Dubuque. That's where we all lived. We'd just graduated from high school that summer," Father Lavarato replied.

"You were able to drink in a bar at that age?" Hank asked.

"Yes," he said. "At least at *Kelly's Tavern* – as disreputable a place as you could imagine. We'd go in there sometimes and play pool. We were under age, of course, but that was Dubuque for you. And Sean had a brother who was a policeman who knew Kelly and, well, we got away with stuff."

"Pat O'Brien," said Hank.

"So you know about him, too?" he said, lifting his eyebrows at Hank.

"A little," said Hank. "But, please, go on. Tell us what happened."

"Well, this one night we caused a scene and were thrown out. We should have gone home but Jack wanted to go to his dad's warehouse. He said he knew about some homemade beer hidden in the basement. It was stupid, so stupid. But Sean and I didn't argue. We went. When we got to the warehouse we saw this black man walking down the street all alone. It was the strangest thing we'd ever seen – not only that he was black, which was odd enough in those days, but that he was walking alone down those dark, nasty streets. So we thought we'd have a little fun. We grabbed him and started giving him a hard time. He tried to leave but we wouldn't let him. We all went into the warehouse and started drinking some more. Soon there was a scuffle and things got out of hand. It was terrible. An accident ... "

"Accident? What kind of accident?" said Hank, interrupting.

"During the scuffle he bit Sean who reacted by hitting him in the head with a bottle – an uncontrollable reflex, I believe. Anyway, he fell and we thought he was just knocked out. We had no idea he was – dead."

"But why did you take a picture?" Katie asked.

"It was Jack's nutty idea. His dad kept a camera there and he thought it'd be a neat idea to stage this photo so we could show to our friends."

Hank and Katie looked at one another and shook their heads.

"I know, I know, we should've known better," Father Lavarato continued, "but we were just punk kids and we'd all had too much to drink and somehow, you know the saying – *it seemed like a good idea at the time.* So, Sean and Jack propped him up and I quickly took the picture before he woke up, but of course, he never woke up."

Shaking and lowering his head, he continued in a low voice, almost to himself. "Dear Jesus, what were we thinking? We all knew better. We'd been brought up better than that."

"What happened then?" asked Hank.

"Pat O'Brien showed up. Came in the back way. Caught us 'red handed' and scared us half to death. At first he didn't say anything, but just walked over and took a good look at him. He checked for a pulse, looked at his eyes. Then he turned with a twisted grin that I'll never forget and told us he was dead. You can't imagine the horror we all felt. As I said, up to then we still thought he was just knocked out. My God, I could have died right then and there I was so shocked. Then he flipped out."

"Who flipped out?" asked Katie.

"Pat O'Brien. You only had to see him – this big, mean cop completely out of control. He started kicking furniture and smacking Sean around and screaming at all of us. He told me to get out of there, and don't even think of talking about it or coming around Jack or Sean again, ever. He grabbed me and pulled me to the front door and literally kicked me out into the street. I was so scared I ran all the way home."

Hank said, "But what happened to the body?"

"To tell you the truth I never knew *for sure*. I didn't even have *an idea* until years later. You see, that night was the last time I ever saw or spoke to Sean again. I saw Jack just once, a few days later. He came by my house to ask me if I knew anything about the camera. I didn't, of course, and told him that."

"What *did* happen to it?" asked Katie.

"I don't know. Last I saw of it Sean's brother had it. Threatened he would show the picture around if we made any trouble. I really think he was referring to Jack's folks. They were wealthy and influential and he could have made trouble for him if he wanted. Then Jack told me *he* was leaving the next week, going away to school. And that was the last I saw of him – at least alive."

"But what did they do with the body?" Hank insisted. "You said, 'you don't know for sure.' You obviously have some idea."

"After I left the warehouse, Jack told me Sean and his brother carried it out the back way – that's where the patrol car was parked. A few years later, when I was in the seminary, I got a phone call from Jack. It was the first time I'd heard from him since he left Dubuque. It was quite a shock. He was in his sophomore or junior year at Brown by then and was calling from some bar, sounding quite drunk. He told me Sean had recently called him from California and told him he'd joined the Marines. He said he was being shipped overseas, heading to war – a short war for him as it turned out. Anyhow Jack had asked Sean the same thing. What happened to the body? Sean told him was that if it were him, he wouldn't eat any more fish out the Mississippi again."

Katie gasped.

"Yeah, I know," said Father Lavarato. "It doesn't take a genius to figure out what that's supposed to mean. Up to that point I had

182

actually hoped there had been a big mistake – that the black man was not dead – that Sean's policeman brother was trying to scare the devil out of us. But after I heard that, I knew the worst had happened. But wait a minute," Father Lavarato said as something just occurred to him. "Let's back up a bit. How did *you* get the camera? And how in the world did you know that *I* took that photo? How did you know *any* of this?"

"Well," Hank said, "as I said, I bought the camera at an auction in Illinois – not that far from Chicago, actually. Just recently we learned Patrolman Pat O'Brien had been fired from the Dubuque Police Department in the early '40s and supposedly went to the Chicago area. He obviously never had the film developed but how the camera ended up at an auction is anybody's guess. At any rate I did get it developed and from that point on it was mainly a lot of luck. The only reason we guessed the picture was taken in Dubuque was because Katie recognized the Grettsmer House."

"So one day we went to Dubuque," Katie jumped in, "and found the house. And what's stranger still, Jack's sister, Anna, still lives there."

"You're kidding," broke in Father Lavarato. "I knew her as a kid. She *still* lives there? But I heard she was married."

"She was," Katie said, "but she's now a widow and living by herself. She's a lovely lady and invited us in and told us about Jack and the rest of the family. Showed us some old photos and told us where he went to high school. That eventually led us to you."

"You didn't tell her anything about *this*, about me, did you?" Father Lavarato asked with alarm.

"No, of course not," Hank said. "She doesn't know anything and we don't plan to tell her. Actually, we got hold of some old Columkille year books and found the photos of Jack and Sean there. They were the only people we could identify at the time. We knew someone had to have taken the picture but didn't know who. But later we found this photo of the three of you – 'The Three Musketeers' and suspected it had to be you. Jack's sister, Anna, confirmed the fact that you three were pretty close."

"We were," said Father Lavarato smiling sadly at the old photo. "We had been since grade school. We were a pretty unlikely trio, at that. 'A Wop, a Kraut and a Mick,' as Kelly used to say. Dubuque, in those days, was a pretty segregated community. And I'm not talking about just blacks. I don't believe *any* blacks lived there. There were lots of Germans and Irish, though. And although both groups were

Catholic, they hated each other. They fought all the time – even had separate churches. I was the 'oddball' Italian. So it *was* strange to see us hang out together, I guess. But I can tell you one thing for sure, no one messed with us."

"Why's that, Father?" asked Katie.

"Well, Jack was a mean one, but by this I mean mean-spirited. Sean was just plain mean but had a good heart, I really believe that. He was always in trouble. Jack would have been, too, but his folks always bailed him out; old Dubuque family with lots of money. And they sure didn't like Sean and I hanging around their place. I *tolerated* Jack, but I really liked Sean. Scratch his thick Irish skin and you'd find a pretty nice guy, a loyal friend, for sure. Jack, on the other hand, was fun to be around, but I never really trusted him. He was smart as a whip but spoiled rotten. He died young, too, you know. Not even 50 years old. I went to his funeral."

"Really?" said Hank.

"My mother called and told me about it. He became a lawyer, lived in Boston, and that's where the funeral was held. I happened to be in New York at the time and decided to drive up. I'd heard he'd become a bad alcoholic and when I saw him in the casket, I hardly recognized him. He'd had a failed marriage and the funeral was very small, just a few business associates. He had no children, too busy I suspect. His ex-wife was there and his sister, Anna. I shook her hand and told her how sorry I was but she had no idea who I was and I let it go at that. His father had already died, and his mother was apparently too ill to make the trip. Quite a sad ending."

"When did you leave Dubuque?" asked Katie.

"The condensed version? Not long after Jack. I think I was in shock for a couple of weeks, hardly ate anything, seldom left the house and when I did I was scared to death the police would grab me. My mother knew something was wrong but I never told her, of course. Finally I ended up telling our old Irish parish priest, Father O'Malley. I knew he was terribly upset but he hid it pretty well. Actually, he's the one who kept insisting that the man was most likely never killed in the first place. He always suspected I had a religious vocation so he arranged for me to enroll in a seminary in Illinois. After I was ordained I eventually gravitated toward mission work and soon ended up in Africa. It became my life work. I love what I do. I love the people I work with. I love my life. I see it as God pushing me in the right direction and I thank Him every day of my life.

"But you'd be right if you think I still feel guilty. Even after all these years, a day doesn't go by when I don't think of that young black man, his life full of promise, ending up like that. Accident or no accident, I'll always feel guilty because of the part I played. And just like you've probably heard many times before – *I'd do anything if I could change what happened.* If *only* I hadn't gone to Kelly's that night. If *only* I'd headed home instead of to that warehouse. If *only* we'd just let the man go rather than make him come in and drink with us. If only. Yeah, if only."

"Well I think you're being too hard on yourself," said Hank. "Remember, it *was* an accident."

"He seemed quite intelligent, you know," Father continued, ignoring Hank. "Older than we were and appeared completely unafraid of us. I think that's what probably irritated us, Jack the most – that he acted like he was as good as we were. Can you imagine even *thinking* like that now? I remember him saying he was from the south and he had the unlikely name of '*Glory*,' I remember that. Said he worked on a barge. That's all we ever knew about him."

Hank and Katie exchanged quick glances.

"Alexander," said Hank in a quiet voice.

"Excuse me?" said Father Lavarato.

"Alexander," repeated Hank. "His name was Glory Alexander. He was 25 years old, lived in Hardeman County, Tennessee. His wife's name was Elizabeth and they had a baby daughter named Angela."

CHAPTER THIRTY-SIX

After Hank dropped his second information bombshell regarding the specifics of Glory Alexander, Hank and Katie really *did* think Father Lavarato would faint.

He turned and stared at Hank as if he were looking at a ghost, his mouth dropped open and his eyes grew wide. Although he didn't actually faint, it was clear he was once again deeply shocked.

Hank apologized and said he didn't mean to startle him again but somehow in their discussion, they just hadn't gotten that far. He went on to explain by showing him the 'Missing Person' ad in the paper and then told him about his phone calls to the shipping company.

He then dug out copies of the reports the tugboat captain had filed and all the other miscellaneous pieces of information he and Katie had gleaned over the last several weeks.

Through it all Father Lavarato sat silently absorbing it. It was only when Katie told him that her grandmother and her genealogy club were busy running down the family history, and when Hank added they believed there was a good chance they'd be able to find some living relatives that Father Lavarato came alive again.

"My God, I can't believe all this!" he said in a voice mixed with confusion and admiration. After all these years, you two, with no vested interest in this at all, and with the barest scraps of information have managed to piece all of this together. I don't know what you're studying in school but seems to me you have a rosy career waiting for you with the CIA or FBI, or something."

"No," laughed Hank. "We've heard that before, but as we said earlier, Katie is an architecture major and I'm in psychology. It just – I don't know – it captured our imagination and the more we found out, the more we felt the need to see it through to completion."

"And for you, what is 'completion'?" asked Father Lavarato. "Turning me in? I'm guilty – I won't argue that."

"No, Father. That's not why we came," Hank said.

"Bringing closure to his family, the family of Glory Alexander," said Katie. "That's what we'd like to do if we can. Just think, as far as we know his family has no idea what happened to him; why he didn't return home or where he'd gone. Did he fall into the river and drown? For all they knew, he ran off with another woman or just took off and headed west to find his fortune. It must have been heart-wrenching to his wife and daughter waiting for him, not to mention his parents whom we assume were still alive at the time."

"And we suspect there are descendants still alive," broke in Hank. "Family who are wondering the same thing. We know he had a daughter. We know his wife's name, and where they lived. With all the information tools available to people today, I suspect we should learn something soon."

"And if you do?" said Father Lavarato, excited now, "What will you tell them?"

"If you mean, will we tell them about you, that's up to you," said Hank. "Our purpose here today is not to make any judgments. We're merely trying to tie up as many loose ends as possible. We're so far into this thing already, we just want to find out everything we can."

Hank then looked at his watch and said, "I'm afraid we're going to have to leave pretty soon. We have a flight back to Chicago at 5:45 and we should be at the airport at least an hour ahead of time. When are you returning to Africa?"

"Hopefully within the next few weeks. I'm giving a couple more fundraising talks and I'm waiting for a medical report to come ..."

"Are you okay?" asked Katie. "I mean, you're not ill or anything, are you?"

"No, no. Just a few routine tests," he said with a veiled attitude of indifference. "When you get to be my age they never tire of prodding and pulling, always convinced something is wrong with you."

"Will Mariama be going with you?" asked Hank.

"No. Mariama will be staying here," he said. "This will most likely be my last trip to Africa and I don't want to take any chances. Last time we went, there were some awkward questions regarding her papers. I have the feeling they want to keep her there and I can't let that happen. At any rate, I don't plan to stay too long, a month or two at the most. I'm actually going with a new, young missionary fresh out of language school – my replacement. I want to see him get off to a good start. It's going to be difficult for me, though, these people have become my family and I've come to love them very much. I'm going to miss them a great deal."

"I'm sure you will," said Hank. "May I use your phone to call a cab?"

"I'll have Mariama do it for you. But I hate to see you go so soon. I have a thousand questions I'd like to ask you. Can't you stay for an early dinner or something?"

"No, I'm afraid not this time. If I don't get Katie home tonight, her parents will kill me. We can't take a chance we'll miss our flight. But I'll leave you my address and phone number."

When Mariama entered the room Father said, "Mariama, our friends have to leave soon. Would you be so kind as to call a cab for them?"

"Yes, Father."

Before she turned to leave, he said something else to her in whatever foreign language they were using.

"Normally, I make her talk in English," he chuckled. "She needs the practice. She's going to have to get by without me for a while and I know she's a bit nervous. But, as I said earlier she's already pretty good. She's really extremely bright."

"Father, thank you so much for meeting with us," Katie said reaching over to grab his hand.

"That goes for both of us," said Hank standing up and giving him a firm shake. "I promise to keep you informed what we find out, and I hope this whole thing didn't upset you too much. I can just imagine the shock it gave you after all this time."

"On the contrary," he said and smiled. "It's actually taken a lot off my mind. I haven't spoken about this to anyone, other than Father O'Malley – the priest I mentioned earlier, and Jack, and they're both gone. Believe it or not, it feels good to get it off my chest. Usually *I'm* the one who hears confessions," he said, smiling. "But before you go I have something I want to give you. I've had it for a long time and I believe it's time to pass it along."

Mariama returned carrying a small wooden box and handed it to Father Lavarato.

"Here," he said, handing it to Hank. "I want you to take this with you."

"What is it?" asked Hank as Katie moved in closer to see. "It's gorgeous and smells wonderful," she said.

"The box is made of *Tamboti* wood. In my opinion it's one of the most beautiful woods found in Africa. Similar to Sandalwood, but I believe more elegant and has a more persistent and pleasant scent. But it's what's in the box that I really mean for you to have. Go ahead and open it."

Hank worked the lid off and he and Katie peered inside. The box was lined with a lustrous, short napped black fur and contained only a single item; a small square piece of thin metal with writing on it. A hole had been punched or drilled at one corner. Hank lifted it out and handed it to Katie.

"It looks like English," she said. "I can make out the letters, *S. A. M. – SAM!* A name?" Then, "*No. 312. CHARLESTON. 1859* – a place and date?" And finally, "*P. O. R. – PORTER.* What is it?" She looked quizzically at Father Lavarato.

"Remember when I told you that Sean hit Glory with a bottle?"

They nodded.

"I never told you why. Sean was trying to force him to finish drinking the bottle of beer. But the poor guy didn't want to. So Jack and I were holding his arms while Sean was trying to pour it in him. Somehow, during the struggle the young man's shirt got ripped and Sean saw something around his neck and grabbed hold of it to see what it was. When he did, Glory bit down on Sean's hand – deep enough to draw blood. Sean screamed, in great pain, I'm sure, and instinctively swung the bottle and hit Glory in the head. And that was it. I know he didn't mean to really hurt him, Sean just wasn't like that. And kill him? No way. It was purely an instinctive reaction. Later, when we were told he was dead Sean was even more shocked than Jack and I. I could tell he was *really* shaken up."

"And this was around his neck?" said Katie, holding up the item.

"Yes. It was on the floor of the warehouse where Sean had dropped it. I was supposed to throw it away on my way home that night but I forgot and later, when I found it in my pocket, I just couldn't."

"But what is it?" asked Katie turning it over and over in her hand.

"It's a slave tag," said Father Lavarato.

"A what?" Hank and Katie chimed in simultaneously.

"A slave tag, or slave badge. I didn't know what it was myself for years. I was forever curious, of course, but didn't dare show it around or ask anyone. Then one year when I was back in the states I was sent to Charleston to attend a missionary convention. One afternoon a bunch of us went to visit the Charleston Museum and there it was, or at least one very similar to it, sitting in a display case. I was amazed! I later studied up on them and learned that they were issued to slave owners who, at that time in our history, were legally allowed to 'rent out' slaves for short-term employment. Moreover, hired slaves, by wearing a tag, or badge, could be easily distinguished from runaways or free blacks."

"But Glory couldn't have been a slave, he was way too young," exclaimed Hank.

"No, of course not," said Father Lavarato. "All that ended after the Civil War. He was probably wearing it as some sort of 'statement' or 'reminder' of racial inequality or, and I thought of this later, it could have belonged to one of his ancestors. I don't know. All I do know is that he treasured it enough to fight for his life for it. And that's exactly what it cost him."

"But why are you giving it to us?" asked Katie.

"Because somehow I think you'll find a better home for it. I've had it for 60 years. It's your turn now. Find the family. Return it to them."

Just then Mariama appeared in the doorway to tell them the cab was there. Father put his arms around their shoulders and turned and led them to the door.

"I can't tell you both how delighted I am that you two came all this way to see me. I can't believe how you've managed to pull this mystery together. Promise you'll let me know how it all ends, I'll be praying for both of you," he said giving Katie, then Hank a final hug.

"That's a promise," said Hank as they left the house and hurried to the cab, waving goodbye to him and Mariama.

As they pulled away, Father Lavarato smiled and waved back, his arm now protectively over his ward's shoulder. When the cab turned the corner and headed toward the airport they wondered if they'd ever see him again.

CHAPTER THIRTY-SEVEN

Sean Joyce was waiting for them when their flight arrived. They said their hellos – and goodbyes and Hank retrieved his car and headed home. He pulled into his parents' driveway at sunset. A slippery snow had started to cover the ground with estimates of five to six inches by morning. It promised to be a proper setting for the holidays.

He couldn't wait until Katie called him Sunday night – Christmas Eve – after she'd opened the present he'd given her. After vague promises of not spending "too much" on each other, he hoped he'd done the right thing. By now he admitted to himself they were getting pretty serious in their relationship. In fact they'd already had a few discussions that skirted around the idea of long-term permanent relationships, but he wasn't quite ready to give her a ring yet.

His prior relationship with Wendy had ended rather badly. He still felt guilty that he had let it develop into something more serious, at least more serious in *her* mind, than he had ever planned. They dated steadily throughout their junior and senior years and when they graduated and no ring was forthcoming, she made quite a scene.

Was a ring expected? They'd never talked about marriage that he could recall. He liked her well enough but marriage had really never entered his mind. As he looked back on it, he admitted he was pretty naive about the whole thing, and he didn't want to go through that again. So when he returned to school and began his graduate studies, he was pretty reluctant to start dating. And though he wouldn't admit it, he now paid a little more attention to Pete, who seemed to have a sixth sense about women and their "conniving ways," as he put it.

Anyway, this was different. Katie was different. He liked her lively spirit and easy-going ways, her personality and her family. Damn, he thought to himself, perhaps he should have given her a ring after all. Well, too late for that now. He was pretty sure she'd love the pendant.

It wasn't just any pendant. It was an antique pearl pendant set in a rich, ornate silver mounting. His grandmother had quietly willed it to him years earlier when she'd started divesting herself of her collection of antique jewelry acquired over years of foreign travel with his grandfather.

"It's Russian," she had confided to him at the time. "And very old. I found it in a small shop in *Ordu*, Turkey, on the Black Sea. I don't wear it anymore. Keep it until you meet someone special."

He had called her a few days ago and told her of his intentions and hoped it was all right with her. She reminded him that it was his to do with as he saw fit – but thought it was an excellent idea. The clasp had broken on the chain and he'd taken it to a jeweler to get repaired, but other than that, he really hadn't spent much on it.

Christmas Eve. The rest of the family started arriving early in the afternoon. Al and his family arrived around 1:00, followed shortly by his sister, Sarah, and her family.

After dinner, when all the kids had finished and descended to the basement to play, Hank told them about the trip to Philadelphia. They were mesmerized with the story and got particularly excited when Hank showed them the box and contents.

"Holy crap," said Al. "Wait till Gary hears about this. He'll go ape! Can I take it and show him?"

"No way, bro," said Hank. "This thing is staying right here with me. But I'm not heading back until Tuesday, if he wants to get together before then."

It was a mad house; but it was wonderful. Five kids screaming, seven adults *oooing* and *ahhhing*. Ribbons and wrapping paper strewn everywhere.

Hank saved Katie's gift until last. He'd guessed right, it *was* a book but he was totally surprised when he opened it and found a copy of *Babe Ruth: The Idol of the American Boy*. By Daniel M. Daniel, Sports Writer of the New York Telegram. With a Foreword by Babe Ruth. Published 1930.

"Hey, is this cool or what?" shouted out Hank. "Check out this book Katie gave me."

"This *is* great, Hank," his dad said paging through it. "Wow, look at these old photos. Oh boy," he exclaimed. "It's autographed!"

"Yeah, I noticed. By Daniel Daniel," said Hank. "Never heard of him ... "

"No," his dad yelled again. "By Babe Ruth!"

"What?" said Al reaching for it. "Lemme see. If it's really Ruth's signature, that puppy could be worth some serious dough."

Now everyone was crowding around as they checked the signatures. Mr. Torney was right. Both Daniel M. Daniel, the author, *and* Babe Ruth had signed the book; Daniel on the title page and Ruth on a page with his photo.

"Hank," his mother said in an alarmed voice. "Did you know Katie was going to spend that kind of money on you? I know you're fond of each other and all, but really, dear... "

"Mom, relax! I have *no* idea what she paid for it. I'll ask her about it when she calls and ... "

Just then his nephew, Josh, ran into the room and yelled, "Uncle Hank. Phone!"

"That's probably her," Hank said. "Back in a few minutes."

"Oh Hank," Katie exclaimed before he could say a word. "The pendant's absolutely beautiful. It's gorgeous! I just love it. I'm wearing it right now. All the women here are terribly jealous. But we promised we wouldn't spend much money on each other, remember."

"Well, we need to talk about that. The book you gave me ... "

"No matter. You're not getting it back," she broke in. "I'm never taking it off. I'm going to solder the clasp shut and ... "

"Katie! Hold on a minute. I'm glad you like it, but I've got to admit, I really didn't spend that much on it. It used to be my grandmother's and it's really old. She gave it to me a few years ago and all I did was get the clasp repaired. But *your* present is something else! It's great! But it must have cost a fortune. Did you know it's autographed by Babe Ruth? *The* Babe Ruth? And I know it must have cost a mint!"

"Well, you're wrong, too," she said, laughing. "Dad found it in a crate of old books and almost threw it away. All I did was have the binding repaired. You really like it?"

193

"Are you kidding? It's a *collector's* piece. And I really do think it's valuable, with both signatures and all. Not that I'd ever even think of selling it."

"Well, we're even then," she said. "Neither one of us spent very much on the other and we both like our gifts. I'd say we did pretty good."

"Yeah, I guess we did," said Hank relieved. "Did you tell your folks about our visit with Father Lavarato?"

"I did and – ohmygosh, I almost forgot. Grandma wants to talk to us. She won't tell me anything without you being here. Something about what her genealogy club found. She wants us to come to one of their meetings so they can *all* tell us – the *Girls*, as she calls them. Can you come? Maybe on the way back to school? What do you think? Could be kinda fun?"

"Sure, I'm heading back Tuesday. I'll just leave a little earlier than planned and pick you up around noon. Then you could ride back to school with me. Would that work?"

"Hold on. I'll ask."

Hank heard her place the phone down while she left to get an answer. She was back in a moment.

"Grandma says that'll work out great. Mom says to plan on having lunch here and then you and I'll meet with grandma and the *Girls* and leave from their place. Sound okay?"

"Sure. I miss you."

"Yeah, miss you too."

CHAPTER THIRTY-EIGHT

The next few days at the Torney household passed quickly. It had been hectic as expected, but well worth it. The snow had been deep enough that the grandkids had a blast racing down his folks' sloped backyard on new sleds and mini-skis. Of course, this meant helping them put on and take off warm and dry winter gear about every hour. And his mom had insisted on doing it all herself. She loved it, but was clearly exhausted.

Gary Woodard stopped by early Monday afternoon to see the slave tag and get the complete story. He said he'd heard about them before, but had never actually seen one. He was amazed at how things were falling in place and was very complimentary of Hank's efforts.

Around nine the next morning Hank left to pick up Katie. He said goodbye to his folks, packed up his Christmas loot, mainly new socks, underwear, shirts, and such, and backed out of the driveway, waving to his folks. The main roads were clear but the country roads were a little greasy so he took his time and pulled up in front on her house shortly after 11:30. When he got out of the car, he was promptly smacked by a couple of snowballs.

The war was on!

After a fast and furious two-way volley, Hank versus Michael and Brennan, the front door opened and Katie came out yelling at her brothers.

"You guys knock it off. Lunch is ready!" Again, the magic *food* word put an immediate halt to the battle and a headlong rush toward the front door ended in a three-way tie.

"You're as bad as they are," she chided with a grin and quick kiss. "Glad you're here. Merry Christmas!"

Lunch consisted of warm leftovers from what must have been a sumptuous Christmas dinner. Sliced ham and turkey sandwiches, hot dressing, garden salad and two kinds of pie from which to choose.

"I hope this is all right, Hank," said her mother. "Certainly nothing fancy."

"This is perfect, Mrs. Joyce," Hank said. "Hits the spot. Thanks very much."

"Well, you're welcome. I knew you wouldn't have a lot of time. Mother's expecting you both at 2:00 and will be calling here if you're even one minute late. I don't know what you're getting yourselves into but it should be interesting. She's been quite secretive about the whole project and I know she and the *Girls* seem quite excited."

Hank and Katie said their goodbyes and left the house a few minutes after 1:00. The back seat of his car loaded with her stuff.

"Looks like Santa was extra generous this year," Hank said nodding toward the back seat. "You must have been a very good girl."

"Really good," she said, smiling and holding up her new pendant and swinging it back and forth. "Did I tell you I just love it?"

"You did. And I hope I told you how much I and every sports nut in my family was impressed with the Babe Ruth book. I'll have to put it under lock and key to keep Pete away from it."

They pulled into the driveway of *Pine Grove Acres* around 1:45. Built just a few years earlier, the sprawling three-story brick building had been cleverly nestled back in the woods and landscaped to look like it'd been there forever.

"You're going to love this place," Katie said as they parked the car and headed up a circular walkway. "It's more like a mini-country club than a retirement home. And whatever you do," she cautioned as they walked up to a wide set of automatic opening glass doors, "don't refer to is as a 'retirement home' or Granny and the *Girls* will brain you.

Elsie was waiting just inside, all smiles and hugs for both of them. A fire was burning in a massive stone fireplace that took up most of the rear wall, and the pungent smell of pine filled the large room. In the corner stood a huge, tastefully decorated Christmas tree surrounded at the base by a mound of large pinecones. A table covered with plates of Christmas cookies and urns of coffee, spiced cider and hot water for tea lined another wall. And scattered around were comfortable looking easy chairs and couches where small groups of elderly and young alike were chatting away.

Katie fielded several "Hello, Katherines" from some of the residents before her grandmother impatiently grabbed them both by the arms and led them off down one of the side hallways to a cozy meeting room. The *Girls* were waiting.

They entered and found several women sitting around a large oval table, smiling expectantly. Three vacant seats remained along one side for the three of them. It was hard to tell how old they all were, sporting an interesting selection of hair colors ranging from jet black to gray blue to one outrageous orange. But the twinkle in their collective eyes belied their ages at any rate. If they were anything like Elsie, thought Hank, they should prove to be a lively bunch.

"Ladies, you all know my lovely granddaughter, Katherine."

Murmurs and smiles all around.

"And this handsome, young gentleman is her *friend*, Hank."

The ladies giggled and smiled at one another.

"As you may remember," Elsie said, "they go to college together and have come here today to hear what we were able to find out about our assignment."

Nodding toward the ladies as she introduced each one, she said, "This is Gladys Worthington, Iris Snyder, Opal Howard, Mary Buckley, who I understand canceled her hair appointment to be with us today, we appreciate that, Mary, Elizabeth Goetzman, Mae Howes, and Alice Anderson. Jeannie Duffy would have been here but she's in Florida visiting her grandchildren. She'll be distressed when she finds out we had to go ahead without her. But at any rate, kids, this is your team."

"Very pleased to meet you, ladies," said Hank. "Katherine and I are really interested in learning anything you can tell us. We certainly appreciate your help."

He noticed Iris Snyder was black. He couldn't help but wonder what was going through her mind during all this. He didn't have to wait long. Almost immediately she leaned over and whispered something to Elsie.

"Hank," Elsie said. "Katherine told me about your trip to Philadelphia – most interesting. I told the ladies about it earlier. They were wondering if you happened to bring the tag with you so they could see it?"

"You bet," Hank said as he quickly dug into his briefcase and retrieved the box. "Here it is," handing it to Katie.

Katie opened the box, lifted out the tag and placed it on the table while the ladies crowded around, clucking and murmuring.

"This is the man's name," Katie said. "*SAM*, and here's his number, *312*. Here you can see the name of the port town, *CHARLESTON* – the date, *1859* – and the type of job his owner hired him out for, *PORTER*."

The ladies were fascinated and began chatting among themselves, and most likely would still be chatting had not Elsie brought the meeting back to order.

"All Right now, ladies," she interrupted. "We need to get back to business. Hank and Katherine have to drive back to school today, and we don't want them driving in the dark now, do we? And besides I know they're both very anxious to hear what we have to say. So let's begin with a report from Gladys Worthington and Mary Buckley. They, together with Jeannie Duffy, worked on the census records."

Then, with a wide grin, she said, "As they say, girls, let's 'knock their socks off'!"

Clearly, neither Hank nor Katie was prepared for what followed; Hank least of all. He knew enough to appear polite and interested, and he'd certainly be appreciative of whatever they could find but he didn't expect much. After all, they were only a bunch of little old ladies, right?

Gladys and Mary, census gurus, explained that since Glory had been 25 years old when he died in 1940, he had to have been born in 1915. So they began with the 1920 Census, in Hardeman County, Tennessee, the place his wife and daughter were living at the time of his death. However, they said there was a problem right off the bat. Since they didn't know the names of Glory's parents, nor *where* the family lived in Hardeman County, and since the census was not indexed, they had to do a name-by-name search of the thousands of families that lived there.

To further complicate things, they explained, early census records often missed young children and, for all they knew, the Alexander family may not have even lived in Hardeman County when Glory was a child. In other words, they were looking for the proverbial needle in a haystack as Gladys politely pointed out.

Well, Hank thought to himself, at least they tried.

"*But*," Gladys said with glee, "we got lucky. We found them!"

What? Hank and Katie shared startled looks. *Good Heavens,* Hank thought to himself. *They found them? They actually found them?*

Gladys handed them a copy of a Hardeman County census record page and pointed out the highlighted Visitation Number 246 on Page 212 which showed the household of Thomas Alexander, farmer, age 35, living with wife, Abigail, age 32, son, Glory, age 5, and daughter, Marissa, age 2.

"It took the three of us almost two weeks," said Mary proudly, "and just when we thought we were on the wrong track and about ready to give up – there it was, jumped right off the page!"

"Yes indeed," added Gladys, "it was quite a relief. It was actually Jeannie who first spied it. Pity she couldn't be with us today but she's in Florida visiting with her ... "

"Yes dear, her grandchildren," interrupted Elsie, "but we'll be sure she gets proper credit for being such an eagle eye. Now do you have anything else for us?"

"Not at this time," said Gladys, slightly miffed at being cut off so quickly just when she was warming up. "Now if we were working backwards, we could probably trace the family back quite a ways but, if I understood our assignment correctly, we were interested in following it *forwards*, trying to find a present day descendent of Mr. Alexander. Am I correct?"

"You're perfectly correct, dear," said Elsie.

Hank had sat quietly through the last few exchanges but you could tell he was dying to say something and suddenly blurted out, "So did you look for him in the next census? The 1930 Census?"

"Oh, I'm afraid that's impossible, dear," said Mary with a condescending look on her face. "The 1930 census information hasn't been released yet, not until seventy-two years have passed. And even then, it will be some time before the information trickles down to the public."

"I guess I don't understand," Hank said. "Someone has that information already, don't they? Isn't there someone we could call who could look it up for us? I'd be happy to pay, of course."

"No, Hank," said Gladys. "You don't understand, dear. That information *can't* be released until seventy-two years has elapsed. It's the law – a *privacy* issue."

"So it's a dead end? That's as far as we can go?" said Katie in a disappointed voice.

"I didn't say *that*, dear," replied Gladys. "In fact we've learned lots of interesting things about the family. If you look at the census sheet you can see that Mr. Alexander, Glory's father, *owned* his house. That's valuable information. But more importantly, we can tell by looking at the locations of the census taker's visits, both ahead and after the Alexander visit, that the house was most likely situated on a farm near the town of Pineview. That should prove *very* valuable."

"And, for what it's worth," Mary said, "we also found a listing for an Andrew P. LeClaire living on a farm nearby. I believe he was the 'family friend' who went with Glory's wife to pick up his pay from the shipping company. We really weren't looking for the name, but it was so unusual that it also sort of lit right up, so to speak. He was one of seven children living in a rented home in the same general area."

"That's amazing, Grandma. This is excellent information," said Katie.

"Yes indeed, and thank you, ladies, excellent job," said Elsie to a polite smattering of applause as Gladys and Mary smiled and sat down.

"Now's let's hear from Opal Howard and Elizabeth Goetzman and see what *they* can tell us. Ladies?"

"When Betsy and I learned that Mr. Alexander was a home owner," began Opal, an attractive and impeccably dressed, gray headed lady who could have been any age between 55 and 75, "we immediately thought of tracking him down through the tax records. Unfortunately we quickly learned Hardeman County tax records aren't on any databases, so we contacted the Hardeman County Genealogical Society, had a nice chat with some of their volunteers and worked out a trade with them. We agreed that if they would do some local searches for us, we would reciprocate for them when they needed any work done in our area. So we arranged for them to do a quick search of the tax records."

"We gave them the name, Thomas Alexander," jumped in her sidekick, Betsy, who stood, at most, five feet tall, and was wearing a Green Bay Packer sweatshirt and sporting a head of bright orange dyed hair. "We gave them his approximate location and told them he was a homeowner. We asked them to check the county tax rolls starting in 1920 and to fax us the results. We do have our own fax machine here, you know," she added proudly. "We also asked for the names, addresses and telephone numbers of all the cemeteries, and daily and weekly newspapers in the area, especially those most likely to carry news about black families.

"We've got back most of what we asked for within a couple of weeks and we have it all listed in your final report," Opal said, beaming. "We then went back online and checked for any nearby cemeteries that had web sites. We only found one that had indexed burials recorded. Unfortunately we found no hits for the name Alexander. However we suspect there are other cemeteries, especially black only, that would be small and perhaps not in any database at all. Might be something to look into if you ever plan a trip down there."

"Finally," Betsy added, "when reviewing the tax records, we noticed that Thomas Alexander, indeed, owned his house and a small farm of 20 acres. He faithfully paid taxes on the property until 1943. After that date another name appears as owner. As it turned out that led to another key piece of information about which you'll soon learn. And that's all *we* have to say at this point."

"Excellent work, Opal and Betsy, very professional. Now, let's hear from Iris Snyder and Mae Howes, our Public Records Experts. Ladies what can you share with us?"

Iris stood up, smiled and began her report in a very cultured voice.

"I'm afraid Mae and I aren't as proficient as the other ladies with computers. But we're pretty good with *old* technology, especially when its combined with unlimited minutes," she said smiling and waving a bright red cell phone.

"We started calling various departments in the County Seat," she began. "The first thing we were interested in was any death records, and we started with the year 1943. You'll recall that was the last year Thomas Alexander paid taxes on his property."

"We were surprised when we found him right away," continued Mae, the last of the the *Girls* to speak. "Unfortunately, records in those days were very sparse, particularly when it came to black people – sorry about that, Iris."

Iris acknowledged with a wave of her hand and a smile.

"All they could tell us was his death had been recorded on April 15, 1943, at the age of 52 of heart failure. We had hoped there would be additional names we could recognize and, actually, there was one more Alexander, a John Alexander who died "accidentally" on

August 9, 1933, age 11. We assume he was related, but we're not sure exactly how at this point."

"We also found out there was only one weekly newspaper in the entire county," Iris said. "We called the local library in Bolivar and they were gracious enough to check the microfilm of the paper on the weeks covering those dates as well as weeks on either side. Unfortunately, there was nothing of interest regarding the two men. Again, not a surprise for the same reasons mentioned earlier."

"The last thing we checked," said Mae, "were marriages recorded during the early 1900s on up to 1940. And here we were a bit luckier, because we found a listing for a G. Alexander and Elizabeth Johnson in April 1937. Even though his entire name is not shown, we strongly believe it's him, Glory. The 'G' and 'Elizabeth' and the time frame match perfectly. We ran out of time but recommend you order a copy of the license that should show his complete name. We've included the address where you can order it."

"Great job, you two," said Elsie while they received their fair share of polite applause.

"Well, kids,' she said turning to Hank and Katie, "that's as far as we got. What do you think? Anything there you find helpful?"

"Are you kidding?" said Hank jumping to his feet and giving them all his own round of applause. "I'm flabbergasted! I had no idea if you'd find anything at all let alone all this valuable information. I'm really overwhelmed. Thank you all so very much."

All the ladies positively beamed, turning and nodding to one another.

Elsie handed a black folder to each of then and said, "We took all the information, along with supporting documents, and combined them into one folder and here's a copy for each of you. Unfortunately, we weren't able to provide you with names of any *living* relatives, which is what we know you want to end up with. But recapping," she quickly added, "we did manage to find where the Alexanders lived, the names of his parents and the death notice of his father. We also learned the actual date Glory and Elizabeth were married and more importantly, that they were married in Hardeman County."

"That's absolutely wonderful, Grandma," said Katie giving her a big hug.

"Thank you, dear," said her beaming grandmother.

"What do you suggest we do now?" Katie asked. "What do you think are the best next steps?"

"Actually we talked about that and think you have a couple of options," said Elsie. "First you could hire a local genealogist. The downside to that is the expense, and unfortunately, you never know for sure how thorough or accurate he or she has been. On the other hand, they *are* local and should have an idea of the best places to look.

"Or, you can take a trip to Hardeman County and check out some places for yourself; the court house, local black churches; old cemeteries, places like that. Hardeman County is not that large and you might be surprised at what you find. Then, you could always fall back on the local genealogist option if you needed some follow-up research."

After another hour of questions and answers, more 'show and tell' of the slave tag and photos Katie had taken, and after hugs all around with promises to keep them informed, Hank and Katie finally said their goodbyes and headed to school.

"I've gotta tell you," Hank said as they turned onto the main highway, "I hope I'm that with it when I reach their age. I can't believe they found out that much in such a short time. They all seemed so involved and anxious to help."

"Yeah, I know," Katie said. "Mom told me that's all they've been talking about for weeks."

"Well they were great. But tell me, was I wrong in my impression that Gladys Worthington might have been hitting on me?"

"Don't flatter yourself, Romeo," Katie laughed. "She's old enough to be your – sister!"

CHAPTER THIRTY-NINE

All signs of the mild, Midwest winter vanished on New Year's Eve. The first week of January witnessed the beginning of a nasty cold snap that kept students hunkered down inside for days on end. A little snow would at least have made life bearable, but if you could believe the farmers, it was too cold to snow.

Hank didn't mind. He was seriously entangled with several assignments and the preparation of his thesis was hanging heavily over his head. He'd already handed in an outline to his advisor and was looking forward to going over it with him. During the week he and Katie regularly met for lunch or coffee in the Commons and most weekends went to a campus play or a movie and pizza. Katie still helped out at her dad's auction barn almost every week and Hank, schedule permitting, would see her there from time to time.

Pete even seemed to be taking classes more seriously as the school year shifted into the winter semester. He and Hank still managed to get into a few quick basketball games but other than that, Hank noticed Pete's normal late evening carousing seemed to have really tapered off. He was impressed and was sure Amy had something to do with it.

Sundays, Hank and Katie had gotten into the routine of going to church together; one week he'd go with her to Mass at the Newman Center and the next week she'd go with him to St. Mark's Lutheran. He knew that on the weeks she went with him she'd still go to Mass but she never mentioned it, so neither did he.

The "Glory Project" had been put on temporary hold although it was never that far out of either of their minds.

One evening in early January, Hank received a surprise phone call from Lt. Rea from the Dubuque Police Department.

"Hank? This is Lieutenant Rea, how're you doing?"

"Uh, fine. Just fine. How are you, Lieutenant?"

"Great. Wanted to call you and let you know I had an interesting chat last week with a Lieutenant Shaunessy in Chicago. I was there for a convention and he noticed my Dubuque name tag. Never met the guy before. An old-timer."

"Uh huh."

"Well anyway, like I said, he noticed I was from Dubuque, and he asked if O'Brien was a common name in Dubuque."

"O'Brien?" said Hank, perking up. "You mean like Pat O'Brien?"

"Yeah. Said his wife was originally from Dubuque and she was an O'Brien. Said there was a photo of a Sgt. O'Brien on his precinct wall; originally from Dubuque. No relation, he said, but it caught his interest."

"But it was Pat O'Brien?"

"I asked him that. And yes, he thought it was Pat – a typical Irish name he remembered."

"Know what happened to him?"

"Asked him that, too. Said he just remembered seeing it in a grouping of photos of precinct guys that had died in the line of duty and that he'd check and let me know the details. Anyway, he called me back yesterday."

"And?"

"Well, seems Officer O'Brien – 1910-1945 –was killed during a raid on a local Chicago bootleg operation, apparently under very questionable conditions."

"What's that mean?"

"He either didn't know that much or was unwilling to say more except that it usually meant there was something dirty going down and O'Brien was most likely involved. Kind of what we were talking about last time."

"Yeah, sure is. Did he say anything else?"

"No. Except he wondered why I was interested. I told him I was just curious and we left it at that. How are you coming by the way?"

"In school, you mean?"

"In school – and with your project."

"Well, school's fine. Busy of course, I'm finishing up this year. Working on my thesis now. And the project's fine, too, but temporarily on hold. We're making progress, slowly but surely."

"You know I'm still interested, really curious you might say. Anything I can do to help?"

"No, but thanks. And, don't worry. I'll fill you in when I can. It's just too early now."

"Can you tell me if this O'Brien guy was involved?"

Hank didn't reply for a moment and finally said, "Yeah, looks like he was. We suspected as much but weren't sure until we learned he was on the force at the time. Then it seemed to make sense why the crime was never reported. And I might as well tell you, that black guy, Glory Alexander, *was* killed there after all, although under somewhat accidental conditions."

"No kidding! How'd you learn that?"

"Well, I talked to an eye witness."

"You talked to an eye witness! From that long ago? Where in the world did ... "

"I know you're curious and all but I won't say more about it at this point – perhaps later."

After a long pause Lieutenant Rea said, "Fair enough. But you're right. I'm more than curious, and sorry if I bothered you. Just thought you'd be interested in the Chicago angle. You take it easy and study hard now, hear?"

"I will, and thanks for calling, Lieutenant."

"Who was that?" asked Pete who had come into the room just as Hank hung up. "Your friendly neighborhood cop?"

"It was. How'd you know?"

"You don't have that many *Lieutenant* friends. What'd he want?"

"Not much. Wondered if I knew your Social Security number."

"Yeah? What'd you tell 'im'?"

"Told him you'd never worked a day in your life. Never needed one. So he asked me about the project."

"Tell him you ran down one of the guys involved?"

"Yeah, but no names. I suppose we're being too secretive about it, but I think it's best to keep it to ourselves for now. And by the way, Pete, this *is* privileged information, you know. I expect you to respect that, too."

"Yeah, yeah, I know. Don't worry. My lips are sealed!" He proceeded to run his fingers across his mouth like closing a zipper.

"I'm serious. If you ... "

"Hey. I know! Don't worry. Who'd I tell anyway?"

CHAPTER FORTY

Dr. Angelo Pascuzzi's office was on the second floor of the Cambridge House on the north end of campus. Built in 1920, Cambridge House was once a private home the college acquired during an expansion in 1954 and didn't have the heart to demolish. Instead, they built around it and turned it into comfortable offices for a handful of senior staff.

Dr. Pascuzzi was a clinical psychologist who'd given up a lucrative private practice in Chicago ten years earlier in favor of teaching; a decision he still believes was one of the best he'd ever made. Income was no longer a concern of his. Over his career, he'd earned plenty and invested wisely. He now enjoyed a light and predictable schedule that afforded him time to devote to his newest interest – writing "psycho mysteries." He'd been modestly successful and managed to get three novels published in a series that attracted a small but loyal audience of readers.

Dr. Pascuzzi still looked forward to teaching, and Hank was one of the reasons. He'd been an advisor to Hank ever since he'd declared his major and was one of the main reasons Hank had decided to enroll in the master's program. He was now looking forward to meeting with him and reviewing the rough draft of his thesis. He didn't often run into students with Hank's degree of enthusiasm and natural ability. He loved what he'd read and was anxious to see the final product: *The Emergence of the Black Athlete and Its Effect on the American Psyche.*

Where in the world had he come up with that, he wondered? Did he realize what he was getting himself into? If it'd been anyone else but Hank, he would have tried to dissuade him. But in Hank's case, and from what he'd read so far, Pascuzzi believed he could pull it off.

Hank arrived promptly at 10:00, and knocked.

"C'mon in, Hank!"

"Morning, Dr. Pascuzzi," Hank said, entering the office taking off his jacket. "How are you?"

"Just fine, Hank. Take a seat. Coffee?"

"Sure, that'd be great. It's freezing out there. Thanks for meeting with me this morning, seeing it's Saturday and all."

"No problem. I'm usually in here anyway. Cream? Sugar?"

"A little cream. Working on your next book? I'm one of your fans, you know"

Dr. Pascuzzi laughed. "No, I'm not as a matter of fact, but thank you. I've been looking through your rough draft. How long have you been working on it?"

"Well, for the last several weeks, I guess," said Hank. "I've already started writing the final version, but thought I better run it by you before I went too far. What do you think? I mean, do you think it'll be okay?"

Dr. Pascuzzi handed Hank a cup of coffee, placed his own cup on his desk and sat down and stared at Hank. His face became very solemn before he said, "No Hank, I don't think it'll be okay."

Hank's heart skipped a beat. *Oh no*, he thought to himself. *Was I that far off?*

Suddenly Dr. Pascuzzi's face broke out into a broad smile. "Hank. It's not going to be just *okay*. I think it'll be terrific! If the final product is half as good as your draft it'll be one of the best I've ever had the pleasure of reading. And I sincerely mean that. And so do a couple of colleagues I've shown it to. Hope you don't mind."

Hank's look of relief must have been apparent to Dr. Pascuzzi because he quickly added, "I'm sorry. I didn't mean to tease you. But you gave me such a *great* lead in, I couldn't resist. I think it's a terrific subject and I love the way you're handling the time sequences."

"Whew! You had me going there for a minute. Thank you, sir."

"You're welcome. But tell me something, how did you choose this particular subject in the first place?"

"Well, it's something I've been interested in for a long time. Baseball is my sport, you know, always has been. As a kid I remember reading about the challenges the early, black baseball players went through, especially some of the all time greats like Satchel Paige and Jackie Robinson. I've always been fascinated by how they were able to succeed despite having so much going against them. Later, I discovered the same was true in lots of other sports. Jesse Owens in track and field, Arthur Ashe in tennis, Jack Johnson in boxing. There's quite a list. I can't help but think that in my field of sports psychology, I'll be working with athletes of all colors and nationalities, and understanding all I can will be very helpful to me."

"I totally agree with you, Hank. I think it's perfect. How far along are you on your final draft and when do you think you'll have it finished?"

"I'm probably a third finished now, so I'm guessing within the next month or so," said Hank. "I've still got some holes to fill in, and I'm wrestling with the finish a bit, but I plan to be done well before the deadline."

"That's great, Hank. Let me know if I can help. I can't *directly* contribute anything, you understand, but I can sure listen and give my opinions."

"I will. And I appreciate your positive comments. You scared the devil out of me for a minute, you know."

"I know. I'm sorry," he grinned. "By the way, I was talking to your roommate the other evening. He told me an interesting story about you and your lady friend. Is it Miss Joyce?"

"Yes sir. Katie Joyce. You were talking to Pete?"

"Yes. Peter Lang. He's your roommate, isn't he?"

"Yeah, but ... "

"Peter took a sophomore class in business psychology from me a while ago and I've sort of been following his basketball career. He's quite talented, you know."

"Yeah. I've told him I thought he had a good chance of being drafted if he wanted but, well, you've got to know Pete. He definitely loves to play, and he really does have the talent but he's just not interested in the commitment it would take to get in the pros. He said he doubted it would be much fun at that point. And you know, in a way he's right."

"Well anyway," said Dr. Pascuzzi, "I ran into him in the Commons. Told him I was meeting with you today. He mentioned you'd received a great Christmas gift – an old baseball book with Babe Ruth's autograph in it. Is that true?"

"Yes, Katie gave it to me for Christmas. Her father runs an auction house and he found it in an old box of books. I'll bring it over next time we visit if you'd like to see it."

"I surely would. It must be quite rare. I hope you keep it in a safe place. He also said you two were trying to solve an old murder mystery? Something about a racial crime? What's that all about?"

Hank felt a wave of irritation. *What's wrong with that nitwit,* he thought to himself. *Didn't I tell him to keep that to himself?*

"Pete tends to exaggerate a bit, Dr. Pascuzzi. But Katie and I *have* gotten involved in little amateur detective work lately. Probably spending more time that we should be – we're looking now for some folks down south, and they *are* black. We have some information for them we suspect they would appreciate getting. It's kind of a long story and ... "

"No, Hank, that's fine. You don't need to tell me. I didn't mean to pry, it just sounded interesting is all."

Dr. Pascuzzi paused, and then said, "I suspect you don't know this, but did you realize *I'm* part black?"

Hank, momentarily taken off guard, replied, "No – no, Sir, I didn't. I'm sorry if I said anything that might have offended you."

"Not at all. My grandmother was black. A lovely woman, very attractive. She lived in Louisiana and married a Creole gentleman when she was still in her teens. They had four children, including my mother who married an Italian, hence the 'Pascuzzi' name. Most people think I'm Italian and proportionately I guess I mostly am. In reality, I'm a *'quadroon'* – one quarter black."

"Really? *Quadroon?* I've never heard the term before. And you're right. I've always considered you to be Italian."

"Well, I do too. It's not that I'm ashamed of my black heritage. In fact I'm rather proud of all my ancestors. However, I've got to admit that where I grew up, telling people you were part black was not doing yourself any favors. By the time *my* kids came along and grew up, it wasn't that big a deal although they sure didn't want to be called *octoroons* which is what they officially are."

"Octoroons? Sounds like some kind of fancy cookies."

"Just labels people think up. They don't mean much. But it's something you should be aware of when you are dealing with black athletes."

"How do you mean?"

"Well, take Tiger Woods, for example. He's no more black than I am. In fact, he's one quarter black, just like me. He really doesn't want to be labeled as black either, and he's said as much. His father is half black, and a quarter American Indian and a quarter Chinese. His mother is half Thai and a quarter Chinese and a quarter Dutch. And there are other famous black athletes with similar backgrounds.

All I'm saying is be careful with your research. Don't get blindsided by someone out to pick a fight with your results."

"Thanks, Dr. Pascuzzi. That's great advice. To tell you the truth, I really hadn't thought about that aspect of it. Have you ever done any research on your family?"

"Oh my, yes. Are you asking because that's what you and Katie are doing with your research?"

"Well, partially, yes. We're having trouble locating some people. We know where they lived years ago and the time frame in which they lived but we're trying to locate living descendants and aren't sure where to look."

After a brief reflection, Dr. Pazcuzzi said, "Let me give you one suggestion you may find helpful, I know it helped me. First you're going to discover that public records on black people aren't always complete, particularly as you go back toward slavery times. I eventually found one ancestor, for example, listed under 'property owned.' I never did find her in the census records."

"How *did* you find her?"

"Through a church. You see, I learned early on that religion was of major importance to black families in the South. It was their point of connection; the church gave them hope and security and a real sense of community. Still does. So if you're looking for someone you can't find through public records, and you have an idea where they lived, you might try the local black churches, most likely a Baptist church. It may not be the kind of hard, written evidence you'd like. And you may not get it from the pastor. But I've yet to find a black southern church that didn't have at least one person, most likely an elderly woman who may not even know how to read or write but whose phenomenal memory has kept track of the families who've worshipped there over the years. That's where I'd look."

CHAPTER FORTY-ONE

By the time Hank got back to his apartment it was almost dark. He put some soup on to heat, set out some crackers and cheese, and cracked open a beer. After eating he went to the living room and began studying but had a hard time concentrating. He was intrigued about what Dr. Pascuzzi had told him about tracing Glory's family back though local churches.

He went into his bedroom for his "Glory" files to check something and couldn't help noticing things had been moved. He distinctly recalled stacking everything on the corner of his dresser; the folder the *Girls* had prepared, photographs, the letters, newspaper articles, and the box with the slave tag. But when he looked it was obvious things had been shifted around and the box was missing.

"What the hell?" he mumbled.

In a panic he searched through everything again thinking he'd missed it or it'd somehow slipped and fallen on the floor. But it hadn't. It was gone. Someone had taken it.

"Pete!" he said aloud. "I'm gonna kill him!"

Furious, he stomped back into the living room and plopped down on the sofa facing the door. Waiting.

Pete finally returned at 10:30. He entered like a bear, slightly unsteady on his feet, humming to himself and sporting a silly grin. As he locked the door and turned into the living room he jerked to a stop to see Hank sitting there in the dark. Alone. Silent. Staring at him.

"Hank, ol' buddy!" he said, recovering quickly, pleased he had someone with whom he could share his late night escapades. "What's with you up so late. Little past your bedtime, isn't it? You should have been with me tonight over ..."

"Where's the slave tag, Pete?" Hank asked in a low voice.

"What?" Pete said, slightly put off his stride and looking at Hank with confusion – having trouble comprehending the icy atmosphere. "Where's what?"

"The slave tag, Peter." Hank said in a louder, more menacing voice as he stood up and approached him. "Where's the slave tag? It's gone!"

Peter stood still for a second staring at Hank and suddenly, in a terrible flash, it came back to him. He froze and his eyes grew wide as his mouth dropped open.

"Oh damn!" he exclaimed. "I left it at Tank's."

"TANK'S!" shouted Hank grabbing hold of the front of Pete's jacket. "You took it to Tank's?"

"Oh jeez, I'm sorry, Hank," he choked out, raising his hands, palms out. "I didn't mean to leave it. Just wanted to show it to them. I'll go back right now and get ..."

"Didn't I tell you to leave it *alone*?" Hank bored in. "And didn't you *promise* to keep quiet about the whole thing? Everyone seems to know all about it, including Dr. Pascuzzi. And *now* the tag's gone. What were you doing at Tank's and why would you think those nitwits would be interested in a slave tag anyway?"

"Tank had a poker party going," Pete said, stammering, "and Garrison was there and Jackson and well, they're black you know, and I just thought, well, they'd be interested in seeing it. Jeez, I'm sorry, Hank. I shouldn't have done it. I'll go back right now and get it."

Hank could see Pete was obviously very upset and he backed off a little but not much.

"No, you shouldn't even be driving. You're half drunk."

"I walked over. I'll walk back."

"Walked?" Hank exclaimed. Tank's apartment was way on the other side of campus, at least a couple of miles. "No. I'll drive. I want to be sure I get it back." He grabbed his jacket and headed out the door. "C'mon. I can't trust you out of my sight. And I don't trust any of those guys either, that's for sure. You didn't tell 'em what it's worth, did you?"

"Well, I might have said something, not sure," he said, sheepishly.

"Damn it, Pete. You haven't got a brain in your head."

John "Tank" Andrews played center on the varsity football squad. The nickname was appropriate. A walk-on from Springfield High who, during his third year of high school, stopped getting taller only wider. He stood 5'8" and weighed 285 pounds, most of which was solid muscle.

Hank knew Tank, of course. He knew most of the team. Tank was all right; a little slow perhaps, but a nice enough guy. He also knew Mike Garrison and Tom Jackson. Jackson played tackle on defense and Garrison was a running back. They were both from the Chicago area and were known as street smart, in-your-face characters, and seldom seen apart.

They'd both received athletic scholarships and thought quite a bit of themselves; Garrison justifiably so. He was 6'2", a well-proportioned 190 pounds, and fast. According to the instructors Hank talked to, he also did well in his classes.

Jackson was not quite as tall but fifty pounds heavier and had a reputation for playing "to the death" football, showing no mercy to the opponents he went after. But whereas Jackson was universally liked by almost everyone, Garrison had a racial chip on his shoulder that had been the cause of more than one problem on and off campus.

Tank lived in a small apartment with the reputation of being a party place. Most weekends there was a gathering of people there, drinking, playing loud music and generally letting off steam. The campus police knew about it and had been called there several times by neighbors complaining about the noise and general rowdiness. One complaint usually took care of things until the next time.

About once a month Tank hosted a poker party that usually started in the middle of the afternoon and went late into the night. These were more subdued affairs and were normally restricted to the community of jocks on campus. Pete, who loved a good poker game, usually attended. Stakes were kept reasonable and the only cost of admittance was a six-pack. That assured you a seat at a table and an ample supply of chips, pretzels and, occasionally, a couple of Sloppy Joes.

When Hank and Pete walked into the apartment, there was still a game going on. Tank and Garrison and three other guys were deeply absorbed in the middle of a hand. A sizable pile of poker chips was in the middle of the table and a stack of empty beer cans gave witness to some steady drinking. Jackson and couple of other guys were slouched on Tank's couch playing a video game.

Hank and Pete stood mostly unnoticed by the table until Tank finally looked up and saw them standing there.

"Pete my man! Back for more punishment? And you brought fresh blood with you. Pull up a couple of chairs."

"Sorry, Tank," Pete said. "Can't stay. Just came back to get the slave tag."

No one said anything. Tank looked down and began shuffling the cards.

Pete paused a few seconds and when there was no reaction, said a little louder, "Said I came back to get the slave tag. Where is it?" Another few moments of silence before Pete shouted, "Damn it, you guys, where's the tag? It's not even mine – it belongs to Hank. Quit screwing around and hand it over."

Again no one said anything. And just when Pete, who was getting redder by the second, was about to blow up, Hank nudged him aside and stepped up to the table.

"Listen. We've been polite and asked nicely. But if that tag doesn't show up in the next 10 seconds, I'm going to call the police and report theft of a very valuable piece of jewelry. And no one's leaving this room until they come."

At this alarming and unpopular piece of news, heads started to turn and look at each other, but still no one said anything.

"Fine," said Hank. "Pete, give me the phone."

At that point Tank stood up and glowered at Garrison who was seated at the table, smirking at Hank. "Give 'em the damn tag, Garrison," he said. "Just what I need, another visit by the Keystone Kops."

"Like he's gonna keep me from leaving?" said Garrison rising to his feet with a scowl on his face. "I wanna leave, this little man ain't gonna stop me. I'll give him the tag later. I want to show it to a couple of brothers who'd appreciate it for what it is. Something 'Whitey' here'd never understand. C'mon Tom, we're outta here."

Hank immediately stepped between Garrison and the door and said, "That's my property you've got, Garrison. You're not taking it out of here."

"And who's gonna stop me," he said pushing Hank hard. "You keep it up, little man, and you'll *never* get it back."

When Garrison shoved Hank out of the way, Pete moved in and grabbed Garrison before he reached the door. Garrison whirled quickly and took a swing at Pete, who quickly ducked, pivoted and threw Garrison hard up against the wall while twisting his arm up behind his back. He slammed him so hard, his head bounced twice knocking all the pictures onto the floor and shaking the entire house.

Garrison screamed in pain. "YEOWWWW! YOU'RE BREAKING MY ARM – YOU DAMN MANIAC – LET LOOSE!" Everyone stood still in shock. It looked for a second like Garrison's pal was about to leap to his rescue, but Tank quickly froze everyone with a stare and said, "Let 'em have at it."

Hank quickly recovered and said, "Easy Pete. Give him a little air."

"Where's the tag, Garrison?" Pete yelled in his ear. "Give us that tag or I swear to God, I *will* break your ... "

"My jacket," Garrison screamed. "In my jacket pocket."

During the melee Garrison had dropped his letter jacket on the floor. Hank quickly bent down and went through the pockets. The box was there. He checked and the tag was inside.

"Got it. Let him go, Pete."

Quickly, Pete released him and stepped back ready for anything. But Garrison was in no condition to give anyone anymore trouble. He stumbled back and fell on the sofa, moaning and holding his arm. Without another word out of anyone, Hank and Pete left the apartment and headed home.

"Good Lord, Pete, where'd you learn a move like that? He didn't know what hit him."

And, in a rare moment of soul bearing, Pete replied, "He's not the only one brought up in the projects."

CHAPTER FORTY-TWO

By mid-March, winter was starting to release its icy grip on campus and the tantalizing hint of spring was in the air. It wasn't exactly shirtsleeve weather yet, but the ice and snow were mostly gone, and days were warm enough to get by with a light jacket. Winter term was over and exams were finished. After being cooped up inside for several weeks, students were joyously scrambling outside making up for lost time.

Mountain bikes were flashing up and down the streets, baseball gloves were dug out and oiled, and Hank had already competed in his first 10K run of the season; *The Gaelic Gallop*, a St. Patrick's Day romp that was an annual favorite and drew a large crowd of semi-serious runners. He came in 16th out of 223 finishing with a time of 37:58 – an average of 6:07 minute miles. Not his best, but not bad for the limited time he'd taken for training.

Katie, of course, thought it was wonderful!

He'd also finished the final draft of his thesis, and Katie had "volunteered" a friend to proofread and type it for him. All it took was the promise of a deep-dish pizza and a pitcher of beer at *Zoey's*; a pretty slick deal, Hank thought, considering the final draft had mushroomed to 124 pages. With that out of the way, he relaxed a bit and started to enjoy his last few weeks in school.

Then he received a strange phone call.

Pete was in the apartment quietly listening to vintage Dave Brubeck and actually doing schoolwork, when Hank returned after spending most of the afternoon studying in the library. The aroma of home cooking put a grin on his face and notched his appetite into third gear.

"Peter, lad, what culinary surprise do you have in store for your poor old roomie today?" Hank said, lifting his nose into the air and taking in a deep breath. "Something smells wonderful."

"Old fashioned pot roast, complete with potatoes, onions and carrots, Parker House dinner rolls and an apple pie, M'Lord," Pete replied, not looking up from his work.

Surprisingly enough, Pete really was a pretty good cook when he wanted to be which was very seldom. He and Hank usually took turns fixing dinner, but both agreed Hank was kitchen-challenged so Pete fixed the majority of meals. Usually they weren't this fancy – mainly hamburgers, chili, spaghetti, things quick and easy.

Hank realized Pete was still feeling guilty about leaving the slave tag at Tank's, as well as blabbing to Dr. Pascuzzi, so he figured this was his way of saying "sorry". That was fine with him.

"Peter, you're going to make some woman very happy if you keep this up. Now if there were just something we could do about your toilet training."

"Dinner in 30 minutes," Peter said, ignoring the jab. "Wash your hands before coming to the table, and by the way, you got a strange message on the machine. You may want to listen to it first. Sounds like a mysterious lady to me. You're not seeing some foreign exchange student on the side, are you?"

"Very funny. Foreign exchange student?"

"Listen to the message."

Hank threw his jacket on a chair and punched the message button.

Hello. This is Mariama. I wish to speak to Mr. Hank Torney. Please call Mariama when comfortable. My number is 267-342-8945. I say again. 267-342-8945. Thank you.

"All Right," said Pete. "Is that weird or what? Don't tell me that's not a foreign voice."

"Yes, Einstein. But it's not a foreign exchange student. That's the young African girl who's Father Lavarato's ward." He played the message again.

"Sounds scared to death," said Hank. "Bet it's the first time she's made a long distance call. Wonder what's going on?" He dialed the number. After a few rings a woman answered.

"Hello. May I speak with Mariama, please?"

"Who's calling?"

"This is Hank Torney. I'm a friend of Father Lavarato. Mariama called me earlier today and left a message to call back."

"Oh yes, just a minute, please. She's in her room studying."

218

Hank heard the sound of the phone being put down before Mariama's voice came on the line."

"Hello?"

"Mariama? This is Hank Torney calling back. How are you?"

"I am well, thank you. And you? Are you all right?"

"Just fine, Mariama, thank you. Is there something the matter?"

"Father Tom called yesterday. He asked me if I hear from you. I tell him no. He say to call you and say hello and ask if everything is all right. You are helping him with something, is right?"

"Yes, Mariama, I am and everything's fine. I'm working on it, but very busy with school. Who was the lady who answered the phone?"

"That is Mrs. Bevins. She stays with me when Father Tom is gone. Please give me your address."

"My address? All Right. Do you have a pencil and paper?"

"Yes."

Hank gave her his address as well as his phone number at home. He then asked how school was going, and complimented her on her English. They chatted a little and before saying goodbye he asked to speak to Mrs. Bevins again.

"Yes? This is Ruth Bevins."

"Ms. Bevins, is Father Lavarato all right?"

"Just a moment, Mr. Torney."

Hank heard her tell Mariama it was okay and that she could go back and finish studying.

"Father Lavarato called from Africa yesterday," she said, "from a French hospital. And no. I strongly suspect he is not doing well. His cancer has come back."

"Cancer! Oh my. I'm sorry to hear that, I didn't realize – I mean he never said anything about cancer."

"Well, that sounds like him, doesn't it? Hardly will talk about it. Tends to pooh-pooh everything. And even yesterday said he was fine. But I could tell he wasn't. Sounded weak and tired. I know the hospital is quite a trip from the mission and he'd only go there if he were *really* sick. I mean, the mission has its own doctor. I'm guessing the reason he went is he needs special treatment. Anyway, he said he was coming back early and to expect him within a few weeks."

"Does Mariama know?"

"She knows he's got a problem of some kind. I'm not sure if she knows how serious it is, poor lamb. He's all she's got."

"Yes, I know. I appreciate your frankness, Ms. Bevins. Please keep me posted. Mariama has my phone numbers and address, so call anytime if I can help."

"Thank you, Mr. Torney, we will. Apparently Father Lavarato thinks a lot of you. Please remember him in your prayers."

"That was about the priest guy you saw in Philadelphia?" asked Pete. "The African missionary? He's got cancer?

"Afraid so. Doesn't sound good. He's coming back home sooner than planned."

"Bummer. That's why the girl called?"

"Yeah. Wanted to know how I was coming with our project. I'm guessing he's hoping I find some of Glory's family before he, well, before something happens. You know, get the tag back in their hands. Sort of make things right in a way. Damn, suppose I'd better get at it again. I was planning on waiting until this summer, but looks like we may be running out of time."

CHAPTER FORTY-THREE

Easter break seemed to be the logical time for the trip to Tennessee. Hank told Katie about his call from Mariama and his concern for Father Lavarato. He told her he'd decided to move things up and go down earlier than they'd talked about. He also expressed his concern about whether or not he'd be able to get every thing done in one day and thought it might be best if he went alone this time.

"Forget it, pal. There's no way I'm not going," she'd said in a huff. "Even if I have to buy my own ticket. No way."

It wasn't the ticket Hank was worried about. It was the possibility of having to stay overnight that bothered him. They hadn't had to do that before and he expressed his concern about what her parents would think.

"Good heavens, Hank Torney. I'm 21 years old! Don't you think my parents trust me by now?"

"That's not the point," he said. "I want them to trust *me*, too. At least give them a call and find out how they'd feel about it."

Katie's admiration for Hank continued to grow daily. He was so wonderfully old-fashioned and she loved him all the more for it. Apparently her folks felt the same way and readily agreed to her going when she convinced them how strongly she felt – even if it meant staying overnight.

Schoolwork-wise, both were in good shape. Midterms would be over by then and they'd have the time. Hank's only major concern at this point was lining up a job. He'd already taken visitation trips to three different colleges although the two schools he was most anxious to hear from – Northwestern and Notre Dame – were disappointingly silent. He was convinced at this point he wanted to stay in the Midwest, and he was going to hold off on any decisions until the last moment. As far as Katie was concerned, she was a straight "A" student to begin with, and was even more excited than Hank about the hunt for Glory's descendants.

Their flight left on time; a puddle jumper to St. Louis and a short flight from there to Memphis. Hank went ahead and scheduled return flights the same day although he was assured, space available, he could change them if he had to, with a minor penalty. Flying seemed like a stupid way to go and they'd talked about driving the 500 or so miles, but that would take a day just to get there and another day back. Besides, he still had scads of frequent flyer miles, thanks to his grandmother.

By the time they deplaned and arranged for a rental car, it was almost 9:00. They quickly left the airport and hopped on Interstate 240 heading east to Highway 57, the scenic highway paralleling the Tennessee-Mississippi state line. Hank figured it would take them around an hour to reach Pineview.

Their plans were loose. First they'd stop at city hall and the local newspaper. Then, the *Girls* had told them about a small local cemetery. And what Dr. Pascuzzi had said about checking with the local black churches seemed to make good sense to both of them. Other than that, they'd just wing it.

Car windows down, it was a perfect, glorious, warm spring day to be zipping through the magnolia-scented south. With radio blaring, they sang along with the local Top 10 until Hank turned off Highway 57 onto a blacktop road twisting its way through the pine covered countryside.

After a few false starts and stops, they passed a small gravel road intersection with an arrow pointing to "Pineview Cemetery." And when they passed over a shallow hilltop they finally saw a sign: **Pineview, Tennessee. Unincorporated**. The road led down a lovely tree-lined street into the center of town.

"Gee, sure doesn't look very large, does it?" said Katie as they coasted down a gentle incline. "Can't be more than two or three hundred, tops."

"If that much," said Hank. "Let's drive around a little and see what we can find.

Entering the downtown district they drove through slowly. It didn't take long, seeing it was only three blocks long. Several of the buildings appeared closed. Of the ones that were open they spied a hardware store, a cafe, a farm implement store, gas station and bar. And they weren't sure about the gas station. The garage bay was open, but the lights weren't on and the front door was closed.

The Southern Savings Bank on the corner and the Avalon Theater were definitely closed. A few cars and pickups were parked along the storefronts, but there was very little activity as far as people were concerned.

"That didn't take long," quipped Katie as Hank turned the car around. "So much for a city hall and newspaper. Now what?"

"Well," replied Hank sounding slightly discouraged, "let's go back to the cemetery we passed on the way in and check that out first. Then we'll come back and stop at one of the stores, maybe the cafe, and ask around a bit. We'll find something."

Pineview Cemetery was tiny, less than a quarter block square. There was a small gate Katie opened while Hank drove in and parked the car in a shaded parking area.

"It'd be faster to just divide up and walk the rows than try and find where the records are kept," Hank said. "You start at that end and I'll start here."

"Right you are, Commander. Race ya," Katie said and started off in a brisk pace to the far side.

Fifteen minutes later they met in the middle. Neither had seen any familiar names.

"Okay," said Hank. "Nothing here. We need to find a *black* cemetery. Let's find someone to ask." They returned to town and stopped at the cafe – *Betty's*. One car and three pickups were parked in front. They entered and headed to the counter. Along the right wall were a few booths, one of which held four men drinking coffee and talking. They looked up and nodded. A young girl and an elderly lady were sitting at a small table in front.

"Morning," smiled a middle-aged waitress walking toward them. "How're y'all doing? I'm Betty."

"Just fine, thanks, Betty," said Hank. "Couple of coffees, please."

"You betcha. Got a fresh pot right here," she said, turning to the back wall and grabbing a pot in one hand and a couple of cups in the other.

"Hah. Betty's idea of fresh coffee is 1995," quipped one of the men in the booth; all of whom had stopped to watch the strangers. The others snickered.

"Just can it, Ralph," said Betty. "I see it hasn't slowed you down any. You're on your what, third refill? No wonder I'm not making any money in here."

That, of course, set the other three men off and they all started in on poor Ralph.

"Don't pay 'em any mind," she said. "This is hot *and* fresh." Then in a louder voice and a nod of her head she said, "I save the drippings for the likes of them who don't seem to know the difference."

"Tastes just fine," said Hank as he sipped the hot coffee. "Thank you."

"You're welcome. What brings you to Pineview? Are you lost or something?"

"No, not lost. We're looking for any old cemeteries in the area."

"Cemeteries? Well, there's Pineview Cemetery. Right on the edge of town."

"Yes, we stopped there already. I'm wondering if you know of any others nearby."

"Looking for some relatives? What're their names?"

"Last name's Alexander. And, uh, we're not related. These are *black* folks we're looking for."

Of course, everyone in the cafe had been listening intently to the conversation and as Hank said this, all eyes in the restaurant turned to one of the four men sitting in the booth, who just happened to be black.

"Black folks? Alexander?" asked the black man who now took center stage.

"Yes sir – Alexander," answered Hank turning around.

"Don't know any Alexanders. When they die?"

"Well," said Hank, "I know they lived around here some 60 or 70 years ago. And I know *some* of them died here since. Actually, we're trying to find any *living* family members. Thought we'd start by checking names in the cemetery."

"Wow," he said, turning and looking at his friends. "That's going back some. I'm not surprised you didn't find any in the city cemetery. You need to find an older black cemetery."

"How about that little ol' cemetery back in Jordon's Grove, Henry?" offered one man. "That's an old 'un."

"No," said Henry. "I know 'bout that one. That's a private place for the Tanger family. All white folks. But I do know of one old black cemetery. Has no name that I know of, just an old metal sign that says, "Cemetery" – down Jackson Hollow road. Backs up to a thick timber 'long Bush Creek."

His friends looked blank. So did the waitress.

"*Eden's Rest*," piped up the little old lady sitting at the table.

Everyone turned and stared at *her* now.

"What's that, Mabel?" said Betty.

"Name of the cemetery. *Eden's Rest*. My mama had an old colored washer lady who's buried there. Lived out back of our place for years. Good old nigra, she was, too."

"Yes, well thank you, Mabel," said Betty. "But I believe we call them black folks now-a-days."

"Black, colored, whatever. You know what I mean," she said in a small huff.

"*Eden's Rest*, then," said Henry, rolling his eyes to his friends. "Might be hard to find, though. You know your way around these parts?"

"No, we're just visiting. From up in Illinois, but we've got a county map," said Hank pulling out a folded up piece of paper from his shirt pocket and smoothing it out on the table.

They all looked at the map before Henry said, "Well hell, half the roads aren't even shown there, but it's just about – here." He marked the map with a small "x."

"There's a little gravel road you turn on here," he said, drawing in a dotted line. "And there's a Dead End sign where you turn. I deliver propane to an elderly couple that lives just off the gravel road. Name on the mailbox is Wilson. Cemetery's on down the road past their place 'bout a quarter section or so."

"Thank you very much. We appreciate it," said Hank.

"Glad to help and hope you find who you're looking for."

"Yeah, so do we. You don't happen to know of any black churches in the area?" added Hank hopefully.

"Well, I go to the Methodist Church here in town. There are a few other black folks that go there, but it's not very old, fifteen or twenty years, I'd say," said Henry looking at his friends.

"Built 1987!" one replied.

"I suspect you're looking for an older church, right?" asked Henry.

"Yes, sir. At least fifty years old."

"Well then I'd try Ebenezer Baptist," he said, reaching for the map again. "It's not far from the cemetery, maybe a mile or two, right about – here." He marked another "x" on the map and handed it back to Hank.

"It's a nice little church and pretty old, I believe. Have some friends who go there. You won't have any trouble finding it. Pastor lives in the house just off to the side."

"Thanks again," said Hank. "You've been most helpful."

"Yes, thank you *all* very much," added Katie.

They paid for the coffee, said their goodbyes and left. Little did they realize how much diversion their little stop provided for the locals who would spend the rest of the morning and part of the afternoon discussing what in the world two, young, white Yankees were doing in Pineview looking for old, dead, black folks.

The possibilities seemed endless.

CHAPTER FORTY-FOUR

There was no way in the world Hank and Katie would've found *Eden's Rest* without a map. And even then, they almost missed the gravel road that sloped down toward rich, freshly tilled bottomland.

"This *must* be Jackson Hollow road," said Katie studying the map. "But I didn't see any sign, did you?

"No," said Hank, "but this *has* to be it."

With a joint sigh of relief, they soon passed the Wilson farm. In another half mile they came to the cemetery. An old metal sign was nailed to a tree by the road. It read "Cemetery" just as Henry remembered.

It *was* small, not much bigger than a good-sized yard; maybe a couple hundred feet on each side. Bordered on the north by a plowed field and on the other three sides by a thick stand of rough timber, it was completely enclosed by a short, mostly white, picket fence.

Hank pulled over and stopped. "Looks like someone takes care of it pretty well," he said. "Least it's mowed, and the fence is standing."

Katie was already taking pictures. Ever since their first trip to Dubuque, she'd been visually recording all the people and places they've visited, including their meeting with Father Lavarato and the *Girls*, and an occasional, interesting old home.

"Let's walk it together. Shouldn't take long," suggested Hank.

Henry was right, it *was* an old cemetery. Several headstones showed dates back into the early 1800s. Walking slowly through the rows, they found several unmarked graves, and several with broken and illegible headstones. It was when Hank was bending down trying to decipher one of them that Katie yelled out.

"Hank, over here. Think I found something."

Hank rushed over and saw a particularly well cared for plot with three headstones. "Thomas Alexander, 1885 – 1942," he read, excitedly. "Abigail Alexander, 1888 – 1954. John Alexander, 1922 –

1933. Bingo! I think you found them! Those names sound familiar all right. But who's John?"

"I don't know. Brother or cousin maybe? I think I remember Iris mentioned a John Alexander listed in the County Death Records. Gosh, he died awful young, only eleven."

"I'm going to get the folder," said Hank. "We need to check those dates and names against the census report."

Katie started taking more pictures.

"That's them!" he yelled as he ran back with the report in his hand. "Names and dates match exactly. Can you believe it? Thomas and Abigail were Glory's parents and John is probably his brother. He was born after the 1920 census was taken so he wasn't recorded. We know Glory was born in 1915, so he'd have been five years older. What do you think?"

"It fits," agreed Katie. "But didn't he have a sister?"

"Yeah. According to the report he had a younger sister, Marissa, who was two years old when the census was taken, so she'd been born around 1918 or so."

"But if *she* got married, her name would have changed to her husband's and she would have been buried with him, assuming she's dead, of course."

"That's right. But she *could* still be alive," Hank said.

"Looks like someone's been taking care of these graves on a regular basis," said Katie. "Could be her. As long as we're here, let's split up and see if we can find any headstones with the name, Marissa 'Whoever.' Not sure how it will help, but it'd be another clue for us to check on."

They had almost completed their search when Katie yelled out again.

"Hank, over here."

"Find her?"

"No, but look at this headstone. Remember him?"

"Andrew P. LeClaire. 1914 – 1978," he read out loud. "Well, I'll be. That's the guy who worked with Glory on the tugboat. Andy LeClaire."

"That's right!" Katie said. "The same guy who later went with Elizabeth, Glory's wife, to pick up his paycheck. Wow! Look at all the other LeClaire names. A large family."

"Now we're making some headway. Let's go find that church."

Ebenezer Baptist Church was easier to find than the cemetery. And from the number of cars and pickups parked outside, it seemed they'd picked a good time to visit. Unlike the cemetery's weatherworn picket fence, the church fence sported a freshly painted, sparkling white look.

The building itself was snuggled back in a copse of dark green pines. Lining the front were two large magnolia trees along with several azalea bushes, all in full bloom. A sign was embedded in the lawn along the front walk.

Ebenezer Baptist Church. Serving God's Children Since 1863. Sunday Services: 9:00 AM. Wednesday Prayer: 7:00 PM. Brother Luther Pittern, Pastor.

"Wow, how lovely," Katie said. "And looks like someone's there. C'mon."

They opened the front door and walked inside, where several ladies were busy cleaning, washing windows, arranging fresh flowers and chatting away in robust good humor. Of course, everything came to a screeching halt as they spied Hank and Katie walking up the aisle toward them. They got almost to the front before one of the ladies smiled and said, "Well, hello there. Can we help y'all?"

"Yes," said Katie. "We're looking for Pastor Pittern. Is he here today?"

"He surely is. Just in back. I'll go fetch him for you."

"Thank you," Hank said, smiling. "Uh, lovely day, isn't it?"

There were general smiles and murmurs of assent from them all. Yet no one moved. Everyone just stood in place and stared at them as if they might have just stepped naked off a spaceship.

Shortly, a handsome middle-aged man came in through one of the rear doors, unrolling his shirtsleeves and generally straightening his appearance as he broke into a smile and approached them with his hand stretched out.

"Welcome to Ebenezer Baptist Church. I'm Pastor Luther Pittern. I apologize for my appearance, but we've been busy cleaning all morning."

"Pleased to meet you, Pastor Pittern. I'm Katherine Joyce and this is Hank Torney. And please, don't apologize. The church looks lovely, absolutely beautiful, especially with all the fresh flowers."

"Getting ready for Easter, you know," he beamed. "We'll all be celebrating Jesus' triumph over the grave. And thanks to the hard work of all these Sisters we're getting His house spic and span. Now, I have the strangest feeling you folks aren't from around here. Am I right?" The Sisters got a kick out of that.

"No sir," said Hank. "Just visiting from Illinois."

"Is that right? Come all this way. Tell me what I can do for you."

"Well, Pastor Pittern," said Hank. "Katherine and I are college students working on a research project. We're looking for some folks who used to live around here. At least their *family* was from around here."

"I assume these are *black* folks you're looking for?" he asked and then noticed all the ladies were slowly closing in to hear better. "Now, Sisters, please continue with your holy work," he gently admonished. "Things looking fine. Mighty fine."

They backed off some and halfheartedly continued their chores, but kept silent and focused on this interesting and totally unexpected visit.

"Yes sir," Hank said as Pastor Pittern turned back and smiled, satisfied they'd get at least a modicum of privacy. "The last name's Alexander. We just came from *Eden's Rest* cemetery and found three of them buried there. Do you have any Alexanders who attend church here?"

"Alexander?" His face pinched up in heavy thought. "No. I can't say we do. And the name's not familiar to me, either. When did they pass, the folks you found in the cemetery, I mean."

"The earliest burial was in 1933, and the most recent, 1954," said Katie referring to her notes.

"Oh my. That's way before my time," Pastor Pittern said. "The church has been here since Civil War days you know, but I've only been pastor for the past six years."

"Are there any records we can look at?" asked Hank.

"None that go back *that* far. I understand there were old records at one time, but they were lost in a fire quite some time ago. Pastor Johnson, who preceded me, started keeping new records in 1985. I'm pretty familiar with *them* but don't recall any Alexanders. But let's ask the ladies. I know some of them have been attending here for a good long time."

Pastor Pittern ushered Katie and Hank up toward the front and said, "Sisters, I'd like you to meet our two guests, Katherine and

Hank. They're college students from up north. They've come all this way looking for some folks who used to live in these parts. I don't recognize the name, but perhaps one of you might."

He then turned and smiled at Hank, nodding to go ahead and ask.

"Uh, good afternoon, ladies. We're looking for any family members with the name Alexander. I know they lived here back in the '30s, '40s and '50s."

The ladies looked quizzically at each other and murmured among themselves, but no one volunteered anything.

"We just came from *Eden's Rest* cemetery," he added, looking down at his notes. "We found graves of a Tom Alexander who was buried there in 1942, his wife, Abigail, buried in 1954, and a young man, John, age 11, buried in 1940. Any of those names sound familiar?"

Again, all they received were some sympathetic stares and shaking heads. Pastor Pittern gave them a few moments to think about it but it was apparent the name was not familiar.

"I'm sorry," he said, "but there's another cemetery in Pineview you might try."

"We've already been there, Pastor," said Hank. "No Alexanders."

"Well, leave me your name and telephone number and I'll ask around. Maybe there's some ... "

"Excuse me, Pastor," interrupted Katie. "May I ask the ladies something?"

"Certainly, child. You go right ahead."

Katie turned to the ladies and asked, "Do any of you know any LeClaires?"

Again, blank stares until finally one of the ladies timidly ventured, in an uncertain voice, "I guess I knows some LeClaires."

"Sister Dorothy. Excellent! Come on down here, dear," said Pastor Pittern.

Then, to the general dismay of the other ladies, he said, "Please, let's go to my office where we can be more comfortable."

Sister Dorothy was a heavyset, sixty-something lady dressed in a green cotton print dress and apron, long black stockings and sensible shoes. She laid down her duster, turned and gave her friends a triumphant smile and followed Pastor Pittern as he ushered them into a small office in the front part of the church.

The looks of disappointment on the remaining ladies were painful to see.

"Sit. Please sit," said Pastor Pittern as they entered a small but tidy office. There was a desk, two or three file cabinets, and shelves filled with books. A small conference table with several chairs sat off to one side. Once they were all settled he continued, "Now then, I assume the LeClaires are kin to the Alexanders?"

"Not kin, we don't believe," replied Katie, "but we know they were close friends at one time and we found quite a few LeClaire headstones in the cemetery."

"Sister Dorothy," Pastor Pittern said, turning to face her. "You say you know the LeClaires?"

"Yes, Brother Pittern. Least ways I know Henrietta LeClaire *Tucker*. She lives with her mama down by the *Hatchie*."

"And Mr. Tucker?"

"He be gone, Brother Pittern. Long gone."

"I see. Church going people?"

"Old Mandy was at one time. She's the mama. But she's all feebled up these days. Hardly gets out of the house any more."

"So you're friends with these folks?"

"I stops by now and then. Sometimes takes 'em a pie, or maybe some chicken. They lives – well, kinda simple like."

Turning to Hank and Katie he asked, "Sound like some folks you'd like to visit with?"

"Yes sir, absolutely," said Hank.

"Well then, let's give them a call and see if there're home," he said starting to reach for his phonebook.

"They ain't gots no phone, Brother Pittern," Sister Dorothy said. "I ain't even sure they gots 'tricity. Like I say, they lives kinda simple like."

"I see. Well, can you tell these nice folks how to get to their house?"

Sister Dorothy stared at Hank and Katie for a while and said, "No. I don't think I can. Not even sure I could tell *you*, Brother Pittern. It's kinda – well, tucked away some."

"Well then, I don't see how ... "

"But I can take 'em – it ain't fur," broke in Sister Dorothy. Then she looked at Katie and asked, "You bring me back?"

"Absolutely," said Katie.

"Well, let's go then!" she said and was up and out the door before another word could be spoken.

CHAPTER FORTY-FIVE

The roads got narrower and narrower as they drove. Sister Dorothy, sitting up front, was steadily feeding Hank directions.

"Take the next right, Mr. Hank. Best slow down here, bad bump. Turn left here. Take it slow. Mind the chickens ..."

She was right about one thing. There was no way they could have found it on their own. After 20 minutes of bouncing down broken up tarmac roads that eventually turned to gravel which soon became dirt lanes, they still weren't there.

"All Right, Mr. Hank, slow way down now. There's a little rutty lane right ahead on the left, hard to see, there! There tis! Turn down there and take it real easy. Gets kinda bumpy from here on. A short ways is all."

Hank didn't have to be told to slow down. The lane was barely wide enough to admit the small rental car. Dense bushes brushed the sides as they bounced and wobbled along until they came to a small clearing. In the middle stood a small wooden house.

"Best stop here," advised Sister Dorothy. "We'll just sit a spell."

The second they pulled into the clearing, the sound of barking dogs shattered the rural silence. Hank could see a large, fenced pen with what looked like a dozen, large hounds jumping up against the side of the house, frantic to get out.

A young man came around the other side of the house and stopped when he saw the car. He was dressed in ripped jeans and a dirty tee shirt and was holding a large wrench in one hand.

"That be Jesse," whispered Sister Dorothy. "He a bit slow."

In another moment or so, the front screen door opened and a woman stepped out on the porch and stared at the car. She was very dark, her hair tied up in a small bun. She was wearing a brown nondescript dress and apron. She turned to the boy and said, "Jesse, quiet them hounds."

"That be Henrietta," said Sister Dorothy, "Jesse's mama."

The young man looked over to the pen and said something too soft for Hank to make out but the dogs immediately settled down. Another word and they went around the side of the house and out of sight. The house itself looked very rustic – part log and part rough-hewn pine boards. It was a low slung, one-story affair, with a porch stretching clear across the front. Sitting on the porch was a small wooden table and a few mismatched wooden chairs.

A large stone chimney interrupted a colorful, multi-patched shingle roof. A fire was burning and a wisp of smoke escaped into the air. The two windows on either side of the front door were framed by white curtains with flowerpots showing from inside.

The yard was bare, hard-packed dirt, but smooth and freshly swept. On the opposite side of the house from the dog pen was a large vegetable garden. It appeared well tended and already showed tiny, leafy rows. A crudely constructed chicken coop stood off to the other side with its gate open. Several hens were out scratching.

Sister Dorothy told Hank and Katie to stay put and she got out of the car, waved a greeting and walked up to the porch. They could see her smiling and talking to the woman, and turning back and nodding toward the car. After a minute or two, she waved for them to come on up and join them.

"Henrietta," she said as they approached the porch. "This here is Hank and Katie, friends of mine from up north."

"Pleased to meet you, Henrietta," said Katie. Hank nodded and smiled.

"Come sit," the petite woman said, gesturing toward the table and chairs. Unsmiling. Uncertain. Wary. "I'll fetch some sweet tea." Turning to the boy who was standing quietly nearby watching with wide eyes she said, "Jesse, that well fixed yet?"

"No, mama."

"Get to it then. We be needing water tonight."

"Yes'm."

As the boy turned and left, staring at the newcomers all the while, Henrietta entered the house. The three of them sat at the table.

"Best let me talk first," said Sister Dorothy in a soft voice. "They a little skittish with strangers."

In a short while Henrietta returned with a tray of fruit jar glasses and a large pitcher of tea. She didn't say anything, just poured out the tea and sat down and began quietly sipping and staring at Hank and Katie.

"Jesse look fine, 'Etta. A good looking boy, how old he be now?" said Sister Dorothy.

"Fifteen last month. Don't talk much, but he can fix 'bout anything that needs fixing. Eats like a mule, though," she said with a small smile.

"Ain't dat the truth," laughed Sister Dorothy. "Knows what you mean, hard to fill 'em up at that age. How's your mama?"

"Poorly last week. Doing better."

"Well, that's good. That's good. Fine looking garden. How many tomatoes you put out this year?

"'Bout a dozen," said Henrietta, warming up a little. "Last year we had so many ... "

"What's all the racket?" interrupted a scratchy voice from inside the house. "Can't an old lady take a nap in peace no more?"

"Mama's up," said Henrietta smiling. "I'll go fetch her."

Henrietta went back into the house and soon came back helping a little slip of a woman out the door. Couldn't have weighed 75 pounds soaking wet, Hank thought. White hair pulled back in a tight bun, old-fashioned black wool dress, heavy, grey wool stockings and well-broken in slippers. Hank jumped up and got a chair for her. Sister Dorothy stood up and smiled.

"Hello, Mandy. How you doing? Heard you were feeling poorly last week."

"Well, my goodness, lookee here," the old woman cackled. "It's Dotty. Was that you making all that noise? And who you got widsha, some kin folks?" she said, cackling again.

"Now you stop joshing, Mandy," said Sister Dorothy, smiling. "This here be Hank and Katie. They friends from up north."

"Well sit down. Sit down. What's you up to these days anyhow. I gots a feeling there's a story coming. I like stories."

They all settled around the table again making small talk until Sister Dorothy eventually got around to telling them how Hank and Katie had earlier stopped by the church looking for information on an Alexander family. She told them how no one at the church knew any Alexanders. She also told them how they'd been to the old cemetery and had found some Alexanders buried there. LeClaires, too, who they believed were friends with the Alexanders.

"Well, I didn't know any Alexanders," continued Sister Dorothy. "But when I says I knows some LeClaires they say they like to meet widsha. Hope that was all right – I bring 'em and all."

The two women had been sitting quietly listening and staring at both Hank and Katie during all this. When Sister Dorothy finished there was complete silence.

Finally, Mandy asked, "You folks like crawfish gumbo?"

At first Hank and Katie were thrown by the shift in the discussion, but soon discovered that *You folks like crawfish gumbo?* wasn't a rhetorical question. Apparently they'd been invited for lunch.

They were at a loss of what to say but Sister Dorothy quickly accepted for all three of them while giving little nods of assurance to let them know that this was a good thing.

"But what about the Alexanders?" Hank asked her quietly.

"She thinking on it," Sister Dorothy replied. "Don't rush. Might as well relax and enjoy things. You in for a treat."

Sister Dorothy was right again. Without apologies for the chipped bowls or mismatched tableware, they were soon served steaming bowls of crawfish gumbo, hot cornbread with whipped butter and more sweet tea. Hank later admitted it was one of the best meals he'd ever had. Even Katie, who wasn't even sure what a crawfish was, enjoyed it enough to have a small refill.

Not a word had been mentioned about the Alexanders. The bowls and plates were removed and glasses refilled with sweet tea.

"Sorry we got no ice for the tea," said Henrietta. "Cooler's acting up some."

"No, please," said Katie. "It's wonderful just the way it is. Everything was absolutely delicious." Hank nodded his agreement vigorously.

"Why you think the Alexanders and LeClaires were friends?" asked Mandy, clear eyed and staring at them, all business now. Hank sensed the moment of truth had arrived. He needed to be careful.

"Well, in the research we're doing, we found some papers that showed they were very close."

"What papers?" Mandy asked, her eyes suspicious again, boring into his.

"Well, um, some old papers from a tugboat company. A company that they both worked for," he said.

"Who's they?" she said, boring in.

Hank, who was not expecting this direct line of questioning paused and said, "Well, it was a long time ago and ... "

"Andrew LeClaire and Glory Alexander," blurted out Katie observing Hank's discomfort. She decided it was not the time to be secretive.

The effect of Katie's revelation was immediate. The old lady jerked back and she looked at her daughter, then with widened eyes at the three of them. "Glory Alexander!" she exclaimed. "Heavens to Betsy, there's a name I haven't heard in a month of Sundays!"

"You knew him?" said Hank, excitedly.

"No," she said in a sad voice but I did know 'bout him. "But I knowed Andrew better. 'Course we called 'im Andy!" she said, chuckling.

"Were you related?" asked Hank.

"Suppose you can say that. Was married to 'im for 32 years!"

"Andrew LeClaire was your husband?" said Katie with surprise.

"Yes indeedy. I be wife number three. The other two punied up and died."

"He and Glory Alexander *were* friends, weren't they?" Hank said after the shock had worn off.

"They were but I never met 'im. Andy told me 'nough 'bout 'im, though. Told me he come up missing when them two was barging up river. But I knew Lizzy, his wife. And Issy, his sister, *we* was good friends. Her name Marissa. We called her Issy."

"What happened to them?" asked Katie.

"Well, Issy married up and moved away. She passed now."

"And Elizabeth, his wife?"

"Lizzy? She passed, too. Almost five years. She stayed around for some time after Glory went missing. Tried hard to find him. 'Specting him to show up one day, but he never did. Andy said it done broke her heart. Then, when Glory's folks died, she left the farm and moved up to Bolivar for work. Needed the money, I 'spect. She had two small childs to raise. She come back now and then to tend the graves and all, and she'd usually stop to visit."

"Two children? So that's *her* son, John, who's buried here with Glory's parents?" asked Hank.

"John?" said Mandy quizzically squeezing up her face deep in thought. "No, no," she said, finally figuring out what he was talking

238

about. "John was Glory's *brother*. Got 'imself kilt riding an ol' mule in a dern thunderstorm. Lightning kilt 'em both."

"But you said Elizabeth had '*two* small children to raise," said Hank, getting more confused by the minute.

"Dat's right. Lemme see, there was Angie – Angela, must have been around four when she left and Tommy be around two."

"What? Tommy? Glory had a son?" exclaimed Hank.

"Why didn't I just say dat? Lordy, boy, you gots to listen up better. Sure, he had a son. Tommy. Course I 'spect Glory never knew dat. Baby come after he went missing."

Hank and Katie looked at each other speechless. Everything was coming at them faster than they could absorb it. Locks were being opened and, as it turned out, this simple, old black woman was the key just as Dr. Pascuzzi had predicted.

"Why you two care 'bout Alexanders anyway?" asked Henrietta, getting a little nervous. "I know you ain't kin."

This time there was no laughter.

"We have something to give to them," said Katie.

"Is it something they want?" asked Mandy.

"Yes, I think it is," said Hank. "We been looking for them for some time now."

"You know what happened to Glory, don't ya?" asked Mandy looking at them carefully now.

"Yes," said Katie. "We know."

"Glory's dead, ain't he?" she said, unfazed.

Katie looked at Hank for a second and said, "Yes ma'am. He's dead – a long time ago.

"Do you know what happened to Angela?" Hank asked.

Mandy sat quietly. Then she turned and looked at Henrietta who shrugged with a "might as well tell them" look. Finally, she sighed and seemed to make up her mind.

"Angie go up in Bolivar with her ma. Heard years later she was married. Dat's been quite a spell now."

"Do you know who she married? Could you tell us her husband's last name?" asked Katie.

"No I can't. Least ways I can't say if I ever did know." She looked at Henrietta who merely shook her head.

"And Tommy?" said Hank with apprehension.

"Mr. Tom, now. Izzy bring him to visit one time. He drivin' a great big ol' black car. Tried to come down the lane yonder. Got stuck in the mud good," Mandy said, smiling. "Jesse had to hook up old Jack and John to pull him out. 'Dat was years ago and he ain't been back since."

"Do you know where he is now?" asked Hank.

"Heard he still lawyers up in Memphis," she replied. "Must be doing right well driving a big ol' black car like that."

By the time Hank, Katie and Sister Dorothy left the LeClaire's porch it was after 2:00. The exhilaration Hank felt after their visit was tempered by the fact they had less than five hours before their return flight.

Sister Dorothy was beside herself with curiosity, and on the ride back to the church tried every which way she could to pry out of them the rest of the story. It was to no avail. Hank and Katie had earlier decided how far they'd go revealing things. They'd already stretched things at the LeClaire's, but felt they'd still maintained the integrity of the family secret.

When they finally drove up to the Ebenezer Baptist Church, the cleaning crew was just filing out the front door. Hank helped Sister Dorothy out of the car and thanked her heartily for her help. Katie gave her a great big hug.

As they drove off, Sister Dorothy waved, turned and strutted toward her flabbergasted friends with a wide grin on her face, undoubtedly assured of several weeks of major bragging rights.

CHAPTER FORTY-SIX

"Where to now?" said Katie as they turned onto the main blacktop. "Bolivar or Memphis?"

"Memphis," Hank said. "Since Marissa's already dead, Tom's our best bet. Let's just hope he's still there. Besides we have to go there anyway. Remember, our flight leaves at 7:15 and it's the last one. If we have to stay over, I'll need to alert the airline soon. By the way, that was brilliant of you to think of asking the church ladies about the LeClaires. We might have been at a dead end right there if you hadn't thought of that!"

"Well, thank you, Mr. Torney," she said as she slid over to give him a quick kiss on the cheek. "You were pretty brilliant yourself."

They arrived at the outskirts of Memphis by 3:15. Hank exited the highway into a small strip mall and pulled up to a phone booth. They'd decided to call the Chamber of Commerce and ask for information about any lawyers in Memphis with the surname Alexander, or preferably, any lawyers with the name Thomas Alexander.

"Good afternoon. Memphis Chamber of Commerce," a chipper voice said.

"Good afternoon, m'am," Hank replied. "I wonder if you can help me. I'm from out of town and looking for Thomas Alexander, a lawyer here in Memphis."

"Please hold a minute. I'll look through our directory." After a short pause, "It looks like we have four Alexanders who work for law firms here in the Greater Memphis area, and two of them work for the same firm – *Alexander, Williams and Pearson*. And yes, one of them is a Thomas."

"Can you tell me if any of the other Alexanders are Thomases?" he asked.

"No, just the one I mentioned. Would you like the address and phone number?"

"Please," he said, giving Katie a big thumbs up. After getting the information, he thanked her and hung up. "Okay, kiddo," he said to Katie, "keep your fingers crossed, here goes."

"Alexander, Williams and Pearson. Attorneys at Law. How may I direct your call?"

"I'd like to speak to Mr. Thomas Alexander."

"One second, please, I'll transfer your call."

After a moment, a woman answered, "Mr. Alexander's office. May I help you?"

"I'd like to speak to Mr. Alexander, please."

"May I ask who's calling?"

"My name is Hank Torney."

"Mr. Torney, I'm Rachel Guiden, Mr. Alexander's private secretary. Mr. Alexander is attending the firm's annual partner's meeting this week. I'm afraid he'll be occupied all day."

"Ms. Guiden, it's extremely important I see Mr. Alexander today. I'm from out of town and only here for a few more hours."

"I'm very sorry, Mr. Torney, but that is simply not possible. Perhaps I could arrange for another attorney to see you."

"Ms. Guiden, can you tell me where your office is located?"

"Yes, of course. We're in the Jackson Building. Are you familiar with downtown Memphis?"

No, ma'am, I'm not. But if you give me the address I'm sure I can find it."

"Very well. The Jackson Building's on the corner of Front Street and Jefferson Avenue facing Confederate Park. Take the elevator to the 19th floor and they can direct you from there."

"Thank you very much, we'll be there soon."

Hank reviewed his conversation with Katie as they headed downtown; the skyline of which he could see off in the distance.

"Get out the city map and find Front Street and Jefferson Avenue. Should be right downtown. We're heading west now on Poplar – 3500 block."

Katie scrambled to unfold the map and studied it. "Got it. We're not too far away. Keep going straight and turn left on 2nd Street, it's one-way. Then three blocks to Jefferson, and right to Front, then maybe another two or three blocks. Looks like it's right on the bank of the Mississippi."

Although they had no preconceived notions of what the Jackson Building would look like, they were stunned when they drove up to it. A towering structure of glass and granite, it commanded a prominent position in the downtown area.

Hank pulled into a parking garage, grabbed his briefcase, and he and Katie hurried across the skywalk to the mezzanine and took an elevator to the 19th floor. When they arrived they were surprised to find the entire floor comprised the law offices of Alexander, Williams and Pearson. Tastefully decorated in birch and dark maple, a large receptionist's desk faced the entrance off to one side. A long, dark blue carpet stretched in both directions down the hallway.

"We're here to see Mr. Alexander," Hank said to an attractive young lady. "Ms. Guiden is expecting us."

"And your names, please?"

"Katherine Joyce and Hank Torney."

"Please have a seat," she said smiling. "I'll let Ms. Guiden know you're here."

They no sooner sat down before an attractive, impeccably dressed woman appeared from the hallway to their right. "Ms. Joyce, Mr. Torney – I'm Rachel Guiden," she said stretching out her hand. "I'm pleased to meet you. After you called I contacted Lawrence Wood, one of our associates. Mr. Wood happened to have some time free this afternoon and can meet with you right away. If you'll follow ... "

Hank broke in, "Ms. Guiden. I appreciate the trouble you've gone through for us, but I must insist. It's Mr. Alexander we need to talk to. It's *very* important."

A flicker of annoyance briefly passed across her face before her professionalism kicked in. She smiled politely and said, "But as I explained to you, Mr. Torney, Mr. Alexander is busy all day in an important meeting. I'm afraid that's impossible."

"Ms. Guiden," Katie said, smiling. "What we've failed to explain is that this is a *very* important matter. One, I can *assure* you Mr. Alexander will want to hear about *personally*."

That stopped Ms. Guiden. A bit more cautiously she asked, "Are you clients of Mr. Alexander's?"

"No, ma'am," Hank responded. "We've never met before."

"Then surely, there are other members of the firm who could help you."

"Ms. Guiden," Katie said patiently. "You don't understand. This is a very sensitive *family* matter."

"Well then, you're correct," Ms. Guiden said with an impatient look. "I don't understand. Of which of your families are we talking?"

"Neither of *ours*," said Hank. "It's Mr. Alexander's family."

That did the trick. After a moment of silent reflection as she studied their faces, she said, "Very well, please come with me."

She led them back to the executive wing of the building and into the foyer of Mr. Alexander's office. She was clearly mystified at what was going on, and was trying to temper her feelings with protecting her boss. There was something about the demeanor of both of them that indicated they really did need to talk to Mr. Alexander. She only hoped they weren't a pair of deranged nut cases or some offbeat religious zealots looking for a financial contribution.

"Now, I can't promise you anything," she said, "but the group is scheduled to take a short break at 4:00 – just a few minutes from now. Mr. Alexander *generally*, but not always, comes back to his office to check for messages. If he *does* come back and he *does* agree to see you, you'll have, maybe, five minutes tops, all right? There really *is* an important meeting in process."

"Yes, ma'am," Hank said. "We understand and we appreciate what you're doing for us."

"Well, please sit down and be comfortable. Can I get you some coffee or iced tea?"

"Nothing, thank you," said Katie. "We'll be just fine."

True to her word the hallway door opened shortly after 4:00 and a tall businessman, dressed in a tailored dark blue, pin stripe suit entered the office. All business. On a mission.

He headed straight for his office door when out of the corner of his eye, he spied the two of them sitting there. He looked curiously to Ms. Guiden who got up and intercepted him.

"Mr. Alexander, there are no messages, but these two young people would like a brief word with you."

He stopped, glanced at Hank and Katie and back to Ms. Guiden.

"I'm in a meeting, you know that," he said to her in a low voice, looking slightly perturbed. "I just came back to get something. Can you make an appointment or better yet, see if ... "

"Mr. Alexander?" said Hank, rising and stepping toward them. "We're sorry to intrude like this. Ms. Guiden did explain you were busy but this is very important."

"Do I know you?" he asked.

"No sir. My name's Hank Torney," he said sticking out his hand. "And this is Katherine Joyce. We're students at Western Illinois State, in Blighton, Illinois. If you could just give us a minute to explain ... "

"Mr. Torney, did Ms. Guiden tell you I'm in the middle of an important annual meeting? I can't possibly see *anyone* today?"

"Yes sir, she did," Hank replied, "but this is ... "

"I'm not sure what advice you are looking for, young man, but we have a large staff of well-qualified attorneys. I'm sure we can find one to help you."

"Mr. Alexander. We need to talk to *you*. And I'm confident you'll want to hear what we have to say."

"I don't mean to be rude to either of you," he said turning toward his office, "but I'm afraid I'm just too busy to see anyone now."

As he reached his door, Hank said, "Sir, does the name, Glory, mean anything to you?"

With his back to them, and his office door already half open, Mr. Alexander froze in place. He stood there, frozen in place, and you could almost visualize gears rotating slowly in his head. When he turned back, his face displayed a sober, quiet expression; staring first at Hank, then Katie before asking in a quiet voice, "What do you know about – *Glory?*"

"Quite a bit, sir." replied Hank.

Again, he stood quietly; studying them, trying to figure out what exactly was going on. Finally, he stepped aside and wordlessly motioned them into his office.

"Ms. Guiden," he said in a tight voice. "Please hold my calls and find Mr. Williams. Tell him something's come up that needs my immediate attention. Ask him please to take over the meeting. Say I'll rejoin them as soon as possible."

"Yes, sir. Right away," Ms. Guiden said, visibly shaken at the strange and unexpected turn of events. "Is there anything else ... ?"

But the door had already closed.

CHAPTER FORTY-SEVEN

Mr. Alexander enjoyed a corner office with floor to ceiling windows offering a drop-dead view of the Mississippi River on one side, and downtown Memphis on the other. Elegant and simple, it positively reeked of corporate power. He was obviously at the top of his game.

He motioned Hank and Katie to a small conference table and pulled up a chair to join them. For a moment or two he remained silent, studying them, waiting until they had made themselves comfortable.

"All Right," he said. "I don't know who you are or what you're up to, but you've got my attention. I don't know where you came up with that "Glory" business, young man, but ... "

"Hank Torney, Mr. Alexander. My name's Hank Torney and her name is Katherine Joyce."

"Yes, I'm sorry, *Mr. Torney*," he continued, not really appearing sorry at all, "Please tell me what you meant by that reference."

"I think you know what we mean, Mr. Alexander," answered Hank, getting slightly irritated at this point. After all, he thought to himself, they'd gone to a lot of trouble to find this man, and he didn't appreciate the way they were being treated. "In the interest of time, why don't we just get to the point. Like *you*, we're also under a severe time constraint. The reference I used was to help determine if you are the correct Thomas Alexander."

"Very well," he said with a patronizing smile. "Then for which Thomas Alexander *are* you looking?"

"The Thomas Alexander who is the only surviving son of Elizabeth and Glory Alexander." replied Hank looking straight into his eyes.

The effect was electric. His mouth dropped open, his eyes grew wide and he seemed to jerk back in his chair as if slapped by a strong hand. For a few seconds he didn't say a word but just sat trying to compose himself.

"All Right," he finally said with a constricted voice. "You've made your point. I *am* the Thomas Alexander you're looking for. But who *are* you two and how do you know about my father? What – for whom are you working?"

The change that came over Mr. Alexander was alarming to witness. From the tough, in-your-face attorney he had been a moment earlier, Hank and Katie were now looking at an unsure, nervous individual. His eyes flashed back and forth between the two of them searching for understanding, trying desperately to find some meaning in this insane situation.

"Are you with one of those search agencies I've dealt with in years past?" he asked in a nervous voice. "Do you have some new information that ... "

"Mr. Alexander, sir, please relax," said Katie in a soothing voice. She leaned over and patted his stretched arm. "We're just students, like we told you earlier. We don't work for anyone."

"Well then, I don't understand," he said. "How do you know my father's name? Is this some kind of joke? Are you looking for reward money? Is that it?"

"Mr. Alexander, please, let me just explain for a moment," said Hank glancing quickly at his watch. "I know this all must come as quite a shock to you, and I'm sorry we had to be so blunt. But we represent no one. We're not looking for money. We're not looking for anything. We're just students, like Katherine said. And unfortunately, we have a plane to catch."

"But this *is* about my father, isn't it?" he asked. "You do know something about him don't you? He's dead, isn't he?"

Hank sighed and in a soft voice replied, "Yes, sir, he's dead. It was an unfortunate accident, but he was killed. In Dubuque, Iowa, in August of 1940."

Mr. Alexander took this piece of news in stoical good grace. Yet he seemed to sag ever so slightly, like a large balloon leaking gas and sinking slowly into the ground. His eyes teared up and he looked past the two of them as if focusing on some far off scene. The silence became uncomfortable.

"We're so sorry, Mr. Alexander," said Katie. "It must be very hard for you after all this time."

He turned slowly and looked at her, focusing, and said in a soft voice, "You have no idea. One day she used to tell me – my mother – she'd say that one day you'll learn what happened to your father.

You'll learn the truth. Do you know how long that's been? Almost sixty years. *Sixty* years!"

Then, shaking his head as to fight off the fuzziness, his eyes cleared and he looked at them both with renewed interest and curiosity. "But I still don't get it. Why you two? Where did you say you're from? How much *do* you know? How did you get involved in the first place ... ?"

"Mr. Alexander, as we said, Katie and I are both students at Western Illinois State. And we got involved in this quite accidentally starting over a year ago when ..."

"Wait. Please, hold on, just a second. Let's back up. Did I just hear you say a moment ago that in addition to knowing my father is dead, you know the *circumstances* of his death? You said something about an *accident*?"

"Yes, sir," said Katie. "We do. That's what we've been trying to tell you. "We know the when, where, who and how!"

Again, Mr. Alexander looked stunned – as if he were waking up from a deep sleep.

"But how in the world do you know *anything* about him? You don't know my family or me. For heaven's sake, you weren't even alive then. I've never allowed any publicity of my search to go public. This just doesn't make sense."

"No, sir. I'm sure it doesn't," said Hank, reaching into his briefcase. "But it all started when we came up with this photograph taken from an old camera I bought." Hank laid the photograph in front of Mr. Alexander. "It was taken in a Dubuque warehouse."

Mr. Alexander picked up the photo and studied it in grim silence. "That's my father? How do you know? I'm not sure if even I recognize him – I've only seen one photo of him. And who are those other people?"

"They're the young men who accidentally killed him – apparently hit him with a beer bottle. They didn't even know he was dead when the picture was taken. When they found out, they disposed of the body and fled town."

"Whoa! Where in hell are you coming up with all this? How do you know that's what happened?"

"Because," said Katie, "we met with the man who took this photo a few months ago. He told us the whole story."

"What? This is insane! You're telling me my father was killed by these young men over 60 years ago and that a different one told you all this? How do I know you're telling the truth? How do you know he – whoever he is – was telling *you* the truth?"

"Well," Hank said, reaching again into his briefcase, "he gave us something. Perhaps it will help prove ... "

At this moment, Ms. Guiden, opened the door and hurried over to her boss, obviously very distraught.

"I'm very sorry to interrupt, Mr. Alexander, but your son just called. He's terribly concerned. He said they're ready to vote, but they won't move ahead without you. What should I tell him?"

With a look of intense frustration, Mr. Alexander jumped to his feet, paced back and forth a moment, and finally said, "All Right, tell them I'll be right down."

Turning to Hank and Katie he said with a pained expression, "Please, I *must* attend to a critical matter. I've got a room of 20 of our top management waiting for me. We only get together like this once a year and we have a very important issue to vote upon. It'll only take a few minutes, I promise, and I'll rush right back."

"But Mr. Alexander," said Hank quickly getting to his feet. "Unfortunately, Ms. Joyce and I have a plane to catch at 7:15. It's already after 4:30 and we've got to get to the airport and return a rental car first. I'm very sorry, perhaps we can call you when we get back."

"No. Please," he said in a voice louder than he intended. "I've waited a lifetime to hear this. Please, don't leave." He paced for a moment in deep thought and said, "I'll tell you what. We have our own company plane, a jet, and if you miss your flight, we'll fly you back ourselves, wherever you want to go. I'm afraid we got off on the wrong foot and I'm sorry if I was short with you but I hope you understand how much of a shock this has been to me. Won't you please wait? It would mean so much to me and my family?"

Katie and Hank exchanged glances and after a moment came to an unspoken agreement. Katie nodded her willingness and Hank said, "All Right. We'll wait but I don't see any way we can make our flight, which is the last one out today, by the way. I think we could get one tomorrow, but if you're serious about flying us back, ok, we'll wait. But we still have a rental car to worry about."

With a grateful smile, a greatly relieved Mr. Alexander said, "Thank you. Thank you both very much. I'll make it worth your while, trust me."

Then, without giving them a chance to reconsider, he turned to his astonished secretary and told her to make them both comfortable and get them anything they needed. Anything at all.

Gripping both their hands, he stressed again that he'd be back just as quickly as he could, and then turned and rushed out the door.

CHAPTER FORTY-EIGHT

Twenty minutes later, Mr. Alexander returned accompanied by a handsome young man who he introduced as his oldest son, Andrew, a member of the firm.

"Thank you both so much for waiting," he said. "I appreciate it more than you can imagine. I haven't had a chance to explain anything to Andrew, and I'm sure my colleagues wondered why I appeared so – shall we say, distracted."

Meanwhile, Andrew was looking back and forth between the two of them and his father; a puzzled look in his eyes.

"Now listen," he said, "I've had a little time to think about this and I have a proposal to make to the two of you. And another request, a big one, I'm afraid. But I'll make it up to you, I promise. I suspect what you've got to say isn't a simple story, am I right?"

"Well, no, I suppose it isn't," said Hank reaching for his briefcase. "But we've got everything recorded right here and I can leave ... "

"Wait, Mr. Torney, may I call you Hank?" Mr. Alexander interrupted holding up his hands, palms facing out. "Hear me out, please. What I'm proposing is you both remain here tonight as my guests and join my family for dinner. I'll get you back to school first thing in the morning. I promise. Please, my sister needs to hear this, too."

"Angela? Are you saying Angela lives in the area?" Katie broke in.

The two Alexanders looked at each other and then at her.

"Yes, Katherine, she lives nearby," replied Mr. Alexander after a thoughtful moment. "You obviously know more about my family that I gave you credit for. Angela, as well as my children, need to hear what you've got to say. Please ..."

His voice started to break as he teared up and turned away to compose himself.

"Dad, what's wrong?" Andrew said going to his father. "We need to hear *what*? Who are these people? Have they threatened you in any way?" He turned and gave Hank a dangerous glance.

"No – no, Andy, hold on," Mr. Alexander said placing his hand on his son's arm. "These two have found out something I've been waiting a long time to hear. I don't understand how they know, or even *what* they know, but I need to hear them out. And I hope they'll stay. He looked at them with desperate eyes. "Will you please stay?" he implored.

"Yes, Mr. Alexander. We'll stay," said Katie.

"Katie!" exclaimed Hank. "Are you sure? We have no room reservations – no change of clothes, and I've still got to get that car back to the airport."

"C'mon, Hank" said Katie in a patient voice. "We knew when we came down that there was a chance we wouldn't be able to get everything done in one day. You were thinking you might have to stay over anyway if you'd have come alone. If I hadn't made you take me, there wouldn't be a problem. We just can't leave now. They need to hear the whole story. Isn't this what we've been working for all these months? We owe it to them – heck, we owe it to *ourselves*. I'll call my folks and explain."

Hank remained silent for a moment, looking at Katie. Finally he said, "You're right, of course." Turning to Mr. Alexander he said. "Looks like we'll stay. *If* we can find a place with a couple of rooms."

Mr. Alexander was all smiles. His son was even *more* confused. And poor Ms. Guiden was more amazed than ever when Mr. Alexander issued her a flurry of instructions.

"Set up an immediate conference call with my wife and sister. Reserve our two suites at *The Grambling*. Schedule the company jet for a morning trip. Cancel Ms. Joyce and Mr. Torney's return flight and pressure the airline for a full refund. Arrange for the rental car's return. More to follow."

As Ms. Guiden rushed off in a tizzy he said, "I am so pleased and excited. I can't thank you two enough. I need to make a few arrangements and I know you must be tired, and perhaps a little anxious. I'm going to ask Andy to walk you up the street to *The Grambling*, one of our nicer little hotels here in Memphis. I realize you're traveling light so, please, *please*, ask André, the manager there, who will be informed you're coming, to get you anything you need. I really mean it."

"Mr. Alexander," said Hank, "There's no need to do anything special for us. Honestly, on the way into town I spotted a *Motel 6*. That'd be just fine with us, really."

"Listen you two. You don't realize yet what this means to me. Let me treat you a little special, will you? And one more thing, don't eat anything. I'll have a car come and pick you up at say – 6:30. We'll have dinner at my home. All Right? That'll give you a little over an hour to relax. I hope you like barbecue."

"We *love* barbecue," said Katie quickly – excited now, all smiles.

"Splendid. Off you go then. Oh, and one more thing. I want to keep this a secret for the time being, even from Andy here. All Right?" Turning to Andy he said, "Sorry, son. I've got my reasons. We can all hear their story for the first time together."

Andrew Alexander led Hank and Katie out of the office and up the street to the hotel. He was burning with curiosity and tried several times, without actually coming right out and asking, to get some hint as to who they were and what their secret was. Hank and Katie didn't budge on their promise and he was too polite to force the issue.

The Grambling was less than three blocks away, on the same side of the street as the Alexander law offices. When they entered the lobby through heavy glass and bronze doors, a nattily dressed, middle-aged man of European extraction met them.

"Ah, Mr. Alexander," he said, "How nice to see you again. And this must be Ms. Joyce and Mr. Torney. We're delighted to have you with us. I understand you had not planned to spend the evening and are traveling rather lightly. So I insist you let me know if there is anything at all you need. Although I think you will find your suites most complete, should either of you need, for example, sleeping attire – or a special cosmetic, do not hesitate to inform your attendants immediately."

While he was talking a bellhop quietly appeared at his side and André, without missing a beat, turned and said, "Louis, please escort Ms. Joyce to the *Versailles* suite and Mr. Torney to the *Belvedere*."

"This way, please," the bellhop said, while reaching for Hank's briefcase and Katie's camera and large purse.

"Well, okay you two," said Andy. "Looks like you're in good hands. Dad said to be in the lobby at 6:30. I'll guess I'll see you both at dinner." Then noticing Katie's pained expression as she looked down to inspect her outfit, he added with a knowing smile, "And listen, sounds like we're having barbecue. It will be *very* casual. Trust me."

Louis dropped off Hank at his suite first. *The Belvedere*. A valet was waiting at the door to greet him. Katie was escorted down the hall and found a maid was waiting for her at *The Versailles*. When she entered she almost fainted. Much later, when she tried to explain to her college roommates what it was like, all she could remember was gold and mirrors – everywhere! Gold curtains. Gold slip covers. A gold colored, silk bathrobe spread across the bottom of a huge Marie Antoinette bed. Gold brocade chairs in the sitting room. And gold gilded mirrors, of course.

Twelve-foot ceilings over heavily brocaded walls. And in the huge living room, a French provincial fireplace. The maid discreetly ignored Katie's stunned disbelief as she stood in the middle and looked around her. And when the heavy curtains were pulled back, the sudden shock of floor to ceiling glass caused her to take a step back in surprise, and then forward again to take in a panoramic view of the Mississippi River Valley.

"The bath is this way, mademoiselle," smiled the maid, obviously enjoying the reaction the suite was having on Katie.

The bath was huge – "about the size of her entire dorm room" she later told her friends. Black marble with – what else? – gold fixtures and gold monogrammed towels. Complete with shower, whirlpool tub, sauna and his and her toilets, sinks and bidets. And a black marble cabinet containing about every name brand cosmetic she had ever heard of and many she hadn't. Talcs, perfumes, shampoos, lipsticks, blushes for the female guests and razors, after shaves, shaving soaps for the men.

Completing the tour, the maid asked, "Is everything satisfactory, mademoiselle?

"Oh yes," Katie stammered. "Quite satisfactory." Then, after looking around a second asked, "but I'm wondering if there are any pajamas I could borrow. I mean, we weren't planning on staying ..."

"But, of course, mademoiselle. Perhaps a size seven?"

"Perfect," gushed Katie in relief. "That'd be just great, if it isn't too much trouble."

"No trouble at all, mademoiselle," she said as she turned and left quietly.

Left alone, Katie walked back through the suite slowly turning as she walked, taking it all in.

She noticed the fresh flowers. "Ohmygosh," she said out loud. "How could I have missed all these flowers?" And the four crystal chandeliers. The entertainment center tastefully tucked away in the corner. The antique French telephone on the bed stand. And the bowl of fresh fruit in the sitting room. She'd never in her life seen any thing even remotely as lovely as this. Her head spun. There was a knock on the door.

There stood Hank, all grins. "Well if you don't like it, I suppose we could still go back to *Motel 6.* "

Katie jumped out and grabbed him and gave him a big hug and kiss. "Oh Hank, come in here. You've gotta see this," she said dragging him into the room. "I've never seen *anything* like this. Ever. Just *look* at this place!"

Laughing, Hank came in and let Katie show him around. She raced from room to room, bubbling with excitement. He'd never seen her like this before and it really tickled him.

"Ohmygosh," she said. "I've got to take some pictures of this place. No one's going to believe this. *I* can hardly believe it. What do you think it cost to stay here for a night?"

"No idea. But I'm glad *we* aren't paying."

"Ohmygosh, isn't it magnificent?"

"It's acceptable," he said in a teasing voice, "if you like this kind of thing. Personally, I feel more comfortable in more sedate surroundings, say in the genre of *Antebellum Southern Gentleman* complete with portraits of every Civil War General I've ever heard about and enough weaponry to kick start a war, including a field cannon aimed down river ... "

"Oh that's right, I was so excited I forgot about *your* room – *The Belvedere?* Come show me ... "

She was interrupted by a knock on the door. The maid was there and handed Katie a wrapped box. Inside the box was a lovely pair of gold silk pajamas. Resting on top was a card that read, "With Compliments – The Grambling."

"Ohmygosh," Katie exclaimed as she lifted them out of the box totally embarrassed. "What did I just do? Oh no, *ETAM – PARIS!* Oh Hank. All I asked was if they had a pair of pajamas I could borrow. I didn't mean for them to do this. *ETAM* is horribly expensive. What should I do?" she said, moaning.

"If I were you I'd wear 'em. Hey, don't worry about it. He said to ask for anything you wanted, didn't he? For the price he's paying for these rooms, I'd think a pair of fancy PJs would be the last thing he'd worry about. If it makes you feel any better, I won't ask for any for myself but I am thinking about ordering some gunpowder and a cannon ball. There's a suspicious looking boat tied up down there in the river and ... "

"Oh Hank," she laughed and threw her arms around him. "This is so cool! I can't believe it! Would you have thought this would happen when we left this morning?"

"No, and I couldn't have written it if I tried. But I'm a little nervous about tonight, I'll tell you that."

"Well you shouldn't be. You've done a wonderful thing here and I think it's very exciting, meeting the family and all. Can you believe how successful Mr. Alexander is? I can't wait to see his house, can you?"

"No, I guess not. By the way," he said looking at this watch, "we're supposed to be in the lobby in 35 minutes!"

"WHAT? 35 MINUTES? Ohmygosh. Get out of here. I've got to get cleaned up. Go – go – GO!"

CHAPTER FORTY-NINE

Forty-five minutes later Hank and Katie were rolling through the countryside of north Memphis. A uniformed driver had met them in the hotel lobby and ushered them into a vintage Mercedes; black, leathery and sleek.

Earlier Katie had managed to call home and explain the circumstances to her parents. Her father had actually heard of the *The Grambling* and was quite impressed. Both parents were as excited as she was with the turn of the day's events, and told her to call home with all the details later that evening.

Soon they were passing through a private entrance and up a long, tree-lined lane to a large, handsome stone house. It sat on a rise surrounded by a well-manicured lawn. A wide, circular drive hosted several cars. As they pulled up in front, Mr. Alexander came down the steps to meet them. Hank was relieved to see he was dressed in khakis and a light blue sports shirt.

"Welcome, you guys," he said. "I'm *so* happy you decided to be with us tonight. Did your find your rooms comfortable?"

"Oh, Mr. Alexander," Katie said, "my room is absolutely gorgeous. I've never stayed in a place like that before in my life. My friends at school are going to drip with envy when I tell them. Thank you so much for your hospitality."

"Nonsense," he said, turning them toward the house. "I'm glad you like them. Now come on in and meet the rest of the family. I was able to rustle up quite a few even with such short notice. Everyone's dying with curiosity to know what's going on, especially my sister. She's not here yet but will be shortly. But before we go in, I need to ask you something and please be forthright with me. Apart from what you told me earlier, is there anything you're going to say that could be an embarrassment to the family?"

"No sir, absolutely not," said Hank. Then he paused. "But I do have some other things to show you and if you'd like to see them first, we can do that right now."

"No. No. I trust you. As long as there's nothing to cast an unfavorable light on my father's reputation, I want the family, that is, I want *all* of us to hear the story at the *same* time for the *first* time. Earlier I considered calling you with questions but decided against it. So thanks – but save what you have for all of us. Now let's go in and meet everyone. Angela should be here soon and then we'll eat, and afterwards you and Katherine can take over. Does that sound all right with you two?"

"Fine with us," said Hank. Katie nodded.

"All Right then, let's go. Oh, one more thing," he said pausing on the stairs leading to the front door. "My youngest son, Philip, couldn't be with us tonight. And there're some others I didn't even *try* to contact on such short notice so if it's all right with you, I'd like to videotape your presentation. That way, I'll be able to share it with them later. Would that be okay?"

"Sure, I guess so." Hank said turning to Katie. She nodded her agreement.

The house was not new. Mr. Alexander told them a local banker who built it in the '30s lost it soon thereafter when the bank was closed due to a series of bad investments. It stood vacant for several years until the Alexanders purchased it and spent a lot of time and money returning it to its original condition. Katie immediately recognized the Prairie Architecture design and Mr. Alexander told her that a student of Frank Lloyd Wright had, in fact, designed it.

He guided them through a spacious entrance and up a wide stone staircase to a central hallway broken up by a series of tall windows. The view of the valley was magnificent. They paused a moment to take it all in. In the distance they could see occasional, flashing pewter glints of the Mississippi as it flowed south toward Memphis.

"This is my private hide-a-way," he said as they approached a cozy retreat off the main hallway. "C'mon in and take a quick peek."

The room wasn't large but it was cantilevered out over the back of the house with a splendid view of the river valley. A small gas fireplace stood in one corner and a large, old-fashioned roll-top desk was placed against the far wall. Two walls were completely taken up by shelves; one wall with a large grouping of photos and the other with various memorabilia. The remaining wall was glass top to bottom.

"If you look around a little you're bound to notice that most everything on display here are items that depict aspects of Black History. I'm very proud of my heritage, and I've spent most of my life collecting items of interest. Some of these items are quite rare. Look at this, for example," he said, leading them over to one of the shelves where he picked up what looked like an old set of handcuffs.

"These are leg irons used to secure slaves being brought to this country from Africa. My great great grandfather was a slave so they have special significance to our family. I bought them in Bedford, Massachusetts, from a descendent of a ship's captain who had actually owned and operated such a vessel.

"And here is an early transcript of Abraham Lincoln's notes from which he composed the Gettysburg Address," he said, picking up a glass display case and handing it to Katie. "I came across it at an auction of notable Civil War documents in Atlanta, Georgia. Most of these things I tracked down myself but some were gifts from friends, family and clients."

He led them over to the far wall and said to Hank, "Andy told me about your interest in sports. Tell me, what do you think about this?"

It took Hank less than ten seconds to recognize what he was looking at. Turning to look at Mr. Alexander with a wide grin he said, "Holy Smokes, you've got an early Brooklyn Dodger uniform." He turned back to stare at it for a moment. "And not just any uniform. Number 42 – Jackie Robinson's number! Was this *really* his?"

"Yes, indeed it was," he said pleased Hank recognized it. "Came right off his back when he retired from baseball in 1957."

"He was one of the *world's* best baseball players," Hank explained to Katie, "with a lifetime batting average of .311! Inducted into the Baseball Hall of Fame in 1962. And the first black player in over fifty years to break the infamous baseball 'color line.' He accomplished some amazing things despite terrible racial injustices. A man's man and one of my genuine heroes."

"Wow!" said Mr. Alexander. "Impressive. You do know your sports trivia. But c'mon, we'd better go now. We can return later if you want. I need to introduce you to the rest of the clan."

They found several people chatting away on a large, flagstone patio. Others were inside an adjacent game room playing pool and generally just horsing around. Hank quickly counted at least eight or nine. As they came into view, all eyes turned to watch them with open curiosity.

"Everyone!" shouted Mr. Alexander in a loud voice and paused to be sure they were listening. "I'd like to introduce our special guests this evening." Turning toward Hank and Katie he said, "This is Katherine Joyce and Hank Torney. They're not clients of the firm but students at Western Illinois. I know you're all wondering what this is about and, I promise, you shall soon know. But for now, understand they are our honored guests for the evening. So please introduce yourselves while I go check on a few things.

"Mary," he said turning to a tall, attractive, middle-aged woman standing nearby, "Would you please take Hank and Katherine around and see they meet everyone? I'm going to call Angie to see how she's coming. I'll check on the food, too. Guys, this is my wife, Mary."

Mary Alexander, who had to be at least as curious, if not more so than the others, smiled graciously, shook their hands and told them how delighted she was they were able to come.

To Katie's relief, she was also dressed in casual, yet lovely clothes. A light tan cashmere sweater over matching slacks. Simple, but very tasteful Katie thought. She asked if they'd like something to drink and Hank, after doing a quick look around to see what others were drinking, said a beer would be great. Katie said an iced tea would be perfect. Once that was taken care of, she began to lead them around the room. First stop were four people playing a game of pool. They recognized Andy among the group.

"This my daughter, Lorraine, and her husband, William. William's a software programmer and Lorraine teaches in one of our local high schools. I know you've already met Andy. This is his wife, Theresa. Theresa is a gynecologist in private practice here in town. Tom said you are both students. What you are studying?"

"I'm a junior in architectural design," said Katie, "and I just love your home, Mrs. Alexander. Prairie Architecture has always been a favorite with me. I understand it was designed by one of Frank Lloyd Wright's students."

"Yes, it was," she said, obviously pleased. "And Hank? How about you? Are you in architecture, too?"

"No, Mrs. Alexander. I'm just finishing my graduate program in sports psychology."

"Really? How interesting. You've got to tell us more about that later. And by the way, it's Mary," she said smiling.

There were other friends and family and they met them all, one by one, each sizing the other up. Finally, she led them over to a middle-aged couple.

"This is Grant LeClaire and his wife, Maureen. The LeClaires are old family friends and Tom wanted them here this evening to meet you both. And although I'm dying to ask *why*," she said, chuckling, "I've been told I'd have to wait to find out."

"Happy to meet you," said Mr. LeClaire. "Welcome to Memphis, and to some fine southern cooking I've been led to believe we'll soon be enjoying."

"Grant owns and operates one of the nicer hardware stores here in town," said Mrs. Alexander, "and Maureen's got her hands full running a daycare center for underprivileged children. How's that going, Maurie?"

"Well, they keep me hopping, that's for sure," happily responded Mrs. LeClaire, a heavyset, smiley-faced woman. "But I love each and every one of 'em."

"Mr. LeClaire," said Hank. "I'm wondering if by any chance you're related to Mandy and Henrietta LeClaire over in Hardeman County?"

After a moment's pause while the LeClaires and Mrs. Alexander stared at Hank in open surprise, he said, "Well, indeed I am. Henrietta's my sister and Mandy's my mother! But, how would you know them?"

"Oh, we all had a wonderful lunch together today" blurted out Katie, "Crawfish gumbo, corn bread and sweet tea. You're sure right about delicious Southern cooking."

"Say *what*?" exclaimed the astonished Grant LeClaire. "You did *what*?"

"Well," Hank quickly said, "We're planning to tell you about that after we eat. I'm sure you ... "

"Hey, everyone," yelled Mr. Alexander stepping out on the patio, saving the day. "Food's ready and Angie's close behind. Let's go ahead and begin eating!"

Grabbing Hank and Katie's arms, Mr. Alexander led them away from the shocked trio to another side of the terrace where a local caterer had set up tables laden with platters of food. Hank and Katie were each handed a plate and an apron. "There's no delicate way to eat good barbecue," said Mr. Alexander. "So here's protection. No sense getting your nice clothes all messy. You and Katherine jump right in. Manners take a back seat at this point in the game."

Hank and Katie had never seen anything like it. Platters of barbecued pork and beef sat on one large table; half racks, burnt ends, pulled pork, chicken and spicy smoked sausages on another. On yet another table were large bowls of coleslaw, potato salad, sliced pickles and French fries. And mounds of sliced bread and butter. On another table were pitchers of water, iced tea, beer and soft drinks and a heaping pile of napkins. It looked like a combination of an old fashioned 4th of July picnic, local political rally, and homecoming celebration on steroids.

And standing behind each table were a pair of smiling, uniformed waitresses ready to help. Their starched white hats were embroidered with the restaurant name: *Rendezvous*.

To the delight of their hosts, Hank and Katie didn't hold back and were soon balancing overloaded plates. They were led to a long picnic table and seated among all the family who, at this point, had forgotten they were "honored guests" and were just concentrating on their own food. (All, that is, except Grant LeClaire who was still staring at them trying to figure out how in the world they knew his mother and sister ... and what was that business about crawfish gumbo ...?)

They had no more than gotten started eating when a whoop and holler from the stairs announced the arrival of the latecomers; Mr. Alexander's sister, Angela, her husband and two of their grown children.

"That's fine, y'all," Angela yelled with a wide grin on her mouth. "Don't mind us. Feel free to go right on ahead and eat without us even though I *am* the senior member of this here family."

After a flurry of catcalls, introductions and apologies for arriving late, they too filled their plates and dug in. Soon the sound of eating and laughing and good-natured family banter almost made Hank and Katie forget who they were, and what they were there for. It all seemed so natural and they were made to feel so comfortable that they almost forgot they were the only two white folks for miles around.

"So," said Angela, who had been slipped in between Hank and Katie. "You two are the reason Tommy's so excited. Well, whatever it is, it must be good. I haven't seen baby brother so turned-on since he won his first court case. Now," she said, bending down in a secretive way, "can you whisper to me what this is all about?" Hank and Katie both laughed and told her they were sorry but had been sworn to secrecy by "baby brother."

They learned Angela was dean of a nearby women's college, and her husband, Randall, was a sales manager for a Memphis computer software company. They'd arrived with their two grown children and spouses: Nat, athletic director of a local community college and his wife, Tanya; and Laura, a stay-at-home wife and her husband, Larry, assistant manager of a local grocery store.

The group was growing and everyone was having a great time. It was obvious to Hank and Katie that this was a close family, and one that enjoyed each other's company. The kindhearted jabs were numerous but short-lived. This was a group that held each other in mutual respect and it showed.

After about an hour of constant eating, when people had finally slowed down and were patting their stomachs and groaning, Mr. Alexander stood up and caught their attention by banging a spoon against a glass.

"All right," he said. "Looks like everyone's 'bout done so before we head inside to learn why I've asked you all over tonight, let's take a moment now to say a word of thanks."

Everyone knew it was time to get serious. The laughing and chattering stopped, the shuffling of chairs ceased and people bowed their heads.

"Dear Lord," he began, "we want to thank You for the wonderful meal we've all greatly enjoyed. We need to remember how fortunate we are when so many of Your children go to bed at night hungry. And we want to thank You for the blessings of family. May we always show each other abundant love and respect and never take each other for granted. For these things and for all the countless blessings bestowed upon us every moment of every day, we praise Your holy name. Amen."

"Amen!" everyone responded in unison.

"Okay. Everyone inside. We'll gather in the den. I think there are enough places for everyone to sit."

CHAPTER FIFTY

The den was on the second floor – not exactly another full floor up but somewhere in between, reached by a short flight of steps from the living room. A large television screen occupied one corner and a massive stone fireplace another. There were lots of family photos scattered around on walls and tables. Floor-to-ceiling book shelves monopolized one whole wall and the other was taken up by a large picture window looking out over the wooded valley.

Several leather couches and chairs were sitting around and people started settling in, curious about what they were going to hear. Mr. Alexander motioned for Hank and Katie to stand next to him at one end of the room until he was satisfied that everyone was sitting and comfortable.

"I first want to thank all of you again for coming," he said. "I'm really pleased we were able to gather up so many on such an impossibly short notice. I know several of you had prior plans this evening yet you respected my last minute invitation and came anyway. I deeply appreciate that. And I hope you understand I would not have asked you if I didn't think it was important.

"There are *still* several that could not be here tonight – either out of town or traveling. So I plan to videotape our meeting," he said turning and gesturing to a camera that had been set up in one corner, "and later I'll see everyone gets a copy. It was my decision to ask you to leave the youngsters at home tonight. It was a hard decision. But to be perfectly honest I'm not sure if what we're about to see and hear would be appropriate for their young ears. Afterwards you can decide for yourselves whether or not you want to share it with them."

He then paused, took a deep breath, turned to Hank and Katie, smiled and said, "This has been a very interesting day, to say the least. Early this afternoon, Hank and Katherine showed up in my office, unscheduled and uninvited. Their timing couldn't have been worse."

He smiled apologetically at Hank and Katie and then continued, "As many of you may know, I was smack in the middle of our company's annual partners' meeting and we were about to have a very important vote. I had gone back to my office to check my messages and these two were waiting for me. Bad timing, you might think. And you'd be right! I tried to get rid of them. Even the unflappable Ms. Guiden tried to steer them off."

A ripple of laughter spread among the group who were familiar with the "unflappable Ms. Guiden" – still all eyes stayed focused in on Hank and Katie.

"At any rate, they were not so easily dissuaded. And I thank God for that because they told me a few things that stopped me in my tracks; certainly enough for me to ask them to stay and come here tonight to talk to all of us."

He paused for another moment, looked down at his hands while he seemed to collect his thoughts and continued. "It's no secret to any of you that all my life I've tried to find out what happened to my father, as has Angie. I guess you could say it's become an obsession with us."

Slowly, one by one, it dawned on the rest of the family that somehow the meeting had something to do with his father? But how could that be?

"I never knew my father," he continued. "I was born after he went missing. Angie was just a small child. You all know the story. He left one day and never came back. We never knew what happened to him – where he was or why he disappeared. Was he dead or alive? Was he injured and in a hospital somewhere? Had he run off with someone, perhaps another woman?"

Sounds of denial filled the room and heads were shaking.

"I know. I know," he said, holding up his hands to quiet them down. "But people can be cruel. And I've been told that many nasty stories *were* circulated at the time. I can only imagine how much they hurt my mother. She *also* spent the rest of her life wondering what happened. It was a mystery that we never solved.

"Over the years we must have spent hundreds of hours writing letters, chasing rumors and talking to anyone we could think of. And we've spent a small fortune on private investigators looking for clues. Most of you don't know this, but we even offered a sizable reward for information that would tell us what happened. We never publicized this because we didn't want it to turn into a three-ring circus. Perhaps we were too cautious. Whatever, we were always disappointed with the results but we never gave up. Mother wouldn't let us. She was tough. Just when we'd be feeling down and feeling sorry for ourselves, there was one thing she always said to us – to Angie and me."

He paused and turning to face his sister asked, "Angie, you remember what mama always told us?"

Angela, who had been sitting quietly during all of this, looked at Hank and Katie and said in a quiet voice, "I do. She always said that 'one day, someone would show up at our front door and tell us'."

"That's right," Mr. Alexander said. "One day someone would show up at our front door and tell us what happened to our father. And, as you know, when she died, her request was to be cremated, with the hope of someday being reunited with him.

"Well, I think you've probably figured out where this is heading by now so I'm going to stop right here and ask Hank and Katherine to take over. As I said a moment ago, they showed up today out of the blue, and I wouldn't let them leave even though they had a plane to catch. They tried to tell me more at the office but I stopped them. I heard enough. I wanted *all* of us to hear the *whole* story together, for the *first* time."

Mr. Alexander stepped aside and nodded, smiling at Hank and Katie and said, "All right you two, take your time and start at the beginning."

Hank stepped forward. He never felt so nervous in his life. He took a deep breath, looked out at the room full of openly fascinated faces, smiled and began.

"Well, it all started at a country auction ..."

CHAPTER FIFTY-ONE

It was well over an hour before Hank finished. The room had become totally silent while family members sat staring at him, several crying softly.

He'd been interrupted only a few times; first, in the very beginning when he told them about the old photo that started the whole process. It was probably a mistake not to have waited to show them until he was finished. At first they hadn't quite grasped what he was talking about so he asked Katie to pass the photo around to the shocked family members. They excitedly gathered in small groups, inspecting it with distress.

Mr. Alexander asked Hank to hold up before continuing. He quickly left the room and soon returned with an old marriage photo of Glory and Elizabeth. It was in a small metal frame and showed a young couple dressed in what were obviously their Sunday best clothes. Neither were smiling, but staring intently at the camera in quiet dignity. Glory was sitting with his legs crossed. His young wife, Elizabeth, stood beside him, her right hand resting on his shoulder. It was a surprisingly good photo for its age, in black and white of course, but clear and sharp.

Everyone compared the two faces and ended up uncertain the man in Hank's photo could actually be Glory. They questioned Hank on why *he* thought it was. After all, they pointed out, Hank wasn't exactly a family member. How could he possibly know all this about their ancestors? Some suspected an ugly hoax in the making.

Hank then created another mega shock when he told them the reason he knew the person was Glory was because the man who took the photo told him so. When he said that, the room exploded!

"You mean one of the killers is still alive?" a person shouted out.

"Who is he?" another cried. "What's his name?"

"How do you know all about this anyway?" came a voice from the rear. "How could you possibly know that this guy was actually involved?"

By this time, several people were standing and arguing among themselves.

Hank raised his hands in surrender turning to Mr. Alexander for help. Mr. Alexander quickly and forcefully asked everyone to sit back down and let Hank finish. Slowly they began to sit back and be quiet. Hank, and when it seemed appropriate, Katie, carefully and slowly took the family through the entire progression of events, pausing and answering questions as best they could. When things would again get out of control Mr. Alexander would interrupt and ease Hank and Katie back on track.

Serious as the discussion was, the family members were relaxed enough to smile when Katie told them about her grandmother's genealogy club, known affectionately as the *Girls,* and explained the important part they played in the puzzle, particularly leading them down to Hardeman County.

Eventually, Hank brought them all up to the present day. He told them how they had left school that morning and came and visited Pineview, the cemetery and the old church.

They were further amazed to learn that someone at the church – namely Sister Dorothy – knew the LeClaire family. And the fact that Hank and Katie had actually found, let alone had lunch with, Henrietta and Mandy earlier that day, was a source of great amusement.

"And, of course," Hank said in conclusion, "once we got that far, the rest fell into place pretty quickly."

It was several moments later before anyone said anything. Most sat silently staring at them, trying to make some sense out of what they had just heard. Others whispered among themselves and looked again at the photos, passing around copies of the "Reward" newspaper ad and the old census reports and other materials Katie made available.

Finally, Andy Alexander stood up and said, "Well, I've got to admit, that's the most amazing story I've ever heard. But, if you'll forgive me for a moment, the lawyer in me keeps asking myself, *Why*? Why, out of the blue, can these two people, college students, to boot, show up with something some pretty fine private investigators couldn't find? Why? And how? It all seems a little – *fishy* to me."

"Now hold on, Andy," said Mr. Alexander, "before we go passing judgment too soon, let's think it through."

"But Dad," said Andy, "C'mon. Let's be realistic. Why would these two *white* folks spend all that time and money doing something like this anyway? I mean, what's in it for them? Maybe – somehow – they heard about the reward and ... "

"That's enough, Andrew," said Mr. Alexander in a firm voice. "Keep in mind, Hank and Katherine are guests here. And remember, I'm the one who insisted they stay. It was not their idea."

"But Tom," said Grant LeClaire getting to his feet. "Andy has a point. I've listened as carefully as I could and I agree that this is one fantastic tale, but you're a lawyer, too. One of the best. Yet, I suspect none of these things would stand up in a court of law beyond being circumstantial evidence. We can't even agree the photo is actually Glory. I'm not sure you could prove a case with this information. Now I'm not a family member," he continued, "although I feel like one. Our families go back a long ways and I'm as hopeful as you are that this is the real McCoy. All I'm saying is we need to look into this a little more carefully."

A loud murmur of agreement swept the room.

"Thanks, Grant," said Mr. Alexander, "I do appreciate your thoughts but I don't see how anyone could think that what you've heard here could be faked. And why, for heaven's sake, would anyone want to do that anyway?"

"The money!" a voice shouted out.

"Yeah, the reward!" joined another.

Again the room erupted. People jumped up and started to argue among themselves again. Others got on their feet trying unsuccessfully to be heard. During this newest episode of confusion Katie was excitedly talking to Hank while motioning to his briefcase at the same time. Hank paused a moment and his mouth dropped open in sudden recognition of what she was saying and *he* jumped to *his* feet.

"Excuse me everyone," he said with no results. "HELLO! Excuse me! May I say something ... ?"

It was Angela who first saw Hank trying to talk, but with no one paying any attention. So *she* stood up, put two fingers to her lips and let out an ear-piercing whistle. Shocked into silence, everyone turned and looked at her. "Will everyone please relax and be quiet for a moment?" she said. "Hank is trying to tell us something."

All eyes turned to Hank, many of them frowning. People started to sit back down.

When he felt he had all their attention, Hank said, "I can understand your misgivings about what we've told you. Honestly, I really can. Sometimes Katie and I feel the same way. I mean when we started all this, we had no idea what we'd find, if anything. But keep in mind what I've told you has been boiled down from almost a year into – what? – an hour or so?

"Many of you are wondering why we got involved in the first place. A good question. Some of our own friends have asked the same thing. The best way I can answer it is by telling you that we, that is, Katie and I, are inquisitive by nature. When we had the film developed, we were intrigued with what we found. I must admit it started off as kind of a game to us – a challenge. Yet the more we discovered, the more troubled we became. It soon became painfully obvious that a crime *had* been committed and we wanted to do what we could to solve it. At first we had no idea where to start or where it might lead us. And it actually wasn't until earlier today that we learned that any family members were even still alive!

"As far as any reward goes, Mr. Alexander told you the truth. We never discussed anything about any reward. The first time we heard about one was a few moments ago. Katie and I have no interest in receiving money for what we've done and we'll be happy to sign a release to that effect. We did what we did because we felt it was the right thing to do. We hope you'd do the same thing if you were in our places."

At this point Mr. Alexander stood up and started to say how embarrassed he was for his family when Hank cut him off. "No, Mr. Alexander," he said. "That's all right. I meant what I said. This is almost as unbelievable to Katie and I as I'm sure it is to you and I think it's perfectly understandable that your family would find it hard to believe, as well."

Reaching into his briefcase he continued, "However, I may have something that will help convince all of you that what we've told you is the truth. I'm sorry, Mr. Alexander. I was planning to show this to you earlier today, but things got a little frantic and I was, well, distracted and I forgot all about it.

He had their attention now. All eyes were riveted on him and what he retrieved from his briefcase.

"I told you about the priest we found who was present when Glory was killed. What I didn't tell you was how deeply it's affected

270

him. As a matter of fact he's devoted his entire life to working in an African mission. For your information he's there right now. He's obviously an old man and is dying from cancer."

There were more gasps as they all stared at him in wide-eyed curiosity.

"I guess you could say it was another miracle that we found him when we did. Actually Katie and I have come to believe that God has had a hand in this entire affair. There were just too many amazing coincidences. At any rate, he gave us this."

Everyone's eyes immediately turned to the box Hank held in his hand.

"It's made from a rare African wood," Hank said, "and from what we learned is quite a treasure in its own right. But it's what's inside that we think you'll appreciate. He told us if we were ever able to find any family members, that we were to give this to them. So, Mr. Alexander, I guess this belongs to you – to you and your family."

Having said that, he handed the box to Mr. Alexander. No one in the room moved and again an eerie silence settled in. Mr. Alexander silently accepted the box and held it in his hands for a moment admiring its beauty. Then slowly, he opened it and looked inside.

For a moment he just stared, trying to understand what he was seeing. Then, as comprehension settled in, he began to shake ever so slightly and tears began rolling down his cheeks.

For a moment no one knew what to do. People turned to one another with alarmed looks on their faces. Angela, surprised at seeing her normally stoical brother loose his composure, quickly got to her feet and went to him and he handed her the box.

She looked inside as the other family members searched *her* face for clues.

After a few moments, as it also dawned on her what she was looking at, her mouth suddenly dropped open, her eyes widened and she exclaimed, "Oh my God. The slave tag."

CHAPTER FIFTY-TWO

It was almost eleven o'clock before everyone left. The last two hours had been an emotion-filled period of sadness tempered with elation. To finally learn, once and for all, what had happened to Glory Alexander, and gain possession of the family's beloved slave tag at the same time, was almost too much for the family to handle.

Once the shock of the slave tag revelation had worn off and everyone had a chance to hold and admire it, Mr. Alexander produced several bottles of Dom Pérignon and initiated a series of toasts that passed from family member to family member.

Hank and Katie received their share of kudos, of course, as did the memory of Glory and Elizabeth. But Maureen, wife of Grant LeClaire, gave the most moving toast of all.

When she slowly stood up with raised glass, everyone smiled. The room quieted down.

"I'd like to propose a toast," she said in a quiet voice, "to the inherent goodness of mankind. To all those God-fearing people, living and dead, who have demonstrated unselfish love for their fellow man, regardless of race, color or creed."

There was a moment of silence until finally someone jumped to their feet and cried, "Here, here." In a magical moment everyone was on their feet, clinking glasses, hugging, weeping and shouting, "Here, here!"

Andy and his wife drove Hank and Katie back to the hotel. Mr. Alexander told them he'd pick them up at 9:00 in the morning and drive them to the airport himself.

They were exhausted. No one said much on the ride back. Just small talk. Mainly questions about family and school. Andy kept silent until they pulled up in front of *The Grambling* when they all got out to say good-bye.

"Hey, man," he said to Hank as they shook hands a final time. "I apologize for what I said earlier – 'bout you guys trying to pull some kind of stunt or something."

Hank started to protest but Andy cut him off. "No. Dad was right. I was out of line and I'm sorry. What you guys did for us – for the family – for Dad and Aunt Angie was above and beyond. You know what I'm saying? I mean, you guys made his day. Hell, you made his whole year, or decade, or whatever. Maureen hit the nail on the head, and you guys are two of the good people she was talking about. You've made some solid friends in Memphis, man, I can tell you that."

Then he grabbed Hank and gave him a big bear hug.

André met them at the front door. He already knew Mr. Alexander would be coming to pick them up at nine the next morning and suggested a 7:30 wake up call and a breakfast in Hank's room at 8:15. Katie and Hank quickly agreed.

On the elevator ride up to the top floor, Katie snuggled against Hank and told him this had been one of the most marvelous days in her entire life. Looking directly into his eyes, she whispered, "Hank Torney. You are *my* hero. And I love you so very much!"

Breakfast arrived promptly at 8:10 the next morning. A large trolley of silver-service covered food and drink was rolled out to the balcony off his living room. Hank called Katie and told her she had five minutes to get over.

"Wow, I could get used to this in a hurry," she said later as she worked her way through a large glass of fresh-squeezed orange and mango juice, an order of eggs Benedict, a tantalizing selection of fresh sweet rolls and a cup of strong chicory coffee. Hank laughed and told her she'd better get over it soon because it was all going to come to a screeching halt at 9:00.

Katie quickly snapped off a bunch of pictures of Hank's room, including one of him poised by the canon, and they reluctantly left for the lobby.

Downstairs, they found Mr. Alexander already waiting. He led them to his Mercedes and they headed to the airport.

"Hank," he said as they were on the freeway, "I didn't want to make an issue of this last night, but there really is a reward, you know. And you two have more than earned it. It's quite substantial, and regardless of what you said at the house, I want you two to have it."

"Whoa, Mr. Alexander," Hank quickly said. "Katie and I are serious about this and in no way will we accept one dime for what we did. And please, don't make us feel uncomfortable about it. We did it because we wanted to and, well, to receive any money would kinda ruin it for us. So, please, you can give the money to your favorite charity if you wish. But we won't accept any of it although we appreciate the gesture."

Mr. Alexander didn't say anything for a moment, just kept on driving. Finally he said, "I thought you might say something like that. But surely there's something I can do. It would make *me* feel a lot better."

"I really can't think of anything, sir. How about you, Katie?"

"Well," she said after a moment, "How about this? If Mr. Alexander really wants to make the gesture, how about buying a new computer for the *Girls*. Granny is always complaining that the one they have is so old, and slow. Her genealogy club does a lot of research online and anything to help them out would be a nice thing to do. After all, they spent weeks researching for us and without their help, we might never have found the family."

"That's a marvelous idea, Katherine," said Mr. Alexander. "Just tell me where to send it and consider it done."

When they arrived at the airport, Mr. Alexander drove on to a private hanger area where a shiny new Lear Jet sat waiting, the pilot standing by.

One more set of emotional goodbyes and they were finally ready to board. Katie gave Mr. Alexander a slip of paper with the address of her grandmother's retirement center and he gave each one of them a copy of the videotape that had been duplicated earlier that morning.

"Let's keep in touch with each other," he said as Hank and Katie stepped up into the plane. "I have a feeling we'll be crossing paths again."

The plane taxied down the tarmac, turned and after a few seconds of muted conversation between the pilot and the control tower, sped down past where Mr. Alexander stood waving and quickly lifted off. Hank and Katie furiously waved back and were soon airborne and on their way home.

Sitting back and admiring the plush, leather interior of the passenger cabin they smiled at one another.

"Really think our paths will cross again?" Katie asked.

"Doubt it," said Hank. "And I have to admit, I'm kinda glad the whole thing's over. Aren't you?"

"Oh, I don't know – sorta – I guess – maybe," she replied with an impish smile.

Hank grinned. "You're really something you know. And by the way, I love you, too."

PART THREE

THE RIVER

2001 – 2003

CHAPTER FIFTY-THREE

It was an exciting Easter break. Katie arrived home early in the afternoon to an expectant family wanting to hear all about their adventures. When she showed them the videotape, everyone sat and watched mesmerized. Even Michael and Brennan seemed interested. When she told her grandmother about Mr. Alexander's promise to outfit the Girls with a new computer, her grandmother immediately got on the phone and relayed the message. After Easter Mass, several friends stopped by to see the videotape for themselves. Apparently there were more people who knew about their project than she thought.

Pretty much the same thing happened at Hank's. After the initial flush of excitement, his brother invited Gary Woodard and his wife over to watch.

"Hank," Gary said after he saw the tape, "I can't believe you actually pulled it off. That is one amazing story you've got there. I've gotta give you credit, man. You oughta write a book or something."

"Oh sure," said Hank. "Like I've got the time. I'm gonna be looking for a job in a couple of months. But, thanks anyway. You had a lot to do with it, you know. If we hadn't had a photo, we wouldn't have even known about the crime. Actually, the whole project was kinda weird that way. Everything fell into place when it had to. If you've never believed in divine intervention before, you'd have to after this."

A week later Hank received a very nice note from Tom Alexander. It was enclosed with a newspaper clipping of a two-column story that had appeared in the Memphis paper. The headline read: *60 Year-Old Mystery Solved. Precious Family Heirloom Returned.* There was a large photo of a smiling Mr. Alexander holding up the slave tag.

That evening Hank called Philadelphia and spoke with Father Lavarato's housekeeper. She told him he was still in Africa. He learned the mission now had email access so he fired off a long message explaining what had transpired and attached a copy of the Memphis newspaper article.

Two days later he received a reply from Father Lavarato saying how happy and relieved he was and congratulating both of them on a job well done. He told him he was feeling much better and felt he was on the mend. He said he is making plans for them all to get together as soon as he returned home to discuss another important matter.

"Plans? Important matter?" Hank said to himself. "What's he got up his sleeve now?"

The remainder of the spring semester was flying by with a vengeance. Hank spent about half his time getting ready for his finals and the other half following up on job inquiries. He'd already received a few promising leads but the majority of them were either from the east coast Ivy League schools or from schools on the far west coast. And he just wasn't interested in moving that far away at this time.

His top three choices, in order of preference, were Notre Dame in South Bend, the University of Illinois in Champaign and University of Michigan in Ann Arbor. He'd been invited to all three at least once, and to Illinois twice. He felt his interviews had gone particularly well and his grades and references were strong. It was time to wait and see what happened. He felt quite confident he'd soon be receiving an offer from Illinois but, at this stage, nothing was a sure thing.

He and Katie still got together almost daily. He knew he wanted to be with her as much as possible, and she seemed to feel the same. She'd kept her thoughts to herself about his job search, but she prayed daily he'd stay in the Midwest and worried he wouldn't. She easily admitted to herself how much she loved him.

Her roommates were constantly quizzing her about her "pending engagement". The fact that she and Hank had been spending so much time together and, in fact, had crossed that critical line of visiting each other's homes, just added fuel to their fire. And now, after the trip to Memphis where they had stayed overnight the kidding had heated up. Although she was quick to point out they had separate rooms, that didn't seem to slow it down much. It irritated her at times, but she understood they were just having fun at her expense. They knew what kind of girl she was, and while some may think she was dismally behind the times, her real friends admired her for her strong moral convictions.

She also was looking for a job, at least for the summer, and was zeroing in on the Chicago Architecture Foundation. She had a strong connection there through her senior advisor who had several friends on staff. The Foundation normally only hired graduate students but during the summer there were occasional openings for qualified undergrads to work as researchers and tour directors. It would mean sharing an apartment with someone, but the pay was decent and she'd be able to go home weekends. And it sure wouldn't hurt to have the working experience with such an icon on her resume.

Mr. Alexander followed through with his promise to help the *Girls*. Katie's grandmother called her one evening with the exciting news that he'd arranged with a local computer store to come out and install not one, but two, top-of-the-line, large screen Macintosh computers with the newest genealogy software already loaded. He also had a color laser printer installed that was networked to both.

It seemed as if he'd thought of everything and prepaid for a three-year service contract that covered just about anything that could possibly go wrong. Of course, the *Girls* were absolutely ecstatic and wanted his address so they could all send him thank you notes.

One evening in early May, Hank returned to his apartment from the library and Pete told him that Mr. Alexander had called two or three times and was very anxious that Hank call him back as soon as possible.

"Man, that Alexander dude's all hopped up," Pete said. "You'd better be calling him right now!"

"Did he say what it was about?"

"No. I asked if I could give you a message, but he said he had to talk to *you*. Like I'm chopped liver or something?"

"I don't know, it's pretty late. I'd better wait till tomorrow."

"C'mon man! Don't say that. It's 7:15! Don't be messing with me. I'm dying to find out what he wants. I can't even study. Call. Do it now. C'mon. Here's the phone."

"For heaven's sake, relax," said Hank, smiling. "You're as bad as Katie's roommates. Take a chill pill or something."

Mr. Alexander must have been waiting by the phone because it was answered immediately. Before Hank could even say anything he heard him ask, "Hank?"

"Yes, sir. How are you? I'm sorry I didn't call back sooner but ... "

"Are you ready for this?" Mr. Alexander broke in with an excited voice. "We're gonna be on the *Oprah Winfrey Show!*"

CHAPTER FIFTY-FOUR

When finally Hank got off the phone his head was spinning.

"What'd he want?" Pete asked in an excited voice. "I heard you talking about being on some type of show. What was that all about?"

"He said we're gonna be on Oprah! I can't believe it."

"Cool! The Opry! But that's the Grand Ol' Opry to you, son. Nashville. Johnny Cash, Little Jimmy Dickens, Merle Haggard, Minnie Pearl! VERY COOL! Count me in. I'm invited too, right?"

There was a long-standing joke that Pete was a closet hillbilly. The funny thing was Hank knew for certain he was raised in a rough Detroit neighborhood. Pete didn't talk much about his family and quickly changed the subject when it came up. Hank had learned not to discuss it around him although he had pieced together the fact his dad worked in the automobile assembly plants and had originally come from somewhere in the southwest – Texas or New Mexico he thought.

Pete never mentioned his mother or any sisters or brothers. He knew he learned basketball the hard way, in vacant lots playing street hoops, and he knew he could hold his own against the best. He also knew it didn't pay to play rough on the court with him, and had seen more than one episode where it required several people to pull him off some wise guy who tried to get cute with swinging elbows and tripping feet.

And Hank knew Pete was pretty handy with a Western-style guitar. He came back to the apartment more than once and found him playing and singing some mournful ballad on the back porch, only to stop when he spied Hank. He really did have a great voice but would get embarrassed if Hank said anything. So he didn't.

Occasionally, if the right group was playing at *Grumpy's*, and if Pete had had enough beer, he'd join in on a set. When that happened, it wasn't long before the hooting and hollering died down, and he'd mesmerized the crowd with some decades-old country western tune, the kind he seemed to prefer.

Hank was there one night when you could have heard a pin drop as Pete, eyes closed, and off in some far away, secret place, sang *The*

Streets of Laredo. The rest of the band had long stopped playing and listened along with everyone else.

Hank decided it was way too early to pop Pete's bubble about the *Oprah* versus *Opry* show so he ignored him and called Katie right away. He told her he had some important stuff to share and asked if she could meet him for a cup of coffee.

"Sure. I guess. What's up?"

"You ain't gonna believe this, kiddo. Gotta tell you in person."

"Hmmm. Sounds mysterious. I can be there in 10 minutes. Can't stay late, though. I've got two finals next week."

Hank zipped over to the Commons and was waiting with two coffees when Katie arrived.

"Okay, Mystery Man. Another surprise? You're full of surprises, you know. What's so important that it couldn't wait until tomorrow?"

"Man, this is way freaky. Listen up. When I got back to the apartment tonight Pete told me Mr. Alexander had been trying to reach me all evening."

"*Our* Mr. Alexander?"

"One and the same. I called him back and he told me he'd had a call that day from Oprah Winfrey and she wants him, his sister, and us to be on her show. A special!"

There was a moment's pause while Katie stared at Hank in disbelief and then her eyes grew wide and she screamed, "What? We're gonna be on the *Oprah Winfrey Show*?"

"Shhhhhh, not so loud," said Hank looking around as people were turning to stare at them. "But yeah, I guess so. At least that's what Mr. Alexander said."

"Ohmygosh," she cried again in a loud voice. "I can't believe it. When? How did this ... " Suddenly her eyes narrowed and she stared hard at Hank. "This is a joke, isn't it? Are you kidding me, Hank Torney, because if you are, I'm never going to speak to you again?"

"Easy now," Hank said, laughing. "Take it easy. I'm not kidding. Let me tell you what he said and then we have to make some decisions – fast. I've got to call him back first thing in the morning."

Hank proceeded to tell Katie that after the story had appeared in the Memphis paper, Mr. Alexander received a call from someone at the Museum of African American History in Chicago. Apparently they had been mailed a copy of the story and were interested in learning more about it. They were particularly keen on getting him to donate the slave tag to the museum. He told them that wasn't going to happen but offered to send them a copy of the videotape, which he did.

Around a week later he received another call from them to express their thanks and tell him they were absolutely fascinated with the story. They had shared it with their board of directors, one member of which is a self-proclaimed history buff who also happened to be a producer for the Oprah Show, and ..."

"Are you making this up?" broke in Katie again. "This is the most bizarre thing I've ever heard."

"No. I swear this is exactly what he told me. Then that producer person apparently showed it to Oprah herself, who promptly came unglued after seeing it and said something to the effect – 'We've got to get that story on my show. Who do I call?'

"So the other night he was at home eating dinner," Hank said, "when the phone rang and it was Oprah Winfrey. He thought it was a joke at first but when she started asking him specific questions about the video: Who filmed it and why? Exactly who you and I were and what our involvement was? When did it all happen? Stuff like that. He knew she was questioning the authenticity of it – like she couldn't believe it was really true. But he must have convinced her – 'course he's a lawyer – and she got very excited, telling him what a great human interest story it was, and that it was perfect for her audience, which I guess is quite large ... "

"Yeah, I'd say so," interrupted Katie again, by this time squirming in her seat. "Like the number one daytime program on television – with a bezillion viewers. Ohmygosh, I can't believe this."

"So anyway," Hank went on, "she wants him and Angie, and you and me on her show. And she wants to do it as soon as possible, before someone else hears about it. Can you believe it? Fly everyone into Chicago, put everyone up in a fancy hotel, limos back and forth – yadda yadda. I don't get it. I mean, I know it's an interesting story and everything, but c'mon. Will people really be *that* interested?"

"Oh Hank!" Katie said, taking his head between her hands and looking into his eyes. "Oh sweetie, don't you know it's a *fabulous* story? It's a *perfect* story. It's warm and it's kind and mysterious and intriguing. And it starts so sad, but has such a warm, happy ending. Oh yes, Hank. People will be very interested. They'll love it. They'll eat it up."

"You think? Well, maybe. Anyway I promised I'd call him back by tomorrow morning with a date. We've got three choices," he said, referring to a scrap of paper he pulled out of his pocket. "Next Friday or Saturday or Monday of the following week; that's the 11th, 12th or 14th. But we need to be there the day before ... "

"WHAT?" exclaimed Katie. "You are kidding now, right? About next week?"

"Well – no," said Hank, "and I've got a final on Monday so Monday's out. And I kinda promised Pete I'd go to the intramural playoffs with him Friday night, but if we got done in time, I suppose that would work. But actually I think Saturday would be best ... "

"HANK TORNEY!" Katie shouted and jumped up, spilling her coffee and causing every head in the room to turn to them again. "Are you CRAZY? INTRAMURAL PLAYOFFS? What are you talking about? What about me? Are you even interested in what *I* think?"

"Well, sure," said Hank shocked at her reaction. "That's why I called you right away. I guess I can forget the playoffs on Friday, and then there's Saturday. So there's still two different times. What would work best for you?"

"Oh Hank, you don't understand," said Katie starting to walk in circles as the reality set in. "That's only *ten* days from now! What am I going to wear? Look at my hair! I have to call Mom."

She started to turn and head toward the door, obviously in a mild state of shock.

"Katie, wait!" shouted Hank jumping to his feet. "When? What should I tell Mr. Alexander? I've gotta call him back. What day? Friday? Saturday? Remember, can't be Monday. I've got a final ... "

"Late as possible!" she replied as she reached the door. "Tell him Saturday. Although I'm not sure where I'll find an outfit in that amount of time."

"Good grief, you sound just like Pete. He's talking about buying new cowboy boots."

"PETE? What's he got do with this? *COWBOY BOOTS?*"

"Don't ask," said Hank, sinking back into his chair, shaking his head at the mess he apparently had gotten himself into.

CHAPTER FIFTY-FIVE

The following week Oprah promoted the upcoming special on her show every day. She promised "one of the most fascinating shows of the year." And although she didn't give away much she managed to reveal enough snippets of information that even Pete was interested in watching. By this time, he'd learned the difference between *Opry* and *Oprah* and was very disappointed to say the least. He'd had his heart set on Nashville.

"Hell, I can go to Chicago any time I want," he complained. "And it wouldn't be to go to the *Oprah Winfrey Show*, I can guarantee you that."

All of Hank and Katie's family and friends had been alerted and would either be home watching or sitting in the audience. Since the show is produced in Chicago, their families planned to drive in Friday night and stay at the hotel rooms provided by the studio. Tom Alexander and his sister, Angela, along with their children were flying in and staying at the same hotel.

Early that evening, everyone had an opportunity to meet at the studio with Oprah and talk about what was going to happen the next day. It was an informal and joyous reunion of sorts and everyone had a chance to meet Oprah and get her to sign autographs.

"The main thing is, just be natural," Oprah said during her briefing. "I'll chat with Mr. Alexander and Angela first and set up the situation. Then we'll have a station break and Hank, you and Katherine will be invited on to tell your story. Try to relax and have fun and just be yourselves. Here's a list of questions I'm liable to ask. Just look them over and if I do ask one of them, try to keep your responses as short as possible. I don't want it to look too rehearsed – spontaneity is good. If you ramble on too long, I'll break in to keep us moving along. You have a wonderful story to tell, and remember, I've reserved the entire show for you guys. It's gonna be just great. And by the way," she added, "you may not have realized it, but over the last few days we've had a couple of camera crews out filming some of the key locations in your story. Assuming it all goes as planned, we'll show them as we're talking about them."

Before they were all dismissed, Hank privately approached Oprah and asked if he'd be able say something before the show ended – just a minute or so.

"Depends. What do you want to say?" she said, curious. "You're not planning on doing anything goofy, are you?"

"No, no, of course not," Hank said, "and I'll tell you if you insist, but I'd like to keep it a secret if it's all right."

"No, not necessary. I trust you. Am I correct it has something to do with you and Katherine?"

Hank just smiled.

"Well let's see how it goes," she said. "If there's time, that's no problem. Our stage crew does a pretty good job letting us know exactly how much time we have left. You watch me – I'll cue you."

That night Hank called Lieutenant Rea at his home and told him to watch the Oprah Winfrey show the next day telling him it should answer all his questions. He left him more confused than ever.

Oprah was absolutely right. It was the spontaneity of the show that made it so remarkable. It unfolded exactly as she'd said, with the first segment featuring Tom and Angela who talked about their early childhoods and the story of their missing father. They were natural and compelling. Oprah really played up the fact that even with such a shaky start in life, each of them had achieved marvelous successes.

It was after the first break, when Hank and Katie joined them on stage, when things really got interesting. Hank, with Katie's help, succinctly told their story. Oprah's crew had done a marvelous job shooting footage of scenes in Dubuque, Pineview (including a short visit at *Betty's Café*), and the campus of Western Illinois State to match their dialogue. And, to everyone's surprise, there was even footage of the Girls. The audience absolutely loved it.

Of course, the presentation of the slave tag created the biggest stir, just as it did when Hank and Katie first revealed it to the Alexander family. Oprah made sure the camera shots were in tight so the entire studio audience could get a good look at it.

But no one was prepared for what was to happen next.

With approximately two minutes left before sign off, Oprah remembered Hank's request.

"Hank," she said. "That was a truly awesome story. It just gives me the goose bumps, doesn't it all of you?" turning to the studio audience who responded with thunderous applause. "Is there anything you'd like to add before we close?"

"Yes there is," Hank said getting up from the couch and walking over and standing in front of Katie. Everyone's eyes were glued to him and all of a sudden you could hear a pin drop. What was going to happen now, people were wondering?

Reaching down and grabbing hold of Katie's hand and bringing her to her feet, and before anyone had a second to even think about it, he said, "Katherine Ann Joyce. In the presence of God, and our parents and family members, the studio audience, and everyone watching this program this evening, I would like to take this opportunity to ask for your hand in marriage."

For a heartbeat, everyone on stage, as well as the entire studio audience were frozen in shock. Then, as if on cue, the whole building erupted. People who'd never heard of Hank or Katie before, jumped to their feet and cheered in a thunderous roar.

The cameraman, in obvious confusion – this part was not scripted – cut from the audience to the stage to Hank and Katie and finally to Oprah, who was grinning from ear to ear and doing a slow turn to the audience as if to say, *Can you believe this*? Finally she signaled for everyone to quiet down and directed the camera to Katie who was in obvious shock herself. Hank was still holding her hand and smiling directly at her as if they were the only two people around.

"Oh Hank," she said looking around in confusion, turning first to the people on stage, and then toward the audience where her parents were standing and grinning at her. "I didn't expect this. What – when – oh dear ... "

"I've already spoken to your father," Hank said, "and he's fine with it."

The audience again erupted in laughter at this new revelation.

Katie was starting to come out of it and was still unsure of what was going on and how to react. She started to stammer, "Oh Hank, I don't know. This is so sudden. I don't know what to say ... "

At this moment, Oprah, seizing the magic moment stepped up to Katie, put her arm over her shoulder and good naturedly said, "C'mon girl, you'd better say *something*. We've got about 40 seconds of airtime left ... "

Another roar of laughter and finally Katie snapped out of it and said in a loud clear voice, "Yes, Hank Torney. I will marry you. I will. I will!"

Well, if you thought the crowd got crazy before, you should have seen and heard them now. Everyone was jumping around and cheering. It was a joyous, wacky scene and the cameras went wild with cuts of Hank and Katie hugging and kissing – their parents hugging and shaking hands. The whole audience was hugging each other. It was magic, just plain magic!

Oprah rushed over and embraced them both and then turned to the camera and in the final seconds of the show smiled broadly and said, "This is *supposed* to be *my* show but this afternoon I'm not so sure. Well, I hope you all enjoyed it. I know I did. Gotta go. Thanks for watching ... "

The final scene showed general pandemonium as the camera pulled back and both Hank and Katie's families streamed on stage initiating a new round of hugging and hand shaking, then slowly faded to black.

Before the show was even over, the station's phone lines started to light up, and by the time it ended, they'd maxed out. It ended up receiving one of the highest ratings of any daytime show that ran that season. Segments of it were picked up and ran on numerous stations throughout the country and it was actually rebroadcast in its entirety a few weeks later on a rare Oprah Special.

CHAPTER FIFTY-SIX

For days after the show, calls had streamed in to Oprah's studio, ranging from oddball marriage proposals to both Hank and Katie "in case things didn't work out" to offers for the story rights of their adventure. One major airline called in with a "Deluxe All Expenses Paid Honeymoon" package to their choice of Hawaii or Greece if they would agree to come and talk at the company's national sales convention.

There were offers for other TV appearances and radio shows, but there were also final exams to think about, so Hank and Katie quickly let it be known they were not available. When they returned to campus the following week, there was an offer of free pizza and beer for Hank and Katie and "a *limited* number of their friends" at *Zoey's* the following weekend. This offer they definitely accepted.

Pete took full credit for orchestrating the entire event and let it become common knowledge that without his "firm friendship" with Oprah, the whole thing would never had happened. Of course, the fact that just a few days prior he didn't know the difference between Oprah and the Grand Ol' Opry never came up.

As far as Katie's friends were concerned, everyone agreed the "amazing proposal" on live TV was the stuff matrimonial legends were made of. Many a night during the next couple of weeks was spent in her dorm room replaying that portion of the show. It never failed to elicit a thunderous round of squeals and teary hugs and laughter.

To Hank, one of the more satisfying things that happened took place with no fanfare at all.

One afternoon, as he and Katie were sitting in the Commons having a cup of coffee, he spied Mike Garrison and Tom Jackson, along with a sizable bunch of their groupies, heading their way.

Hank had seen both of them around campus several times since their run in at Tank's apartment but no words had been exchanged. He knew it was just a matter of time before they'd meet again. Apparently now was the time. Hank told Katie to stay seated as he stood to face the approaching group.

The Commons quickly became silent as other students noticed and solemnly watched the ensuing drama. It was no secret on campus what had happened that night at Tank's apartment and there had been lots of speculation on how it would play out.

Mike walked right up to Hank and stopped. Then, in a voice loud enough that everyone in the silenced hall could hear said, "Hank, I came over to apologize for the way I acted at Tank's that night. I'd had too much to drink, but that's no excuse. I was dead-ass wrong and I'm sorry, man. What you did for that Alexander family was over the top. And I'm hoping you'll forgive me and take my hand."

With that astonishing statement, both to Hank as well as to Mike's group who had been expecting a little get back action, Mike stretched out his hand to Hank.

Hank smiled and grabbed it and said, "Hey, Mike, no harm done and no offense taken. I appreciate you doing this, I really do. Couldn't have been easy." Then turning and gesturing toward Katie, he said, "I'd like you to meet my fiancé, Katie Joyce."

"Hi, Katie. Pleased to meet you and congratulations, that must have been some shock. The proposal, I mean, right up on the stage, in front of the whole world and everything."

"Yes, it was," said Katie. "And thank you, pleased to meet you, too."

"Can I buy you a cup of coffee?" Hank asked.

"No man, thanks. I'm going over to the gym and talk to Pete. Best get it out of the way now. He's a good man to have watching your back. I'd better be careful," he said with a grin.

"Pete's okay." Hank said, "and he'll appreciate it."

"All Right then. See you around." With that Mike and his subdued friends filed out of the Commons and headed toward the campus gym.

Eventually, as these things often happen, people soon forgot all about the Oprah Event. After the initial burst of fame, all the hoopla faded away, and Hank and Katie slipped back into a normal routine.

Well, almost.

CHAPTER FIFTY-SEVEN

Thursday evening before finals week, just as things were finally getting back to normal, another bombshell exploded.

Hank was just returning from an early evening meeting with Dr. Pascuzzi when he found Pete waiting for him at the door of their apartment.

"Hey, man, where've you been?" Pete said with a nervous smile on his face. "I've been sitting here for an hour waiting for you. You've got a visitor!" Hank followed him into the living room. There sitting on the couch was Mariama, Father Lavarato's ward. She turned toward him and smiled.

"Mariama!" he said, "What are you doing here? I mean, how are you? Are you here alone?"

"I asked her the same thing," said Pete. "She won't talk to me. Would only say she wanted to see you. Is this the girl that you talked about? The one from Africa?"

By this time Mariama had gotten to her feet and walked over to Hank.

"Father Tom is dead," she said with teary eyes.

Hank, in a bit of a daze as to what was happening said, "Father Lavarato's dead? Oh, Mariama, I'm so sorry to hear that. When did he die?"

"He died last week, at the mission. They call and told us. I talk to him two days before. He tell me to come and see you." Having said that she reached into her small travel bag and retrieved an envelope and handed it to Hank.

"But, I don't understand," Hank said. "He told you to come see me? What exactly did he say – oh jeez, where's my manners, please sit down. Can I get you something to eat?"

"We've got some beer and pizza left over from *Zoey's*," blurted out a nervous Pete. "Want I should ... "

"Hot tea would be very nice, please," Mariama said sitting back down on the sofa."

"Pete," said Hank. "Would you please fix us some hot tea?"

"Tea?" Pete said with a puzzled look on his face. "I don't think we have any tea ..."

"Go downstairs and borrow some." Hank said through clenched teeth turning to stare at Pete.

"Right!" said Pete, startled. "Hot tea. No problem. Back in a jiff." He rushed out.

"I'm very sorry to hear about Father Lavarato, Mariama. We only knew each other a short while, but I know he was a good man. I'm glad we met and had a chance to help each other. But, you didn't come all this way just to tell me he died, did you?"

"When I talk to him, he said he mailed me a letter and some instructions. He was sick, I know. I did not know he was dying ..." She started to cry softly.

"Oh Mariama, I'm sorry. I know he loved you very much."

"Soon I get his letter," she started up again. "He told me to come to see you."

"See me? Father Lavarato told you to come see me? I don't understand. Why were you to come to see me?"

"I think he write you something," she said, nodding to the letter Hank still had in his hand. "I was not to talk to anyone and give only you the letter."

By this time Pete had come charging back up from downstairs and into the kitchen with a box of tea bags and soon started to bang around with pots and pans. Hank sat down on a chair near Mariama and opened the envelope.

It was several pages long, neatly written in dark blue ink. There were also two smaller envelopes inside that Hank set aside. He started to read:

Dear Hank,

If you're reading this letter, you know I'm no longer with you. I imagine you must be in a state of shock. Sorry to do this to you, my friend, but let me explain. When I learned I didn't have much time left, I made the decision to stay in Africa. Actually, I must admit that when I left Philadelphia, I strongly suspected it would end this way. I just didn't think it would be this soon. Please understand that Africa, for all practical purposes, is my home. And other than

Mariama, whom I treasure and will deeply miss, I love the people here and consider them all to be my family.

Besides, I'm a practical man. I didn't see much sense in hastily returning to the inevitable. I wanted to be buried here in the mission cemetery and that's the way it will be.

But – what about Mariama? For some time I've been agonizing what to do about her.

First of all, she can never return here. I've seen and heard too much that's convinced me she would not be safe. We talked a little about that before I left, remember? Well, things really haven't changed. Perhaps they will one day – but not now.

Neither do I think it in her best interest to remain in Philadelphia. She has no family. She really has very few friends. Part of that is my fault. I now believe I was overly protective of her because of what she's gone through. Perhaps "going through" would be more accurate. Believe me, she's come a long, long way since I brought her to the U.S.

Anyway, I've looked into many options before I left, and was never able to feel comfortable about any of them.

And then you came to see me. You and Katherine.

Immediately I sensed a basic goodness in both of you. Goodness and honesty and integrity. And cleverness. What an adventure you two undertook, and for no personal gain. Without being overly dramatic, I believe it was a sign from God.

I can't tell either of you how overjoyed I was to learn you were able to return our object to the family. I can't express enough the internal peace I now have because of this simple act of kindness.

Who knows what my life would have been if that terrible night had never occurred. Good heavens, I could have turned out to be a banker – or a bus driver – or a skid row bum! But I became a missionary and I couldn't have imagined a more fulfilling life. God truly moves in mysterious ways.

I continue to pray daily for Glory, that poor man. I continue to suffer from guilt. But the fact that his family knows the truth at least offers me some degree of solace.

So, why is Mariama now with you?

Because of the things about you and Katherine I mentioned earlier – and because of your resourcefulness – I believe you are the logical choice. Somehow I know you two will figure out what to do! I trust you both to make the correct decisions.

About the two smaller envelopes; one contains a Transfer of Guardianship. It passes guardianship of Mariama to you, Hank, if you agree to sign and accept the responsibility. It's perfectly legal. I took care of this with a Jesuit lawyer friend of mine over the last couple of weeks. If you agree to this, Mariama will be your ward!

Don't panic! It's not as scary as I'm sure it must sound. She'll soon be sixteen and in a couple of more years, an adult. She's already completed her sophomore year in high school and received excellent grades. And she's working on her citizenship papers – it's important she become a full-fledged American. She's very bright and this should not be a problem.

In the second envelope you'll find some practical help (read that financial help). The key is to a lock-box at Dubuque Bank and Trust, Dubuque, Iowa. Please be patient with me as I explain.

I never had a chance to tell you about my strange Aunt Ophelia. She came to live with us after my father was killed in an accident. She just showed up one day. I don't know where she came from and she wouldn't say. Nor would my mother. Ophelia didn't speak much English and, in fact, didn't speak much at all.

She seldom left the house yet seemed to have an inexhaustible supply of funds. On several occasions I recall, she would come quietly into the kitchen and lay down a wad of bills on the kitchen table in front of my mother. And turn and leave. That was it.

She dressed in the old style of rural Sicily with lots of black, to-the-floor dumpy dresses, long black wool stockings and black low cut shoes. All my friends were scared to death of her. She reportedly had the evil eye! At least that's what everyone thought, and she very well may have. (Just kidding.) At any rate I used that to my advantage from time to time dealing with childhood enemies. There were many strange stories about her I could tell you if I had the time.

When my mother died in 1952 I went back to Dubuque for the funeral. I was in town for just a few days to settle up her modest affairs. I signed over the papers of the house to my aunt and the evening before I left, she came up to me and gave me a quick hug. I almost died of shock. She handed me an envelope with the key you're now holding along with a business card of a Herman Weister, senior trust officer at Dubuque Bank and Trust. She told me it was for me but would not say what it was or what I was supposed to do with it. Unfortunately I had to leave Dubuque the following morning and was soon back in Africa.

I pretty much forgot all about it until I returned to Dubuque several years later. By that time Ophelia was gone. Just gone. No one knew where. The house had been sold but the new owners knew nothing about her. I had earlier sent an occasional letter and postcard to her but never received any replies. And believe it or not, we never had a phone when I was living there.

I went to my old parish and high school to give a talk and raise some money for the mission, and later stopped at the bank. There I met and talked to this Mr. Weister and he told me that shortly after my mother had died, Ophelia had come to see him.

She wanted a safety deposit box and insisted on a perpetual rental agreement. Paid cash and left. He knew all about me and told me the box and all contents had been transferred into my name. Another big surprise!

When I finally looked in the box I almost had a heart attack. I found a leather pouch filled with four large diamonds, nine gold coins, a string of 22 perfect, black pearls and a large and peculiar looking gold brooch. There was also a piece of notepaper scrawled with the words – Not For Church!!!!

I was stunned, of course. I had no idea what everything was worth. I didn't know what to do, but took one of the coins and one of the diamonds with me and left the rest in the lock box. Before I returned to Africa I took them to an appraiser in New York who subsequently referred me to two different specialists; a diamond merchant and a rare coins dealer.

The diamond turned out to be an old European cut with a little over five carats and was appraised at $60,000!

The coin was Etruscan and created quite a stir at the coin dealers. They wouldn't tell me what it was worth until they'd had a chance to do more research but were mentioning figures among themselves in the $20,000 to $30,000 area. They were extremely curious where I came by it and wanted to buy it but I left hurriedly without telling them anything.

The whole thing made me nervous as the dickens, I'll tell you that – walking around with around $90,000 in diamonds and rare coins in my pocket so I put them in a bank until I could figure out what to do with them.

Eventually I sold them both and received slightly over $62,000 for the diamond and $28,500 for the coin! Can you believe that?

The money was a godsend for the mission. At the time we were struggling financially and it kept us afloat. Over the next several years, when the contributions were just not coming in as planned, I sold two more of the coins for around $30,000 each.

Eventually, the mission was financially stable and I never took anything else, and I never touched the pearls or the brooch. Heaven knows what they're worth. But that was many years ago. I tell you all this now to let you know there should still be three diamonds and six coins, plus the jewelry that has never been shown to anyone as far as I know.

I must admit I felt a little guilty selling what I did because, as a priest, I agreed to a vow of poverty! And then there was Ophelia's note in the lock box to think about. However, although the mission is indeed a Catholic-run operation, the money did not go into the church "coffers," which I believe was at the root of her concerns.

Her strange admonition did not surprise me in the least. I recall when she first came to live with us, I had many questions about her. Although my mother never told me much (and I'm not sure she knew much), there were isolated comments made with her Italian neighbor cronies, usually over a glass of grappa, and when no one knew I was around, about a love affair with a wild Sicilian young man of questionable employment integrity (read that as bandit) who, after vague promises of marriage, had been sought after by a nasty group of brigands and left Ophelia in a rush to enter a monastery. His option was losing his life.

I realize how strange this all must sound to you, but I believe there is more than a kernel of truth to it. And it would help explain the "treasure" in the box.

Anyway I was willing to risk her dreaded evil eye, and placed the majority of the proceeds in an endowment fund for my African mission. I am happy to say it has grown substantially over the years and now allows them a modest, yet steady annual income.

I'm also enclosing a Power of Attorney naming you the sole owner of the contents of the box, along with the key and business card.

In closing, I'm saying I trust you, Hank, implicitly. Use the money the best way you can in Mariama's behalf. For travel, clothing, food, shelter, and most importantly, education. Whatever it takes to help her achieve the potential she is capable of. And most importantly, to be God's child.

It may be a lot of money, but it's not family. It's not friends. And it's not her immortal soul. Those are the things that really count and I believe you understand and live by that.

Know that I'm praying for you all, and will continue to pray for you no matter what. Please don't mourn my passing. I go to the Lord willingly and with great joy. And I go secure with the knowledge that one day we'll all be together again and rejoice in His presence.

Father Thomas Lavarato
Missionary

Hank read the letter. Then he read it again. By the time he'd finished, Pete, who had brought in some hot tea in three mismatched mugs, was sitting quietly watching him.

"Hey, ol'' buddy," he said when he saw the expression on Hank's face. "You all right? Here, have some tea."

"Everything okay?" asked Mariama. "Father Lavarato explain?"

"Sure," said Hank forcing a smile. "Everything's fine, Mariama. Please, enjoy your tea. You and Pete sit and visit for a moment. If you'll excuse me, I need to make a phone call."

CHAPTER FIFTY-EIGHT

Hank quickly recovered from his initial shock and called Katie. He summarized the situation the best he could. They both agreed Mariama couldn't stay in the apartment with him and Pete so Katie suggested she stay in the dorm with her; a response Hank was hoping for. A few quick arrangements were made and he drove Mariama over later that evening. She had one small suitcase and an over-the-shoulder bag; all her earthly belongings.

Mariama seemed relieved. She recognized Katie right away and they exchanged hugs and Katie smoothly settled her into a small cot in her room. Exhausted from the long trip and subsequent anxiety of presenting herself to Hank and Pete, she gladly went to bed.

Later that evening Katie called home and filled her parents in on the unexpected turn of events. They invited her and Hank to bring Mariama home that coming weekend. Hank agreed that was a great idea, and after classes on Friday all three of them drove to her house.

As it happened, Katie's folks fell in love with Mariama the minute she walked in the door. And before the weekend was over, they insisted she stay with them — at least until she had a chance to relax and get a feeling for the quietness of the Midwest.

It was an easy decision for both Hank and Mariama, so they moved her into Katie's old room. Her parents admitted they missed having a young lady around the house and her two brothers seemed excited at having such an exotic houseguest. Hank started to feel better about the whole thing and when he later called and talked with Mariama, he was greatly relieved to find out she loved it there. The feel of the country, her own room, two "brothers" to pal around with.

"Yes, Hank," she said excitedly. "I like it here very much. They are very nice people. They want me to live with them for a while. Is that all right?" And that's how it turned out. Mariama had a place to stay. Hank and Katie were able to concentrate on exams. And Pete never did figure out what was going on.

Katie completed her junior year with top grades – no surprise to anyone. By taking extra credits the past two years, and passing out on a couple of subjects, she planned to graduate the following March, a full quarter early.

Hank's thesis received top accolades from the relatively small sports psychology community and he graduated with Honors. Mr. and Mrs. Joyce came to his graduation, as did most of Hank's family, who finally got to meet Mariama. They were equally mesmerized by her charm.

The night before Hank and Katie's families returned home, he took advantage of the noisy crowd at *Zoey's* to inform them that Mariama was his legal ward, a small technicality he had failed to mention earlier. He had visited with his Pastor about it a few days earlier and came to the conclusion that under the strange circumstances, it made the best sense.

"Your what?" Mr. Torney exclaimed with wide eyes. "She's your *what*? Your *ward*?"

There was an awkward silence for a moment before his grandmother cleared her voice and said, "But Hank, dear, aren't you a bit young to have a ward of your own. Why you're not even married yet."

Somehow that seemed to be just the right thing to say and after the laughter died down, the Joyces told of their fondness for the girl and how much they enjoyed having her stay with them. They stressed that things seemed to be working out splendidly for everyone. And that's how it played out.

Hank got the job offer he wanted from Notre Dame. Actually he had offers from all three colleges on his target list, but he was especially delighted to get the nod from *The Fighting Irish* – as were all male members of both families, especially Sean, Katie's brother. He hired a small U-Haul, headed to South Bend and found a convenient, little apartment close to campus.

He went on the payroll in August and kept extremely busy meeting and planning with the various coaching staffs. He also had lesson plans to go over for the two freshman level psych courses he was required to teach. He later discovered he enjoyed the teaching almost as much as interacting with the teams.

Katie also got the job she was hoping for at the Chicago Architecture Foundation. It was a job to die for, she later confided, and set her up perfectly for her short senior year.

They were both very busy, but still managed to get together every couple of weeks, alternating between South Bend and Chicago. Not a bad arrangement according to her grandmother, "... for two youngsters absolutely smitten with each other."

It was during one of his summer visits to the Joyces, that Hank told Katie and her folks about the lock box; a secret he'd been keeping to himself. Mr. Joyce, although intrigued, would not even consider taking any money for having Mariama stay with them. But he thought it was a prudent idea to at least check to be sure everything was still in the lock box that was supposed to be there.

"If we're really talking about the kind of money Father Lavarato suggested, it might be a good idea to visit with a financial advisor to determine what course of action would be in her best interest."

"I agree totally," responded Hank quickly. "You folks and my parents, and Katherine, of course, are the only ones who know about it."

"Okay then," Katie's father said. "I suspect one of the first things you might consider would be to have the contents professionally appraised and insured. Then, depending on what the various markets are for those particular assets, it may be best to leave them alone, or liquidate them and put the money into some kind of investment contracts. Either way, I think Mariama needs some type of legal trust fund set up, one that will assure her of ample funds for any educational endeavor she chooses, and a comfortable income when she needs it."

Hank vigorously nodded his agreement.

"Then, if it's all right with you, Hank, I'll talk, discreetly, of course, with some of my financial friends and see what the consensus is. In the meantime, let's sleep on it. That lovely young lady has enough to worry about the way it is. I just want her to know she's got a home here as long as she wants."

Mariama seemed to flourish under the doting attention of Mrs. Joyce. Everyone agreed it was the missing ingredient of a strong mother figure that she desperately needed. Her English soon became flawless and when she enrolled in the local high school that fall, her grades were enviable.

She was the only black student at the school but that didn't seem to slow her down or interfere with her developing friendships with the other students. And, as far as anyone could tell, there was never a hint of any racial incident. Whereas this was most likely due to her friendly attitude and winning smile, the fact that she lived with the Joyce family which, by default, included the ever-protective Joyce brothers, would be enough to discourage any tawdry behavior.

Hank and Katherine were married the following spring. The quiet celebration took place at St. Patrick's where she'd been baptized and confirmed, went to school and spent much of her earlier life.

One of Katie's best friends at college was maid of honor and Pete was Hank's best man. Family members on both sides, including Mariama, made up the rest of the wedding party. It was a lovely affair, which took place on a picture perfect day.

To Hank's surprise, Andy Alexander and his wife showed up . Neither Hank nor Katie expected that and had only sent an invitation to the family as a formality.

Andy told him his father was heartsick he couldn't come but was deeply involved in a trial and just couldn't get away. The next day, they opened the wedding gift from the Alexander family. The note accompanying it from Mr. Alexander said that if they didn't accept the gift he would sue them – and win.

It was the Jackie Robinson uniform Hank had admired so much the night he and Katie visited the Alexander home.

"Dear Hank and Katherine," the note read. *"I hope you both realize how much I wish I could have been there to help you two celebrate your wedding. But I know Andy and Theresa will express my regrets in person.*

Please accept this gift that I wholeheartedly offer. Hank, it will look great in your office at Notre Dame.

I have replaced it with something that means so much more to me and my family – my great grandfather's slave tag – that you two so graciously returned to us.

When you two come back to Memphis, and I hope you do soon, I want to show you the place of honor it has on my wall. Already it has brought immeasurable joy to us all. God bless both of you.

Your friends always, The Alexander Clan."

CHAPTER FIFTY-NINE

Hank's first year at Notre Dame had gone better than he'd ever envisioned. He easily fit in and became a valuable member of the famous Fighting Irish sports world. His access to Notre Dame tickets made him an instant hero to both sets of families, not to mention Pete and Amy, now also married and living in Chicago. There was no shortage of guests, particularly during the football season weekends. The house, with two extra bedrooms, was usually full of family and friends.

Katie took a job with a well-known, local architectural firm doing what she always dreamed of doing; designing renovations for historic homes throughout the Midwest. Her specialty was the expansion of present facilities without damaging the integrity of the original structure.

They loved the neighborhood where they lived and were quickly becoming enamored with the house they were renting. It belonged to a retired Notre Dame history professor who had moved to North Carolina after the last term, and was thinking of permanently settling there. There was already talk of him selling the home and Katie and Hank had first grabs if they were interested.

That Thanksgiving weekend Hank and Katie returned to Dubuque. It was their first trip back since the infamous "Flatfoot" episode. They were planning to meet the Alexander family for lunch at the Julien Dubuque Hotel.

A couple of weeks earlier Hank received a call from Tom Alexander. He told them that this year, specifically over Thanksgiving vacation, was the first opportunity the entire Alexander family had to get together since Hank and Katie had visited them. He told them he was flying the whole crew up to Dubuque to put some closure to his father's death by visiting the place where he had lost his life and leave behind his mother's ashes. He hoped Hank and Katie could join them and offered to send them airplane tickets.

After a quick discussion with Katie, Hank told him they'd be honored to join them but since they were less than three hours away, they'd drive.

They said their goodbyes to Katie's family around 9:00. It was a crystal clear, cloudless, fall day, unseasonably warm but with just enough snap in the air to require a light jacket. They enjoyed a leisurely drive to Dubuque, arriving at the hotel a few minutes early.

Mary and Tom Alexander were waiting for them in the lobby and after exchanging hugs, led them up and into a private dining room on the second floor. The rest of the family was lounging around; chatting and joking with each other. When they entered, Mr. Alexander boomed, "Listen up everyone. Come over and say hello to our good friends, Katherine and Hank Torney."

All his children were there; Andy and his wife, Theresa, Lorraine and her husband, William, and Phillip, the son they hadn't yet met, now home after spending three years in Europe working for the U.S. Foreign Diplomatic Corps. Tom's sister, Angela, and her husband, Randall, were there also.

It was a joyous and raucous get together with lots of good old-fashioned male banter about the comparative abilities of *The Fighting Irish* versus the *Tennessee Volunteers* while Katie, now visibly pregnant with their first child, fielded questions about her new career and the soon-to-come changes when the baby arrived. After a splendid lunch, Tom Alexander rose, and striking his spoon against his water glass, quieted the room down.

"All Right folks, it's almost 1:30 and we need to be at the marina at 2:00. It's a fine day and as you know we're going to take a little cruise up the river so we can pay our final respects to my father. We need to stay on schedule. Hank and Katherine still have to drive back to Chicago this afternoon, and our plane leaves at 5:00 so let's finish up here and get downstairs."

Although the majority of trees had already turned color, it was still a wonderfully scenic trip as the 35-foot houseboat Mr. Alexander had rented exited the marina and slowly motored up river. The wind was almost nonexistent and the sun was warm on their shoulders as they passed Dubuque's old downtown district and headed upriver toward Eagle Point Park.

When they reached the park, they also reached Lock and Dam No. 11. It was time to turn around and head back. The houseboat captain was careful not to get too close to the turbulent water, and as he slowly turned the boat back downstream, he paused, as earlier requested by Mr. Alexander, and let the current take over.

In the back of the boat, the group had formed into a semicircle and linked themselves together, arm over shoulder, facing up river. The captain heard one of them talking. The others, heads bowed, remained silent. Some private family thing, he imagined, although he couldn't figure out the white couple's involvement. He couldn't hear what was being said and really didn't care. He was being paid a full day's rate for only two hours!

He turned his attention back down river. Better concentrate on where he was going. So it was that he didn't notice that after Mr. Alexander finished his remarks, an urn of ashes was slowly emptied into the water. Roses were handed out to all family members, as well as to Hank and Katie, who, one by one, dropped them over the side.

By the time the Alexanders' plane left the airport, and long before Hank and Katie pulled into his parents' driveway in Evanston, the ashes and roses had intermingled and been swept down river by the swift current.

Down they flowed past Dubuque. Heading toward Memphis.

Toward home.

About The Author

Robert E. Buckley was born and raised in New York. A graduate of Iowa State University with majors in Psychology and American Literature, he spent his career in the advertising agency business, as copywriter and creative director of Young & Rubicam affiliated agencies. Buckley lives with his wife, Lois, in Marion, Iowa. They are the parents of three grown sons and have seven grandchildren.

The Slave Tag as well as Buckley's other two books: *Ophelia's Brooch* and *Two Miles An Hour*, are available in both print and ebook formats at Amazon.com.

Printed in Great Britain
by Amazon